I0818652

# KERABAN THE INFLEXIBLE

OR, ADVENTURES IN THE EUXINE.

BY JULES VERNE.

TRANSLATED BY HENRY FRITH.

**Fredonia Books**
**Amsterdam, The Netherlands**

Kéraban the Inflexible:
Or, Adventures in the Euxine

by
Jules Verne

ISBN: 1-58963-464-0



Reprinted from the original edition

Fredonia Books
Amsterdam, The Netherlands
http://www.fredoniabooks.com



In order to make original editions of historical works available to scholars at an economical price, this facsimile of the original edition is reproduced from the best available copy and has been digitally enhanced to improve legibility, but the text remains unaltered to retain historical authenticity.

# KÉRABAN THE INFLEXIBLE

## OR, ADVENTURES IN THE EUXINE.

## PART ONE

# KÉRABAN THE INFLEXIBLE

## OR, ADVENTURES IN THE EUXINE.

By Jules Verne.

### Chapter I.

### How Van Mitten and his Valet walked and talked.

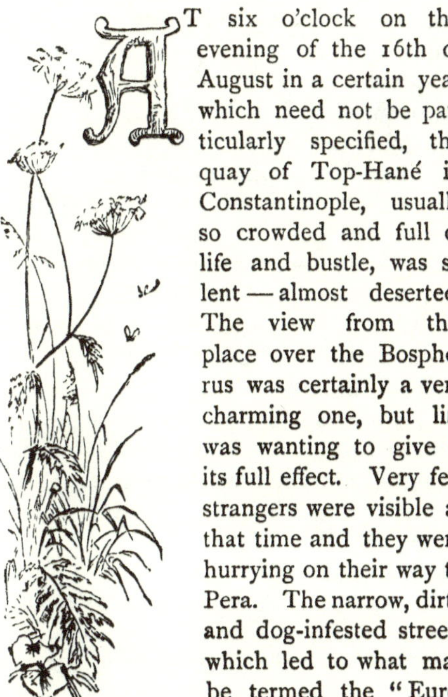

AT six o'clock on the evening of the 16th of August in a certain year which need not be particularly specified, the quay of Top-Hané in Constantinople, usually so crowded and full of life and bustle, was silent — almost deserted. The view from this place over the Bosphorus was certainly a very charming one, but life was wanting to give it its full effect. Very few strangers were visible at that time and they were hurrying on their way to Pera. The narrow, dirty and dog-infested streets which led to what may be termed the "European" quarters were almost free from the presence of the representatives of western civilization. Pera is more especially affected as a residence by the Franks, whose white-stone mansions contrast vividly with the dark cypress groves upon the hill.

But the quay is always picturesque, even when deprived of the rainbow hues of the various costumes worn by the passers-by. The Mosque of Mahmoud with its graceful minarets, its pretty Arabic fountain (now deprived of its elegant roof) its shops where sweatmeats of all kinds are vended; the stalls piled with gourds, Smyrna melons, Scutari raisins, contrasting with the wares of the vendors of perfumery, and the bead sellers—the landing place, or port, where lie hundreds of gaudy caïques, double banked, the oars of which caressed rather than struck the blue waters of the Bosphorus or the Golden Horn.

But there were at that particular time many of the habitual loungers of the Top-Hané—Persians, coquettishly crowned with head-gear of Astrachan; Greeks, balancing the many folded *fustanelle;* Circasians, nearly always in military dress; Georgians, still Russian in their costume though many miles from the frontier; Armenians, saturnine and swarthy, whose sun-browned skins were perceptible between the folds of their embroidered vests; but the Turks—the Osmanlis—the sons of ancient Byzantium and old Stamboul—where were they?

Where were they? It would have been no use to question two Western strangers who with inquisitive eyes, noses in the air, and with somewhat undecided steps, were walking almost apart upon the terrace. They could not have answered you.

But there is something more yet. In the town properly so called, beyond the port, a visitor would have remarked the same characteristic air of silence and desertion. On the other side of the Golden Horn—a deep indentation between the old Serail and the landing place of Top-Hané on the right bank, which is united with the left by three bridges of boats—the whole of Constantinople appeared to be asleep. Was no one awake in the Palace of Serai Bournou? Were there none of the Faithful, no Hadjis or pilgrims in the mosques of

Ahmed of Bayezidièh, Saint Sophia, or Suleimanieh?

Was this the hour of repose, of siesta, for the careless guardian of the tower of the Seraskierat following the example of his colleague on the tower of Galata, on both of whom devolved the duty of giving warning of the frequent fires which break out in Constantinople? The stillness even appeared to extend to the port, notwithstanding the presence of the Austrian, French, and other steamers—the boats, steam launches, and caïques which passed and repassed upon the waters that laved the bases of the houses.

Was this, then, the much vaunted Constantinople, the vision of the east realized by the will of Constantine and Mahomet II.? That is just what the two strangers above referred to were asking each other as they walked to and fro; and if they did not answer the question in Turkish it was not for want of acquaintance with that language.

They were both well acquainted with the native tongue: one of them because he had been employed for twenty years in correspondence and merchants' business in the country; the other because he had frequently discharged the duties of secretary to his master, even while he acted in the capacity of a domestic servant.

These men were natives of Holland, and hailed from Rotterdam. Their names were Jan Van Mitten, and Bruno, his valet, whom destiny had driven to the extreme borders of Europe.

Van Mitten, a well-known individual, was a man of forty-five or forty-six years of age, still fair haired, of fresh complexion, with blue eyes and yellow whiskers. He wore no mustaches. His nose was rather short relatively to his face; his head was massive; he had broad shoulders; stood somewhat below the middle height, and inclined to stoutness. His feet were more remarkable for usefulness than elegance. Altogether he had the air of a brave, resolute man; he was a good specimen of his nation.

Morally speaking, perhaps Van Mitten was of a plastic temperament, of a somewhat pliable disposition—one of those men who, while of an extremely sociable and indeed humorous turn of mind, are ready to avoid discussion and ready to cede points; more fitting to obey than to command—quiet, phlegmatic individuals, who are supposed to have no decided will of their own. They are by no means the worse for that. Once and once only during his former life Van Mitten had been engaged in a discussion, the consequences of which had been very serious.

On that occasion certainly he had come out of himself, but before long he had re-entered his shell, so to speak. It would have been better perhaps had he yielded, and no doubt he would have done so could he have foreseen the consequences. But it will not do to anticipate the events which form the ground-work of this tale.

"Well, sir?" said Bruno, when he and his master had reached Top-Hané.

"Well, Bruno!"

"Here we are, sir, in Constantinople."

"Yes," replied Van Mitten; "and some thousands of miles from Rotterdam."

"Don't you think, sir, that we are quite far enough from Holland by this time?" said the valet, drily.

"I do not think I can ever be too far from it," replied his master in a low voice; as if he were afraid of Holland hearing him.

In Bruno, Van Mitten possessed a most devoted servitor. This faithful valet in some respects resembled his master, as much so, indeed, as his deference would permit him to resemble that personage, with whom he had been so many years associated. For twenty years master and man had not been separated for a day. If Bruno in the house was something less than a friend, he was more than a servant. He performed his service intelligently, methodically, and did not scruple to give advice, of which Van Mitten might take advantage; or make complaints which his master would accept without remonstrance. He was very much annoyed, however, when he had to obey the orders of any but his master; yet he could not resist—in a word, he wanted "character."

It may be added that Bruno, who was at this time forty years of age, was of a rather lazy temperament; he could not bear to move about. To be able to endure an active life, one must train and get thin; but Bruno was in the habit of having

himself weighed every week so as to ensure his maintaining his rotundity of form.

When he entered the service of Van Mitten he turned the scale at only one hundred pounds, which was a miserable weight for a Dutchmah. But within a year afterwards he had gained thirty pounds in weight, and was not ashamed to go anywhere. To his master therefore he owed it that he had reached the hundred and sixty-seven pounds of flesh which he then carried about with him, and which put him in such a good position amongst his countrymen. He found it necessary also to be modest and reserved, so that in time he might arrive at the proud distinction of pulling down two hundred pounds in the scale.

In fine, Bruno, who was greatly attached to his native land, which he looked upon as the finest in Europe, or in the world for that matter, would never, unless under very urgent circumstances, have quitted Rotterdam, the first city in Holland in his estimation, on the banks of the Niewe Haven canal. Nevertheless it was a fact that Bruno was then at Constantinople, the capital of the Ottoman Empire.

But what was Van Mitten?

Nothing less than a rich merchant of Rotterdam; a dealer in tobacco; a consignee of the best products of Havana, Maryland, Virginia and Porto Rico; and particularly of those of Macedonia, Syria, and Asia Minor.

For twenty years Van Mitten had done a considerable business of this kind with the house of Kéraban of Constantinople, who exported tobaccos all over the world. Thus it happened that in his dealings with this large Eastern house Van Mitten had picked up something of the Turkish tongue, which he soon spoke like one of the "Faithful." So also Bruno, from sympathy, and in order to be better acquainted with his patron's business, made it a point to learn the language too; and spoke it scarcely less fluently than his master.

This pair of originals had made an agreement with each other, only to speak the Ottoman tongue in Turkey. In fact, but for their dress they might have passed for natives. This was by no means unwelcome to Van Mitten, and Bruno was too obedient to manifest his objections.

So he compelled himself to say every morning to his master

"Efendum emriniz nè dir?" which means, being interpreted, "Sir, what do you require?"

Then Van Mitten would reply—

"Sitrimi pantalounymi purtcha," which signified that he required his clothes brushed.

From what has been said, the reader will now understand that Van Mitten and Bruno had no difficulty in finding their way about Constantinople, firstly because they understood the native language, and secondly because they were sure of a welcome at the "house" of Kéraban, the chief of which firm had already been in Holland, and according to the law of contracts had struck up a great friendship with his Dutch correspondent.

For this reason Van Mitten, when he quitted Rotterdam, made up his mind to go to Constantinople, and Bruno made no objection though he only resigned himself to the move unwillingly. So it came to pass that master and servant found themselves in the quay of Top-Hané in the city of the Faithful.

About this time of the evening some passers-by appeared, strangers chiefly. Then two or three Turks walked past conversing, and the keeper of a café established at the end of the square arranged his unfilled tables leisurely, pending the expected arrival of his customers.

"In less than an hour," remarked one of the Turks, "the sun will have dipped beneath the waves of the Bosphorus, and then—"

"And then," continued another, "we shall be able to eat and drink in comfort, and smoke at our ease."

"This Fast of Ramadan is very long."

"All Fasts are tedious," was the reply, as the interlocutors passed on.

Meanwhile two strangers were exchanging opinions upon the same same subject, as they paced in front of the *café*.

"These Turks are extraordinary fellows," said one. "Really, a traveller who happened to arrive in Constantinople during this melancholy Lenten season would have but a poor opinion of the capital."

"Bah," replied the other, "London is no more gay on a Sunday. If the Turks fast during the day, they make up for their abstinence at night. When the sunset gun is fired, the odour of cooking and the smoke of tobacco will arise simultaneously with the people, and the streets will resume their wonted gaiety."

It would seem that the stranger was right in his estimate, for at that moment the proprietor of the *café* called out to his waiter—

"See that everything is prepared. In an hour we shall be overwhelmed by the flood of customers."

The two strangers meanwhile continued their conversation.

"I think that Constantinople is best worth visiting during this period of the Ramadan. If the days are sad and *triste*, like a succession of Ash Wednesdays, the evenings are gay and festive as a carnival."

"There is the contrast, you see, to emphasize it."

While these men exchanged their views the Turks were regarding them not without a kind of envy.

"They are happy, those Franks," said one of the subjects of the Sultan. "They can eat, drink, and smoke as they please."

"No doubt," replied his companion; "but they cannot at this moment procure a *kébal* of mutton, nor a *pilaw* of nice fowl and rice, nor a cake of baklava—not even a slice of water-melon or cucumber."

"Because they are ignorant of the right places in which to find them. By means of a few piastres one can always find willing vendors who have received the dispensation of the Prophet."

"By Allah," said his friend, "my cigarettes are drying up in my pocket, I cannot lose so much good tobacco."

So at the risk of his future happiness the "Believer," who paid little attendance to his creed, took out a cigarette and lighting it puffed rapidly the perfumed weed.

"Look out," said his companion; "if some Ulema less tolerant than usual should see you——"

"Oh, I can soon swallow the smoke—he will see nothing," replied the faithful one.

Thus these men continued their promenade, lounging up and down the square, and subsequently disappearing up one of the narrow streets which lead to Pera and Galata.

"This is certainly a singular city," said Bruno as he gazed around him. "Ever since we left our hotel I have scarcely seen even the 'ghost' of a native. There are only phantoms in Constantinople apparently. The people and the place seem to be equally asleep—even the dogs, yellow and lean as they are, will scarcely trouble themselves to bite you. After all that travellers have said I cannot see the object in travelling. What do you gain by it? I would rather be in our own city of Rotterdam, under the grey sky of Holland."

"Patience, Bruno, patience," said the calm Van Mitten. "We have only been here a few hours yet. Nevertheless I cannot say this is altogether the Constantinople I had pictured to myself. I fancied we should plunge into the *Arabian Nights* at once, into all the dreams of the East, and we actually find ourselves imprisoned in the depths of——"

"An immense convent," added Bruno, "in the midst of a people as sad as a Trappist Priory."

"My friend Kéraban will explain to us what it all means by-and-by;" said Van Mitten.

"But where are we at this moment?" asked Bruno. "What is this place? what do they call this quay?"

"If I am not mistaken we are in the Top-Hané," replied Van Mitten—"at the end of the Golden Horn. There is the Bosphorus, which laves the shores of Asia, and on the opposite side you may see the Seraglio Point and the Turkish town which is raised above it."

"The Seraglio!" exclaimed Bruno. "Is that the palace of the Sultan wherein the eighty thousand odalisques live?"

"Eighty thousand?" repeated Van Mitten smiling; "I fancy you have estimated the number somewhat too highly—even for a Turk. In Holland we find one wife sufficient for a household, and even then one cannot always have peace!"

"Quite so; certainly, sir; let us not speak of that unless we must." Then Bruno turning towards the *café*, said—

"This looks like a *café*, and after his exertions combined with this baking Turkish sun I should not be surprised if my master would like some refreshment."

"That is one way of saying that you are thirsty," replied Van Mitten. "Well let us enter this *café*."

So they seated themselves at one of the small tables on the *façade* of the establishment.

"Cawadjii," cried Bruno, rapping on the table, European fashion.

But as no one answered the summons, he called again more loudly.

After this second summons the proprietor of the *café* appeared at the end of the shop, but made no signs of approaching nearer.

"Strangers," he murmured, when he caught sight of his customers. "Do they really believe they can be served?" Then he came to the table.

"Cawadjii, let us have some cherry-water, quite fresh," said Van Mitten.

"At gun-fire," replied the man.

"What!" exclaimed Bruno. "Cherry-water with gun-fire? No, cawadjii—no—with mint!"

"If you have no cherry-water," continued Van Mitten, "let us have a glass of rose-rahtlokoum. I remember it—it is very nice."

"At gun-fire," was the answer of the proprietor as he shrugged his shoulders.

"What does he mean by gun-fire?" asked the valet of his master.

"We shall see," replied the latter, who, always willing to be accommodating, said, "If you have not rahtlokoum, let us have a cup of coffee, some sherbet—what you please!"

"At gun-fire!"

"At gun-fire?" repeated Van Mitten.

"Not before," said the *café*-keeper as he unceremoniously re-entered his shop.

"Let us come away from here," said Bruno. "There is no use in remaining with this stupid Turk, who deafens us with his 'gun-fire!'"

"Come along, Bruno," said Van Mitten. "I daresay we shall find a more complaisant *café*-keeper presently."

So they made their way across the open space once more.

"I am quite of opinion, sir," said Bruno, "that we cannot meet your friend, M. Kéraban a moment too soon. We should have known what was in store for us had he been at his house of business."

"Yes, Bruno, but we must have patience a little longer. They told us we should find him here."

"But not before seven o'clock, sir. It is hither that his caïque will come to take us across to his villa at Scutari on the opposite side of the Bosphorus."

"Quite so, Bruno; and my estimable friend will soon put us *au courant* with all that is going on. He is a true Turk, one of the old Conservative party, who will not permit any innovations to be made in existing circumstances; who protest against all modern inventions—one of those men who still prefer a coach (when they find one) to the railroad, and a sailing vessel to a steamer. During the twenty years I have know Kéraban, I have never known him to change ever so little. When, three years ago, he came to visit me in Rotterdam he arrived in a post-chaise, and instead of eight days he had been quite a month on the journey. I have known a good many obstinate people in my time, Bruno, but of all Kéraban is the most 'pig-headed' person I ever met."

"He will be considerably astonished to meet you again in Constantinople" said the valet.

"I fancy so," replied Van Mitten, "and I would rather take him by surprise. At least in his company we shall be thoroughly the Turk. My friend Kéraban is not the man to adopt the costume of the Nizam and to wear the blue coat and red fez of the modern 'believer.'"

"When they take off their fezzes they look like bottles with the corks out," remarked Bruno.

"Ah, my dear and inimitable Kéraban will come dressed just as he was when he visited me at the other side of Europe; he will have his turban and caftan on—"

"Just like a date merchant," interrupted Bruno.

"Yes like a date merchant who sells golden fruit, and who might even eat them at every meal," replied Van Mitten. "He has the very business for this country—a merchant in tobacco. How could he fail to make his fortune in such a business in this place, where every one smokes, morning, noon, and night."

"Smoke!" exclaimed Bruno. "Where have you seen anyone smoke? I have not seen any smokers at all—not one, yet I quite expected to find groups of Turks at every door smoking long curling pipes or tubes of cherry with amber mouthpieces. But no! Not even a cigarette much less a cigar!"

"There is something we do not understand, depend upon it, Bruno. Why even in Rotterdam we shall find more smokers than in the streets of Constantinople."

"Are you quite sure that we have not mistaken the route and gone somewhere else?" continued Bruno. "Are you certain that we *are* in the Turkish capital, sir? Perhaps after all we have come wrong, and that is the Thames yonder and not the Golden Horn in the Bosphorus. That mosque yonder may be St. Paul's instead of St. Sophia. This Constantinople? Never. It is London!"

"Be quiet, Bruno. Moderate your spirits, you are much too volatile for a native of Holland. Be calm, patient, phlegmatic, as I am, and never be surprised at anything. We left Rotterdam, as you know——"

"Yes, yes," assented Bruno, shaking his head in a melancholy manner.

"We came by way of Paris, St. Gothard, Italy, Brindisi, and the Mediterranean, and yet you would have me believe that the Messageries steamer landed us at London Bridge after eight days' steaming—and not at Galata at all?"

"Nevertheless——" began Bruno.

"I trust," continued Van Mitten, "that you will not give way to these little eccentricities before my friend Kéraban. He might take such joking in ill part, and begin to argue in his obstinate way."

"I will take care, sir," replied Bruno. "But though one cannot obtain any refreshment, I suppose it is permissible to light a pipe. Do you see any objection to that, sir?"

"None whatever," replied his master. "In my capacity of tobacco importer nothing pleases me more than to see people smoking. Indeed I am extremely sorry that Nature has only endowed each individual with one mouth. It is true we can consume snuff by the nose."

"And by the teeth in chewing," added Bruno.

So saying he pulled out an enormous pipe of painted porcelain, and having lighted it, puffed it contentedly and with evident satisfaction.

But at this moment the Turks, who had so emphatically protested against the abstinence of the Ramadan, reappeared upon the quay, and the individual who had been indulging in the cigarette at once perceived Bruno smoking his pipe.

"By Allah," he exclaimed, "here is one of those accursed Franks defying the ordinances of the Koran. I cannot suffer it."

"At least put out your own cigarette," said his companion.

"Of course," he replied; and throwing it away he marched directly up to the Dutchman, who by no means expected such a meeting.

"Not till gun-fire," said the Turk, as he snatched the pipe from Bruno's lips.

"Here; my pipe!" exclaimed Bruno, whom his master vainly tried to control.

"Dog of a Christian—not till gun-fire," said the polite Turk.

"Dog yourself, Turk," retorted Bruno with Christian spirit.

"Be quiet, Bruno," said Van Mitten.

"Let him give me my pipe then, at least," said the valet.

"At gun-fire," replied the Turk, as he placed the pipe in the folds of his caftan.

"Come, Bruno, it is no use to transgress the customs of the country one visits," said his master.

"Robbers' customs," said Bruno indignantly.

"Come along, I say. My friend Kéraban will not arrive before seven o'clock. Let us resume our promenade, and we will meet him when the time comes."

So Van Mitten dragged away Bruno, who was much disgusted at being separated from his pipe, to which he clung with all the tenacity of a confirmed smoker.

As the strangers walked away, the Turks remarked one to the other.

"Truly these Frankish strangers think they can do anything they please."

"Even to smoke before sunset!" said the other.

"Do you want a light?" enquired his friend.

"Yes, thank you," replied the other as he lighted a fresh cigarette.

# KÉRABAN THE INFLEXIBLE

## OR, ADVENTURES IN THE EUXINE.

BY JULES VERNE.

### CHAPTER II.

### HOW SCARPANTE THE STEWARD AND CAPTAIN YARHUD DISCUSSED PROJECTS WITH WHICH THE READER MUST BECOME ACQUAINTED.

HILE Van Mitten and Bruno were promenading upon the Top-Hané, and at the moment they reached the fiıst bridge of boats which puts Galata in communication with the ancient Stamboul, a Turk rapidly turned the corner of the Mosque of Mahmoud and halted in the open space beyond it.

It was then six o'clock in the afternoon. For the fourth time that day the muezzins were mounting the minarets to call the people to prayer, and their voices were soon heard calling out the formula—"There is but one God and Mahomet is His Prophet."

The Turk who had arrived so hastily upon the scene, turned about and gazed intently at the few passers-by. He then advanced to the meeting-place or axis of all the streets, with a view to obtain the greatest range in all directions. But the object of his quest had not appeared, and the Turk manifested considerable impatience.

"So Yarhud has not come," he muttered. "He knows he ought to have been here punctually at the appointed time!"

The Turk then took a few turns up and down the open space, and advanced as far as the northern angle of the barracks, whence he gazed in the direction of the cannon-foundry, as he stood tapping his foot upon the ground impatiently. Then he turned back again to the café at which Van Mitten and Bruno had vainly demanded refreshments. Here he seated himself at one of the empty tables, but was too careful to summon the waiter, for being a scrupulous observer of the Ramadan, he knew the time had not yet arrived for indulging in any of the various products of the Ottoman distilleries.

This individual's name was Scarpante, the intendant or steward of the Seigneur Saffar, a rich Turk who lived at Trebizond.

Saffar himself was at that particular time travelling in Southern Russia, and intended to return to Trebizond when he had visited the Caucasian provinces, never doubting that his intendant would meanwhile have succeeded in carrying to a successful termination an enterprise with which he had been specially charged. Scarpante was to rejoin him at his palatial residence when he had accomplished his mission, which Saffar never admitted to himself even was likely to fail. He could not conceive that any emissary of his should not succeed when he had commanded success, and backed his orders with the powerful aid of money. In everything he acted with the ostentation which is characteristic of these "nabobs" of Asia Minor.

The steward was a very audacious fellow, an adept at all enterprises which required skill and force to carry them out. He hesitated at nothing to carry out his master's designs, which were put through *per fas et nefas*. It was upon one of these desperate undertakings that he arrived in Constantinople, and that he was then awaiting the meeting with a certain Maltese captain, who was no better than himself.

The captain's name was Yarhud; he was commander of a felucca—the *Guidare*—and made periodical voyages across the Black Sea. To his ordinary smuggling he added even a less creditable trade, that of carrying black slaves from the Soudan,

"Are you certain of your crew?"

Ethiopia, or Egypt, and others from Georgia and Circassia. The market for these human commodities was at that very corner of Top-Hané—a market in regard to which the Government, very conveniently, shut its eyes.

Scarpante was still waiting, but the captain did not come. Although the intendant remained outwardly impassible and nothing betrayed his feelings, he was inwardly boiling with indignation.

"Where is the dog?" he muttered. "Has any accident happened to him? He ought to have quitted Odessa the day before yesterday. He should now be here on this spot at this café at this hour, for which I gave him rendezvous."

As he finished his half-articulate speech, a Maltese sailor appeared at the angle of the quay. This man was Yarhud. He glanced right and left and perceived Scarpante, who immediately rose and advanced to meet the captain of the *Guidare* in the midst of the increasing numbers of the passers-by.

"I am not accustomed to be kept waiting, Yarhud," was Scarpante's address, in a tone the Maltese could not fail to understand.

"You must forgive me," said the captain; "I made all possible haste."

"You have only this moment arrived?"

"This instant by the Janboli and Andrinople Railway, and had not the train been late——"

"When did you leave Odessa?"

"Two days ago."

"Where is your vessel?"

"Waiting for me there,— in Odessa harbour."

"Are you certain of your crew?"

"Absolutely. They are all Maltese like myself; and devoted—to generous paymasters!"

"They will obey your orders then?"

"Certainly; in everything."

"Good. What news have you, Yarhud?"

"Well, both good and bad news," replied the captain, lowering his voice.

"Let us have the bad news first, then;" said Scarpante.

"Very well. The bad news is that the girl Amasia—Selim's, the Odessa banker's, daughter—is about to be married, soon. So her kidnapping will be a more difficult matter, and will have to be accomplished more hurriedly than if she were not to be married so quickly."

"The marriage must not take place, Yarhud," said Scarpante, in a tone louder than was altogether prudent. "No, by the Prophet, it must not take place."

"I did not say that it *would*," replied Yarhud. "I said that it had been arranged to take place."

"Quite so. But my Lord Saffar is under the impression that in three days the young lady will have been carried on board your ship and bound for Trebizond. Now, if you think that impossible——"

"I never said it was impossible, Scarpante. Nothing is impossible when audacity and money are combined. I merely said that the enterprise will be more difficult under the circumstances; that is all."

"Difficult!" exclaimed Scarpante, contemptuously. "This will not be the first time that a Turkish girl, or a young Russian lady, has disappeared from Odessa!"

"And it won't be the last time, or the Captain of the *Guidare* will know the reason why," replied Yarhud.

"Who is the fellow who wants to marry Amasia?" asked Scarpante.

"A young Turk; of the same race as Amasia herself," was the reply.

"From Odessa?"

"No; of Constantinople."

"What is his name?"

"Ahmet."

"Who is this Ahmet, then?"

"Nephew and sole heir of a rich merchant of Galata, Seigneur Kéraban."

"What is his business?"

"Tobacco, in which he has made an immense fortune. Selim the banker is his correspondent at Odessa. They have put through some very important business together, and often pay each other visits. Under these circumstances, Amasia and Ahmet have become acquainted; and so the marriage has been arranged by the father of the girl and the uncle of the young man."

"Where is the marriage fixed to take place?" asked Scarpante, "Will it be solemnized here, in Constantinople?"

"No; at Odessa."

"When?"

"I do not know; but if young Ahmet's wishes are consulted, it may be any day."

"So we have no time to lose, eh?"

"Not an instant."

"Where is this Ahmet now?"

"At Odessa."

"And Kéraban?"

"Here; in Constantinople."

"Did you see this young man, Yarhud, while you were passing through Odessa?"

"I had a particular object in seeing him, and in taking notice of him. I have seen him, and know him!"

"What kind of man is he?"

"A young, and rather interesting fellow;

very acceptable to the banker's daughter too."

"Is he to be feared, think you?"

"They say he is both brave and resolute, and in this business at any rate we must reckon with him."

"Is he independent, in fortune, I mean?" continued Scarpante, who kept putting leading questions concerning the young man who gave him some uneasiness.

"No," replied Yarhud: "Ahmet is entirely dependent upon his uncle and

"Leaving the Top-Hané in a sort of penumbra."

guardian, Kéraban, who loves him as a son; and he will no doubt soon go to Odessa, so as to be present at the marriage."

"Cannot we find some means to prevent the Seigneur Kéraban from going thither?" suggested Scarpante.

"That certainly would be a good thing to do, and would give us more time; but in what way do you propose to prevent him?"

"The way I must leave to your invention," replied Scarpante. "But bear in mind the wishes of Seigneur Saffa *must* be carried out, and the young Amasia must be carried off to Trebizond. It will not be the first visit of the *Guidare* to that part of the coast, and you know how your services will be remunerated."

"I know!" replied Yarhud, briefly.

"My patron, Saffar, saw the girl, though only for an instant in his house at Odessa. Her beauty has made a deep impression on him, and she will not complain of the exchange from the banker's home to the Palace at Trebizond. Amasia will surely be carried off, Yarhud; and if not by you, by some one else."

"I will do it: you may depend upon me," replied the Maltese simply. "But as I have told you the bad news, let me now tell you more favourable tidings."

"Speak!" said Scarpante, who, after pacing up and down in a thoughtful attitude, returned to his companion.

"If this projected marriage renders it more difficult to carry the girl off, since Ahmet will not be long absent from her, I will find opportunity to enter the banker's house. The fact is, I am not only the captain of the *Guidare*, but a merchant. My vessel carries a rich cargo; silk stuffs, brocades enriched with diamonds, and a hundred kindred articles, calculated to attract the attention of a young girl about to be married. At that time too she will be all the more easily tempted. I shall be able to attract her on board and then, taking advantage of a favourable wind, I shall be able to put to sea before her absence has caused any alarm."

"That seems a good notion, Yarhud;" replied Scarpante: "and I have no doubt you will succeed. But you must be very careful to keep all this a profound secret."

"You may make your mind quite easy on that point, Scarpante."

"You are not in want of money, I suppose?"

"No: there is no fear of that when your generous patron is concerned."

"Well, now lose no time. The marriage once contracted, Amasia will be Ahmet's wife, and it is not in that capacity that my lord wishes to see her at Trebizond."

"I quite understand."

"Very well. As soon as the banker's daughter is on board the *Guidare* you will set sail."

"Yes, for before I make my advances I will wait for a favourable breeze—a steady westerly wind."

"How long do you anticipate it will take you to run from Odessa to Trebizond?"

"With possible delays, calms or changes of wind—for the wind is very uncertain in the Black Sea—the voyage may perhaps occupy three weeks."

"Good!" replied Scarpante. "I will make my way to Trebizond about that time, and my patron will not be long after me."

"I hope to be there before you," said Yarhud.

"The orders of my master," continued the intendant, "are very strict concerning the treatment of the young lady. Every consideration possible is to be shown her. There must be no violence or ill treatment, mind!"

"She shall be treated with as much respect as the Seigneur Saffar can desire, and with as much deference as if he were present himself," replied Yarhud.

"I count upon your zeal, Yarhud."

"You shall have it, Scarpante."

"And upon your skill and address."

"In truth, I shall be all the more certain to succeed if the wedding be postponed," said Yarhud; "and it will be, if some obstacle can be put in Seigneur Kéraban's way so as to prevent his departure."

"Do you know this great merchant?"

"It is always as well to know one's enemies, or those also may become such," replied the Maltese. "Thus my first care on my arrival here was to present myself at his office under the pretext of doing some business."

"You have seen him, then?"

"Just for an instant, but that was enough; and——."

At the same moment Yarhud suddenly approached Scarpante and whispered—

"Eh! this is a singular coincidence, isn't it? Perhaps it may prove a happy chance for us."

"What do you mean?" enquired Scarpante.

"Look at yonder stout man descending the Rue de Pera, accompanied by his servant."

"Is that he?"

"The very same," replied the captain. "Let us keep aloof, but we will not lose sight of him. I know that he returns every evening to his house at Scutari, and if necessary I will follow him to the other side of the Bosphorus and find out when he proposes to start for Odessa."

Scarpante and Yarhud then mixed with the other pedestrians, but in such a manner as to observe Kéraban and to overhear his orders. A feat all the easier inasmuch as "my lord Kéraban," as they called him, always spoke in a very loud tone, and never attempted to conceal his imposing person nor his sentiments.

## Chapter III.

### How Kéraban met Van Mitten, and was greatly surprised at his appearance.

"My lord Kéraban" was very much "on the surface," to employ a modern term. This was the case physically as well as morally. He was, in face, about forty years old, at least fifty in his figure, and actually forty-five. Yet his face was intelligent, his figure majestic. He wore a beard, turning grey, which was cut rather close, and divided into two points. His eyes were black and piercing, as sensitive to passing impressions as the most delicately adjusted scales to the weight of a grain. His chin was square, his nose somewhat hooked, and this feature added to the natural piercing appearance of the dark eyes. His lips were parted sufficiently to display his white and even teeth. His forehead was high, and displayed a vertical fold or line—a true type of obstinacy—between the bushy black brows. Kéraban's face was peculiar, and one not easily forgotten by anyone who had ever seen it, if only once.

Kéraban, in his dress, remained faithful to the old Turkish costume of the time of the Janissaries. The large turban, the capacious trousers, the sleeveless waistcoat garnished with enormous buttons, the shawl around the waist already sufficiently developed by nature, and finally the caftan with its majestic folds. There was nothing European in this style of dress, which contrasted strongly with the modern costume of the Orientals. It was designed to repress the invasions of industrial enterprise, a protest in favour of local colour which had a tendency to disappear, a defiance hurled at the edicts of the Sultan Mahmoud, who had upheld the modern costume of the Turk.

It is scarcely necessary to add that Seigneur Kéraban had a servant—a man about twenty-five years of age, named Nizib, so thin as to drive Bruno to desperation, and clad in the same ancient costume as his master. As he never contradicted his master in words, so he assimilated himself to Kéraban in dress. He was a devoted valet, but absolutely devoid of any ideas of his own. He always said "Yes" in advance; and, like an echo, repeated unconsciously the last phrase of the influential merchant. This was the surest way of being of his master's opinion and to avoid reprimands, of which the Seigneur Kéraban was prodigal.

Both master and man reached the Top-Hané by one of the narrow streets which descend from Pera. Kéraban as usual was speaking in a very loud voice without caring whether or not he was overheard.

"Well," he was saying, "may Allah protect us, but in the time of the Janissaries everyone had the right to do as his fancy dictated, when evening had set in. No; I will not submit to these new police regulations, and I will go by the streets without a lanthorn, if it please me to do so, although I may tumble into a puddle or break my legs over a stray dog."

"Stray dog," assented Nizib the Echo.

"So you need not worry me with your stupid remonstrances," continued Kéraban, "or by Mahomet I will pull your ears so long that an ass will be jealous of you, as well as the driver."

"The driver," said Nizib; who by the way had not ventured upon a single expostulation, as one may imagine.

"If the inspector of police fine me, I will pay the fine: if he put me in arrest, I will go to prison. But I will never give way on this point, nor on any other."

Nizib made a sign of assent. He was quite ready to follow his master to prison if circumstances so fell out.

My Lord Kéraban

"Ah, you new-fashioned Turks," exclaimed Kéraban, as some Constantinopolitans, clothed in their modern dress, passed him. "Ah, you would make laws, and alter our old customs, would you? Ah, when I cease to protest. . . . Nizib, did you tell my caidji to wait with the caique at the steps of Top-Hané at seven o'clock?"

"Yes; at seven o'clock."

"Why is it not there?"

"Why *is* it not there?" echoed Nizib.

"I suppose because it is not yet seven."

"It is not yet seven."

"How do you know that?"

"Because you say so," replied Nizib.

"Suppose I were to say it was five o'clock?"

"Then it would be five o'clock," said the human echo.

"One is not so stupid as that!"

"No, not so stupid," was the answer.

"This fellow by such constant agreement will end by causing disagreement," muttered Kéraban.

At this moment Van Mitten and Bruno reappeared, and the latter kept urging his master to leave the city.

"Well, monsieur, I may pass, surely!"

"Let us go on," he said, "by the first train. This Constantinople, indeed! This the capital of the Commander of the Faithful! Never!"

"Be quiet, Bruno," said Van Mitten; "calm yourself."

The sun was setting and had already dipped behind the hills of old Stamboul, leaving the Top-Hané in a sort of penumbra. The twilight prevented Van Mitten from recognizing Kéraban as they crossed the quay from opposite directions; but it so happened that they met, and each in his anxiety to pass got in the other's way. This produced a balancing movement which is ridiculous to a beholder.

"Well, monsieur, I may pass, surely!" said Kéraban, who was not a man to yield the path to anyone.

"But—" said Van Mitten, who in his

anxiety to be polite effectually precluded the passage.

"I tell you I will pass, sir."

"But," again said the Dutchman, and he was about to explain when he suddenly recognized the man with whom he had such important business.

"What! My friend Kéraban?" he cried.

"You!" exclaimed Kéraban. "You! here—in Constantinople!"

"Yes, 'tis I," replied Van Mitten.

"Since when have you been here?"

"Since this morning."

"And you did not call on me the very first—!"

"On the contrary," replied the Dutchman, "I went to your office, but you were not there, and they told me I should find you here at seven o'clock."

"They were right," replied Kéraban shaking the hand of his correspondent with great vigour. "My dear Van Mitten, I never—no never—expected to see you in Constantinople. Why did not you write?"

"I quitted Holland so hurriedly."

"On business?"

"No, simply travelling for a change. I had never been in Constantinople, nor in Turkey at all, and I wished to return the visit you paid me in Rotterdam."

"Very good. But how is it Madame Van Mitten is not with you?"

"Well, the fact is, I did not bring her," replied the Dutchman hesitating. "Madame Van Mitten is not so easily moved. So I came alone with my valet Bruno."

"Ah, yonder lad," said Kéraban nodding at Bruno, who believed he ought to bow to the Turk with his hands to his forehead, like the arms of a semaphore.

"Yes," replied Van Mitten. "He wished to leave me just now and go——"

"Go away!" exclaimed Keraban. "Go home again without my permission!"

"Yes, he finds your capital too dull. There is no life about it, he thinks."

"It is nothing but a mausoleum," said Bruno. "There is no one in the shops, there are no carriages in the streets. There are only ghosts in the city, and one cannot even smoke a pipe!"

"But it is the Ramadan, Van Mitten," said Kéraban. "We are in full fast!"

"Ah, so this is the Ramadan," said Bruno. "Well now, if you please, what *is* the Ramadan?"

"A time of fasting and abstinence," replied Kéraban. "While it lasts we are forbidden to drink, smoke, or eat—that is between the rising and setting of the sun. But in half an hour hence a cannon will signify the close of the day."

"Ah, now I understand what those fellows meant by their cannon-shots," exclaimed Bruno.

"We recompense ourselves fully during the night, though, for the abstinence practised by day," continued Kéraban.

"So," said Bruno to Nizib, "you have had nothing since morning because it is Ramadan?"

"Because it is Ramadan," replied Nizib.

"Well, that system would very soon make me thin," exclaimed Bruno. "Why it costs me a pound a day to live, at least!"

"At least," assented Nizib.

"But," continued Kéraban, addressing Van Mitten, "wait until after sunset: you will be astonished. You will perceive a complete transformation—a dead city will prove a living one. Ah, you new-fashioned Turks, you have not yet entirely concealed the old customs under your modern veneer. The Koran holds good against all your absurdities. May Mahomet strangle you!"

"Good friend Kéraban," replied Van Mitten, "I perceive you are still faithful to your ancient usage."

"It is more than fidelity, Van Mitten; it is obstinacy. But tell me, my worthy friend: you will remain some time in Constantinople, will you not?"

"Yes; and even——"

"Well, then you belong to me. I will take care of you and be responsible. You shall not leave me."

"So be it; I am yours," said Van Mitten.

"And you, Nizib, you must look after

yonder valet," adding Kéraban indicating Bruno. "I charge you particularly to modify his ideas concerning our wonderful capital."

Nizib made a sign of assent, and at once carried Bruno away into the midst of the crowd which was becoming more and more compact.

"Now I think of it," said Kéraban suddenly, "you have come very opportunely,

"I will carry you across"

Van Mitten. Six weeks later I should have been far away from Constantinople."

"You, Kéraban?"

"Yes; I should have embarked for Odessa by that time."

"For Odessa! Indeed!"

"Well, if you remain so long, we can go to Odessa together. Why should you not accompany me, eh?"

"Why, you see——"

"Nonsense: you will come, won't you?"

"I rather counted upon resting after such a long and fatiguing journey."

"Very well, you shall rest here. Then you can repose at Odessa afterwards for three weeks."

"Kéraban, my friend,——" began the Dutchman.

"I won't listen to you, Van Mitten. You are not going to annoy me at our very first meeting, I suppose? You know I am right, and am not easily put off."

"Yes, I know," said Van Mitten; "yet——"

"Besides," continued his friend, "you do not know my nephew Ahmet, and you really must become acquainted with him."

"You have already spoken of your nephew to me——"

"Say rather, my son: but I have no child. Business, you know; all business. I never have had five minutes to spare to get married in!"

"One minute is enough," replied Van Mitten seriously; "and very often one minute is too long."

"You will meet Ahmet at Odessa," said Kéraban. "A charming fellow. He detests business, for instance; he is somewhat of an artist, and trifles with The Muses; but charming, charming! He resembles his uncle in nothing, and obeys him without argument."

"Friend Kéraban——"

"Yes, yes; I understand: it is for his wedding that we are going to Odessa."

"His wedding!"

"Certainly. Ahmet is going to marry a lovely girl, Amasia, daughter of my banker Selim—a true Turk—like myself. We shall have a regular *fête*; it will be splendid. You will be there."

"But I should prefer—if——"

"It is all arranged," interrupted the inflexible Kéraban, cutting short Van Mitten's last feeble protest. "You can never have the face to resist me."

"I should like to——"

"But you can't. There!"

At that moment Scarpante and the Maltese captain, who had been walking up and down the open space, approached the two friends. Seigneur Kéraban was saying to his companion:

"That's understood. In six weeks at latest, we will start for Odessa together."

"And the wedding will take place——"

"As soon as we arrive," replied Kéraban.

Yarhud whispered to Scarpante—

"Six weeks! We have plenty of time."

"Yes, but not too much; however, the more the better," replied his friend. "Don't forget, Yarhud, that before the six weeks have passed, Seigneur Saffar will have returned to Trebizond."

So they continued their promenade, but with eyes and ears open.

Meantime Kéraban had continued his conversation with Van Mitten.

"My friend Selim," he said, "is always hurried, and my nephew is in tremendous haste and more impatient still for the conclusion of the marriage. I must tell you that they have some reason for their impatience. The young lady must be married before she is seventeen, or she will lose a fortune of one hundred thousand pounds (Turkish*) which an old fool of an aunt has left her under that condition. Her seventeen years will expire in six weeks. So I made her listen to reason, and told her that the marriage need not take place till the end of next month."

"Your friend Selim has no objection, then?"

"Naturally, none."

"And Ahmet——"

"He is most willing, of course. He adores Amasia, and I approve. He has plenty of time for marrying and has no business at all. You can understand his anxiety, being a married man, Van Mitten."

"Yes, oh, certainly!" replied the Dutchman. "But it is a long time ago, and I can scarcely remember all about it."

"But, though in Turkey we are forbidden by etiquette to enquire concerning the health of our friends' wives, it is not forbidden in the cases of strangers. I hope Madame Van Mitten is quite well?"

"Oh yes, thank you. Quite well; very well indeed," replied Van Mitten, who did not appear very much at his ease. "Yes, perfectly well. But always suffering, you know. Women, as you are aware——"

"No, no; I don't know anything about them," interrupted Kéraban. "Women!

* About £90,000 English money.

No. Business, as much as you like. Macedonian tobacco for the cigarettes, Persian for the narghilés. My correspondents at Salonica, Erzeroum, Latakia, Bafra, Trebizond, not omitting my good friend Van Mitten of Rotterdam. For thirty years, I have exported tobacco from these places to the four corners of Europe."

"And smoked them too!" said Van Mitten.

"Yes, smoked too, like a factory chimney; and may I ask you, do you know anything better in the world?"

"Certainly not, friend Kéraban."

"I have smoked for forty years, my friend: faithful to my chiboque and my narghilé. They constitute my whole harem, and there is not a woman in the world that I value at a pipe of tompéki."

"I am quite of your opinion," replied the Dutchman.

"Now that I have got you here," said Kéraban, "I am going to keep you. You shall not escape me. My caïque is coming to meet me to carry me across the Bosphorus. I dine at my villa at Scutari and will carry you across."

"That is, of course if——"

"I will carry you across," reiterated Kéraban, "do you hear? So, make up your mind; are you going to make excuses?"

"No, I accept," replied Van Mitten. "I am yours, body and soul."

"You shall see what a charming place I have got. I built it myself, under the cypress trees, half way up the hill of Scutari, in full view of the Bosphorus and Constantinople. Ah, your true Turk is always on the Asiatic side. Here we have Europe—yonder is Asia, and our progressionists in frock coats cannot carry their ideas so far. They would stultify themselves if they crossed the Bosphorus. Come, let us go to dinner."

"You may do as you please with me," replied Van Mitten, resigning himself to his impetuous friend.

"And you cannot help yourself," he replied. Then turning round he called out, "Nizib! Where is Nizib?"

The valet, who was walking about with Bruno, came hurrying up with him when he heard his master's voice.

"Has the caidji arrived with the caïque?" enquired Kéraban.

"With the caique!" said Nizib.

"I will thrash him, he may be sure. Yes, he shall have a hundred strokes of the stick."

"Oh!" exclaimed Van Mitten.

"Five hundred," continued Kéraban angrily.

"Oh!" exclaimed Bruno.

"A thousand," cried the merchant, "if he disappoints me!"

"Seigneur Kéraban," said Nizib, "I see your boatman. He has quitted Seraglio Point, and in ten minutes will have reached the steps yonder."

While Kéraban loitered about with impatience, leaning upon the arm of Van Mitten, Yarhud and Scarpante did not cease to observe him closely.

# KÉRABAN THE INFLEXIBLE;

## OR, ADVENTURES IN THE EUXINE.

By Jules Verne.

### Chapter IV.

### Showing how Seigneur Kéraban, more headstrong than ever, came into collision with the Turkish Authorities.

OWEVER, as it proved, the caidji had arrived, and he came to inform Kéraban that his caique was waiting at the steps.

These "caidjis" may be numbered in hundreds on the waters of the Bosphorus, and the Golden Horn. Their boats are impelled by two rowers, one in front, the other astern, and can be rowed in either direction at will. They are about fifteen or twenty feet long, made of beech or cypress wood, carved and painted. It is astonishing with what rapidity these graceful boats glide about and cross each other's course on the splendid stretch of water that separates the two continents. The influential corporation of watermen, (caïdjis) is charged with maintaining the service from the Sea of Marmora as far as the Château d'Europe and the Château d'Asie, which face each other at the mouth of the Bosphorus.

The caïdjis are generally respectable men, dressed in a kind of shirt of silk—a many coloured "yelek" embroidered with gold, and short white cotton drawers. They wear a fez, and shoes, their arms and legs are naked.

If the caïdji daily employed by Seigneur Kéraban to row him from Scutari to Constantinople had been harshly received for his delay, one must not be surprised. The phlegmatic boatman did not make any complaint, he knew very well he had an excellent customer, and made no answer. He merely indicated the steps at which the boat was moored.

Then Kéraban, accompanied by Van Mitten and followed by Bruno and Nizib, proceeded to the place of embarkation, but halted when a movement was perceived amongst the crowd on the Top-Hané.

"What is the matter yonder?" asked Kéraban.

At that moment the chief of the police of Galata, accompanied by several of his men, was perceived upon the "place." A drummer and a bugler accompanied them. The former beat the "ruffle" and the latter blew a "call," and by these means succeeded in imposing silence upon the crowd, which was composed of very heterogeneous elements—Asiatic and European.

"Here is some other iniquitous proclamation, no doubt," muttered Kéraban, in the tone of a man who was determined to stand upon his rights everywhere and always.

The chief of police then drew from his pocket a paper, which was embellished with the official seals; and in a loud voice read the contents as follows:—

"By command of the Muchir, President of the Council of the Police:—An impost of ten paras from this day will be demanded from everyone who may cross the Bosphorus from Constantinople to Scutari, or from Scutari to Constantinople, by caïque, or by any other species of vessel, by steam or sail. Whosoever refuses to pay this tax shall be arrested, sent to prison, and fined for his contumacy.

"Given at the Palace, the 16th of the present month,
(Signed) "THE MUCHIR."

Murmurs of discontent arose when this novel tax was thus proclaimed. The impost was equal to about five centimes or one half-penny a head.

"Very good! Another tax!" exclaimed an old Turk, sarcastically, who ought to

Caïques on the Bosphoras.

have been accustomed to these exactions so capriciously demanded by the Financiers of the Padischah.

"Ten paras! The price of a small cup of coffee," remarked another, gloomily.

The chief of police, knowing very well that Turks like other people will grumble but pay nevertheless, was about to quit the Top-Hané when Kéraban accosted him.

"So," said he, "there's a new tax imposed upon all those who cross the Bosphorus?"

"By proclamation of the Muchir," replied the chief of police. "But," he added, "surely the rich Kéraban is not complaining of it?"

"Yes, the rich Kéraban," replied that individual.

"And you are quite well, Seigneur Kéraban, I hope?"

Quite well; as well as taxes will permit. Now is this tax already imposed?"

"Certainly. Since the proclamation was issued."

"And if I wish to go across to Scutari this evening in my caïque, as I usually do——?"

Kéraban objects to the new Tax.

"You must pay ten paras."

"And as I cross the Bosphorus every morning and evening——"

"That will cost you twenty paras a-day," replied the chief of police. "A mere nothing for the rich, Seigneur Kéraban."

"Indeed!" was the answer.

"My master will get into some scrape," muttered Nizib to Bruno.

"He must give way though, eventually," said Bruno.

"He—give way? You don't know him yet," replied Nizib.

Meanwhile, Seigneur Kéraban, folding his

arms and staring into the very soul of the chief of the police, appeared to be working himself up into a nice little passion. He spoke at length in a voice in which his irritation was very evident.

"Well, there is my boatman, who has come to tell me that my caïque is waiting for me; and as my friend Van Mitten, and my servant and his will accompany me——"

"You will have to pay forty paras," replied the officer; "and, as I said before, you can very easily afford such a trifle."

"That I have the means to pay forty paras, or a hundred, or a thousand, or a hundred thousand is nothing to the purpose," replied Kéraban. "But I will pay nothing, and I will cross just the same."

"I am very sorry to oppose Seigneur Kéraban," replied the chief of the police, "but he cannot pass without payment."

"He will pass without paying."

"No, indeed!"

"Yes, indeed!"

"Friend Kéraban," began Van Mitten, with the laudable intention of making this headstrong individual listen to reason, "My friend——"

"Let me alone, Van Mitten," retorted Kéraban, angrily. "This tax is perfectly iniquitous, vexatious. It ought not to be submitted to. Never--no never would the old *régime* have dared to levy a tax upon the caïques on the Bosphorus."

"Well, at any rate, the new *régime* have need of money," remarked the chief of the police, "and they have not hesitated to do so."

"We shall see about that," said Kéraban.

"Guard," said the chief, addressing his men, "you will see that the new proclamation is carried out."

"Come, Van Mitten," said Kéraban, stamping his foot. "Bruno, Nizib, follow us."

"You must pay forty paras," remarked the chief of police quietly.

"Forty blows of the stick," replied Kéraban, irritably. But scarcely had he advanced towards the steps where the caique lay, when the guard surrounded him and his friends, and obliged them to retrace their steps.

"Let me pass," he exclaimed, putting himself into a defiant attitude. "Do not dare to touch me, any of you, even with the tips of your fingers! I will pass, by Allah; and that too without the loss of a single para."

"Yes, you may pass, certainly; through the prison-door," replied the chief of police, who was getting rather excited also; "and you will pay a pretty fine before you come out again."

"I will go to Scutari."

"Not by crossing the Bosphorus; and as it is impossible to go any other way——"

"You think so, do you?" sneered Kéraban, who with clenched hands and red face looked quite apoplectic. "You think so; well, then, I will go to Scutari, and I will not cross the Bosphorus, neither will I pay the fine."

"Really!"

"Even if I have to go all round the Black Sea," said Kéraban in conclusion.

"Seven hundred leagues to save ten paras!" exclaimed the chief of police, shrugging his shoulders.

"Seven hundred leagues! A thousand, ten thousand, a hundred thousand," shouted Kéraban the obstinate; "were it a question of only five—two—or even a single para."

"But, my friend," began Van Mitten.

"Let me alone, I tell you," exclaimed Kéraban, putting him aside.

"He is off now," muttered Bruno.

"And," continued Kéraban to the chief of police, "I will go through Turkey and the Chersonese, I will cross the Caucasus, walk through Anatolia, and reach Scutari without having paid a single para of your iniquitous impost."

"We shall see about that," responded the chief of police.

"You shall see it all," retorted Kéraban, now thoroughly roused, "and I will start this evening."

"*Diable*," exclaimed captain Yarhud to his friend Scarpante, who had not lost a word of this discussion. "This will rather disarrange our plans!"

"Yes, indeed," replied the other. "A very little would induce this headstrong fellow to persist in his mad project; and if so, he will pass Odessa when the marriage may be concluded."

"But," again said Van Mitten to Kéraban, with the hope of dissuading him from his mad project, "you must——"

The Summons to Evening Prayer.

"Will you be quiet! Leave me alone!" said Kéraban.

"Remember the marriage of your nephew Ahmet," said Van Mitten, persistently.

"We will see that is completed."

Scarpante then whispered to Yarhud aside:—

"We have not an hour to lose!"

"You are right," replied the Mal tese captain, "and early to-morrow morning I will start for Odessa by the railway."

Then these two worthies withdrew from the crowd, and as they turned away, Kéraban called out to his servant:

"Nizib," he said.

"Yes, sir!"

"Follow me to the counting-house."

"To the counting-house," replied Nizib.

"And you too, Van Mitten," added Kéraban.

"I?"

"And you also, Bruno."

"Yes, but——"

"We will go all together."

"Eh!" exclaimed Bruno pricking up his ears.

"Yes; I have invited you to dinner at Scutari," said the Seigneur Kéraban to Van Mitten; "and, by Allah, at Scutari you shall dine—when we return."

"But we shall not be back for——how long?" said Bruno.

"Not for a month, a year, ten years perhaps," replied Kéraban, in a tone that admitted of no discussion. "You have accepted my invitation to dinner, and my dinner you shall eat!"

"It will have got cold by that time;" muttered Bruno.

"Will you allow me, friend Kéraban——"

"I will allow you nothing, friend Van Mitten. Come."

So saying, Kéraban advanced a few steps towards the end of the promenade.

"We are quite unable to withstand this 'pig-headed' fellow," said Van Mitten to Bruno.

"But are you really going to yield to such caprice, sir?"

"Whether I remain here, or go elsewhere, it is all the same to me, so long as we do not touch Rotterdam," replied his master.

"But, sir——"

"And since I follow my friend Kéraban, you have no alternative but to follow me," continued Van Mitten.

"Here is a pretty complication!" remarked the valet.

"Let us be off," cried Kéraban, who then addressed himself to the chief of the police in a sneering tone, calculated to exasperate that official.

"I am going," he said. "I shall depart despite all your arrests. I will go to Scutari without crossing the Bosphorus."

"I will do myself the pleasure of witnessing your return from such a strange journey," replied the chief of police.

"I shall be extremely glad to meet you on my return," responded Kéraban politely.

"But I may as well inform you that if the tax is still in force when you come back——"

"Well?" said Kéraban.

"I cannot let you pass from Scutari to Constantinople across the Bosphorus without paying the ten paras per head."

"Well then, if your iniquitous impost is still in force when I return, I will find out some way of crossing to. Constantinople without paying a single para: there!"

So saying Kéraban took Van Mitten's arm and made a sign to Nizib and Bruno to follow them. The party quickly disappeared, amid the crowd which cheered this partizan of the Old Turkish *régime* who was so tenacious of his rights.

Just then the report of a cannon was heard. The sun was setting beyond the Sea of Marmora: the fast of Ramadan was at an end, and the faithful subjects of the Sultan might now indemnify themselves for the privations of that long day.

As suddenly as by means of an enchanter's wand Constantinople was transformed. To the silence of the Top-Hané succeeded cries of joy and pleasure. Cigarettes and every description of pipe were immediately produced and lighted: the air was odorous with tobacco. The *cafés* were quickly crowded to overflowing by hungry and thirsty customers. All kinds of pastry and sweetmeats and more solid food were eaten, and every known beverage appeared on the tables as if by magic. The shops were brilliantly illuminated, and the transformation was complete in the twinkling of an eye!

Then the old town and its new quarters were lighted up as magically. The Mosques—St. Sophia, the Suleimanieh, Sultan-Ahmed, all the civil and religious edifices from Seraï Burnou as far as the hills of Eyoub, were crowned with many-coloured fires. Luminous verses were suspended from one minaret to another, tracing the precepts of the Koran upon the dark background of the sky. The Bosphorus studded by the lanthorns carried by the caïques which were tossed about by the waves, scintillated as if the stars had fallen upon the water. The palace upon the margin, the villas on both the European and the Asiatic sides, Scutari, the ancient Chrysopolis, and its houses built up in amphitheatre form, by stages; presented only lines of fire which were reflected from the sparkling sea.

From the far distance resounded the notes of the tambourine, the lute, or guitar, the tabourka, the rebek and the flute; mingled with the chanting of hymns and psalms of evensong, for the dying day. And at the summits of the minarets, the muezzins, in the call of three prolonged notes, sent over the city—the city now in festive array—the last summons to the evening prayer, which consists of one Turkish with two Arabic words, *Allah, Hœkk Kébir*!

---

## Chapter V

### How Seigneur Kéraban discussed his journey and how he quitted Constantinople.

Turkey in Europe actually comprehends three principal provinces, Roumania (Thrace and Macedonia), Albania and Thessaly, and a tributary province, Bulgaria. It is only since the treaty of 1878, that the kingdom of Roumania, with the principalities of Servia and Montenegro, have been declared independent, and Austria occupied Bosnia, less the "sanjak" of Novi Bazar.

Seigneur Kéraban, when he made up his mind to follow the littoral of the Black Sea, perceived he would have to proceed by the coasts of Roumelia, Bulgaria and Roumania to reach the Russian frontier. Thence crossing Bessarabia, the Chersonese, Tauridis, or even the Tcherkess country, over the Caucasus and Transcaucasia, the route would turn southward and eastward by the Euxine to the limit which separates Russia from the Ottoman Empire.

Afterwards, by the littoral of Anatolia to the south of the Black Sea, the most headstrong of Ottomans would reach the Bosphorus at Scutari once again without having paid the newly imposed tax.

In fact he had to make a journey of six hundred and fifty Turkish "agatchs," which are equal to about two thousand, eight hundred kilométres, or to reckon by the Ottoman league—that is to say, the distance which a horse will ordinarily walk in an hour—the tour embraced a distance of seven hundred leagues, twenty-five to a degree. Now, from the 17th August to 30th September, there are forty-five days; so Kéraban must make fifteen leagues in four-and-twenty hours, if he wished to return by the 30th September, the last day on which the marriage of Amasia could take place if the conditions of the will respecting the hundred thousand pounds of her aunt must be fulfilled. In any case, Kéraban and his guest would not be able to sit down at his table in Scutari, and eat the dinner there awaiting them, in less than forty-five days.

Nevertheless, by taking advantage of the several railway lines, the journey and the time could have been very considerably abridged. Thus, from Constantinople the railway may be traversed to Andrinople and a branch thence to Janboli. The Varna and Rutschuck line unites with the Roumanian railways, and these extend to southern Russia by Jassi, Kisscheneff, Kharkow, Taganrog, and so on up to the Caucasus. A line from Tiflis to Poti runs to the Black Sea shore, and reaches almost to the Russian frontier. Certainly there is no railway across Turkey in Asia nearer than Broussa, but thence Scutari may be reached by the iron road.

But to argue on the above lines with Seigneur Kéraban, would have been so much time wasted. That he—one of the Old Turks—would condescend to make use of these modern appliances of locomotion, he, who for forty years had resisted all European encroachments! The idea was preposterous! Never! He would rather walk every step of the way than cede the point!

So that same evening when Van Mitten and the merchant had reached the office of the latter at Galata, the question had been already raised and settled. The Dutchman's first suggestion respecting railroads was received with a shrug of the shoulders, and finally with a point-blank refusal, by Kéraban.

"Nevertheless," continued Van Mitten, who thought it right to insist, though without any hope of persuading his host, "Nevertheless, it seems to me——"

"When I say 'No,'" interrupted Kéraban, "I mean No. Besides, you are my guest, I have to take care of you, and you cannot proceed without me," he added.

"So be it," answered Van Mitten. "But putting railways aside, perhaps there are some simple means whereby we may reach Scutari without crossing the Bosphorus, but still without going all round the Black Sea."

"What are they?" enquired Kéraban frowning. "If they are good, I will adopt them; if bad, I decline."

"I know an excellent way," said Van Mitten.

"Speak quickly. We have to make all our preparations yet. We have not a minute to lose!"

"This is my idea," said Van Mitten. "Let us go to one of the nearest ports and cross to Scutari by steamer."

"By steamer! Use a steamboat!" exclaimed Kéraban, raised to "boiling point" at once by the very mention of steam.

"Very well then, by a sailing vessel, a zebec, a felucca, a skiff—anything you please: starting from one of the Anatolian ports, Kirpih for instance. Thence we could reach Scutari in a day, and drink the health of the muchir on our arrival!"

Seigneur Kéraban had permitted his friend to continue without interruption. Perhaps he was already inclined to adopt Van Mitten's suggestion, which promised a solution of the difficulty, and, at the same time saved his own pride and *amour propre*. But after a while his eyes kindled, his fingers clenched and unclenched, and at length his fists, tightly closed, indicated a by no means reassuring temper to Nizib, who knew the signs.

"So, Van Mitten, you counsel me to embark upon the Black Sea to avoid crossing the Bosphorus? That is what your suggestion comes to."

"That would be the best plan, I think," replied Van Mitten.

"Have you ever heard any mention of a certain malady called sea sickness?" enquired Kéraban, quickly.

"Of course I have," replied the Dutchman.

"And you have never experienced it?"

"Never. Besides the transit is such a short one——"

"So short!" exclaimed Kéraban. "And may I enquire what you call 'so short?'"

"Scarcely sixty leagues, I imagine."

"Well, it does not matter whether it be only fifty, or twenty, or ten, or only five," exclaimed Kéraban, who always became excited when contradicted or opposed. "If it were only two leagues, they would be too long for me!"

"But just think for a moment——"

"Do you know the Bosphorus?"

"Yes."

"There is scarce half-a-league of water between here and Scutari?"

"I believe so."

"Well then, whenever there is the least wind, I am always ill when crossing in my caique."

"Sea-sick?" enquired Van Mitten.

"I should be equally upset on a pond or in a bath. So now speak to me again about crossing the Black Sea, if you dare. Just dare to suggest to me any transit by sailing vessel again! try it!"

We need scarcely add that the worthy Dutchman did not discuss the question farther and the suggestion dropped.

But how should they proceed? Communications were not easily made—at least in Turkey; but they are not impossible. On the ordinary routes relays could be found, and the travellers could journey on horseback, with provisions and supplies and with a guide—at least they could put themselves under the care of the Tartar courier who is charged with the postal service. But as the courier has only a limited time to proceed from one station to another, to follow him would induce too much fatigue; and to those unaccustomed to such rapid travelling, rideing "post haste" was out of the question.

In any case the Seigneur Kéraban did not intend to travel in this manner. He would proceed rapidly, but comfortably.

Kéraban's Luggage.

It was merely a question ot expense, and that would have no weight with the rich merchant of Galata.

"Well," said Van Mitten in a resigned tone, "since we can't travel by railway, steam-boat or sailing vessel, how do you propose that we *shall* proceed?"

"By post chaise."

"With your own horses?"

"With relays"

"And do you expect to find relays all along the route?

"Yes, I do."

"They will be very expensive!"

"What it will cost, it *will* cost," replied Kéraban, who again began to feel ruffled.

"You won't get out of this journey under a thousand pounds (Turkish)—perhaps fifteen hundred pounds,* said Van Mitten.

"Be it so! I will spend millions, I tell you: *millions* if necessary. Now have you come to the end of your objections?"

"Yes," replied the Dutchman.

"And time too," said Kéraban, in a tone which suggested to Van Mitten the propriety of holding his tongue.

Nevertheless, he could not refrain from remarking to his imperious host that the journey would be attended with great expense; that he himself was expecting large remittances from Holland which he intended to place in the Bank at Constantinople; that in fact he had not much money with him; and——"

Here Kèraban put his hand upon his friend's mouth, and informed him that the expenses of the journey concerned him (Kéraban) and him only; that Van Mitten was his guest; and that it was his custom to pay his guests' expenses, etc., etc.

At the "etc.s" the Dutchman gave in, and no more was said on that point.

Had Kéraban not been the fortunate possessor of an old English-built carriage, he would have been driven to the necessity of hiring a Turkish "araba" drawn by oxen. But the old post-chaise which had made the journey from Rotterdam was there in the stable and quite ready for use.

This chaise was comfortably arranged for three travellers. In front a great box of provisions and luggage was secured, and behind a seat was carried up in the form of a hooded "rumble," in which two servants could travel comfortably. There was no coachman's "box," so the journey must be accomplished by post-horses.

It no doubt appeared ridiculous to modern *connoisseurs*, but the vehicle was well-built, hung on good springs, had large wheels, and was capable of defying the roughest roads.

Van Mitten and Kéraban occupied the interior of the chaise; Bruno and Nizib were perched up behind in the "cabriolet," which afforded them shelter and was furnished with glasses which they could pull up at pleasure. Under such circumstances they felt equal to the journey to China, but fortunately the Black Sea did not extend so far, or Van Mitten would have been introduced to the "celestial" capital.

Preparations for the journey were at once commenced, and if Kéraban could not start that very evening, as in the heat of the discussion he said he would do, he determined to leave the city at dawn next morning.

One night is not too long a period to make arrangements for such an expedition, and to put business matters in train. So the *employés* at the counting-house were "requisitioned" just as they were about to refresh themselves after a long day's fast. And Nizib was there, invaluable on all such occasions.

As for Bruno he had to return to the Hotel de Pesth, Grande Rue de Pera, where his master and he had arrived that very morning, and arrange for the transfer of their luggage to the business premises of Kéraban. The faithful Dutchman was accompanied by his master, for he would not have dared to leave him.

"So, sir, it is all decided;" he said, as soon as he and Van Mitten had quitted the merchant's house.

"How can it be otherwise with such a man as Kéraban?" said Van Mitten.

"And we are going all round the Black Sea?"

"Yes; unless my friend alters his course, which is almost an impossible contingency."

"I never thought we should ever find such a pig-headed Mussulman as he is," remarked Bruno.

"Your comparison, if not polite, is nevertheless correct," replied his master; "so, as I have hurt my hand in trying to hammer sense into him, I will abstain from attempting it in future."

"I was hoping to rest a little in Constan-

* The Turkish pound is a gold coin equal to 2 paras, 25 cents, about 100 piastres.

tinople," said Bruno. "This journey and I——"

"This is not a journey, Bruno; it is simply 'another way' that Kéraban is taking me home to dine with him!"

But this way of looking at things did not suit Bruno. He did not like moving; and here he was destined to be travelling about for weeks—perhaps months—across various countries; interesting, no doubt, but difficult and dangerous. Besides, the fatigue consequent upon such a journey would reduce him considerably in size and weight, and he would lose some of those hundred and sixty-seven pounds which he valued so highly.

Then his lamentable refrain came to his master's ears over and over again—

"Something will happen to you, sir; something evil will come of it, I tell you."

"We shall see in good time," replied the Dutchman. "Meanwhile collect our luggage, while I go and purchase a 'Guide' of the countries, and a note-book to record our impressions. Then you can return here and go to bed—or rest yourself."

"When?"

"When we have made the tour of the Black Sea, for it is fated we must make it."

With this fatalism, which a Mussulman need not have been ashamed of, Bruno shook his head, and departed. The journey certainly did not commend itself to him.

Two hours later, Bruno came back with the baggage carried by stout porters. These were the natives whom Théophile Gautier called "two-footed camels without humps."

The "gibbosity," however, was not wanting in this instance, for the men carried heavy packs or trunks on their backs. These were deposited in the court yard, and the chaise was loaded.

Meantime Kéraban was putting his affairs in order, and giving instructions to his clerks and managers. He wrote some letters, and drew a large sum in gold, as paper money was depreciated. He required Russian money, too, and he proposed to change his Ottoman gold at the *caisse* of his friend Selim, the banker, at Odessa.

The preparations were rapidly completed. Provisions were packed, and some defensive weapons deposited in the chaise, in readiness for an emergency. Kéraban had not forgotten two narghilés, for Van Mitten and himself, an article quite indispensible to a Turk, and particularly for a tobacco-merchant.

The horses had been ordered to arrive at daybreak. From midnight to sunrise there was time for supper and some sleep. Next morning, when Seigneur Kéraban sent to call the rest of the party, they jumped up and dressed in their travelling costumes.

The chaise was ready; the horses harnessed; the postillion mounted; he was waiting for the travellers.

Seigneur Kéraban repeated his instructions to his men. All were ready to start.

Van Mitten, Bruno, and Nizib waited, silent, in the yard.

"So you have really determined?" whispered Van Mitten to his friend Kéraban.

The latter merely pointed to the chaise, but made no verbal reply.

Van Mitten bowed, and gravely entered the carriage, taking the left-hand seat, Kéraban entered after him. Nizib and Bruno climbed up into the "cabriolet" at the back.

"Ah, my letter!" exclaimed Kéraban, just as the postillion was starting his horses.

Then, letting down the window, he handed a letter to one of his clerks, with directions to put it in the post.

This letter was addressed to his housekeeper at his villa at Scutari, and contained only these words—

"Dinner put off until my return. Change the *menu*. Soup *au lait caillé*, shoulder of mutton *aux épices*. Be sure it is not overdone."

Then the chaise rolled away through the streets, crossed the Golden Horn on the bridge of Validèh Sultane, and quitted the town by Jené Kapoussi, the New-gate.

Seigneur Kéraban has gone! May Allah protect him!

# KÉRABAN THE INFLEXIBLE;

## OR, ADVENTURES IN THE EUXINE.

By Jules Verne.

### Chapter VI.

Showing how the Travellers encountered some Difficulties, chiefly in the Delta of the Danube.

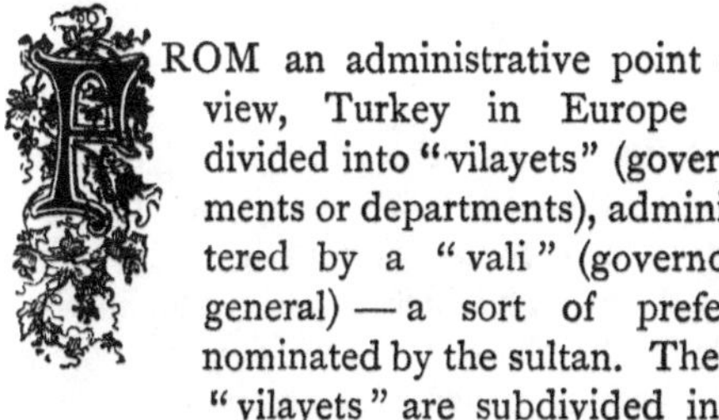

FROM an administrative point of view, Turkey in Europe is divided into "vilayets" (governments or departments), administered by a "vali" (governor-general) — a sort of prefect nominated by the sultan. These "vilayets" are subdivided into "sanjaks" or districts governed by a "moustesarif," into "kazas" or cantons administered by a "caimacan"; and "nahaies" or communes, with a "moudir" or mayor. This, as will be perceived, is something like the French system of administration.

But, as a matter of fact, Kéraban had few if any points of contact with the authorities of the "vilayets" of Roumelia, which cuts the route from Constantinople to the frontier. This route keeps, as nearly as possible, to the shore of the Black Sea, and shortened the journey he had to make.

The weather was very pleasant for travelling. The heat was tempered by a refreshing breeze from the sea, which came in an uninterrupted course across the somewhat flat country. First the fields of maize, barley, and rye, with vineyards, which are widely cultivated in the Ottoman empire, met the eye. Then came forests of oaks, pines, beech, birch; then clusters here and there of plantains, Judas-tree, laurels, figs, St. John's bread-tree, and, particularly near the sea, pomegranates and olives identical with those of the same latitude of lower Europe.

Leaving the gate of Jeni the carriage took the road to Choumla, whence a branch-road leads to Andrinople by way of Kirk-Kilisie. This road follows, and many times crosses, the railway which puts Andrinople, the second capital of the Ottoman empire, in communication with Constantinople.

As the carriage was being driven rapidly alongside the railway, the train overtook the travellers, and a man put his head out of a railway carriage to have a look at the chaise, which was proceeding at a great pace.

This traveller was no other than the Maltese captain, Yarhud, who was on his way to Odessa, where, thanks to the speed of the train, he would arrive long before the uncle of young Ahmet.

Van Mitten could not resist his impulse to call the attention of his companion to the train, which sped past them at a high speed. Kéraban merely shrugged his shoulders.

"Eh, friend Kéraban, they get to their destination very quickly," said Van Mitten.

"Yes, when they *do* arrive at it," replied Kéraban.

Not an hour was lost in this the first day of the expedition. As money in plenty was forthcoming, there were no delays in procuring horses: the animals were quite as willing as the postillions to work for a master who paid so handsomely.

The travellers passed Tchataldje, by Buyuk Khan, by the watershed of the tributaries of the Sea of Marmora, by the valley of Tchorloxa, by the village of Yeni Keni; then by the valley of Galata, across which, if the legend be true, are dug subterranean canals which used to supply the capital with water.

At night fall the carriage stopped, but only for an hour, at the long, straggling village of Serai. As the provisions the travellers carried with them were more particularly destined for consumption in the localities where it would be difficult to procure food even of inferior quality, it was decided to keep the store in reserve. So Kéraban and his companions dined at Serai, and the journey was then resumed.

Bruno, we may venture to say, found it somewhat unpleasant to pass the night in the "dicky" of the carriage, but Nizib had no such feelings, and accepted the situation as a matter of course. He slept soundly, and set his companion such a good example that he could not do otherwise than profit by it.

The night passed without incident, thanks to the long and winding road which formed the approach to the town of Viga, and avoided the rude slopes and marshy ground of the valley. Van Mitten much regretted that he could not see that little town, which contains about a thousand people, almost all Greeks, and which is the seat of a bishop. But he had not come to *see*. He was the companion of the Inflexible Kéraban who did not trouble himself to collect any impressions of his journey.

About five o'clock the next evening, after having passed the villages of Bounar-Hissan, Jena, and Uskùp, the travellers threaded a little wood wherein were several tombs. In the graves underneath lay the remains of the victims of a band of brigands who had at one time infested the neighbourhood. The travellers then reached a fair-sized town containing about 16,000 inhabitants, called Kirk-Kilisse. This name, which signifies "Forty Churches," is justified by the number of religious edifices. It is situated in a valley, the sides and bottom of which are occupied by the houses where Van Mitten and his valet explored in a few hours.

The carriage was put up in the courtyard of a respectable hotel, where Seigneur Kéraban and his companions passed the night, and started again at daybreak.

During the day (19 August) the postillion cleared the village of Karabounar, and in the evening, late, arrived at Bourgaz, which is situated on the gulf of that name. The travellers slept that evening in a "khan," or kind of rude inn, which certainly was not so comfortable as the post-chaise.

Next morning they found the road parted with the coast, and ran inland towards Aidos; in the evening the party arrived at Paravadi, one of the stations of the little railway from Choumla to Varna. They then traversed the province of Bulgaria to the southern extremity of the Dobroutcha, at the foot of the last spurs of the Balkan chain.

At this point the difficulties became serious: there were so many swampy valleys, so many forests of aquatic plants to be passed, through which it was almost impossible for the chaise to make way, and where its progress disturbed from their retreats thousands of wild-fowl.

The Balkans form a very important mountain chain. In its range between Bulgaria and Roumelia it detaches many spurs northward which extend in undulations almost to the Danube.

Hereabouts Kéraban's patience was sorely tried.

When it became necessary to cross the extremity of the chain before descending into the Dobroutcha the tremendously steep slopes and awkward corners rendered it quite impossible to drive the carriage round. So the horses had to be unharnessed several times in these narrow roads only suitable for horses alone, and all these arrangements took up a great deal of time, and gave rise to considerable ill-temper and much recrimination. When the horses were taken out, the carriage-wheels had to be blocked and lifted round, and above all "greased" with a considerable handful of piastres, which the postillions put into their pockets, declaring all the time that they must retrace their steps.

Kéraban had good ground for inveighing against the existing government which permitted the roads to get so greatly out of repair, and which did so little to facilitate travelling in the provinces. The "divan" would not put itself out, except to impose taxes and restrictions of all kinds. Seigneur Kéraban knew all about it! Ten paras to cross the Bosphorus indeed! He always harked back to this fixed idea, which continually oppressed him. Ten paras: ten paras, forsooth!

Van Mitten took very good care not to answer Kéraban. The very suspicion of contradiction would have enraged his inflexible companion. So Van Mitten, by way of appeasing his friend, found fault with all governments, and the Turkish administration in particular.

"The tremendously steep slopes and awkward corners."

"But it is not possible that there could be such abuses in Holland!" exclaimed Kéraban.

"On the contrary, there are, my friend;" replied Van Mitten, who was desirous to appease his companion at any cost.

"I tell you there are not," retorted the latter. "It is only in Constantinople that such things are possible. Do you mean to tell me that they would put a tax upon caiques at Rotterdam?"

"We have no caiques there," replied Van Mitten.

"That is no matter."

"No matter—what do you mean?"

"Well, supposing you had them there, your king would never venture to tax them. Now don't tell me that this new-fangled Turkish government is not the very worst in the world."

"The worst! not a doubt of it," responded Van Mitten, who was anxious to bring the discussion to a close.

And so, the better to put an end to what after all was a mere conversation, he took out his long Dutch pipe, and the appearance of the pipe made Kéraban anxious to stupefy himself also with the fumes of his *narghilé*. The carriage was quickly filled with tobacco smoke and the glasses had to be let down to permit it to escape. So, by degrees and under the influence of the weed, the obstinate one became silent and even calm, until some trivial incident aroused him to the realities of the journey.

It became necessary, in the absence of shelter, to pass the night of the 20th of August in the carriage; and it was only when morning dawned that the last spurs of the Balkans were crossed, and the travellers found themselves beyond the Roumanian frontier in the more suitable roads of the Dobroutcha.

This region is almost a peninsula, formed by a great bend of the Danube, which, after turning northwards towards Galatz, bends to the east again towards the Black Sea, into which it discharges itself by many mouths. Indeed, the isthmus, so to speak, which unites the "peninsula" to the Balkans, is circumscribed by the portion of the province situated between Tchernavoda and Kustendjé, which are connected by railway. But south of the railroad, the country being essentially the same as the northern portion, topographical speaking, one may say that the plains of the Dobroutcha have their birth at the base of the last hills of the Balkan chain.

"The good country," the Turks call this fertile tract wherein the land belongs to the first occupant. It is, if not inhabited, at any rate traversed by Tartar shepherds, and populated by Valaques in the portions near the river. The Ottoman Empire owns a considerable portion of this land, which exhibits a succession of plateaux, scarcely intersected by any valleys, which extend almost to the forests by the mouths of the Danube.

Upon the even roads the chaise proceeded rapidly. The post-masters had no occasion to grumble here when their horses were harnessed, or if they did it was only to keep themselves in practice.

Their progress was rapid, so fast indeed that on the 21st of August the travellers "changed" at Koslidcha and the same evening reached Bazardjik.

At the latter place Kéraban determined to pass the night, and let every member of the party enjoy a good rest, of which Bruno was greatly in need, though he prudently kept his opinion to himself on this subject.

At daylight next morning the travellers proceeded with fresh horses in the direction of Lake Karasou, an immense shaft or reservoir, the waters of which pour themselves into the Danube in dry seasons when the river is low. About twenty-four leagues were accomplished in twelve hours, and at eight o'clock in the evening the carriage stopped at the station of Medjidie on the Kustendjé and Tchernavoda Railway. This town is quite a new one, but it already boasts of twenty thousand inhabitants, and promises to become more important.

At this station the travellers were obliged to wait till the line was clear, greatly to Kéraban's disgust, who was in a hurry to reach the "khan" in which he proposed to pass the night. But a train was on the line, and fifteen minutes elapsed before it proceeded. A torrent of invective was accordingly poured forth upon railway administration in general, which permitted all kinds of ill-doing, and not only smashed those travellers who were foolish enough to travel in the carriages, but hindered others who objected to use the railway.

"At any rate," said Kéraban to Van Mitten, "an accident will never happen to me in a train."

"Who knows?" returned the Dutchman somewhat imprudently.

"I know it!" replied Kéraban in a tone which brought the conversation to an abrupt conclusion.

At length the train moved away from the station; the gates were opened, and the carriage was permitted to pass. The travellers then reached the khan, where they were enabled to lodge comfortably in the place which was named after the Sultan Abdul Medjid.

Next day they crossed a desert to Babadagh, but so slowly was the journey made that it was deemed advisable to continue it through the night. In the evening, about five o'clock, Toultcha was reached. This is one of the most important towns in Moldavia, and in such a city, containing representatives from nearly every country under heaven, Kéraban had no difficulty in selecting a suitable hotel. Van Mitten also had time to explore the town and the amphitheatre, which is very picturesquely situated.

"The Carriage was quickly filled with tobacco smoke."

On the next day (24th August) the travellers crossed the Danube, and it need scarcely be said that the origin of the name of the river was the subject of a lively discussion between Kéraban and Van Mitten, who argued from the Ister or Hister of the Greeks to the Roman name Danuvius, which in Thracian language signified "cloudy." They argued from Celtic, Sanscrit, Greek, and whether Professor Windishman was wrong or Professor Bopp was right, till Kéraban as usual reduced his adversary to silence by saying that Danube came from the Zend word "asdanu," which means the "Rapid River."

But rapid as it may be, its course is not sufficiently quick to carry away all its waters; and consequently inundations of the Danube have to be calculated on. Now Kéraban in his obstinacy did not make any allowances for this, and notwithstanding all remonstrances persisted in crossing the Delta of the Danube.

He was not alone in this determination—that is, hundreds of aquatic birds were also crossing; but he ought to have recognized the fact that, if nature had made these residents web-footed, it was because they would have to inhabit a swampy region liable to inundations.

The horses and the carriage were, however, quite unfitted for such a transit; and the route was practically through a marsh which was almost impassable. Notwithstanding the advice of the postillion, and Van Mitten's remonstrances, Kéraban gave the order to go on. So the men obeyed him. The consequence was that towards evening the carriage became embedded in the slough, and the horses were quite unable to extricate it.

"The roads are not properly attended to in this country," said Van Mitten.

"They are as they are," replied Kéraban, "and just what you might expect under such a government!"

"We should do better if we retraced our steps and endeavoured to find another way," said Van Mitten.

"On the contrary—we shall do better by continuing our journey and not changing our route at all."

"But how are we to get on——?"

"Get on? By sending for some more horses to the nearest village. It makes little difference whether we sleep in the carriage or in an inn, does it?"

There was nothing to be said to such an argument as this. The postillion and Nizib were dispatched for extra horses to the next village, which was not so very far away. They could not be expected to return, however, much before sunrise. So Kéraban, Van Mitten, and Bruno had to reconcile themselves to the fact of passing the night in that vast plain, as desolate a "steppe" as the deserts of central Australia. Fortunately the carriage, already embedded to the axles, gave no signs of sinking any deeper in the quagmire.

The night was very dark. Great clouds came down very near the earth, chased by the winds from the Black Sea. Though there was no actual rain, a thick mist from the saturated ground arose like an Arctic fog. Nothing could be seen at a greater distance than ten paces, and the lamps of the carriage threw only a perplexing gleam through the mist, so that it would have been better, perhaps, to have extinguished them. It was possible that the light might attract some undesirable visitor; but when Van Mitten said so, the obstinate Kéraban argued the point to such a length that it was quite lost. The Dutchman was right nevertheless, and had he been sharp enough to suggest their being left lighted, Kéraban would no doubt have had them extinguished.

Ten o'clock came. Kéraban, Van Mitten, and Bruno, after a light supper which consisted of some of the stores in the hampers, walked about smoking for about half an hour, pacing up and down a narrow path which was firm enough to sustain them.

"Now," said Van Mitten, "I think, friend Kéraban, that there is no objection to our going to sleep in the carriage until the fresh horses come."

"I see no objection whatever," replied Kéraban, after a pause. This reply was somewhat extraordinary for a man who was always making objections.

"I do not think we have anything to fear in the middle of such an extensive plain," said the Dutchman.

"I think not."

"There is no attack likely to made upon us?"

"None."

"Except, perhaps, the attacks of mosquitos," said Bruno, who had just succeeded in administering to himself a hard slap on the face, intended as a death-blow to half-a-dozen of those insects.

As a matter of fact, the worries of these insects became very trying. Attracted,

"Towards evening the carriage became embedded in the slough."

perhaps, by the light of the carriage lamps the mosquitos came singing in myriads around them.

"Hum," said Van Mitten, "there is one thing needful, and that is a mosquito-net."

"These are not mosquitos," said Kéraban, as he scratched the back of his neck, "they are gnats."

"I'll be hanged if I can tell the difference then," remarked Van Mitten, who did not wish to enter upon an entomological discussion.

"It is a very curious thing," remarked Kéraban, "that only the female insect attacks man."

"I think I can understand that," remarked Bruno, rubbing himself.

"I believe we should do well to get into

the chaise," said Van Mitten; "we shall be devoured if we remain here."

"The countries of the Lower Danube are particularly plagued with these gnats, and one ought to sprinkle one's bed and clothing with powder of pyrites."

"Of which we have not a grain," remarked Van Mitten.

"Precisely," answered Kéraban. "But who could have foreseen that we should have been stranded in the marshes of the Dobroutcha?"

"No one, friend Kéraban."

"I have heard it stated," continued Kéraban, "that a colony of Crimean Tartars, to whom the government had made a concession in this delta, was obliged to be broken up in consequence of the attacks of these gnats."

"After our own experience, the tale does not seem improbable," replied Van Mitten.

"Let us get into the carriage again," said Kéraban.

"We have remained out too long already," said his friend, as the mosquitos came buzzing round in myriads, beating their tiny wings thousands of times in a second.

Just as Kéraban and his friend were about to enter the chaise, the former said—

"As we have nothing to fear, had not Bruno better remain outside and wait the return of the postillion?"

"He will not object," said Van Mitten.

"I will not object because it is my duty to obey," replied Bruno. "But I shall be eaten alive."

"No," replied Kéraban. "I am informed that these gnats never bite twice in the same place; so that Bruno will soon be free from their attacks."

"Yes, when I have been bitten in a million places," said Bruno.

"That is what I mean," retorted Kéraban.

"But may I not, at any rate, keep watch in the 'dicky'?" asked Bruno.

"Certainly, so long as you do not go to sleep there."

"And how is it possible for me to sleep in the middle of this swarm of mosquitos?'

"Gnats," replied Kéraban; "merely gnats. Don't forget that, Bruno."

So saying, Kéraban and Van Mitten shut themselves up in the carriage, while Bruno climbed into the 'dicky,' to keep watch over his master, or masters; for since Kéraban and Van Mitten had met, Bruno could certainly count upon two masters.

Bruno, having carefully closed the carriage doors, went to see how the horses fared. The poor brutes, quite exhausted, lay prone upon the ground, breathing loudly, and mingling their hot breath with the fogs of the swamps.

"Old Nick himself will not drag them from this quagmire," muttered Bruno. "Seigneur Kéraban must have had some fine ideas concerning this route; but after all that is his business."

Then the valet ascended to his perch, and let down the glasses, through which he could see the luminous bars projected by the carriage lamps through the mist.

What better could Bruno do to keep himself awake and his eyes open than endeavour to review all the circumstances which had carried him in the train of the inflexible Kéraban, the most pig-headed of all Turks?

So he (Bruno), a native of ancient Batavia, a "loafer" in the streets and on the quays of Rotterdam, a fisherman of very slight pretence, a lounger by the canals which intersected his native town, had been carried away to the opposite end of Europe. He had made an enormous stride from Holland to Turkey. Scarcely disembarked in Constantinople, when fate dragged him to the steppes of the lower Danube. And there he was, perched up in the carriage, in the "dicky" of a post-chaise, in the midst of the marshes of the Dobroutcha, lost in the darkness of night, and fixed in the ground as firmly as the Gothic tower of Zuidekirk. And all this because he had undertaken to obey his master, who, without any necessity, had yielded to Kéraban.

"Oh for the strangeness of human experience," muttered Bruno. "Here I am, in a fair way to make the tour of the Black Sea—if we ever *do* make it—all to save ten paras, which I would willingly have paid out of my own pocket! Ah, this headstrong fellow will ruin me: I have already lost two pounds weight, and in four days! How much shall I have lost in four weeks? Oh, hang these insects!"

Though Bruno had carefully closed the

"Bruno went to see how the horses fared."

"cabriolet," some dozens of gnats had found their way in, and were feasting on him. So he rubbed and slapped and scratched, but so that Kéraban should not hear him.

An hour passed; then another. Perhaps Bruno might have slept, had not the mosquitos prevented any repose. But sleep under the circumstances was impossible.

It was nearly midnight when a brilliant idea occurred to Bruno: he would smoke, and so overcome the persistent attacks of the gnats with the puffs of tobacco. How did it happen he had not thought of it before? If the insects could live in such an atmosphere as he designed to create, they must be very hard to kill—these mosquitos of the Danube.

So he drew his porcelain pipe—a sister of that which had been taken from him in Constantinople—and began to discharge thick volumes of tobacco smoke upon his enemies. The swarm hummed louder than ever, but soon dispersed and sought refuge in obscure corners of the cabriolet.

Bruno congratulated himself upon his manœuvre. The battery which he had unmasked had routed his opponents, they had fled in disorder, but as he did not wish to make any prisoners—indeed, quite the contrary—he opened the glass and let the half stupefied insects escape, knowing that the tobacco would effectually keep the others at bay.

So, having gained the victory, Bruno paused to look around him over the field.

The night was very dark, and strong gusts of wind came tearing over the flats. Had not the carriage been so firmly embedded in the ground, it might have been overturned. But there was no fear of that.

Bruno stared northwards, endeavouring to distinguish some gleam of light which would indicate the approach of the postillion and Nizib with the horses. But the darkness was profound beyond the small space illumined by the carriage lamps. Nevertheless, while straining his eyes into the darkness, Bruno fancied he perceived, about 60 yards from his perch, some brilliant points of light, which moved about rapidly, and appeared sometimes on the ground, and sometimes about two or three feet above it.

The valet at first thought that the spots were the effects of "will-o'-the-wisp" or *ignis fatuus*, caused by the escape of gases from the marshy ground. But even if his reason led him into error, the horses would not have been conscious of the phenomenon, and they began to evince symptoms of uneasiness, and snorted loudly.

"Ah! what can this be?" said Bruno to himself. "Some new complication, no doubt. Perhaps they may be wolves yonder!"

This surmise was in no way extravagant; for these hungry animals are very numerous in the Delta of the Danube, and they had on this occasion no doubt been attracted by the smell of the horses.

"Diable," muttered Bruno. "These are worse foes than mosquitos, or the gnats of our pig-headed friend. Tobacco will be no safeguard this time!"

# KÉRABAN THE INFLEXIBLE;

## OR, ADVENTURES IN THE EUXINE.

BY JULES VERNE.

### CHAPTER VI.—(*Continued.*)

EANWHILE the horses displayed great uneasiness which it was impossible not to understand. They attempted to struggle through the slough, and tried to rear, shaking the carriage violently at every attempt. The luminous points which had been observed were approaching. A kind of growling was audible, carried down by the wind to the travellers' ears.

"I think," said Bruno to himself, "that it is about time to rouse my master and Seigneur Kéraban."

The incident was sufficiently serious. Bruno slid down from his perch, let down the steps of the carriage, opened the door, and, having entered, closed it behind him. The two friends were sleeping soundly.

"Monsieur!" said Bruno, putting his hand on Van Mitten's shoulder, "Master!"

"Go to the Devil!" was the Dutchman's reply, as, half asleep, he regarded his servitor.

"There is no use sending people to the Devil when he is so close by," muttered Bruno.

"Who are you?" enquired Van Mitten.

"I? Your servant!"

"Ah, Bruno, is it you? After all you did right to wake me. I was dreaming that Madam Van Mitten——"

"You were seeking a quarrel," replied Bruno; "well, there is food for one now."

"What is the matter then?"

"Will you please wake Seigneur Kéraban!"

"Must I wake him?"

"Yes, we have not too much time."

So Van Mitten, without another word, though still but half awake, shook his companion vigorously.

None can sleep more soundly than a Turk, when the Turk has a good digestion and an easy conscience. This was the case with Kéraban, and many attempts were made to rouse him.

Kéraban, without opening his eyes, grumbled and growled like a man who was by no means disposed to stir. Had he been as headstrong in his sleeping as when waking, they would have been obliged to let him alone.

Nevertheless, the persistence of Van Mitten and Bruno was such that Seigneur Kéraban was awakened. He extended his arms, opened his eyes, and in a thick sleepy tone said—

"Have the postillion and Nizib arrived with the relays?"

"Not yet," answered Van Mitten.

"Why did you wake me then?"

"Because if the horses have not come," said Bruno, "some other animals of a very suspicious appearance are surrounding the carriage and preparing to attack us."

"What animals do you mean?"

"Look!" said Bruno briefly.

Kéraban let down the glass and leant out of the window.

"Allah protect us!" he exclaimed. "There is a pack of wild boars."

He was right. The assailants were wild boars, which are very numerous in the Danubian territory which confines the estuary. The attacks of these animals are greatly dreaded, and they may be well classed amongst the wild beasts.

"What are we going to do?" asked the Dutchman.

"Remain quiet if they do not attack us," replied Kéraban. "We will defend ourselves if they do."

"Why should they attack us?" asked Van Mitten. "Wild boars, so far as I am aware, are not carnivorous animals."

"Quite so," replied Kéraban, "but if we do not run the risk of being eaten, we have the chance of being ripped up by their tusks."

"That's about it," said Bruno calmly.

"Therefore, let us make ready for any emergency," remarked Kéraban.

The travellers accordingly got their weapons ready. Van Mitten and Bruno had each a revolver carrying six shots; and a good supply of cartridges handy. The old Turk—a declared enemy of every modern invention—only carried two pistols of Ottoman make, with Damascus barrels, the butts ornamented with precious stones, but more suitable for ornament than defence. Van Mitten, Kéraban and Bruno had to content themselves with these arms, and determined to use them only when certain of success.

Meanwhile the wild boars, about twenty in number, were continually approaching and surrounding the carriage. By the light of the lamps, which had no doubt attracted them, the travellers could perceive the animals tossing up the earth with their tusks in their excitement. They were enormous specimens, almost as large as donkeys, of prodigious strength, and each quite capable of decimating, if not destroying, a whole pack of hounds. The situation of the travellers in the carriage would be by no means a pleasant one if they were attacked on both sides before daybreak.

The horses quite understood the position; and as the boars approached, the poor beasts plunged so that they seemed likely to break away from the traces altogether.

Just then some shots were heard. Van Mitten and Bruno had each fired twice at the boars which came to the attack. The animals more or less seriously wounded, uttered terrible cries and gruntings as they rolled upon the ground. But the rest, rendered more furious, precipitated themselves upon the carriage, and attacked it with their tusks. The panels were pierced in many places, and it became pretty clear that ere long they would be completely "stove in."

"Fire! fire!" exclaimed Kéraban, as he discharged his pistols. They generally missed fire once in every four times, which was quite in accordance with precedent. The revolvers of Bruno and Van Mitten however did good execution and accounted for a number of the assailants, some of which were boldly attacking the horses.

The latter had no means of repelling the assailants save by kicking. If they had been free, they would have scampered over the plain, and then it would have been merely a question of speed between them and the boars. As it was, the horses did all in their power to break their traces and escape. But the harness was stout cord and refused to part. It was therefore a question whether the forepart of the carriage would give way, or the whole vehicle be pulled out of the mire.

Kéraban and his companions were quite alive to the situation. What they most feared was that the carriage would capsize. Under those circumstances, the boars which the bullets had not kept off would dart upon them. So they seemed quite at the mercy of the furious pack. Nevertheless the coolness of the three men never abandoned them, and they continued to fire upon the assailants.

At length a tremendous pull shook the chaise. They thought the front part had given way.

"All the better," said Kéraban. "The horses will gallop away across the plain, and the wild boars will pursue them; so we shall be left undisturbed."

But the forepart of the chaise resisted with a strength that did credit to its English builder. So, as it would not part, the whole chaise moved, and the shock became extremely violent; so much so, indeed, that the carriage was pulled from its oozy bed, and the horses, mad with terror, rushed at headlong speed across the marshy plain through the thick darkness of the night.

But the wild boars had by no means abandoned the party. They ran beside the carriage and kept worrying the horses while they attacked the chaise, which could not distance them.

Seigneur Kéraban, Van Mitten, and Bruno were very soon thrown to the bottom of the carriage.

"Either we shall be overturned—" cried Van Mitten."

"Allah protect us! There is a pack of wild boars."

"Or we shall not," interrupted Kéraban.

"It would be better to seize the reins," said Bruno judiciously as, lowering the front windows of the chaise, he sought to grasp the "ribbons;" but the horses had in their struggle broken them, and the valet was obliged to abandon his attempts, and to allow the animals to continue their headlong course across the swampy ground. There were no means of stopping them, and if any had presented themselves the boars would also have halted. So the three men had to depend upon their weapons.

Of the travellers, thrown against each other or into the corners of the carriage at every jolt of the conveyance, the one resigned as a true Mussulman ought to be, the others as phlegmatic as Dutchmen, never exchanged a remark.

Thus an hour passed away, and the chaise still was dragged along at the same furious pace; but the wild boars did not abandon the chase.

"Van Mitten, my friend," said Kéraban at length, "I can tell you how a traveller, under similar circumstances to these, when pursued by a pack of wolves in Russia, was saved by the sublime devotion of his servant."

"How was that?" enquired Van Mitten.

"In a very simple way," replied Kéraban. "The servant took an affectionate farewell of his master; then, recommending himself to Heaven, he threw himself out of the carriage; and while the wolves stopped to devour him his master managed to distance them and was saved!"

"It is very unfortunate that Nizib is away just now," remarked Bruno drily.

After this little speech the travellers relapsed into silence, and calmly waited events.

Night was now closing in, and still the horses did not abate their desperate speed, so the wild boars could not gain upon them to make a serious attack. If no accident occurred,—if the wheels did not come off, or if a shock more than usually severe did not overturn the chaise,—the occupants considered they had a chance of safety, even failing the devotion of which Bruno appeared incapable. Meanwhile the horses, directed by instinct, kept safely to the portion of the steppe which they had been accustomed to traverse. They proceeded in a direct line towards the post where relays were to be obtained.

Thus it happened that at daylight the travellers were not far from the much-needed assistance.

The pack of wild boars continued their course for about half an hour longer, and then by degrees fell away, but the horses did not slacken speed for a moment, nor did they halt until they fell, completely foundered, about a hundred paces from the post-house.

Kéraban and his companions were safe, and they all returned thanks to the Supreme Being, the God alike of the Christian and the Mussulman, for their preservation.

Just as the carriage came to a stop, Nizib and the postillion, who had not dared to trust themselves upon the steppe in the dark, were setting out with fresh horses. These were immediately harnessed in place of those which had been so knocked up. For this Kéraban had to pay a large sum; then, without an hour's rest, the chaise, which had been overhauled and attended to, continued the journey and took the road to Kilia, a small town situated on the Danube.

The travellers reached Kilia without further adventure upon the evening of the 25th of August. There they alighted at the principal hotel and had twelve hours' repose, which in a great measure compensated them for the fatigue they had undergone. Next day they started at daybreak and soon reached the Russian frontier.

There they encountered new difficulties. The formalities of the customs officers exasperated Kéraban, who, fortunately or unfortunately, knew enough of their language to make himself understood, and for a time his obstinacy threatened to prevent the continuation of the journey.

At length, however, Van Mitten succeeded in calming him, and Kéraban consented to submit to the exigences of the service and to have his baggage examined. He paid the duties demanded, and consoled himself by repeating the sage remark that "All governments were alike, and he did not estimate any of them at the value of a melon-rind!"

The Roumanian frontier was crossed, and the chaise traversed that portion of Bessarabia which forms the littoral of the Black Sea towards the north-west. Then the travellers were not more than twenty leagues from Odessa.

---

## Chapter VII.

### In which the Reader will be pleased to become acquainted with the Fair Amasia, and her Intended Husband Ahmet.

Amasia, the only daughter of Selim the Banker, was walking and chatting with her personal attendant Nedjeb, in the verandah of a beautiful country-house, the gardens of which extended in terraces to the shore of the Black Sea.

From the last terrace, the steps of which were bathed by the calm water, Odessa could be perceived towards the South in all its glory. This town is quite an oasis in the surrounding desert, forming a splendid panorama of palaces, churches, hotels, and other habitations built upon a steep cliff which rises precipitously from the sea. From the banker's house one could even perceive the great square surrounded with trees, and the staircase which marks the statue of Richelieu. This great man was the founder of the city, and was its ruler until he undertook the liberation of France.

As the climate is dry and "trying" in the season of the northerly and easterly winds, the inhabitants seek shelter during the summer heat under the welcome shade of the Khontors, and the residents have built their villas on the sea-shore; for business will not permit them all to seek relaxation in the Southern Crimea for the whole season. Amongst these elegant houses one would remark the banker's residence, which was so situated as to be not much inconvenienced by the prevailing dryness of the season.

The name "Odessa" signifies the "town of Ulysses," for so the inhabitants formerly petitioned Catharine II. to name their village. The empress consulted the Academy of St. Petersburg, and the *savants* investigated the records of the siege of Troy. These records informed them that at one time a town, more or less problematical, existed there under the name of "Odyssos," whence Odessa arose in the middle of the eighteenth century.

Odessa has been, is, and always will be, a commercial city. Its 500,000 inhabitants consist of Russians, Turks, Greeks, and Armenians—in fact a gathering together of all people who have business tastes. Now, if commerce makes merchants, it equally makes bankers; and amongst the latter, Selim, from modest beginnings, had risen to be one of the most wealthy and esteemed.

Selim belonged to the rather numerous class of monogamous Turks. He had never had but one wife: Amasia was his only daughter, now engaged to Ahmet, Kéraban's nephew. So Selim was the correspondent and intimate friend of the most obstinate Turk who ever wore a turban. The marriage of Amasia and Ahmet was to be celebrated at Odessa. She would be the sole wife of the young man, and return with him to his uncle's house in Constantinople.

People also knew that Amasia's aunt—her father's sister—had left by will to her niece an enormous sum of money, amounting to £100,000 (Turkish), on the condition that she should marry before she was sixteen—a caprice of the old lady, who, never having been herself married, was determined that Amasia should lose no time—and the period fixed would expire in six weeks from the time we refer to. Failing this marriage, the money would go to collateral inheritors.

Amasia herself was charming even in the eyes of Europeans. Had her white muslin veil, her gold embroidered head-dress, and the triple row of sequins across her forehead been removed, her beautiful hair would have been perceived in all its luxuriance. She was in no way indebted to art to heighten her beauty. No *hanum* pencilled her eye-brows, no kohl blackened her lashes, no henna darkened the eyelids. No bismuth or "rouge" improved her complexion: no carmine heightened the colour of her lips. A western woman of the present style would be found more painted than was Amasia. The elegance of her figure, her graceful mode of walking, and her natural ease of movement, were all discernible under the *feredjé*, or cashmere cloak which draped her from neck to heels like a dalmatic.

That day, in the gallery which opened into the gardens, Amasia was wearing a long silken chemise, which was concealed by the ample *chalwar* united to a little embroidered vest, and an *entari* with a silken train slashed on the sleeves, and embroidered with a trimming of *oya*—a

The city of Odessa.

Turkish lace. A girdle of cashmere supported the train, so that it might not impede her steps. A pair of earrings and a ring were her only jewels. Elegant *padjoubs* of velvet hid the lower part of the leg, and her pretty little feet were encased in gold-embroidered slippers.

Her attendant, Nedjeb, a bright and lively girl and a devoted servant — one might say friend—was at this time with Amasia; laughing, chattering, moving hither and thither and making the house quite gay by her good humour and cheerfulness. Nedjeb was a Zingara by descent, not a slave. Slavery is not the less abolished in principle because one occasionally sees some Ethiopians or Negroes sold in the open market. A large number of domestics is necessary for a great Turkish family—a number which in Constantinople includes a third of the Mussulman population—these servants are never reduced to a condition of slavery: and, it must be confessed that, looking to the fact that each domestic has his special work, there is not much to do individually.

The banker's establishment was conducted somewhat on this principle, but Nedjeb

Amasia and her attendant, Nedjeb.

was exclusively attached to Amasia. Having been received quite as a child into the house she occupied, a unique position, and never performed any menial duty.

Amasia was reclining upon a divan, covered with rich Persian stuffs, and was gazing out upon the Bay of Odessa.

"Dear mistress," said Nedjeb, seating herself upon a cushion at Amasia's feet, "Seigneur Ahmet has not yet arrived! what is he about, I wonder?"

"He has gone into the city," replied Amasia, "and perhaps he will bring back a letter from his uncle Kéraban."

"A letter!" exclaimed the attendant. "A letter! We don't want that, we want Seigneur Kéraban himself; and, to tell the truth, this uncle keeps us waiting a good deal."

"Patience, Nedjeb. A little patience," said Amasia.

"Yes, you speak very calmly and take it easily. But if you were in my place, my dear young mistress, you would scarcely be so patient."

"Silly girl!" replied Amasia. "It is not a question of your marriage, but mine."

"And do you not think it is a very important thing to pass from the service of a young lady to that of a rich married dame?"

"I shall not love you any the better," said Amasia.

"Nor could I love you any better, dear lady; but, truly, to see you so happy as the wife of Seigneur Ahmet would re-act on me, and make me very happy too."

"Dear Ahmet!" murmured Amasia, as she veiled her eyes a moment, while she invoked the remembrance of her *fiancé*.

"Ah! there you are, obliged to shut your eyes to see him," cried Nedjeb maliciously, "while if he were here you would open them."

"I tell you that he has gone to meet the messenger from the bank, who will no doubt have a letter from his uncle."

"Yes; a letter from Seigneur Kéraban, in which he will repeat as usual that business detains him in Constantinople; that he cannot as yet leave home; that tobacco is rising—that unless it falls he will arrive in eight days, without fail—unless indeed it happens to be sixteen days. And time presses. We have only six weeks. If you are not married then, you must give up your fortune, and ——"

"It is not for my fortune that Ahmet is going to marry me, Nedjeb."

"Quite so; but there is no need to lose it by delay. Oh! if Seigneur Kéraban were my uncle!"

"What would you do if he were?"

"I would do nothing, dear mistress, as no one can do anything. Nevertheless, if he were here—if he arrived to-day even—or to-morrow, or a little later, we would carry him to the judge, and have the contract completed. Afterwards we would go to the Imaun and be married, and well married too. The *fêtes* should be prolonged for fifteen days, and Seigneur Kéraban might go away then as soon as he pleased, if he wanted to return so particularly."

There could be no doubt that the arrangements as detailed by Nedjeb could be made and carried out, if Seigneur Kéraban did not tarry longer in Constantinople. The contract would be registered before the Mollah, who filled the position of a ministerial officer, a contract by which the future husband bound himself to give his wife furniture and kitchen utensils. Then came the religious ceremony, and the various formalities—all of which could be accomplished within the period that Nedjeb named. But still was it necessary that Kéraban, whose presence as guardian of his nephew was indispensable, should occupy in business the few days which the impatient waiting-woman so anxiously claimed for her charming mistress?

Just then the girl exclaimed, "See what a pretty vessel is just coming to anchor under the garden steps!"

"So there is," said Amasia.

Immediately the two girls proceeded towards the steps which led to the water's edge, so that they might more conveniently observe the graceful little vessel which had just "brought up" opposite.

It was the *felucca*. The sail was still brailed up, and she was running in under the impetus of a light breeze. She came to anchor within a cable's length of the shore, and dipped gently to the wavy undulations of the water which broke on the foot of the steps. The Turkish flag floated from the mast.

"Can you read her name?" enquired Amasia.

"Yes," replied Nedjeb. "See, there it is on the stern. The '*Guidare*.'"

So it was. Captain Yarhud had come to an anchor in this part of the bay, but it did not appear as if he intended to remain, because his sails were not furled, and a sailor would have noticed that the ship was in sea-going trim.

"Truly," remarked Nedjeb, "it would be very pleasant to have a sail in that vessel upon such a blue sea, and with such a gentle wind, just enough to make it bend over with those great sails."

Then, in the mutability of her imagination, the young Zingara perceiving a casket, in which were some jewels, upon a small table near the divan, opened the case and said—

"Ah! look at the beautiful things Seigneur Ahmet has brought for you. It must be more than an hour since we looked at them!"

"Do you think so?" murmured Amasia, taking out a necklace and a pair of bracelets, which glittered as she held them up.

"With these jewels Seigneur Ahmet hopes to make you more beautiful, but he will not succeed!" remarked Nedjeb.

"What do you say?" replied Amasia. "Where is the woman who would not gain by wearing such beautiful ornaments as these? Look at these diamonds from Visapour; they are exquisitely brilliant, almost fiery, and remind me of the eyes of my *fiancé*."

"Oh, dear lady, when yours look at him, do you not offer him a gift equal to his own?"

"Silly child!" replied Amasia. "Look at this sapphire of Ormuz; and these pearls of Ophir; these tourquoises of Macedonia—"

"Tourquoise for tourquoise," said Nedjeb, laughing joyously. "The Seigneur Ahmet will not lose by the exchange."

"Fortunately he is not near, Nedjeb, to hear you say so."

"Ah, but if he were he would tell you the same, and his words would have greater value than mine."

Then, taking up a pair of slippers which were lying near, she continued, "Look at these pretty 'babouches,' all embroidered and trimmed with swansdown, made for a pretty pair of little feet I know. Let me see if I can put them on for you."

"Try them on yourself, Nedjeb."

"I?" exclaimed the girl.

"This is not the first time that, to please me, you——"

"Certainly, certainly," replied Nedjeb. "Yes, I have already tried on your pretty dresses, and I went out upon the terrace, where they took me for you. If I was only pretty enough!—— But no! that never will be, and to-day less than ever. Let me try these pretty slippers on."

"Do you wish it?" said Amasia, as she yielded to the girl's solicitations. So Nedjeb put on her young mistress's feet the slippers which were worthy of a place in a glass-case of curiosities. "Ah, how can you now venture to walk in them?" exclaimed the young Zingara. "Your head may now be jealous of your feet."

"You make me laugh, Nedjeb," replied Amasia. "Yet——"

"And those arms, those beautiful arms, which you leave quite unadorned! Why should you? Seigneur Ahmet has not forgotten them, not he! I see here some bracelets which will suit them to a nicety. Poor little arms!—how badly they have treated you. Fortunately I am here."

And, laughing all the time, Nedjeb passed two magnificent bracelets on Amasia's wrists, and they looked more resplendent upon the white skin than within their case of velvet.

Amasia let her do as she pleased. Every ornament spoke to her of Ahmet, and to the incessant chatter of Nedjeb, her eyes, glancing from one jewel to another, responded in silence.

"Amasia, dearest!"

The girl at these words rose hastily and met a young man whose twenty-two years suited well his *fiancée* of sixteen. Ahmet was somewhat above the middle height, of a good figure; easy, yet somewhat dignified: his black eyes wore a very sweet expression and flashed like lightning in his passionate moments. His hair was brown and curly beneath his fez, his small moustache was trimmed Albanian fashion; his teeth were white—in fact, there was an aristocratic air about him, if the term "aristocratic" is permissible in referring to a man in whose country there is no hereditary aristocracy.

Ahmet adhered strictly to the Turkish dress. He could not do otherwise, being the nephew of such an uncle. His well-made costume became him well; it was of rich material and in good taste.

The young man advanced and seized the hands of his affianced bride, obliging her to reseat herself while Nedjeb said—

"Well, Seigneur Ahmet, is there any news from Constantinople?"

"No," replied Ahmet, "not even a business letter from my uncle Kéraban."

"Oh, the wretch!" exclaimed Nedjeb.

Ahmet, Amasia's *fiancé*.

"I cannot myself understand," said the young man, "why the courier has not brought any letter from him. This is the day he never fails to let us have some information, and to arrange matters with the banker; yet your father has not received any letters from him either."

"For a punctillious man of business like your uncle, this certainly is a circumstance to wonder at, dear Ahmet. Perhaps a telegram——"

"He send a telegram! My dear Amasia, you know quite well he would no more telegraph than he would travel by railway. Utilize modern inventions, even for business! He would rather receive bad news by letter than good news by the telegraph, I believe. Ah, Uncle Kéraban——"

"You have written to him, of course, dear Ahmet?" asked the girl, whose gaze was tenderly fixed upon her *fiancé*.

"I have written to him a dozen times, to beg him to fix an earlier date for our marriage. I have told him over and over again that he was acting a barbarous part——"

"Good!" exclaimed Nedjeb.

"That he had no heart; though the best of men——"

"Oh!" said Nedjeb, shaking her head.

"Yet he had no pity," continued Ahmet, "while acting the part of father to his nephew. But he replied that so long as he came within six weeks we had no reason to complain!"

"Well, we must only wait his good pleasure, Ahmet."

"Wait, wait!" exclaimed the young man. "He is robbing us of so many days of happiness!"

"Men who have done no worse are often arrested," remarked Nedjeb, tapping her foot impatiently.

"What shall I do? await Uncle Kéraban? I declare, if he does not answer my letter by to-morrow, I will go to Constantinople!——"

"No, dear Ahmet," said Amasia, seizing his hand as if to detain him, "I should suffer so much by your absence that the few days gained would not please me at all; they would not recompense me for the separation. No, stay where you are: who knows? Perhaps, something may alter your uncle's determination."

"Alter Uncle Kéraban's determination! You might as well hope to change the course of the stars, to make the moon rise instead of the sun, to change the laws of the universe—as to alter Kéraban's decision," said Ahmet.

"Ah, if I were his niece," said Nedjeb.

"What would you do then?" asked Ahmet.

"I would seize his caftan, so that——"

"You would only succeed in tearing it."

"Well, then, I would pull his beard for him, hard!"

"His beard might even be pulled off altogether," replied Ahmet.

"And yet," said Amasia, "Seigneur Kéraban is the best of men."

"No doubt, no doubt," replied Ahmet, "but so headstrong, so obstinate, that if an encounter were to take place between him and a mule, I should decline to bet on the latter."

# KERABAN THE INFLEXIBLE;

## OR, ADVENTURES IN THE EUXINE.

BY JULES VERNE.

### CHAPTER IX.

SHEWING HOW CAPTAIN YARHUD VERY NEARLY SUCCEEDED IN HIS ENTERPRISE.

WHILE Ahmet was speaking, one of the servants of the house, whose duty, according to Ottoman usage, was only to announce visitors and nothing else, appeared at the entrance of the gallery.

"Seigneur Ahmet," he said, addressing the young man, "a stranger is below and desires to speak with you."

"Who is he?" asked Ahmet.

"A Maltese captain; he insists upon seeing you, and says you will receive him."

"Very well, I will come down," said Ahmet.

"My dear Ahmet, why not receive him here, if he has nothing of a private nature to communicate?" said Amasia.

"Perhaps he commands that pretty felucca," observed Nedjeb, indicating the vessel which was anchored off the steps.

"Perhaps he does," said Ahmet; "let him come in!"

The servant retired, and, almost immediately afterwards, the stranger presented himself.

Captain Yarhud—for he it was—had, greatly to his chagrin, been delayed considerably in his voyage. Immediately he and Scarpante, the intendant, had parted, the captain had started for Odessa by railway, and had thus got in advance of Kéraban by many days. But when the worthy Yarhud had reached Odessa, he found the weather so bad that he could not put to sea. The wind had only moderated that morning sufficiently to permit his making sail, and he had accordingly come out and anchored before the banker's villa. So after all he had obtained but a little start of Kéraban, and the delay might prove very prejudicial to his interests.

Yarhud felt he must commence operations without losing an hour. His plans were all laid; he must try strategy first, and force after if his *ruse* did not succeed. But it was necessary that Amasia should be allured on board the *Guidare* that very day; thus before the alarm could be given and pursuit made, the felucca, he hoped, would be well on her way, running before the stiff nor'-wester.

Such abductions as Yarhud contemplated were by no means infrequent upon the coast—more frequent than one would imagine; nor are they altogether limited to Turkish territory. It is not very many years ago since Odessa was thrown into consternation by a series of abductions, the authors of which could not be traced. A number of young girls belonging to the highest grade of society disappeared, and it was only too certain that they had been carried away into slavery and sold in the markets of Asia Minor.

Now what had been done in the capital of southern Russia, Yarhud hoped to repeat for the benefit of Seigneur Saffar. This was not the first time either that the *Guidare* had been employed in such traffic, and the captain valued his profits on the transaction at more than ten per cent. !

Yarhud's plan was as follows :—To allure the young lady on board the *Guidare* under the pretence of showing her and selling to her many rich stuffs which he had bought from the principal markets on the coast. Ahmet would most likely accompany Amasia on her first visit, but he trusted she would return again with Nedjeb. It would then be possible to put to sea before assistance could be given. If, however, Amasia could not be tempted on board, then Yarhud intended to use force. The banker's house was in a manner isolated at the curve of the bay, and his domestics were no match for the crew of the felucca ; but there might be fighting, and in that case people would quickly ascertain the circumstances under which the abduction had been carried out. So it was much the better policy, in the interest of the abductors, that the affair should be accomplished without any disturbance.

"Seigneur Ahmet ?" said the captain, interrogatively, as he entered the gallery, accompanied by one of his crew, who carried some fabrics in his arms.

"I am he," replied the young man, "and you are—— ?"

"Captain Yarhud, commanding the felucca *Guidare*, which is moored yonder."

"What is your business ?"

"Seigneur Ahmet," said the captain, "I have heard of your approaching marriage."

"You have then heard, captain, of that which most dearly concerns me."

"I can quite understand that," replied the captain, turning towards Amasia ; "so I had the idea that I might perhaps place at your disposal all the rich things which my vessel contains."

"Well, that is not a bad idea of yours, Captain Yarhud," replied Ahmet.

"My dear Ahmet, what can I possibly want with more than I have ?" said Amasia.

"Who knows ?" replied Ahmet. "These Levantine captains have often an extensive assortment of valuable things, and we may as well inspect them."

"Yes ; we must inspect them, and purchase some too," exclaimed Nedjeb ; "and ruin Seigneur Kéraban, which will punish him for his delay."

"What does your cargo consist of, captain ?" enquired Ahmet.

"Valuable stuffs which I have purchased at various places where they are made," replied Yarhud, "and in which I usually trade."

"Very well : we must let these young women see them—they know more about such things than I do ; and I shall be very glad, my dear Amasia, if amongst the cargo of the *Guidare* you can find some pretty things to please you."

"I have no doubt about it," replied Yarhud, "and, besides, I have brought some samples with me, which I pray you to examine before you go on board."

"Let us see them," exclaimed Nedjeb. "But I tell you beforehand, captain, you have nothing in any way too beautiful for my mistress."

"Certainly not. That is true," remarked Ahmet.

At a sign from Yarhud the sailor who accompanied him unrolled some samples, which the captain presented to the young lady.

"Here are some Broussa silks embroidered with silver," he said. "They are intended for sale in the bazaars of Constantinople."

"That is certainly a beautiful fabric," said Amasia as she examined the silk, which under the skilful fingers of Nedjeb scintillated like luminous tissue.

"See ! see !" cried the Zingara. "We could not have found anything better in the merchants' houses in Odessa."

"That really appears to have been made expressly for you, my dear Amasia," said Ahmet.

"I would suggest that you should also examine these muslins from Scutari and Turnova. From this sample you may judge of the exquisite workmanship. But you will be fairly surprised, when you come on board, by the variety of the designs and the colours of the fabrics."

"Well, it is quite understood that we are going to visit the *Guidare*, captain; "said Nedjeb"

"You will never regret your visit," replied Yarhud. "But permit me to show you some other articles. Here are brocades studded with diamonds; chemises of silk crape of diaphanous texture; tissues for *feredjis*, muslins for *jacmalls*, Persian shawls for girdles, taffetas for *pantalons*."

"Yes, yes, let us go on board," exclaimed Nedjeb

Amasia could not sufficiently admire the magnificient stuffs which the Maltese captain unfolded before her, and displayed with such cunning artifice. If he were as good a sailor as he was a skilful trader, the *Guidare* would never meet with any mishap under Yarhud's command. All women—and young Turkish women are no exception to the general rule—permit themselves to be tempted by the sights of fabrics from the best looms of the east.

Ahmet perceived at once how much struck Amasia was with the display, and certainly, as Nebjeb had said, neither the bazaars of Odessa nor Constantinople; not even the great stores of Ludovic the celebrated Armenian merchant, could offer a more extended choice.

"Dearest Amasia," said Ahmet, "you would not like this worthy captain to take all this trouble for nothing. Since he has shown you these beautiful things, and there are even more beautiful ones on board,—we may, I think, pay the vessel a visit."

"Yes, yes," exclaimed Nedjeb, who could not remain still. She ran down to the edge of the water as she spoke.

"And," continued Ahmet, "we shall no doubt find some silk goods which will satisfy Nedjeb too."

"Well, and must not I have something to do honour to the wedding-day?" retorted Nedjeb, who had overheard him; "something to celebrate my mistress's wedding with the generous Seigneur Ahmet?"

"So good as he is too," added Amasia, extending her hand to her affianced husband.

"That is settled then, captain," said Ahmet; "you will see us on board your vessel."

"At what hour?" enquired Yarhud, "for I would like to show you all my fine things."

"Say in the afternoon," replied Ahmet.

"Why not at once?" said Nedjeb.

"Oh the impatient creature!" replied Amasia, laughing. "She is even more anxious than I am to visit this floating bazaar. One might very easily perceive that Ahmet has promised her a present which will make her smarter and more coquettish than ever."

"Coquettish for you alone, my dearest mistress," said Nedjeb in an affectionate manner.

"It only rests with you, Seigneur Ahmet," said Yarhud. "You can go on board at once if you please. My gig can be brought to the steps and in a few strokes we shall be on board."

"Let us go then, captain," said Ahmet.

"Yes, yes, let us go on board!" exclaimed Nedjeb.

"Very well, since Nedjeb wishes it," added Amasia.

Then Captain Yarhud told the sailor to gather up all the samples which he had brought, and while the man was thus occupied he himself advanced to the edge of the terrace and hailed the *Guidare*.

Immediately there was a movement on board. The boat was launched; and in five minutes, under the impulse of four strong rowers, the gig came alongside the steps of the terrace.

Captain Yarhud then signified to Ahmet that he was at the young man's disposal.

Yarhud, notwithstanding his habitual self-command, could scarcely conceal his satisfaction at the turn things had taken, and at the opportunity which had presented itself. Time pressed, for Kéraban might arrive now at any moment, and there was nothing to prevent his remaining for a day or two to celebrate the wedding of the young couple. Now Amasia, as the wife of Ahmet, would not be an acceptable visitor at the palace of the Seigneur Saffar.

Yes: captain Yarhud felt as if suddenly impelled to act by force. It was quite in his line to act without any consideration or scruple. Besides the circumstances were all favourable, and the wind was in the proper quarter for his enterprise. The vessel would be well in the offing before any pursuit could be attempted, even supposing the abduction were immediately discovered. Had Ahmet been absent, Yarhud, would not have hesitated to carry Amasia and her maid on board then and there; and put to sea with them, while they were engaged in examining the various fabrics in the cabin. It would be easy enough to keep them prisoners and stifle their cries until the *Guidare* had gained the open sea. With Ahmet present the difficulties had increased, but were not unsurmountable. The captain would not hesitate to put Ahmet "out of the way," if necessary. The murder would be put in the bill, and Seigneur Saffar would have to pay the increased cost: that would be all!

Yarhud remained standing on the steps and thinking what course would be best when he had persuaded Ahmet and his companions to embark in the boat for the *Guidare*, which lay scarcely a cable's length away, lifting gently to the motion of the waves.

Ahmet, standing upon the lowest step, was about to hand Amasia to her seat in the stern of the gig, when the door leading into the gallery opened, and a man of about fifty years of age, dressed something in the European style, entered hurriedly.

"Amasia! Ahmet!" he cried.

This was Selim the banker; the father

"That is certainly a beautiful fabric," said Amasia.

of Amasia and the correspondent of Kéraban.

"Daughter—Ahmet! Where are you?"

"Father, what is the matter?" exclaimed Amasia. "Why have you returned so quickly?"

"I have important news."

"Good news?" asked Ahmet.

"Excellent," replied Selim. "An express sent by Kéraban has just reached me."

"Really!" exclaimed Nedjeb.

"A special messenger, who has advised me of Kéraban's speedy arrival He was not far in advance of your uncle."

"Uncle Kéraban! Do you mean that he has left Constantinople?" cried Ahmet.

"Yes, and I am expecting him here."

Fortunately for the captain of the *Guidare*, no one perceived the angry gestures with which he received this intelligence. The sudden arrival of Ahmet's uncle was a contingency which would seriously interfere with the accomplishment of the worthy captain's designs.

"Ah! Seigneur Kéraban is good," exclaimed Nedjeb.

"But why is he coming?" asked Amasia.

"For your marriage, my dear young lady," replied the attendant. "What other object could bring him to Odessa?"

"That must be the reason," said Selim.

"I think so too," said Ahmet. "Else why need he have quitted Constantinople? He must be enchanted. Fancy my worthy uncle leaving his business suddenly without any previous intimation of his intention. He wishes to surprise us."

"He will be well received and gladly welcomed," said Nedjeb.

"Did not his messenger tell you the reason for his coming?" enquired Amasia of her father.

"No, nothing whatever," replied Selim. "The man had ridden post from Majaki, where Kéraban's carriage was changing horses. He came to the banking-house and merely announced the immediate arrival of Kéraban at Odessa, and as he will halt nowhere, we may expect him at any moment."

If the contumacious Kéraban was at that time endowed with all the most amiable qualities of mankind as friend, uncle, and "seigneur," by those interested, can we be surprised? His unexpected arrival meant the celebration of the wedding between Amasia and Ahmet, and the happiness of the young people was assured; no fatal delay would mar their future. Ah, if Kéraban were the most obstinate, he was, nevertheless, the best of men.

Yarhud, impassible as ever, was a spectator of this family scene; but he had not sent his boat away. It was very important that he should become aware of the plans of the Seigneur Kéraban; indeed he was afraid that he would insist upon the marriage of Amasia before he continued his journey around the Black Sea.

At that moment voices, which overpowered a more imperious voice, were heard outside. The door opened and Kéraban, followed by Van Mitten, Bruno, and Nizib, entered the gallery.

---

## Chapter X.

### In which Ahmet, in deference to circumstances, makes an Energetic Resolution.

"Good day, friend Selim, good day. May Allah protect you and yours!"

So saying, Kéraban shook Selim's hand warmly.

"Good day, nephew Ahmet;" and then Kéraban folded the young man in his arms.

"Good day, my little Amasia," he continued kissing the girl on both cheeks.

All this passed so quickly that no one had any time to reply to the salutations.

"Now we had better be going," said Kéraban turning to Van Mitten.

The phlegmatic Dutchman, who had not been introduced, appeared like some strange personage in the scene. Seeing Kéraban distributing his hand-shakes and embraces with such prodigality, Van Mitten had no doubt that his friend had come to hasten the marriage; but when Kéraban cried "*en route*" the Dutchman was greatly amazed.

It was Ahmet, however, who first interposed.

"How!" he exclaimed. "Going away?"

"Yes, we are off again, nephew."

"You really are going, uncle?"

"This moment."

The general astonishment was very marked, and Van Mitten whispered to Bruno—

"Certainly this way of acting is very characteristic of my friend Kéraban."

"Very much so," replied Bruno.

Meanwhile Amasia looked at Ahmet, who looked at Selim, while Nedjeb had eyes for no one but this mysterious uncle who was anxious to get away almost before you could say he had arrived.

"Come along, Van Mitten," said Kéraban as he turned to the door.

"Monsieur, will you tell me——" said Ahmet to Van Mitten.

"What can I tell you?" asked the Dutchman turning round suddenly, for he was following his host.

But Kèraban returned as he was at

"The door opened and Kéraban, followed by Van Mitten, Bruno, and Nizib, entered the gallery."

the door and said, addressing the banker,—

"By the way, friend Selim, can you change me a few thousand piastres?"

"A few thousand piastres!" echoed Selim, who did not understand.

"Yes, Selim; for Russian money: I want some for my journey in Muscovite Territory."

"But, uncle, will you tell us,"—began Ahmet who was standing now beside Amasia, "will you tell us——"

"At what rate is the exchange?" continued Kéraban without paying any attention to Ahmet.

"Three and a half per cent," replied Selim, in whom the banker at once predominated.

"What! three and a half!"

"Roubles are at a premium," replied

Selim. "On the Exchange they are asking——"

"Look here, friend Selim, it must be three and a quarter for me: you understand—three and a quarter."

"Oh yes—for you certainly, friend Kéraban—and without any commission at all."

Selim evidently had no longer any definite idea of what he was saying or doing.

All this time Yarhud at the end of the gallery was listening to what was going on very attentively. Would the issue be favourable or unfavourable to his projects?

Ahmet now seized his uncle by the arm, and, not without difficulty, succeeded in stopping him.

"Uncle," he said, "you have embraced us all just when you have arrived——"

"Just as I am about to go away, you mean," replied Kéraban.

"Well, be it so: I do not wish to contradict you. But at least tell me why you have come to Odessa."

"Because Odessa was in my way. Had Odessa not been a stage in my journey, I should not have come here. Is not that so, Van Mitten?"

The Dutchman contented himself by assenting with a nod.

"Ah yes, by the by, you have not been introduced. I must present you." Then, addressing Selim, Kéraban continued—

"My friend Van Mitten, my correspondent at Rotterdam, whom I am bringing to dine with me at Scutari."

"At Scutari!" exclaimed the banker.

"It seems so," said Van Mitten.

"And Bruno his servant," continued Kéraban; "a brave follower who does not wish to be separated from his master."

"It seems so," said Bruno, like an echo.

"Now, let us be off," said the impetuous Turk.

"If it must be so, uncle," said Ahmet, "we will not endeavour to detain you. But if you are only here because Odessa happens to be in your way, may I enquire what route you are taking for Scutari?"

"The route which leads round the Black Sea."

"Around the Black Sea!" exclaimed Ahmet.

A dead silence supervened for a few seconds, and then Kéraban said—

"Well, if you please, what is there so very surprising in that? Is there anything so very extraordinary in our going from Constantinople to Scutari by the sea-coast route?"

Selim and Ahmet looked at each other, significantly. Was the rich merchant of Galata going mad?

"Friend Kéraban," said the banker at length, "we do not wish to oppose you in any way." This was the usual phrase, and a prudent one when dealing with the obstinate Kéraban. "We have no wish to contradict you at all, only it appears to us that you might have perhaps reached Scutari more directly by crossing the Bosphorus."

"There is no longer any Bosphorus!" said Kéraban.

"No longer any Bosphorus!" exclaimed Ahmet.

"Not for me—which is the same thing. There is a strait for such people as will submit to pay an iniquitous tax of four paras a head; a tax which these new Turks have imposed upon waters which have hitherto been free as air."

"What! a new tax?" said Ahmet, who at once comprehended the situation; and that his uncle had had some discussion in which his obstinacy had refused to give way: hence his departure from Constantinople.

"Yes," exclaimed Kéraban, working himself into a pitch of excitement. "Just as I was about to cross in my caïque to dine at Scutari with my friend Van Mitten, this tax was ordained. Naturally I refused to pay it. The officials refused to let me pass. I said that I knew how to reach Scutari without crossing the Bosphorus. They said I could not: I replied that I could. And so I will, by Allah! I would rather have my hand cut off, than pay those ten paras. No, by Mahomet, they do not know Kéraban!"

Evidently *they* did not know Kéraban. But Selim, Ahmet, Van Mitten, and Amasia knew him; and they perceived that, after what had passed, all their efforts to change his resolution would be in vain. There was no use in attempting to argue the point. Discussion would have only led to complications. They must accept the situation, and without any consultation it was accepted unanimously.

"Now we must start," said Kéraban.

"After all, you are right, uncle;" said Ahmet.

"Quite right," added Selim.

"I am always right," replied Kéraban, modestly.

"One ought to resist such iniquitous imposts," continued Ahmet, "even though it cost you a fortune."

"Even my life," said Kéraban.

"You have done well to refuse payment, and to show that you can reach Scutari from Constantinople without crossing the Bosphorus."

"And without paying ten paras;" added Kéraban; "even though the alternative cost me five hundred thousand!"

"But you are not absolutely compelled to leave here at once, I suppose," said Ahmet persuasively.

"Absolutely compelled, nephew," replied

Kéraban. "I suppose you are aware that I must return in less than six weeks."

"Quite so, uncle,—so you can give us eight days in Odessa."

"Not five days—not four—not one day—not an hour"—exclaimed Kéraban.

Ahmet, perceiving that the natural obstinacy of the man was cropping up, signed to Amasia to intercede.

"And our marriage, Monsieur Kéraban?" asked the girl modestly, taking his hand.

"Your marriage, Amasia. That will still be a fixture. It must be accomplished before the end of next month, and so it shall be. My journey will not retard it by a day—if I leave here at once!"

So crumbled the castle in the air which had been erected: the scaffolding of hopes which had been put up on the unexpected arrival of Kéraban fell to the ground. The wedding would not be hastened, but on the other hand it would not be delayed. How could he count upon the accomplishment of the conditions, with a long and toilsome journey in prospect?

Ahmet could not restrain an angry movement, which fortunately his uncle did not observe, any more than he noticed the shade of disappointment on Amasia's brow, or than he heard Nedjeb's whisper of "Oh, the Wretch!"

"Besides"—continued Kéraban in the tone of a person who makes a proposition to which no possible exception can be taken—"besides, I count, upon Ahmet accompanying me!"

"That is a home thrust which will be difficult to parry," whispered Van Mitten to Bruno.

"They will not parry it," said the valet.

In fact Ahmet had received it full in his heart. Amasia also was struck dumb and remained motionless, by the verdict which was to deprive her of her affianced husband. She clung to Nedjeb who would have liked to tear Kéraban's eyes out!

The captain of the *Guidare* did not lose a word of the conversation. Things were taking a turn favourable for him.

Selim now throught it time to interpose, though he had no hope of altering Kéraban's determination; so he said—

"Is it really necessary that your nephew should accompany you on your tour of the Black Sea, Kéraban?"

"Necessary, no; but I do not think that Ahmet will decline to accompany me!"

"Nevertheless——" continued Selim.

"Nevertheless what?" cried Kéraban grinding his teeth,—and this question closed the discussion.

There was again silence for a space which seemed interminable. Meantime Ahmet made his decision boldly. He spoke to his *fiancée* apart, and succeeded in making her understand that, however terrible the parting would be, there was nothing to be gained by resisting the mandate; that, without him, the journey would very likely be prolonged and meet with numerous delays, which his perfect acquaintance with the Russian language would remove. So, by accompanying his uncle, Ahmet decided that no time would be lost, and he would also hasten the journey, even though it cost three times as much; and he would all the more certainly bring Kéraban back in time for the wedding fixed to take place at the end of the following month.

Amasia had not the courage to say yes; but she understood that Ahmet was right.

"Very well, uncle," said the young man, "I will accompany you; I am ready to go; but——"

"Oh, we will have no conditions, nephew."

"Unconditionally, then," said Ahmet; "but," he added mentally, "I will make you run till you are out of breath; pig-headed uncle that you are!"

"Now we must start," said Kéraban: and, turning to Selim—

"Are those roubles ready?" he asked.

"I will give them to you at Odessa, whither I will accompany you," replied Selim.

"Are you ready, Van Mitten?"

"Always ready," replied the Dutchman.

"Well now, Ahmet, embrace your *fiancée* and let us begone."

Ahmet threw his arms round the young girl, who was bathed in tears.

"Do not cry, dearest Amasia," he said: "if our marriage is not advanced, it will not be postponed, I promise you that. Only a few weeks——"

"Ah, my dear mistress," said Nedjeb, "if Seigneur Kéraban would only break a leg or two, before he leaves this place! Shall I see about it?"

Odessa.—The grand Staircase.

But Amasia desired the maid to hold her tongue. Still Nedjeb was quite capable of carrying out her threat, or of finding some other means to stop the intractable uncle.

Farewells were exchanged, the last kisses given; nearly everyone present was more or less affected, even the Dutchman felt an accelerated movement or the heart. Kéraban alone saw nothing, and wished to see nothing, of the general sorrow and tenderness.

"Is the chaise ready?" he asked.

"The chaise is ready," replied Nizib.

"Come along, then. Ah! you new-fashioned Turks, who dress like Europeans, who do not even know how to get fat. (This was evidently an unpardonable sin in Kéraban's eyes.) Ah, you renegades, who submit to the decrees of Mahmoud: I will show you that there is still one of the old believers left, of whom you will never get the better!"

No one contradicted him, yet he proceeded in a still more excited manner—

"Ah! you pretend to monopolize the Bosphorus, do you? Well, I will get to the opposite side of it. *That* for your Bosphorus! I laugh at your Bosphorus. What did you say, Van Mitten?"

"I said nothing," replied Van Mitten, who had taken very good care not to open his mouth.

"Your Bosphorus—their Bosphorus," continued Kéraban shaking his fist towards the south. "Fortunately the Black Sea is there, and it has a coast line not exclusively for caravans. I will follow that road. I will circumambulate it; and you will see the faces of your officials, when I appear upon the heights of Scutari, without having thrown my paras into the box of that set of administrative mendicants."

We must confess that Kéraban, when he reached this crowning invective, was really magnificent in his anger.

"Come, Ahmet; come, Van Mitten. Away, away, away!"

He had reached the door, when Selim detained him—

"Friend Kéraban," said he, "permit me a simple observation."

"I will have no observations."

"Well then, a remark which I wish to make," persisted the banker.

"We have no time."

"Listen to me," continued Selim. "When you have reached Scutari, having made the tour of the Black Sea, what will you do?"

"I—do? why—I—I——"

"You do not, I suppose, intend to remain at Scutari for ever without visiting Constantinople, where your business house is?"

"No," replied Kéraban, with some hesitation.

"In fact, uncle," said Ahmet, "if you still continue obstinate about crossing the Bosphorus, our wedding——"

"Friend Selim," interrupted Kéraban, eluding the main point, "nothing can be more simple. What is there to prevent you and Amasia from coming to Scutari? It will cost you ten paras each, it is true, to cross the Bosphorus, but your honour is not pledged like mine in the matter."

"Yes, yes, come to Scutari in a month," exclaimed Ahmet. "We will meet you there, dear Amasia; and, you may depend upon it, we will not keep you waiting."

"So be it. We meet at Scutari," said Selim, "and then the marriage shall be celebrated. But, after all, Kéraban, when the wedding is over, will you not return to Constantinople?"

"Certainly; I will return—certainly;" said Kéraban.

"How?"

"Well, if the vexatious tax has been abolished, I will cross the Bosphorus, without paying."

"And if the tax be not removed?" said Selim.

"If it be not taken off," said Kéraban, with a superb gesture, "then, by Allah, I will retrace my steps, and make the tour of the Black Sea over again!"

# KÉRABAN THE INFLEXIBLE;

## OR, ADVENTURES IN THE EUXINE.

BY JULES VERNE.

## CHAPTER XI.

### IN WHICH A SOMEWHAT DRAMATIC INCIDENT OCCURS IN THE FANTASTIC HISTORY OF THE JOURNEY.

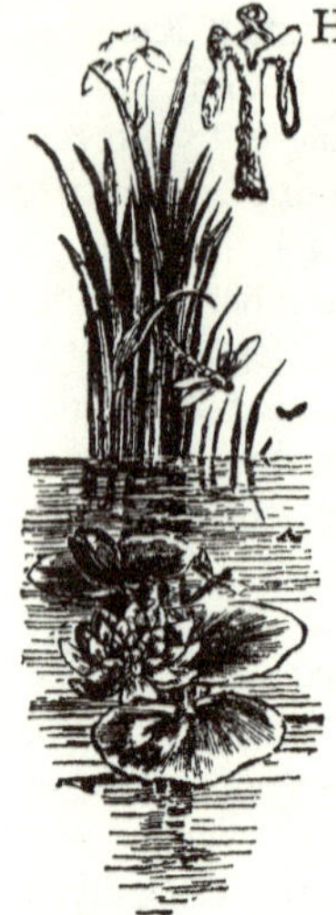

THEY had departed. They had quitted the villa: Seigneur Kéraban to accomplish his journey, Van Mitten to accompany his friend, Ahmet to follow his uncle, Nizib and Bruno because they could not do otherwise. The villa was practically deserted, because we need not reckon ladies and the five or six servants who continued their ordinary avocations. Selim himself accompanied the travellers to Odessa to change the money required for the expedition.

The villa, therefore, now contained only the two girls, Amasia and Nedjeb.

The Maltese captain was quite aware of this. He had followed all the incidents of the leave-taking with unfailing interest. Would Seigneur Kéraban postpone the marriage until his return? He had postponed it for the present—one trump in the captain's hand already! Would Ahmet consent to accompany his uncle? He had consented—trump number two!

Now the Maltese had a third "honour" in his hand. Amasia and her attendant were left alone in the gallery which opened to the sea. The vessel he commanded was lying off shore; his boat was at the steps. His sailors were accustomed to obey his merest sign. He had nothing to wish for.

The captain was sorely tempted to employ violent measures in the abduction of Amasia; but as he was really a prudent man and did not wish to leave anything to "chance," he decided to leave no traces behind him. So he reflected seriously upon the means to be employed.

It was then broad day. If he attempted to carry away Amasia by force, she would call for assistance, and Nedjeb would join in giving the alarm. Perhaps they would be heard by the servants; the *Guidare* would be noticed sailing rapidly away; and the clue to the outrage would be supplied. No; better wait until darkness fell, and meantime act circumspectly. One important point had been already gained—Ahmet was away.

So the Maltese remained aloof, seated in the stern-sheets of his gig, which was partially concealed by the balustrade, and watched the two girls. They scarcely bestowed a thought upon that very dangerous personage in their vicinity.

If, however, the young people, in consequence of the arrangements already made, would consent to go on board the felucca to examine the stuffs, or for any other purpose—and Yarhud had some idea concerning this—he would be able to make up his mind and decide the question without waiting for night.

After Ahmet's departure, Amasia, struck down by the sudden blow, remained pensive and silent, tearfully regarding the distant northern horizon where lay the path which the travellers must follow, and on which route lay so many dangers and delays, that would try the endurance of Seigneur Kéraban and his companions whom he dragged, unwilling, at his chariot wheels.

Had the marriage been solemnized, Amasia would have unhesitatingly accompanied Ahmet. Would his uncle have opposed it? No, he would not have wished to do so. Once she had become his niece, she fancied she would acquire some influence over him, and she would have arrested him in the dangerous course on which his obstinacy

"The Maltese remained aloof, seated in the stern-sheets of his gig."

had launched him. Now she was alone, and had to wait many weeks before she and Ahmet could be again united in the Scutari villa, or their wedding solemnized.

But if Amasia was sad, Nedjeb was furious, and vented her indignation upon the headstrong merchant who had been the cause of the separation. Ah! if her own marriage had been in question, the young Zingara would never have permitted him to carry off her intended. She would have met obstinacy with obstinacy. No; nothing of the kind would have happened in her case!

Nedjeb approached her young mistress, and taking her by the hand led her to the sofa, whereon she forced her to repose; then, taking a stool, she seated herself by her mistress.

"In your place," said Nedjeb, "instead of thinking of Seigneur Ahmet and lamenting his absence, I would think of Seigneur Kéraban and abuse him roundly."

"What good would that do?" said Amasia listlessly.

"I fancy we should be less sad," replied Nedjeb. "If you like, we will heap a series of maledictions upon this uncle's head. He deserves them all, and I assure you I will give him full measure."

"No, Nedjeb," replied Amasia. "Let us rather speak of Ahmet. Of him alone ought I to think, and I only think of him."

"Let us then speak of him," said Nedjeb. "In truth, dear mistress, he is the most charming *fiancé* ever girl possessed; but what an uncle he has! That despot, that selfish wretch, who had only a word to say and did not say it—who refused to remain here for the few days he might have given us. Indeed, he deserves——"

"Let us talk of Ahmet," said Amasia.

"Yes. Ah, how he adores you. How happy you will be with him. He would be perfection if he had not such a man for his uncle. Of what can he be made, I wonder! Do you know, I think he has done wisely not to marry. Against such a disposition as his even the very slaves of the harem would have rebelled."

"There, you are speaking again of him," said Amasia, whose thoughts were running on Ahmet.

"No, no; I was talking of Seigneur Ahmet—I am like yourself thinking only of Ahmet. Yes, in his place I would not have given way. I would have insisted. I really thought he had more determination!"

"People would tell you, Nedjeb, that Ahmet has displayed more energy in yieldng to, than he would have done if resisting his uncle's commands. Do not you perceive that, though it causes me anxiety, it is better he should go and thus endeavour to hasten the journey by all possible means, and prevent the numerous dangers which Kéraban's obstinate rashness would lead to? No, Nedjeb, no; by going away, Ahmet has proved his courage, and has given me another proof of his devotion."

"You may be right, my dear mistress," replied the attendant who, carried away by her native vivacity, could not yield her opinion. "Yes, Seigneur Ahmet certainly showed energy in going away; but don't you think he would have displayed more had he prevented his uncle from going?"

"Was such a course possible?" said Amasia. "Now, Nedjeb, I ask you, *was* such a course possible?"

"Yes—no—perhaps," replied Nedjeb. "It was not a question of breaking an iron bar. Ah, that Kéraban! It is all his fault, and if any accident should happen, he alone will be responsible. When I think of his running into danger, simply because he won't pay ten paras, and imperilling the safety of Seigneur Ahmet, your safety, and consequently mine,—I wish; yes, I wish that the Black Sea extended to the end of the globe, to see whether he would be obstinate enough to make the tour."

"He would do it," replied Amasia, in a tone of sincere conviction. "But let us talk of Ahmet, Nedjeb, and of no else but him."

At that moment Yarhud quitted his boat, and advanced unperceived towards the two girls. At the sound of his footsteps they turned round, and appeared surprised, as well as somewhat alarmed, at seeing the Maltese so near them.

Nedjeb at once arose and said—

"Is that you, captain? How came you here? what do you want?"

"I do not want anything," replied Yarhud, pretending surprise at this reception. "I want nothing; I only came to put my services at your disposal for——"

"Well, for what?" said Nedjeb, as he paused.

"To conduct you on board the vessel," replied the captain. "Have not you decided to inspect the cargo, and to choose such articles as may seem good to you?"

"That is true, dear mistress," said Nedjeb. "We have promised the captain."

"Yes, we promised when Ahmet was here," replied Amasia. "But he has gone away, and it is no longer fitting for us to go on board the *Guidare*."

The captain frowned, but he quickly recovered himself, and replied calmly——

"The *Guidare* cannot remain here long; and I must sail to-morrow, or the day after at the latest. If the lady wishes to inspect my stock, and to purchase any of the goods, she must do so without delay and take advantage of the opportunity now. My boat lies yonder, and we can be on board in a few minutes."

"We thank you, captain," replied Amasia coldly, "but I have no taste for such excursions in Seigneur Ahmet's absence. He must accompany us in our visit to the *Guidare:* he must assist us in our selection. He is no longer here, and I cannot, I will not, go without him."

"I am sorry for that," replied Yarhud; "and all the more because no doubt Seigneur Ahmet will be agreeably surprised on his return to find you have made the purchases you wished. The opportunity will not occur again, and you will regret the loss of it."

"That is possible, captain," replied Nedjeb; "but at this moment, I think you would do better not to press the point."

"Be it so," replied Yarhud, bowing. "In any case, let me hope that, if, a few weeks hence, the chances of trade compel me to remain at Odessa, you will not forget the promise you have made, to honour me with a visit."

"We will not forget it, captain," said Amasia, as she signed to the Maltese to retire.

Yarhud saluted the girls and advanced some paces towards the terrace, when suddenly he stopped as if an idea had just occurred to him, and, approaching Amasia as she was about to quit the verandah, he said—

"One word more—or rather let me offer a suggestion which cannot fail to be agreeable to the *fiancée* of the Seigneur Ahmet."

"What is the man worrying about?" exclaimed Amasia, who was somewhat impatient of the captain's persistency in intruding himself and his opinions at the villa.

"Chance has made me a spectator of the scene which took place before the departure of Seigneur Ahmet."

"Chance?" exclaimed Amasia, who had become distrustful, as if by presentiment of evil.

"Simply chance," repeated Yarhud. "I was in my boat—which is at your disposal."

"What proposition have you to make to us, captain?" inquired Amasia.

"A very natural one," he replied. "I have noticed how the daughter of Selim the Banker has been affected by the sudden departure of Seigneur Ahmet, and if she would like to see him again once more—"

"See him once more? What *do* you mean?" exclaimed Amasia, whose heart was beating tumultuously.

"I mean," said Yarhud, "that in an hour Seigneur Kéraban's carriage will pass along the road which rounds yonder cape."

Amasia stepped forward and gazed at the headland indicated by the wily captain.

"There? Over there?" she said.

"Yes."

"Oh, my dear mistress, if we could only reach that point?"

"Nothing can be more easy," said Yarhud. "Within half an hour, with this breeze, the *Guidare* could get there; so if you like to come you can embark at once."

"Yes, yes," exclaimed Nedjeb, who in this excursion only perceived an opportunity for Amasia to see her affianced once again.

But Amasia was more prudent and reflected upon the suggestion. The captain could scarcely control his impatience at her hesitation, and this anxiety had not escaped the banker's daughter. The appearance of Yarhud was not in his favour either, so she remained uninfluenced by the temptation.

"I await your orders," said the captain.

"No, captain," replied Amasia. "Were I to see my *fiancé* under such conditions, I believe I should give him more pain than pleasure."

Yarhud, comprehending that he had no hope of altering her determination, retired coldly.

The next moment the boat put off, and the captain and his men returned to the vessel. The gig remained alongside, however.

The girls continued together in the gallery an hour or more. Amasia was seated, leaning her elbows upon the balustrade, and was gazing anxiously towards the headland indicated by Yarhud, for at that point the carriage would be visible for a moment. Nedjeb also eagerly watched the place.

After the lapse of an hour or so, the

"Amasia was gazing anxiously towards the headland indicated by Yarhud."

Zingara exclaimed: "Ah! see, look yonder. Do you not perceive a carriage on the road? There on the summit of the cliff."

"Yes, yes," replied Amasia. "That is their chaise. 'Tis he! 'tis he!"

"He cannot see you," said Nedjeb.

"What matter?" replied Amasia; "I know he is looking at me."

"No doubt of it, dear lady. His eyes will discern the villa and perhaps ourselves."

"*Au revoir*, my Ahmet; *au revoir*," cried Amasia, as if the occupants of the carriage could have heard her farewell.

Amasia and Nedjeb quitted the gallery, and as soon as the chaise had disappeared they retired to the interior of the house.

Yarhud from the deck of his vessel perceived them departing, and gave orders to the men to watch for their return as the evening approached. Then he arranged his plan to gain by force what he could not effect by stratagem.

There was no such question of immediate hurry in the execution of the deed he proposed, since the marriage could not take place for six weeks, as Ahmet had gone away. Yet the impatience of Seigneur Saffar had to be considered, as well as his speedy return to Trebizond. Added to these impulses, the navigation of the Black

"The two girls were at once forcibly carried to the boat."

Sea by a small sailing vessel which might be retarded by calms or contrary winds had to be taken into consideration, and fifteen or twenty days might be thus lost. On all accounts, therefore, Yarhud felt obliged to sail at the earliest possible moment if he would arrive at the time agreed upon with Scarpante. Yarhud was, no doubt, a rogue, but he was a rogue who kept his engagements. So he decided to act at once.

Circumstances favoured him. Towards evening—before her father had returned—Amasia re-entered the gallery, and this time alone. The girl wished to gaze on the distant hills which contained in their embrace him she loved best. She took her place again and, leaning upon the balustrade, contemplated the darkening landscape with that fond, "far off" expression in her eyes which no distance could remove.

Thus plunged in reverie, Amasia did not perceive that the boat put off from the *Guidare.* She did not notice its almost noiseless approach by the terrace, nor its bringing up at the steps close by. Nevertheless Yarhud and three of his men were even then creeping cautiously towards her, up the slope; but the girl never noticed their approach.

Suddenly Yarhud leaped up and seized

"Selim fell with a bullet in his shoulder.

her with such force that she had no power of resistance.

"Help! help!" she screamed.

Her cries were immediately stifled, but they had been heard by Nedjeb, who at once came in search of her mistress.

Scarcely had the waiting-maid passed the door of the gallery, when she was seized by two sailors, who at once prevented her from giving any alarm by word or deed.

"On board!" exclaimed Yarhud.

The two girls were at once forcibly carried to the boat and rowed swiftly towards the *Guidare,* which, with her anchor a-peak and her sails hoisted, was lying-to, awaiting the captain's return.

As soon as Amasia and Nedjeb were on board, they were carried to the stern cabin, where they could hear and see nothing of what passed, and the vessel was put before the wind, and her direction was made so that she would pass near the little creek at the extremity of the grounds of the villa.

But, rapidly as all this had been accomplished, the scene had attracted the attention of some of the out-door servants. They had heard Amasia's cries and had given the alarm.

At that moment Selim returned and was informed what had passed. In agony he searched for his daughter—she had disappeared!

But perceiving the *Guidare* making for the point, Selim understood the whole matter in a moment. He quickly crossed the gardens towards the place which the vessel must pass, so as to avoid the rocks at the extremity of the creek.

"Wretches!" he exclaimed. "They are taking away my daughter, Amasia. Stop them! Stop!"

A musket fired from the deck of the *Guidare* was the only response to this appeal. Selim fell with a bullet in his shoulder.

In another moment, the felucca, with a flowing sheet, had disappeared from the sight of those at the villa.

---

## Chapter XII.

### In which Van Mitten discourses on Tulips for, we trust, the Benefit of the Reader.

The postchaise with fresh horses had quitted Odessa about one o'clock in the afternoon. Kéraban occupied the left corner of the interior, Van Mitten the right, and Ahmet was between them. Bruno and Nizib were in the "cabriolet," where they chatted or slept—chiefly the latter. The sun was shining brightly, and the sea broke in dark blue waves against the gray cliffs.

In the interior of the chaise conversation was at first as limited as in the "cabriolet" outside, and if one party slept higher, the other reflected more deeply. Kéraban was thinking of his firm determination, and of the "turn" he was giving the Ottoman authorities. Van Mitten was thinking of the unexpected journey he was making, and did not cease to wonder how it had happened that he, a citizen of Holland, had been launched thus upon a tour of the Black Sea, when he ought to be resting quietly in Pera or Constantinople.

Ahmet had made up his mind to the journey, but he determined not to spare his uncle's purse whenever delay or trouble might be avoided by using it. They would travel by the quickest and shortest route. The young man was ruminating on this as the chaise turned the point, and he could perceive the banker's villa. He fixed his gaze upon it, no doubt at the same time Amasia's eyes were directed to the carriage, and their regards crossed in mid air.

Then, addressing his uncle, Ahmet resolved to open a delicate question, and ask whether he had mastered all the details of the journey.

"Yes," replied Kéraban, "we shall continue upon the shore route all along."

"And whither are we bound just now?"

"To Koblewo, about twelve leagues from Odessa. We shall arrive at the place this evening."

"And after leaving Koblewo?"

"We shall travel all night, and reach Nikolaief to-morrow about mid-day. We shall then have made eighteen leagues more."

"Very good, uncle; we must travel quickly. But after leaving Nikolaief don't you think of reaching the Caucasus district in a day or two?"

"How?" asked Kéraban.

"By taking the train. The south-Russian line by Alexandroff and Rostow would enable us to accomplish a good third of our journey."

"Use a railway?" exclaimed Kéraban.

At that instant Van Mitten touched his youthful neighbour, and said in a low tone—

"It is useless to discuss the question. He has a horror of railways."

Ahmet was not unaware of his uncle's peculiarities in this and other respects, but he fancied that for once he would yield.

But Kéraban would not be Kéraban if he did give way.

"I think you were speaking of railways?" he said.

"Yes, uncle."

"And you wish that I should do what I have never yet done——"

"It seems to me——"

"You wish that I, Kéraban, should permit myself to be dragged like a fool along an iron-rail by a steam-engine?"

"When you have tried it——"

"Ahmet, it is evident you have not reflected upon this suggestion which you dare to make to me!"

"But, uncle——"

"I tell you, you have not thought of what you are saying."

"I assure you, uncle, that in the 'wagons'——"

"Wagons!" exclaimed Kéraban, with an accent impossible to describe.

"Yes, the carriages which run on the rails——"

"Rails? What horrible words are these, and, may I ask you what language you are speaking?"

"Only the language of modern travellers."

"Look here, nephew," exclaimed Kéraban, who was getting excited, "do I look like a modern traveller? Do I look like a man who would permit himself to be dragged along in a 'wagon' by a machine? Is it likely that I should slide along 'rails' when I can drive on a road?"

"When time presses, uncle——"

"Ahmet, look me in the face and listen to me. If there are no carriages, I will go in a cart. If there is no cart, I will ride; if I cannot get a horse, I will hire a donkey. If there are no donkeys, I will walk; and, when I cannot walk, I will crawl; and, when I can no longer crawl, I——"

"For goodness sake, stop," cried Van Mitten.

"When I cannot crawl on hands and knees, I will drag myself along on my stomach," said Kéraban in conclusion—"yes, on my stomach!"

Then seizing Ahmet by the arm, he said—

"Did you ever hear that Mahomet took the train to go to Mecca?"

To this question there was obviously no answer; and Ahmet, who would have replied that had railways existed in the time of Mahomet he would no doubt have used them, thought it best to be silent: while Kéraban sat in his corner grumbling, and condemning all words of a "railway" character.

However, if the chaise did not travel so rapidly as an express, it proceeded quickly. The horses went well upon the level road, and there was nothing to complain of. There was no want of relays. Ahmet, who, with his uncle's consent, had undertaken to pay the expenses, lavished "tips" freely on all concerned with imperial generosity. Bank-notes flew out of his pocket, and he might have been starting a "paper-chase" with rouble currency.

The result of all this liberality was that the travellers reached Koblewo the same day. Thence they turned more inland, and crossing the Bug river, to the heights of Nikolaief, the chaise reached that town easily by mid-day on the 28th August.

Three hours' rest was allowed for breakfast, &c., and Ahmet took the opportunity to write to Selim the banker, telling him of the journey so far and sending all kinds of messages to Amasia. Seigneur Kéraban occupied himself congenially in drinking coffee and smoking. Van Mitten and Bruno explored the town, whose prosperity threatens to outdo its rival Kherson, and to usurp the title of the district from it.

Ahmet was the first to give the signal for departure. The Dutchman did not keep him waiting. Kéraban gave a last puff to his narghileh as the postillion mounted his horse and the carriage rolled away to Kherson.

There were seventeen leagues to travel across an uninteresting country. Here and there were a few mulberry-trees, poplars, and willows. As they approached the Dneiper, the course of which is terminated at Kherson, the travellers came upon long expanses of ground, planted with tall reeds which appeared to be covered with the cornflower. But at the approach of the chaise, these "cornflowers" took to themselves wings, and proved to be blue jays whose discordent chattering was as disagreeable to the ear as their beautiful colours were pleasant to the eye.

At day-break on the 29th of August, Seigneur Kéraban and his companions reached Kherson without incident. Kherson is the chief seat of government, the foundation of which is due to Potemkin. The travellers could not but congratulate this creation of the imperial favour of Catherine II., for they found an excellent hotel, where they stopped several hours, and some good shops, where they were enabled to replenish their stock of provisions—a duty which Bruno, much sharper than Nizib, performed to a marvel.

"Some hours later they changed horses at Aleschki."

Some hours later they changed horses at Aleschki and descended towards the isthmus of Pérékop, which unites the Crimea to Russia.

Ahmet had not neglected to send a letter to Selim from Aleschki, and when the travellers were again seated in the chaise Kéraban enquired whether his nephew had sent his regards also to his friend the banker.

"I did not forget to do so, uncle," replied Ahmet, "and I added that we were using all diligence to reach Scutari as soon as possible."

"You did well, nephew; and he must not neglect to give us news of himself on every possible occasion."

"Unfortunately, as we never know beforehand where we may stop," said Ahmet, "our letters must remain unanswered."

"True," said Van Mitten.

"By the by," said Kéraban addressing his friend, "it seems to me that you do not correspond much with Madame Van Mitten. What will that excellent woman think of you?"

"Madame Van Mitten, do you mean?" asked the Dutchman.

"Certainly"

"Madame Van Mitten is undoubtedly an excellent woman. As a wife, I have not a word to say against her, but as a life companion——But why speak of Madame Van Mitten at all, Kéraban?"

"Eh? Well, because I remember her as a most agreeable woman."

"Indeed!" said Van Mitten, in the tone of a man who hears something for the first time.

"Did not I speak of her in the highest terms, Ahmet, when I returned from Holland?" said Kéraban turning to his nephew.

"Yes indeed, uncle," replied the young man.

"And during my journey, was I not particularly charmed with the reception she gave me?"

"Ah!" remarked Van Mitten.

"Nevertheless," continued Kéraban, "I must allow that at times she is capricious, and has curious ideas on some points. Still, those qualities are inherent in women, and if they cannot get over them it is best to have nothing to do with them—which is precisely how I have acted!"

"And you have acted wisely," said Van Mitten.

"Is your wife as fond of tulips as ever?" enquired Kéraban. "She is a true Hollander in that respect."

"Yes, passionately fond of *them*," replied Van Mitten.

"Look here, Van Mitten. Frankly now, I think you are very cool about your wife."

"Cool! The expression is even too warm, if applied to my regard in that quarter."

"What do you say?" exclaimed Kéraban.

"I say," replied the Dutchman, "that I did not wish you to talk of Madame Van Mitten at all! But since you have mentioned her, and the occasion is favourable, I will make a confession."

"A confession!"

"Yes, friend Kéraban: Madame Van Mitten and I are separated."

"Separated, by mutual consent?"

"Yes."

"For ever?"

"For ever."

"Tell me all about it, unless your feelings——"

"Feelings," exclaimed the Dutchman, "why should I have any feeling in the matter?"

"Very well, then. Go on: speak. In my position as a Turk, Van Mitten, I am fond of tales and, as an unmarried man, I delight in all matrimonial histories."

"Well," said Van Mitten, in a disinterested manner, as if he were telling a story concerning a stranger; "for many years Madame Van Mitten and I did not get on very well. We had disputes upon every subject—bed-time, getting-up time, dinner-time: concerning what we ahould eat, and what we should not eat; on what we should drink; upon what we did; on the time of day it was, and what it ought to be; on the placing of the furniture; whether the fire should be lighted in this or that room; whether the window or door should be shut or open; on what plants should be retained in the garden, and what should be torn up."

"That promised well," remarked Kéraban.

"Yes, but you see it all came to nothing as I am of a mild and long-suffering disposition, and I always yielded without causing an open rupture."

"That was perhaps the wisest plan," said Ahmet.

"On the contrary," remarked Kéraban, "it was foolish."

"I don't know anything about it," continued Van Mitten; "but, at any rate, in our last altercation I wished to resist, and I did resist, like a regular Kéraban!"

"It was a regular rain of bulbs."

"By Allah, that is impossible," cried the individual referred to, who knew himself thoroughly.

"More strongly than any Kéraban," added Van Mitten.

"Mahomet protect me!" replied the other. "Do you mean to assert that you can be more obstinate than I?"

"It seems improbable on the face of it," said Ahmet, in a tone that went to his uncle's heart.

"You will soon see," replied Van Mitten quietly.

"We shall not see that," cried Kéraban.

"Will you permit me to finish? It was concerning tulips that the discussion arose between me and my wife, about those beautiful tulips—so dear to amateurs—*Genners*, which grow straight on the stalk, and of which there are more than a hundred varieties. I had none which cost me less than a thousand florins a bulb."

"Eight thousand piastres," said Kéraban, who was accustomed to reckon in Turkish money.

"Yes, about that," replied the Dutchman. "Now Madame Van Mitten took it into her head one day to root up a *Valentia* in order to put an *Œil de Soleil* in its place. This was too much. I objected. She insisted. I endeavoured to seize her; she escaped, and rushing upon the *Valentias* tore one up by the roots."

"Cost! Eight thousand piastres," muttered Kéraban.

"Then," continued Van Mitten, "I precipitated myself on an *Œil de Soleil* and broke it."

"Cost! Sixteen thousand piastres," said Kéraban.

"My wife destroyed a second *Valentia*."

"Twenty-four thousand piastres," replied Kéraban, as if he were calling over his books at his counting-house.

"I responded with another *Œil de Soleil*."

"Thirty-two thousand piastres."

"Then the battle became general," said Van Mitten; "till madame's ammunition was exhausted. I received two splendid 'cloves' on my head."

"Forty-eight thousand piastres!"

"She received three others full in the chest."

"Sixty-thousand piastres!"

"It was a regular rain of bulbs—such a thing has never been seen—and it lasted half-an-hour. The whole garden was torn up, and the conservatory afterwards dismantled. My entire collection was destroyed."

"And, finally, the cost was—how much?" asked Kéraban.

"Greater than if we had only wanted head-wounds, like Homer's economical heroes," replied Van Mitten. "One way and another I fancy the cost was about twenty-five thousand florins!"

"Two hundred thousand piastres," said Kéraban.

"But I was firm," said Van Mitten.

"That was worth something."

"Besides, I came away, having given orders to have my property realized, and transmitted to the bank in Constantinople. Then I came to Rotterdam with my faithful Bruno, and made up my mind not to enter my house again until Madame Van Mitten had quitted it—for a better world."

"Where tulip-throwing is unknown," remarked Ahmet.

"Now, Kéraban," said Van Mitten, "have you had many fits of obstinacy which have cost you two hundred thousand piastres?"

"I?" said Kéraban, secretly a little annoyed at this question.

"Yes, certainly," said Ahmet, "my uncle has had some—I know at least one."

"What was that, if you please?" asked Van Mitten.

"Why this obstinate fit, which, for the sake of ten paras, is sending us all round the Black Sea. This will cost more than your little eradication of tulips."

"It will cost what it will cost," replied Kéraban drily. "But I think my friend Van Mitten has not paid too dearly for his liberty. That's what comes of having only one wife. Mahomet knew what he was about when he permitted his followers to have as many as they could support."

"Certainly," replied Van Mitten. "I think ten wives are much easier to govern than one."

"What is still more easy," added Kéraban, moralizing, "is to have no wife at all!"

With this observation the conversation ended.

The chaise continued its course: at the post-house relays were found, and the journey was resumed. After travelling all night, the tourists were somewhat fatigued; but, at the instigation of Ahmet, they decided not to lose an hour, and pressed on. Having passed Bolschoi-Kopani, and Kalantschak, they reached Pérékop, at the end of the gulf of the same name—the point where the Crimea unites with Russia proper.

# KÉRABAN THE INFLEXIBLE;

## OR, ADVENTURES IN THE EUXINE.

BY JULES VERNE.

### CHAPTER XIII.

SHEWING HOW OUR TRAVELLERS CROSSED THE ANCIENT TAURIDA, AND WITH WHAT TEAM THEY QUITTED IT.

THE Crimea! the Taurisian Chersonese of the ancients; a quadrilateral, or rather an irregular lozenge, which seems to have been lifted by enchantment from the Italian shores; a peninsula which M. de Lesseps would transform into an island with two strokes of his knife; a corner of the earth which has been the coveted possession, and the objective, of all the jealous peoples who dispute for the empire of the East; an ancient kingdom of the Bosphorus, which the Heracleans subdued six hundred years before the Christian Era; which yielded to Mithridates, the Alains, the Goths, the Huns, the Hungarians, the Tartars, the Genoese; a province which Mahomet II. made a rich dependency of his empire, and which Catherine II. annexed definitively to Russia in 1791!

How is it possible that this country, blessed by the gods, and disputed for by mortals, should escape the network of mythological legend? Have not wiseacres sought in the marshes of Sivach the traces of the gigantic works of the problematic people of Atlantis? Have not the poets of antiquity placed one of the entrances to the infernal regions near Cape Kerberian, the three "moles" of which form the heads of Cerberus. Iphigenia, daughter of Agamemnon and Clytemnestra, become a priestess of Diana "in Tauris," was here on the point of sacrificing to the goddess her brother Orestes, cast upon the shores of Cape Parthenium.

And now the Crimea in its southern part—worth more than all the arid islands of the archipelago—with its Tchadir Dagh rising four thousand feet to a table-land, whereon a feast could be laid for all the deities of Olympus; with its amphitheatres of guests, whose green mantle falls to the sea-shore; its "bouquets" of chestnut-trees, cypress, olives, Judas-trees, almonds, and laburnum, and its waterfalls,—is it not the most beautiful jewel in the crown of provinces which extends from the Black Sea to the Arctic Ocean? Is it not that vivifying and temperate climate that the Russians of the north as well as of the south; unite in seeking, the former to gain a refuge from the severities of a hyperborean winter, the latter to find shelter from the dryness of the east winds? Have they not founded colonies, and built castles, houses, villas, and cottages around Cape Aia, whose Ram-like head defies the attacks of the Black Sea's waves, even to the extreme south of Tauris? Here we find Yalta and Aloupka, which belong to Prince Woronsow—a feudal manor outwardly, a dream of an oriental imagination within; Kisil Tasch, belonging to Count Poniatowski; Arteck, to Prince André Galitzin; Marsanda, Orcanda, Eriklik, imperial properties, and Livadia, a splendid palace with its cascades and streams, and whose winter-gardens are the favourite retreat of the Empress of all the Russias.

Here all dispositions—the curious, the sentimental, the artistic, the romantic—will find something to satisfy them. This little corner of the earth is a microcosm wherein Europe and Asia mingle. Here we find Tartar villages, Greek towns, oriental cities, with mosques, minarets, muezzins, dervishes, monasteries of Russian foundation, seraglios,

Yalta.

thebaïdes in which many romantic adventures are buried; holy places, to which pilgrims converge; a Jewish mountain, which belongs to the tribe of Karaites; and a valley of Jehosaphat filled with tombs, like an ante-chamber to its prototype by the Cedron, where thousands of the justified will unite once again at the summons of the last trump.

What wonderful places Van Mitten had to see; what novel impressions would he not have to note in this country to which a strange destiny had led him! But his friend Kéraban did not travel for the purpose of seeing anything; and Ahmet, besides being familiar with the Crimea, would not allow an hour more than what was absolutely necessary to be spent in even a cursory examination.

"Perhaps, after all," said Van Mitten to

himself, "perhaps I may be able, in passing, to obtain a light impression of this antique Chersonese which has been so justly praised."

But it was not to be. The chaise continued its course by the shortest way, following an oblique line, from north to southwest, without passing through the centre, or

Aloupka.

touching the southern shore of the ancient Tauris. Indeed, such a route as Van Mitten would have followed, had been vetoed at a consultation wherein he had no voice. If, by passing through the Crimea, they could shorten the tour of the Sea of Azof—which route would have lengthened the journey one hundred and fifty leagues at the least—they would gain by cutting direct from Pérékop to the peninsula of Kertsch. Then, from the other side of the Strait of Jenikale, the peninsula of Taman would offer a regular passage to the Caucasian territories.

So the chaise continued its way along the narrow isthmus to which the Crimea hangs like a great orange to a bough. On one side is the bay of Pérékop, on the other the marshes of Sivach, better known under the name of the Putrid Sea—a vast tarn fed by the waters of the Tauris and the Sea of Azof, to which the cutting of Ghénitché serves as a canal.

The travellers as they passed were able to observe the Sivach, which is scarcely three feet deep, and in which the degree of saltness is almost at "saturation point" in certain places. Now as it is in such spots that the salt crystals are deposited, naturally the "Putrid Sea" could be made the most productive salt-marsh in the world. It must be confessed that the odours of the Sivach are not pleasant. The air is impregnated with sulphuretted hydrogen. The fish that penetrate into the lake are quickly killed. The Putrid Sea resembles in this respect the Lake Asphaltites in Palestine.

The railway from Alexandroff to Sebastopol traverses this marsh. So Seigneur Kéraban heard with horror the whistling of the locomotives and the rumbling of the trains upon the rails which are sometimes washed by the dense waters of the Putrid Sea.

Next day, on the 31st of August, the travellers found themselves journeying upon a road through a fertile country. The leaves of the olive trees, blown back by the wind, seemed to be sprinkled with quicksilver; dark green cypresses, magnificent oaks and arbutus of great height were numerous. Everywhere upon the slopes were vineyards, which produce wines little inferior to some good French vintages.

Thanks to the liberality of Ahmet, no delays were met with: the horses were always at hand to be harnessed, and the postillions, frequently rewarded, were always willing to take the shortest cuts. In the evening they had passed the long straggling village of Dorte, and some leagues farther on they would reach the borders of the Putrid Sea again. At this place, the curious lagoon is only separated from the Sea of Azof by a tongue of sand, the average breadth of which is about a quarter of a league. This tongue of sand is called the arrow of Arabat, and extends from the village of that name to Ghénitché northwards, on *terrâ firma*; divided only by a cutting of three hundred feet through which the water from the Sea of Azof enters the marsh, as already stated.

At daybreak Seigneur Kéraban and his companions were surrounded by clouds of damp vapor, thick miasmas, which gradually dispersed under the influence of the sun's rays.

The country was less wooded and more deserted here. A few dromedaries were noticed, animals of great size, and their appearance gave somewhat of an Arabic touch to the landscape. The few carriages that passed were of wood, without a particle of iron, and creaked and groaned loudly. Their appearance was primitive in the extreme, but in the villages and in the more isolated farms, Tartar generosity and hospitality are continually the prevailing features. Anyone may enter, seat himself at table, eat and drink as much as he pleases, and pay his score with a simple "Thank-you."

It need scarcely be said that our travellers never abused these simple customs, which are rapidly disappearing. They left always some sufficient renumeration as a memento of their journey. That evening the team, fatigued by such a long stage, stopped at the *bourgade* of Arabat at the southern extremity of the "arrow." There a fortress has been erected, and is surrounded by houses, scattered in all directions. All about this part of the country are quantities of fennel, the hiding-places of adders; and whole fields of water-melons, the crop of which is very abundant.

It was nine o'clock in the evening when the chaise was stopped before an *auberge* of small pretensions. It was the best in the place. In the forsaken Chersonese it does not pay to be too particular, and our travellers had to put up with the inn.

"Nephew Ahmet," said Kéraban, "we have travelled for many days and nights without any more delay than was necessary to change horses. Now, for my own part, I shall not be sorry to have a few hours' sleep even in a hotel bed!"

"I shall be delighted to do the same,"

said Van Mitten, rubbing his hips to get rid of his stiffness.

"What, lose twelve hours!" exclaimed Ahmet. "Twelve hours, in a journey of six weeks?"

"Do you wish to argue the point?" asked Kéraban, in the slightly aggressive tone he usually adopted.

"No, uncle—no," said Ahmet. "When you have need of repose——"

"The Post-master was standing on the steps"

"Well, I have need of repose now, so has Van Mitten and Bruno, I suppose, as well as Nizib, who is only too glad to get it."

"Seigneur Kéraban," said Bruno, "I regard this idea of yours as one of the best you have ever had, and all the more praiseworthy if supper be included and served first."

This suggestion of Bruno's was very much to the point, as the provisions which had been carried in the chaise were rapidly diminishing, and what remained, it would be necessary to leave untouched, until the travellers reached Kertsch, an important town in the peninsula of the same name, where they could obtain an abundant supply.

Unfortunately, if the beds of the Arabat Inn were pretty good, even for travellers of such distinction, the arrangements of the kitchen left much to be desired. Tourists are not numerous in the Taurida: the principal guests at the *auberge* of Arabat are merchants or salt-buyers, people not difficult to please, who sleep on the hard beds, and eat whatever is put before them.

Seigneur Kéraban and his companions had to put up with a meagre repast—that is to say, a dish of *pilaw*, the national food—but with more rice than fowl, and more bone than flesh. Besides, the fowl was so old and tough, that it nearly resisted and defied Kéraban himself; but the solid molars of the headstrong Turk gained the victory at last, and he did not yield any more than he had ever done.

After this dish, a veritable tureen of *yaourtz*, or curdled milk, came upon the board to assist in the digestion of the *pilaw*: then some cakes, of a not very appetising character, called *katlamas*.

Bruno and Nizib were scarcely as well supplied as their masters, as might be expected. Their jaws would, no doubt, have done justice to the toughest of fowls, but they had not the opportunity to exercise them in that way. The *pilaw* on their table was substituted by a black substance, something like a thin brick from the chimney-back.

"What is that?" asked Bruno.

"I don't know what they call it," replied Nizib.

"What! you a native of the country, and——"

"I am not a native of the country."

"Well, very nearly—you are a Turk," replied Bruno. "Well, my friend, taste a piece of this dried boot-sole, and tell me what you think of it."

Nizib, always willing, took a piece of the said leather sole, and bit it.

"Well?" asked Bruno.

"Well, it is not good, but it is possible to eat it, all the same."

"Yes, Nizib, when one is dying of hunger, and one has no other choice of food."

Then Bruno boldly attacked the dish like a man who has decided not to get thin, but to risk all in the attempt to keep up appearances. And this the men did, aided by several glasses of a certain alcoholized beer.

Suddenly Nizib cried, "Allah protect me!"

"What has happened?" enquired Bruno.

"Suppose what I have eaten prove to be pork?"

"Pork!" exclaimed Bruno. "Ah, just so, Nizib. A good Mussulman, like you, is not permitted to partake of that excellent but unclean animal. Well, it seems to me that if the thing we have eaten is pork, we have only one course open to us——"

"That is——?"

"To digest it as quietly as possible now we have eaten it."

But Nizib was not so easily comforted, for he was a very strict observer of the law of the Prophet, and he felt greatly troubled in mind. So Bruno volunteered to ascertain from the landlord what he had sent up for dinner.

Nizib was quickly reassured, and his digestion was no longer troubled. The dish was not meat at all; it was fish, *shebac*, a kind of "Saint Peter's" fish, which when caught, is split and dried in the sun, and then smoked. These fish are exported in considerable numbers from Rostow on the Sea of Azof.

Masters and servants had accordingly to be content with a very light supper at the Inn of Arabat. The beds appeared even more unpleasant than the gnats in the carriage; but the sleepers were not subjected to any violent jolting, and the rest they obtained in their not too comfortable rooms, was sufficient to recruit their energies.

Next morning, 2nd September, at daybreak Ahmet was afoot, and he set off to the post-house, in search of relays. The team which had brought our travellers to the inn was quite exhausted and unable to continue the journey without a further rest. Ahmet had made up his mind to bring the chaise, all ready horsed, to the inn door, so as to leave his uncle and Van Mitten no excuse—they had only to enter the chaise and depart for Kertsch.

The post-house was some distance off, at the end of the village; and the roof, ornamented with crosses of wood, gave it the appearance of the finger-board of a "double

"The chaise descended the road at a long slinging trot."

bass." But of horses there was no sign whatever! The stable was empty, and the post-master could not supply the animals for any consideration.

Ahmet, very much annoyed at this check, returned to the inn. Kéraban, Van Mitten, Nizib, and Bruno, all ready to start, were waiting for the chaise. Already one of the party—it is needless to say which—was exhibiting signs of impatience.

"Well, Ahmet," cried this individual, "have you returned alone? I thought you had gone to procure horses for us?"

"My errand was useless, uncle," replied Ahmet. "There is not a single horse to be had."

"No horses?" exclaimed Kéraban.

"And we cannot have any before to-morrow," added Ahmet.

"To-morrow!"

"Yes. That means a loss of twenty-four hours."

"Twenty-four hours!" cried Kéraban, "but I do not mean to lose ten, not five, not even one."

"Nevertheless," said the Dutchman," if there are no horses——"

"There shall be some," replied Kéraban, walking away, and signing to the others to accompany him. In a quarter of an hour they reached the post-house. The post-master was standing on the steps, in the easy attitude of a man who knew that one is not obliged to provide what he does not possess.

"You have no more horses, I hear?" said Kéraban, in a far from conciliatory tone.

"I have only those that you brought here yesterday, and they are unfit to travel," replied the post-master.

"And why, if you please, have you no fresh horses in your stables?"

"Because they have been taken by a Turkish seigneur who has gone to Kertsch *en route* to Poti and the Caucasus."

"A Turk!" exclaimed Kéraban. "One of your European Ottomans, no doubt. They are not content with interfering with us in the streets of Constantinople, but they must inconvenience us in the Crimea!"

"Who is this man, this Turk?" he continued, after a pause.

"His name is Seigneur Saffar; that's all I know about him," replied the post-master quietly.

"Why did you permit Seigneur Saffar to take all the horses?" asked Kéraban with contempt.

"Because the traveller arrived here twelve hours before you, and as the horses were available I had no reason for refusing them to him."

"You ought to have done so——"

"Ought to have done so?" echoed the post-master.

"Yes, certainly, when I was on the road hither," replied Kéraban.

Now what could one reply to such arguments! Van Mitten endeavoured to interpose, but was only snapped up by his friend. As for the post-master, he only gazed at Kéraban with a contemptuous expression, and turned away to enter the house. But Kéraban stopped him by saying—

"After all, it does not matter whether you have horses or not: we must proceed at once."

"Proceed at once! Have I not told you I have no horses?" replied the post-master.

"We'll find some."

"There are none in Arabat."

"Find a pair—find one," replied Kéraban, who began to lose his self-control; "find half a one, but find something."

"But if there are no horses," began Van Mitten gently.

"There must be some found."

"Perhaps you can procure for us a team of mules?" said Ahmet to the post-master.

"Very well, mules will do," said Kéraban. "We will be content with mules."

"I have never seen any mules in the province," replied the post-master.

"He has seen one to-day," whispered Bruno to Van Mitten, as he indicated Kéraban; "and a fine one too."

"Are there any asses?" enquired Ahmet.

"No more asses than mules."

"No asses!" exclaimed Kéraban. "You are playing with us, monsieur. No asses in this country—not enough to form a team, not sufficient to relay a carriage? You are joking."

As he spoke Kéraban looked round at a number of natives who had assembled near the post-house.

"He is quite capable of having those people harnessed to the chaise," muttered Bruno.

"Yes, them or us," replied Nizib, who knew his master.

However, since there were neither horses, mules, nor asses, it was evident that the travellers could not proceed; and all they could do was to resign themselves to the delay of twenty-four hours. Ahmet, who was as greatly put out as his uncle, was about to try to make him hear reason in the absolute impossibility of procuring horses, when Kéraban cried out—

"A hundred roubles to anyone who will find me a team."

A shiver passed over the the natives who heard this offer. At length one man boldly came forward, and said,—

"Seigneur Turk, I have two dromedaries to sell."

"I will buy them," said Kéraban.

To harness a pair of dromedaries to a carriage was an experiment never hitherto made; but it was going to be attempted now.

In less than an hour the bargain was completed, and at a high rate. But no matter. Seigneur Kéraban would have paid double the amount. The two animals were harnessed, and with the assurance of a substantial "tip," the late proprietor of the dromedaries, mounting as postillion, seated himself on the hump of one of the animals. Then the chaise, to the great astonishment of the natives, and to the extreme satisfaction of the travellers, descended the road towards Kertsch at a long slinging trot. The same evening the travellers reached Argin, twelve leagues from Arabat.

There were no horses there either, in consequence of the Seigneur Saffar having had them. Our travellers were obliged to sleep at Argin and give the dromedaries a rest.

Next day, 3rd September, the chaise departed under the same conditions and reached Marienthal, seventeen leagues from Argin. The night was passed there, and at daybreak the travellers started again, and after a run of twelve leagues reached Kertsch without accident, but not without some rude jolting consequent upon the "pulling" of the dromedaries, which were quite new to the business.

To sum up, Seigneur Kéraban and his companions, who had started on the 17th of August, had, after nineteen days' journeying, accomplished three-sevenths of the required distance—three hundred leagues out of seven hundred. They had, therefore, done well; and if they continued to progress in like manner during the twenty-six days still remaining—till the 30th of September—they would complete the tour of the Black Sea within the prescribed period.

"Somehow," said Bruno to his master again, "Somehow I can't help thinking that the journey will end badly!"

"For my friend Kéraban, do you mean?"

"For your friend Kéraban, or for those who accompany him," replied Bruno.

# KÉRABAN THE INFLEXIBLE;

## OR, ADVENTURES IN THE EUXINE.

BY JULES VERNE.

## CHAPTER XIV.

### IN WHICH KÉRABAN PROVES THAT HE IS STRONGER IN GEOGRAPHY THAN HIS NEPHEW AHMET BELIEVED.

THE town of Kertsch is situated in the peninsula of that name at the eastern extremity of the Taurida. A hill on which formerly the Acropolis was situated dominates the town. This is Mount Mithridates, so called from the implacable enemy of the Romans who failed to drive them from Asia. The polyglot ancient, audacious general, and legendary poisoner, has justly his place in the front of a city which was the capital of the kingdom of the Bosphorus. There that King of Pontus, that terrible Eupator, fell on the sword of a Gallic soldier, after having vainly tried to poison his iron frame which he had accustomed to poison.

This little historical summary, Van Mitten gave his companions during a short halt. But the relation only called from Kéraban the remark :—

" Mithridates was a stupid blunderer."

" How so ? " asked Van Mitten.

" If he had really desired to poison himself, all he had to do was to dine at that inn at Arabat."

After such a commentary as this, Van Mitten could not proceed with his eulogy of Mithridates, but he made up his mind to visit the monarch's capital in the few hours left to him.

The chaise passed through the town and created considerable surprise amongst the inhabitants in consequence of the pair of dromedaries. Ahmet's first care on arrival at the Hotel Constantine, was to enquire whether horses could be had on the following morning, and to his great satisfaction ascertained that there was no lack of steeds in the stables of the post-house.

"It is fortunate," he said to his uncle, "that Seigneur Saffar has not taken all the relays."

But the little-enduring uncle did not the less cherish a grudge against the man who had dared to travel before him and take his horses. However, as he had no further need for his dromedaries, he sold them to the conductor of a caravan, but only obtained for them living the same price as he would have gotten for the carcases. This loss Kéraban carried in his mind's ledger to the account of Seigneur Saffar.

We may assume that Saffar was not in Kertsch, else a little dispute would probably have arisen which might have had serious consequences. He had quitted the town two days previously, by the Caucasus route. This was fortunate, as our travellers were about to travel by the lower road.

A good supper at the Hotel Constantine, a good night in comfortable quarters, made both the masters and servants forget past troubles. So a letter written by Ahmet to his *fiancée* at Odessa, was the bearer of good news and a report of the journey as regularly accomplished.

As the hour of departure had been fixed for ten o'clock next morning, Van Mitten was enabled to explore the town. Rising with the sun, he found Ahmet on this occasion ready to accompany him. So they walked through the wide streets of Kertsch, which have paved footways and are swarming with multitudes of vagabond dogs. These animals are looked after by a man specially appointed to knock them on the head, but that time he must have been asleep, for Ahmet and the Dutchman had considerable difficulty to escape from the dangerous brutes.

The stone quay, built into the sea at the curve of the bay, afforded them a more secure promenade. Upon the quay are the governor's palace and the custom-house. At some distance out the vessels are anchored, for there is not much water in the bay, though the anchorage is good. The port has become very commercial since the cession of the town to the Russians in 1774, and there is a large salt depot there, the mineral being furnished from the mines Pérékop.

"Have we time to ascend that hill?" asked Van Mitten, indicating Mount Mithridates, on which a Greek temple stands, enriched with the spoils of the tumuli which are so numerous in the province. This temple has replaced the ancient acropolis.

"Hum," said Ahmet, "I would not like to run the risk of keeping Uncle Kéraban waiting."

"Nor his nephew," said Van Mitten, smiling.

"Quite true," replied Ahmet. "All the journey I have scarcely thought of anything but our return to Scutari. You understand, I am sure, M. Van Mitten?"

"Yes, I understand, my young friend," replied the Dutchman; "nevertheless, the husband of Madame Van Mitten might be excused if he did not comprehend you."

With this profound reflection, justified by the condition of things in Rotterdam, the friends, finding that they had two hours to spare, commenced the ascent of Mount Mithridates.

From the summit an extensive view is to be had over the bay of Kertsch. In the south, the extreme end of the promontory is visible. Towards the east, the two tongues of land which enclose the bay of Taman are evident beyond the strait of Yenikale. The clear atmosphere permitted all the features of the country to be seen, and even the *khourghans*, or ancient tombs with which the province is studded, were visible, even to the smallest.

When Ahmet thought that time was up, he led Van Mitten down into the market-place again by a monumental staircase ornamented with balustrades. A quarter of an hour later they rejoined Kéraban, who was endeavouring to discuss some point with his host—a placid Tartar. It was quite time that his friends arrived, for Kéraban was getting angry because there was nothing to put him out of temper. The chaise was quite ready. The horses, of Persian breed, were already harnessed; and when our travellers had taken their seats, they departed at a gallop, which was a pleasant relief from the fatiguing trot of the dromedaries.

Ahmet could not overcome a certain

Kertsch.

anxiety which oppressed him when approaching the strait. He was aware that it would have to be passed, when the route had been changed at Kherson. At his nephew's request, Kéraban had consented not to go round the Sea of Azof, and thus make a short cut across the Crimea. But it never occurred to Kéraban that there was not *terra firma* all the way. He was mistaken, and Ahmet did not undeceive him.

One may be a good Turk, an excellent tobacco merchant, and yet an indifferent geographer. Kéraban was probably unaware that the flow of the Sea of Azof into the Black Sea is carried through a wide "sound," the ancient Cimmerian Bosphorus, known as the Strait of Yenikale, and must be crossed by any one who wishes to pass between the peninsulas of Kertsch and Taman.

Now Seigneur Kéraban had for the sea a repugnance which his nephew was fully aware of. What would he say then when he found himself by the Strait, and if in consequence of currents or want of water it became necessary to cross it at its widest part—a distance of nearly twenty miles? Suppose he refused to venture? Suppose he insisted on remounting the whole eastern side of the Crimea to gain the littoral of the Sea of Azof, up to the spurs of the Caucasus? What a prolongation of the journey this would be—what lost time—what interests would be compromised. How could they then hope to reach Scutari by the appointed time?

These were the thoughts that perplexed Ahmet as the chaise rolled on. In less than two hours the shore would be reached, and the uncle would have to decide. How was he to prepare himself for the event? He must take care that no discussion arose. If the hot-headed Kéraban once took a side nothing would turn him from his idea, and he would insist on turning round and retracing his way to Kertsch.

Ahmet was at a loss. If he confessed his little *ruse* he might put his uncle in a passion. It would be better, he thought, to pass himself off as ignorant of the geographical features of the province and to feign the greatest surprise when he discovered a strait where he quite expected dry land.

"Allah aid me!" muttered Ahmet, and then he waited, with all a Turk's fatalism, the result.

The peninsula of Kertsch is divided by a long trench, made in ancient times, which is called the rampart of Akos. The road which in part follows it is good enough as far as the Lazaretto; then it becomes difficult and slippery in descending towards the coast.

The horses could not proceed very fast during the morning, so Van Mitten had an opportunity to look over this portion of the Chersonese at leisure. He perceived a Russian steppe in all its bareness. Some caravans were crossing the plain, or seeking shade under the rampart of Akos in camp with all the picturesque surroundings of an Oriental halt. Innumerable *khourghans* covered the country, and gave the plain the appearance of an immense cemetery. These, or similar tombs, had furnished antiquaries with the jewels, Etruscan vases, cenotaph stones, and other relics which now bedeck the walls of the Temple and the halls of the museum at Kertsch.

Towards mid-day the travellers came in sight of a great square tower flanked by four turrets: this is the fort which is situated to the north of the village of Yenikale. To the south, at the extremity of the Bay of Kertsch, is Cape Au-Bouroum, dominating the shore of the Black Sea. Then the strait opens with its two points, which enclose the Bay of Taman. In the distance the nearest profiles of the Caucasian range are visible.

The strait certainly resembles an arm of the sea at the point where Van Mitten, aware of his friend's antipathy, gazed at Ahmet in consternation.

Ahmet made him a sign to hold his tongue. Fortunately his uncle was just then dozing, and saw nothing of the Black Sea or the Sea of Azof which confronted him in the sound, whose narrowest part measures five or six miles across.

"Diable!" muttered Van Mitten.

It was certainly annoying that Seigneur Kéraban did not live a hundred years later. Had his journey been made at that time Ahmet would not have felt so uneasy.* For the sand in that strait has a growing tendency to silt up, and this cause will limit the passage to a swiftly running stream in time. If, a hundred and fifty years ago, the ships of Peter the Great were enabled to besiege Azof; at the present time vessels are forced to wait until the south wind heaps up the waves and gives them ten or twelve feet of water under their keels.

* Nor would this tale have been written.—*Translator.*

But our travellers were there in 1882, not in the year 2000, A.D., and were obliged to accept hydrographical conditions as they then existed.

Meanwhile the chaise descended the slopes, which trend down to Yenikale, disturbing, as it rolled on, flocks of bustards from the high grass. The travellers stopped

"Caravans between Europe and Asia."

at the principal hotel, and then Seigneur Kéraban awoke.

"Is this the relay station? Are we having them put to?" he enquired.

"Yes; relays of Yenikale," replied Ahmet simply.

All the travellers alighted, while the carriage went on to the posting-house. Thence it would be conveyed to the quay, where the ferry-barge was lying for the conveyance of travellers on foot, or on horseback, or in carriages, and even for the transport of whole caravans which pass and repass between Europe and Asia.

Yenikale is the headquarters of a lucrative commerce in salt, caviare, tallow, and wool. The sturgeon and turbot fisheries occupy a large proportion of the population, which is almost entirely Greek. The sailors engaged in the coasting-trade pursue their avocation in small, lateen-sail, boats. Yenikale occupies an important strategical position: that is why the Russians fortified it after seizing it in 1771. It is one of the ports of the Black Sea, which hereabouts has two keys of safety, the key of Yenikale on one side and Taman on the other.

After a halt of half an hour Seigneur Kéraban gave his companions the signal to proceed, and they walked towards the quay where the ferry-barge was waiting for them.

Suddenly Kéraban glanced right and left and uttered an exclamation.

"What is the matter uncle?" asked Ahmet, who was not quite at his ease.

"There is a river yonder," said Kéraban, indicating the strait.

"Yes, indeed; so there is," replied Ahmet, who thought it best to leave his uncle under that impression.

"A river!" began Bruno.

But a sign from his master gave him to understand that the point need not be insisted on.

"No," said Nizib. "It is a ——"

He was not permitted to finish his sentence, for a violent blow from his comrade Bruno cut short his explanation just as he was developing his hydrographical attainments.

Meanwhile Seigneur Kéraban was steadfastly regarding the "river" that barred his way.

"It is wide," he said.

"Well, yes—pretty wide—in consequence of a flood, most likely," replied Ahmet.

"Floods, you know; owing to the melting of the snow," added Van Mitten, with the laudable intention to back up his young friend.

"Melting of the snow—in September?" said Kéraban, turning upon Van Mitten.

"Certainly; the melting of the snow. The old snow of course, the Caucasian snow," replied Van Mitten, who had not the least idea of what he was saying.

"But I do not see the bridge by which we can cross this river," continued Kéraban.

"The fact is," said Ahmet, "there is no longer a bridge." As he spoke he closed his hands and looked through them, as through a field-glass, the better to examine the mythical bridge over the pretended river.

"They ought to have a bridge here," said Van Mitten. "My 'guide' mentions the existence of a bridge."

"Ah, your guide mentions the bridge, does it?" said Kéraban, frowning as he gazed at the Dutchman.

"Yes, the famous bridge," stammered Van Mitten, "the—the Pontus Euxinus, you know—Pontus Axenos—of the ancients."

"So very ancient," replied Kéraban, and the words came hissing through his set teeth, "so very ancient that it could not resist the flood caused by the melting of the ancient snows."

"From the Caucasus," added Van Mitten, who had come to the end of his imaginative topography.

Ahmet stood a little apart all this time. He did not know what reply to make to his uncle, and did not wish to provoke any discussion on the topic.

"Well, nephew," said Kéraban, drily, "how are we to pass this 'river' since the bridge has been carried away?"

"We shall find a ford, no doubt," said Ahmet. "There is so little water——"

"Scarcely enough to wet our feet," added Van Mitten, who had better have held his tongue.

"Well, then, my friend, turn up your trousers and wade across this river. We will follow you," said Kéraban.

"But—I——"

"Come, come; tuck them up."

The faithful Bruno here thought it time to interfere to bring his master out the dilemma.

"It is no use, Seigneur Kéraban. We can pass without wetting our feet. There is a ferry close by."

"Ah, there is a ferry-boat, is there? It is very fortunate that we can go in a barge which has no doubt been kindly substituted for the bridge, the famous Pontus Axenos.

Why didn't you say so before? Where is this barge—this raft?"

"Here, uncle," replied Ahmet, indicating the flat-bottomed boat which was made fast to the quay. "Our carriage is already on board."

"Indeed, our carriage is already on board?"

"The boatmen had no trouble to guide the ferry-boat with their poles."

"Yes, and with the horses already harnessed."

"Harnessed? Who gave that order?"

"Nobody, uncle. The post-master has done it as usual."

"Since the bridge has broken down, I suppose?"

"Besides, uncle, there is no other way of continuing our journey," said Ahmet, ignoring the bridge.

"There is another way, nephew Ahmet. We can return and skirt the northern shore of the Sea of Azof."

"Two hundred leagues further, uncle. And my wedding. The date is the thirtieth. Have you forgotten the thirtieth?"

"By no means, nephew; and before that date I shall have surely returned. Let us go."

Ahmet experienced a pang for a moment.

Would his uncle put his mad project in execution and return; or would he take his place in the ferry, and cross the Strait of Yenikale?

Seigneur Kéraban directed his steps towards the boat; Van Mitten and the rest followed him, not wishing to afford him any pretext for the discussion which was threatening.

Kéraban paused for fully a minute upon the quay, looking round him. His companions also stopped.

Kéraban entered the ferry-barge. So did his friends.

Kéraban mounted into the chaise. The others did likewise.

Then the boat was cast off, and the current impelled it towards the opposite side.

Kéraban never spoke. His friends were equally silent.

Fortunately the water was calm and the boatmen had no trouble to guide the ferry-boat with their long "gaffs" or poles according to the exigencies of the transit. Nevertheless there was moment when an accident seemed imminent.

A gentle current turned by the southern point of the bay of Taman had caught the boat obliquely, and instead of landing at that point, it seemed as if the boat would be carried out into the bay, and have to traverse five leagues instead of one. In that case probably Kéraban would have given orders to return.

But the boatmen, to whom Ahmet had said some encouraging words in which the term "rouble" was of frequent occurrence, manœuvred the ferry-boat well and escaped the current. Thus, in an hour after quitting the quay of Yenikale, travellers, horses, carriage, all were landed at the extreme point of the southern side of the bay which is by the Russians called Ioujnaia-Kossa. There was no difficulty in disembarking, and the men were liberally remunerated.

In former times the strip of land had formed two islands and a peninsula; that is to say, it was cut in two places by a channel, and it would have been impossible to cross it in a carriage. But the channels are now filled up. So the chaise had no difficulty in passing over the four versts which separate the point from the village of Taman.

An hour after disembarkation the travellers entered Taman, and Seigneur Kéraban, looking hard at his nephew, merely said—

"Decidedly, the waters of the Black Sea and the Sea of Azof agree wonderfully well in the Strait of Yenikale!"

That was all; and never after was there any mention of the "river" discovered by Ahmet, or of the celebrated "*Pontus Axenos*" of Van Mitten.

# KÉRABAN THE INFLEXIBLE;

## OR, ADVENTURES IN THE EUXINE.

By Jules Verne.

### Chapter XV.

In which Kèraban, Ahmet, Van Mitten, and their servants, play the part of Salamanders.

TAMAN is but a melancholy-looking town, with its comfortless houses, its thatched roofs discoloured by the weather, and its wooden church, the bell-tower of which is continually concealed by the flocks of falcons which wheel around it.

The chaise merely passed through Taman. So Van Mitten was not able to visit the military positions, nor the fortress ot Phanagoria, nor the ruins of Tmoutarakan.

If Kertsch is Greek in population and costume, Taman itself is Cossack, a contrast which the Dutchman could not help remarking upon.

The chaise, invariably proceeding by the shortest routes, followed for an hour the southern shore of the bay of Taman. The travellers saw enough to perceive that the country was full of game, and afforded opportunities for shooting almost unequalled in any other part of the globe.

In fact, pelicans, cormorants, grebes, without counting the flocks of bustards, arose from the marshes in incredible numbers.

"I have never seen such quantities of water-fowl," observed Van Mitten. "One might fire into the marsh at random : not a grain of shot would fail to hit."

This remark evoked no discussion. Kéraban was no sportsman, and Ahmet was occupied with far different thoughts. There was not even the commencement of a dispute, except when a flock of wild ducks rose, alarmed at the approach of the carriage just as it was quitting the coast-road to turn to the south east.

"There is a flock," exclaimed Van Mitten. "It is really a regiment!"

"A regiment! you mean an army," replied Kéraban shrugging his shoulders.

"*Ma foi*, you are right," said Van Mitten. "There are at least a hundred thousand ducks."

"A hundred thousand!" exclaimed Kéraban. "If you had said two hundred thousand now!"

"Oh, two hundred thousand!"

"I should even say three hundred thousand, Van Mitten, and then I should be in no way exaggerating."

"You are right, Seigneur Kéraban," replied the Dutchman prudently, for he did not wish to excite his companion to throw a million wild-ducks at his head. And he was right : a hundred thousand ducks is an immense flight, but there were certainly no fewer in that extensive cloud of birds which threw such an immense shadow on the waters of the bay.

The weather was very fine and the road was fairly passable for carriages. The horses proceeded rapidly, and there was no loss of time at the relays. They no longer had Seigneur Saffar in front of them.

We need hardly say that when night came on they passed it still rapidly journeying on towards the first slopes of the Caucasus, which appeared in the distant horizon. Since the night had been passed at the hotel at Kertsch no one had even thought of quitting the chaise for six-and-thirty hours.

However, towards evening at supper-time, the travellers stopped at one of the post-houses, which was also an inn. They did not know what the resources of the Caucasus were, and whether food was easily procurable there. They thought it prudent, therefore, to economize the provisions taken in at Kertsch.

The inn was of second-class quality, but there was an abundance of food, and they had nothing to complain of on that score. Only the hotel-keeper, perhaps out of his natural distrust, or according to the custom of the country, wished them to pay for everything as soon as they had it. Accordingly, when he brought the bread he said—

"This is ten *kopecks.*"

Ahmet gave him the money.

Then he came in with some eggs. "These are eighty *kopecks*," he said. And Ahmet paid the eighty *kopecks* demanded.

For the *kwass* for the wild ducks, so much: for the salt—yes, even for the salt—so much. Ahmet paid all, even to the knives, glasses, spoons, forks, and plates.

As may be expected such dealings served only to excite Kéraban so much that he finished by purchasing *en bloc* the various necessaries for the supper, but not without certain objurgations which the landlord listened to with an impassibility which would have done credit to Van Mitten. When the meal was finished Kéraban re-sold the utensils at a loss of fifty per cent.

"It is lucky that he does not charge us anything for our digestion," remarked Kéraban. "What a man he is! He ought to be Financial Minister in Turkey. That is a man who would know how to tax every oar that ever rowed a caique across the Bosphorus."

But they had supped well enough, which was an important matter, as Bruno remarked; and they proceeded on their way when night had fallen—a dark, moonless night.

It is quite a curious experience, but one not without charm, to find oneself hurried along in a carriage in profound darkness, through an unknown country in which villages are far apart and even farm-houses are scattered. The jingling of the harness-bells, the measured fall of the horses' hoofs, the sound of the carriage-wheels upon the sandy plain: the jolting in the ruts, the cracking of the postillion's whip, the gleam of the lamps which is soon lost in the darkness when the road is open, and which is vividly flashed back by trees, rocks, drinking sign-boards erected on the embankment of the road; all these constitute an *ensemble* of sights and sounds to which few travellers can remain insensible. They hear the noises; they see the objects in a dreamy manner, in a kind of half somnolence which lends to the surroundings a somewhat fantastic character.

Seigneur Kéraban and his companions were not insensible to this impression, which increased every instant. Through the windows of the carriage they contemplated, with half-closed eyes, the great shadows of the equipage—capricious, undefined, moving shadows—which developed themselves in front upon the vaguely lighted road.

It was about eleven o'clock when a peculiar sound awoke the travellers from their reverie. The noise was a kind of whistle, something like that which is produced by opening a bottle of mineral water, but increased tenfold. One might have imagined it was caused by steam blowing off from the safety-valve of a boiler.

The carriage stopped. The postillion could hardly hold his horses. Ahmet, anxious to know what the matter was, hastily let down the window of the chaise.

"What is the matter?" he cried. "Why do not you go on? What is that noise?"

"It is caused by the mud-volcanoes," replied the postillion.

"Mud-volcanoes!" cried Kéraban. "Who ever heard of 'mud-volcanoes!' This is certainly a pleasant way you are taking us, nephew Ahmet!"

"Seigneur Kéraban, you and your companions had better descend," said the postillion.

"Descend!" exclaimed Kéraban.

"Yes. I must trouble you to follow the chaise on foot, as I cannot manage the horses, and they may run away."

"Let us do so," said Ahmet. "The man is right. We must get out."

"They all quitted the carriage and walked behind the chaise."

"There are five or six versts to be traversed," added the postillion: "perhaps eight, but no more."

"Will you decide, uncle?" said Ahmet.

"Let us get out, Kéraban," said Van Mitten. "We must see what kind of phenomena these mud-volcanoes are."

Kéraban consented, but not without protest. They all quitted the carriage and walked behind the chaise, which only advanced at a slow pace, guided by the light of the lamps. The night was very dark. If the Dutchman had any expectation of seeing the mud-volcanoes he was disappointed, but unless one were deaf it would have been impossible to avoid hearing the curious hissing sound they emitted.

Had it been daylight they would have seen an immense steppe, upon which had been puffed up on all sides little eruptive cones like the large ant-hills one meets with in Central Africa. From these cones escaped gaseous and bituminous springs, which are called mud-volcanoes, though volcanic action has nothing to do with their production. The eruption is simply a mixture of mud, gypsum, chalk, pyrites, with petroleum even, which, under the pressure of carbonetted, or sometimes phosphoretted, hydrogen gas, escapes with considerable violence. These little heaps, which are raised by degrees, give way to permit the eruptive matter to escape, and afterwards fall in when the tertiary formations are exhausted in a space of time of greater or less duration.

The hydrogen gas produced under these conditions is due to the slow but continuous decomposition of petroleum mixed with various other substances. The rocky regions in which it is enclosed is finally broken up under the action of water (rain or springs), the filtration of which is continuous. Then the effusion ceases, just as the effervescence of champagne will cease as the elasticity of the gas is exhausted.

These cones of ejected matter open in great numbers in the peninsula of Taman. There are other localities in the peninsula of Kertsch, for instance, where they may be observed; but our travellers did not see them, for they do not exist near the high road.

However, the travellers passed here between the great mounds surrounded with fumes, in the midst of the outpourings of liquid mud. Sometimes the pedestrians were obliged to approach so close to them that they received puffs of the gas right in their faces, which gave them a most disagreeable sensation, and was of a most unpleasant odour.

"Eh," said Van Mitten, who recognized the presence of gas, "we are in danger here. I trust there will be no explosion."

"You are right," replied Ahmet. "We must be cautious, and ought to extinguish the lamps."

The postillion, who was doubtless conversant with the route, was evidently of the same opinion, for the lamps were suddenly extinguished.

"Mind you do not smoke, you fellows," cried Ahmet to the servants.

"You may be quite easy on that point, Seigneur Ahmet," replied Bruno; "we have no desire to be blown up."

"What!" exclaimed Kéraban; "do you mean that we cannot smoke here?"

"No uncle," replied Ahmet; "we must not smoke for some versts at least."

"Not even a cigarette," added the "headstrong one," who was rolling a pinch of tombéki in his practised fingers.

"Later on, friend Kéraban, later on; it is for all our sakes," said Van Mitten. "It would be as dangerous to smoke here as in a powder magazine."

"A nice country this!" muttered Kéraban. "I should be surprised if a tobacco merchant made his fortune here. Nephew Ahmet, though we had lost a few days, it would have been better to have gone round the Sea of Azof."

Ahmet made no answer. He did not wish to enter into a discussion on this subject. His uncle grumblingly put the cigarette in his pocket, and the travellers continued to follow the chaise, which was a shapeless mass looming in the obscurity of the night.

It was necessary then to proceed with extreme caution for fear of falling. The road was much cut up, and by no means firm under foot. The way ascended gradually towards the eastward. Fortunately there was no wind, so the vapours ascended straight into the air, instead of blowing against the travellers and thus greatly incommoding them.

They advanced very cautiously for about half an hour. The horses "whinnied" and plunged continually, so that the postillion had considerable difficulty to restrain them. The axletrees of the chaise groaned when the wheels slipped into some deep rut or other; but the carriage was pretty strong, as had been already proved in the marshes of the lower Danube.

In another quarter of an hour the region

of the mud-cones would be passed. Suddenly a vivid light appeared on the left of the road. One of the cones had taken fire, and was burning with a tremendous flame. The steppe was illuminated to the extent of a verst around it.

"Hundreds of great cones vomiting fire."

"They are smoking there," muttered Ahmet, who was in advance of his companions. But no one was smoking.

Suddenly the postillion was heard calling out in front. Then the loud cracking of his whip succeeded. He could not manage the horses, which darted forward, and the chaise was dragged away at a tremendous pace.

The pedestrians halted in consternation. The whole plain presented a most terrifying aspect. In fact the flames had been communicated by one cone to another, and they exploded successively with great violence like immense displays of fireworks.

Now the immense illumination quite filled the plain. In the weird light appeared hundreds of great cones vomiting fire, the gas from which burned in the midst of ejected liquid matter; some cones flared with the sinister gleams of petroleum, others were coloured diversely by the presence of sulphur, pyrites, or carbonate of iron. All the time deep growling sounds were audible, and the travellers were afraid lest the earth should open, and form an immense crater under the pressure of so much eruptive matter.

There was indeed imminent danger. Instinctively Kéraban and his companions separated so as to diminish the danger of a common destruction. But they did not stop—they passed on more rapidly: it was absolutely necessary to traverse the dangerous zone as quickly as possible. The way, well lighted, appeared practicable. So winding in and out amongst the cones they traversed the fiery steppe.

"Come on—come on!" cried Ahmet.

The others did not answer him, but they complied. Each one hurried in the direction which the chaise had taken, but they could not perceive it. On the horizon night reigned darkly, and there it was evident the zone of fire terminated.

Suddenly a tremendous explosion burst out in the road itself. A jet of flame rose from a great heap which erupted the ground in an instant.

Kéraban was knocked down, and his companions could perceive him struggling through the flame. What would become of him if they did not go to his assistance?

With one bound Ahmet dashed to the assistance of his uncle. He seized him before the burning gas could reach him, and dragged him, half suffocated, beyond the influence of the vapours.

"Oh uncle, uncle," cried the young man.

Then Van Mitten, Bruno, and Nizib, having assisted to carry him to the thicket near by, endeavoured to reanimate Kéraban.

At length, after some vigorous coughing, Kéraban began to breathe freely. When he was restored to his senses and to life, his first words were—

"Do you dare to dispute, Ahmet, that it would have been better to have made the tour of the Sea of Azof?"

"You are right, uncle," he replied.

"As I always am, nephew, always!"

Kéraban had scarcely finished this little speech, when profound darkness fell upon the plain. The cones had become simultaneously and suddenly extinguished; as if the hand of a machinist had cut off the gas. Everything was pitchy dark, and appeared all the more sombre after the late glow, which had left upon the retina its impression of the light which had so suddenly been extinguished.

What had happened then? How had the cones caught fire, since no light had approached them?

We can offer a probable explanation. To the influence of a gas which will take when it comes in contact with the air, fire the phenomenon, which took place in the vicinity of Taman, in 1840, was due. This gas is phosphoretted hydrogen, generated in phosphates. It is visible in the carcases of dead animals, and in marshy places. It takes fire, and communicates the flame to the carbonetted hydrogen, which is only the ordinary gas we use for lighting purposes. So, under the influence, perhaps, of certain atmospheric conditions, the spontaneous combustion was suddenly produced in a way which could not have been foreseen.

From this point of view, the peninsulas of Kertsch and Taman present serious dangers, from which it is difficult to guard, as they are so very sudden.

Seigneur Kéraban was not far wrong when he said that any other route would have been preferable to that they were pursuing. But, after all, they had escaped the danger; uncle and nephew a little singed, no doubt, but the others without even a burn.

Three versts further on they found the carriage and horses, with the postillion, who had mastered his cattle. The moment the flames had gone out he had lighted the carriage lamps again; and, guided by their gleam, the travellers rejoined him without danger, and without fatigue.

Each one resumed his place. They started again, and the night passed without incident. But Van Mitten preserved a vivid recollection of the scene. He could not have been more astonished if the chances of life had carried him to that part of New Zealand where the springs boil up in the eruptive hills.

"Ahmet dragged his uncle beyond the influence of the vapours."

Next day, the 6th of September, eighteen leagues from Taman, the chaise having turned the Bay of Kisiltasch, traversed the village of Anapa; and, at about eight o'clock in the evening stopped in Rajewskaja, on the borders of the Caucasian district.

# KÉRABAN THE INFLEXIBLE;

## OR, ADVENTURES IN THE EUXINE.

BY JULES VERNE.

### CHAPTER XVI.

IN WHICH THE RELATIVE MERITS OF THE TOBACCOS OF PERSIA AND ASIA MINOR ARE DISCUSSED.

THE Caucasus is that part of southern Russia composed of high mountains and extensive plains, of which the orographic system tends somewhat from west to east for a distance of three hundred and fifty kilomètres. To the north extends the country of the Don Cossacks: the government of Stavropol with the Steppes of the Kalmouk and Nogaïs tribes. In the south are the principalities of Tiflis, capital of Georgia, of Koutaïs, Bakou, Elisabethpol, Erivan, besides the provinces of Mingrelia, Imeritia, Abkasia, and Gouriel. To the west of the Caucasus is the Black Sea, to the east the Caspian.

The whole country to the south of the principal chain of the Caucasus is named Transcaucasia, and has no other frontiers than those of Turkey and Persia: at the point of contact is Mount Ararat, on which the Ark of Noah rested.

There are numerous tribes which inhabit or traverse this important region. These belong to the Kazteval, Armenian, Tscherkess, Tochetschine and Lesghian races. In the north are the Kalmouks, Nogais, Mongolian Tartars; in the south are the Tartars of Turkish descent; Kurds and Cossacks.

If *savants* are to be credited, it is from this semi-European, semi-Asiatic district that the white race emanated—the whites who now inhabit Asia and Europe. So they are by them called the "Caucasian Race."

Three main Russian roads traverse this enormous barrier, which comprises such mountains as Chat-Elbrouz, 4,000 mètres; Kazbec, 4,500 mètres; and Elbrouz, 5,600 mètres, high.

The first of these routes, of both stragetical and commercial importance, runs from Taman to Poti, along the littoral of the Black Sea. The second, from Mosdok to Tiflis, passes by the Col du Darial; the third, from Kizliar to Bakou, by Derbend.

We need scarcely say that Kéraban, in accord with his nephew Ahmet, took the first. What was the use of entangling themselves in the wilds of the Caucasus; so courting difficulty and delay? A road was open as far as Poti, and there are plenty of towns and villages on the littoral of the Black Sea.

There are railways, which it would have been possible to utilize, but Ahmet knew the strong objection his uncle entertained to this mode of locomotion, and avoided the subject which his uncle had tabooed in the case of the Taurus and the Chersonese Railways.

All that was quite understood, and the indestructible chaise, having undergone a few necessary repairs, took the road again, and quitted Rajewskaja early on the morning of the 7th September.

Ahmet was determined to proceed with the utmost possible speed. Twenty days remained in which the journey must be finished, so as to reach Scutari upon the appointed date. On this point Kéraban agreed with him. No doubt Van Mitten would have preferred to travel more at his ease—to receive and record more lasting impressions, and not to be tied to time—but Van Mitten was not consulted. As a guest only had he agreed to accompany and dine with Kéraban at Scutari. Well, was he not taking him to Scutari? What more did he wish for?

Nevertheless, Bruno felt it incumbent upon him to make a few observations as they were entering the Russian Caucasus. The Dutchman having listened, asked his servant to conclude.

"Well," continued Bruno, "why not let Seigneur Kérabanand Ahmet proceed without rest along the Black Sea?"

"To leave them—do you mean?" enquired Van Mitten.

"Yes, leave them, after bidding them *bon voyage!*"

"And remain here?"

"Yes; so then we may see the Caucasus at our ease, since our unlucky star has led us hither. After all, we shall be as well off as in Constantinople within reach of Madame Van ——"

"Hold your tongue, Bruno: do not pronounce that name!"

"I will not if it is disagreeable to you, sir; but it is to her, in fact, that we owe this expedition. To run the risk of being engulfed in marshes, to be roasted in volcanic districts—is too much, it is indeed. I would therefore suggest, not a dispute with Seigneur Kéraban—you would come off second-best there—but just let him understand by a few gentle words that you will see him in Constantinople, when it pleases you to return thither!"

"That would not be quite practicable," replied Van Mitten.

"It would be prudent," replied Bruno.

"You find a good deal to complain of then?"

"Yes, a great deal; and besides—I do not know whether you have remarked it—I am getting thin."

"Not much, Bruno, not much."

"Aye; but I know very well that I am; and if I go on like this I shall soon become a skeleton!"

"Have you been weighed, Bruno?"

"I wanted to get weighed at Kertsch," replied Bruno, "but there was only a letter-weight obtainable."

"And would not that suffice?" said Van Mitten laughing.

"No, sir," replied Bruno, gravely, "but before long it will suffice to weigh your poor servant. Now shall we let Seigneur Kéraban continue his journey without us?"

Certainly this manner of travelling did not suit Van Mitten, who was of a phlegmatic temperament, and disliked hurry. But the idea of abandoning his friend Kéraban was so repugnant to him that he refused to entertain it.

"No, Bruno," he said, "I am his invited guest——"

"A guest!" exclaimed Bruno, "a guest who has to travel seven hundred leagues instead of one league!"

"No matter," replied his master.

"Permit me to tell you that you are wrong, sir;" continued Bruno, "I repeat it for the tenth time. We are by no means at the end of our troubles, and I have a presentiment that you will have your full share of them."

Would Bruno's presentiments be realized? The future will reveal that. In any case he had done his duty as a devoted servant in warning his master; and, since Van Mitten resolved to continue the journey—a journey as ridiculous as fatiguing—the valet had no choice but to follow him.

The road continued almost invariably along the shores of the Black Sea, following the contour of the land. If it sometimes branched away a little to avoid some obstacle of the shore, or to reach some village, it was never more than a few versts. The last spurs of the Caucasus which run parallel to the coast, die away on the boundaries of this little-used route. On the horizon eastward can be perceived the rugged teeth-like, snow-tipped summits, which seem to bite into the sky.

At one o'clock in the afternoon the travellers turned the little Bay of Zèmes, seven leagues from Rajewskaja, so as to reach about eight leagues farther on, the village of Gelendschik. These townships

"This fertile country."

are some distance from one another, you see.

Upon the littoral of the Black Sea we may reckon one little town at this average distance; but beyond these small groups of houses—frequently only a village or hamlet—the country is almost deserted, and is beginning to be even less frequented by the coasting vessels.

This band of *terra firma* between the mountains and the sea is well wooded; trees of various kinds are plentiful, and are united by the wild vines which twine about their limbs as in a tropical forest. In every direction nightingales and warblers sing in the fields of azaleas, which nature has planted in this fertile country.

Towards mid-day the travellers fell in with a tribe of Kalmucks, nomads, who dwell in *oulousses*, comprising many *khotonnes.* The latter are regular "ambulant villages," composed of a certain number of *kibitkas* or tents, which are pitched at random—sometimes on the steppes; sometimes in the verdant valley; sometimes by the side of a water-course—according to the fancy of the leaders. The Kalmucks are of Mongolian extraction, and were formerly very numerous in the Caucasus; but the exigencies of the Russian administration, not to say its "vexations," have compelled a retreat towards Asia.

The Kalmucks have carefully preserved their ancient manners and special costume. Van Mitten was able to note that the men wore large trousers, boots of Morocco leather, a *khalate* (a kind of very ample wadded dressing-gown), and a square cap, trimmed with sheepskin. The women were dressed very much in the same manner, with the exception of the girdle, and a cap, from which their hair, trimmed with particoloured ribbons, escaped. The children were almost naked; and, during the winter, to warm themselves, they crouch in the ashes in the *kibitka,* and sleep amid the hot cinders of the hearth.

The Kalmucks are small of stature, but robust; excellent horsemen, quick, agile, and smart. Their food is a little flour, mixed with water, and cooked with horseflesh. But they are confirmed drunkards, skilful thieves, ignorant, superstitious to excess, incorrigible gamblers, like all the nomads of the Caucasian steppes.

The post-chaise passed through one of the "*khotonnes*" without attracting any particular attention. The people scarcely took the trouble to look at the travellers, one of whom, at least, observed them with great interest. Perhaps they coveted the rapid horses of the vehicle; but, fortunately for Kéraban, they confined themselves to the wish. So the horses reached the next stage without having exchanged their loose box for the picket of the Kalmuck encampment.

The chaise, having skirted the Bay of Zèmes, found the road closed in between the spurs of the mountains and the sea But, beyond the bay, the route widened out, and became more easy.

At eight o'clock the "*bourgade*" of Gelendschik was gained. There the travellers supped hastily, and at nine o'clock continued their journey. They proceeded all night, and at seven o'clock in the morning reached Beregowaja; at mid-day they gained Dschuba; at six P. M., Tenginsh; at midnight, Nebugsk; next morning, at eight o'clock, Golowinsk; at eleven, Lachowsk; and, two hours later, Ducha.

Ahmet would have been puzzled to complain of all this. The journey had been accomplished without accident; but, without incident, which did not altogether please Van Mitten. His tablets boasted only a record of geographical names. He had not seen anything particularly novel; and had not had any new impression worth recording.

At Ducha the chaise remained for two hours, while the postmaster sent to fetch the horses, which were at pasture.

"Well," said Kéraban, "let us dine as comfortably, and for as long a time, as circumstances will permit!"

"Yes, let us dine," assented Van Mitten.

"And dine well, if possible," murmured Bruno, regarding his dwindling rotundity of figure.

"Perhaps this halt will provide us with something of interest, which, hitherto, our journey has lacked. I think my young friend Ahmet will permit no breathing time——"

"Until the arrival of horses," said Ahmet. "This is already the ninth of the month."

"That is the kind of answer I like," said Kéraban. "Let us go and see what we can have."

The inn was but an indifferent one; built on the bank of the little river Mdsymta, which rushes down from the neighbouring hills in a torrent.

The little town of Ducha resembles the Cossack villages, which are known as "*stamisti,*" with palisades and gates, that are dominated by a square tower, wherein a watch is kept day and night. The houses have high thatched roofs, wooden walls, plastered over with clay, and shaded by fine trees. The people are well-to do. The Cossacks, however, have almost completely lost their individuality in the Russians. But they remain as brave and active as ever. They are excellent guardians of the

A village scene.

boundaries committed to their charge, and are justly esteemed the best equestrians in the world, as well in the hunting down of the chronically rebellious mountaineers, as in the jousts and tourneys in which they prove themselves accomplished cavaliers.

The natives are a fine race, remarkable for the beauty and elegance of their forms, but not of their costume, which partakes of the nature of the dress of the Caucasian mountain tribes. Nevertheless, under the high-furred cap, it is still easy to recognize those energetic faces which a thick beard conceals as high as the cheek-bones.

When Kéraban, Ahmet, and Van Mitten seated themselves at table, a repast was served, the elements of which had been taken from a neighbouring *doukhan*—a kind of shop in which the characters, the pork-butcher, the victualler, and the grocer are all preserved in the same individual. There was a roast turkey, maize cakes, buffalo cheese, called "*gatschapouri*"—the inevitable national dish—*blini*, a kind of pancake made with sour milk. For beverages they had some batches of thick beer, and flasks of "*vodka*," a strong brandy, of which the Russians consume a great quantity.

Frankly, one could not expect to dine better at the little inn of a village, situated on the extreme limits of the Black Sea; and assisted by excellent appetites, the travellers did full justice to the repast which was a welcome change from their usual provisions on the journey.

After dinner, Ahmet left the table while Bruno and Nizib took their shares of the remains of the feast. The young man as usual went to the post-house to hurry the relays, and quite prepared to disburse tenfold the five *kopecks* per verst per horse—which the regulations permit—as well as liberal "tips" to the postillions.

Meanwhile, Kéraban and his friend Van Mitten made themselves very comfortable in a kind of summer-house which overhung the river. Now or never was the time to abandon themselves to the luxurious *dolce far niente*, which the Ottomans call "Kief."

Besides the preparation of the *narghilés* became necessary to supplement such a meal. So the pipes were brought from the chaise to the smokers, who yielded themselves to the pleasures of the weed to which they owed their fortune.

The "bowls" of the *narghilés* were quickly filled with tobacco, but it is needless to remark that Kéraban used his own tombéki of Persian growth, while Van Mitten smoked the latakia of Asia Minor.

Then the pipes were lighted: the smokers reclined on the benches, and inhaled the smoke through the long flexible tubes. The atmosphere was soon filled with the odour of the smoke which was not permitted to reach the mouth until it had been cooled by the clear water of the *narghilé*.

For some time the friends smoked in silent enjoyment with half-closed eyes, and apparently supported by the clouds of smoke which appeared like an "aerial eiderdown."

"Ah, this is real enjoyment," said Kéraban at length. "I know of no better way of passing an hour than this chat with one's pipe."

"Conversation without discussion," remarked Van Mitten.

"The Turkish Government has been as usual very badly advised to impose a tax on tobacco ten times its value," said Kéraban. "Thanks to that besotted folly, the use of the *narghilé* is gradually disappearing."

"That is much to be regretted, Kéraban," said Van Mitten.

"For my own part," continued his friend, "I have such a predilection for tobacco, that I would rather die than give up the use of it. Yes, die! Had I lived in the time of Amurat IV., the despot who wished to prohibit it on pain of death, I would have let them cut my head off with my pipe in my mouth."

"I quite agree with you," said the Dutchman, emitting two or three puffs of smoke.

"Gently—gently—do not smoke so fast," cried Kéraban. "You have no time to taste the pleasant smoke. You are like a glutton who bolts his food."

"You are always right, friend Kéraban," replied Van Mitten, who would not have provoked a discussion at that time for the world.

"Always right, Van Mitten."

"But what surprises me," continued the Dutchman, "is that we tobacco merchants experience the greatest pleasure in smoking our own wares."

"And what then?" said Kéraban, who was always ready for an argument.

"Well, because, if it be true that pastry-cooks are usually disgusted by pastry, and sweetmeat sellers by sweetmeats, it seems to me that a tobacco merchant——"

"Permit me an observation—just one remark, Van Mitten."

"What is it?"

"Did you ever hear of a wine-merchant who never tasted the wines he sold?"

"No—certainly I never did."

"Well then, wine merchant or tobacco merchant—it is the same thing."

"Be it so," replied the Dutchman. "Your explanation seems to me conclusive."

"But," continued Kéraban, "as you appear to wish to argue——"

"'Ah, this is real enjoyment,' said Kéraban."

"I assure you I do not," replied Van Mitten, quickly.

"So?"

"No, I declare."

"At any rate you made an observation which reflected on my taste for tobacco."

"Believe me——"

"You did—I say you did," interrupted Kéraban, beginning to get excited. "I can understand insinuations——"

"There was no insinuation on my part," replied Van Mitten, who, without knowing why—perhaps it was the effect of the good dinner—began to wax impatient.

"There was," replied Kéraban, "and it is my turn to make an observation."

"Well then, make it."

"I do not understand—I cannot understand—how you can bring yourself to smoke Latakia in a *narghilé!* It displays a great want of taste in a smoker who has any self-respect."

"It seems to me that I have the right to do so," replied Van Mitten, "since I prefer the tobacco of Asia Minor."

"Asia Minor. Really! Asia Minor is far behind Persia when tobacco is concerned."

"That is a matter of opinion."

"Tombéki, even after being submitted to a double 'washing,' still possesses active properties infinitely superior to those of latakia."

"I quite believe it," replied the Dutchman. "Very active properties; which are due to the presence of belladonna."

"Belladonna, in proper proportion, only increases the qualities of the tobacco."

"Yes, for people who wish to poison themselves by degrees."

"It is not a poison!"

"It is, and a very strong poison!"

"Have I died of it?" exclaimed Kéraban, puffing away.

"No, but you will."

"Well, then in my last hour I will maintain that tombéki is preferable to that dried hay you call latakia," said Kéraban, in a solemnly-nervous tone.

"I cannot let such a mistaken idea pass without protest," said Van Mitten, getting excited in his turn.

"It will pass, nevertheless."

"And you dare to say this to a man who has sold tobacco for twenty years?"

"And you dare to assert the contrary to a man who has sold tobacco for thirty?"

"Twenty years!"

"Thirty years!"

At this point of the discussion the disputants rose at the same moment. While they gesticulated, they let their pipes fall; but they picked them up again, and continued the dispute, getting extremely personal.

"Van Mitten, you are, out and out, the most pig-headed man I have ever met."

"After you, Kéraban; after you."

"I?"

"You," replied the Dutchman, who no longer could control himself. "Just look at the smoke of the latakia which is issuing from my lips!"

"And do you look at the fumes of the tombéki which I puff out in such odoriferous clouds."

Then each one puffed into the face of the other.

"Now just inhale the flavour of my tobacco," said one.

"Just inhale mine," said the other.

"I am obliged to confess," said Van Mitten, "that, as regards tobacco, you are perfectly ignorant."

"And you," retorted Kéraban, "are far behind the merest tyro in smoking."

The dispute waxed so warm that the voices were audible outside; and, certainly, they had reached a point where serious consequences might be expected to ensue, when Ahmet came in. Bruno and Nizib, attracted by the uproar, followed him. All three remained standing on the threshold.

"Look here," exclaimed Ahmet, laughing loudly. "My uncle is smoking M. Van Mitten's pipe, and M. Van Mitten is smoking uncle Kéraban's!"

Nizib and Bruno confirmed the assertion in chorus.

In fact, when they picked up their pipes the disputants had each seized the wrong one; and so, without perceiving the exchange, the disputants had respectively asserted the virtues of their favourite tobacco; Kéraban all the while smoking latakia, and Van Mitten, tombéki.

They could not help laughing, and finally they shook hands like friends whose good feeling no dispute could disturb.

"The horses are harnessed," said Ahmet, "we have only to get into the chaise."

"Let us go then," said Kéraban.

Van Mitten and he then handed the *narghilés* to their valets, and the whole party were soon seated in their travelling carriage. But, as he got in, Kéraban could not help saying in a low tone to his friend—

"Now that you have tasted it, will you not confess that tombéki is far superior to latakia?"

"I willingly confess as much," said the Dutchman, who did not wish to get into another discussion.

"Thank you, my friend," replied Kéraban, much moved by this concession, "that is an avowal which I will never forget."

Then the pair cemented, by a vigorous grasp of the hand, the truce which had lately been proclaimed between them, and which ought not to be broken. The chaise was urged rapidly along the coast road; and at eight o'clock in the evening the frontier of Abkasia was reached. The travellers halted here for relays, and slept soundly until the next morning.

# KÉRABAN THE INFLEXIBLE;

## OR, ADVENTURES IN THE EUXINE.

By Jules Verne.

—♦—

### Chapter XVII.

Wherein is related a very Curious Adventure, which terminates the First Part of this History.

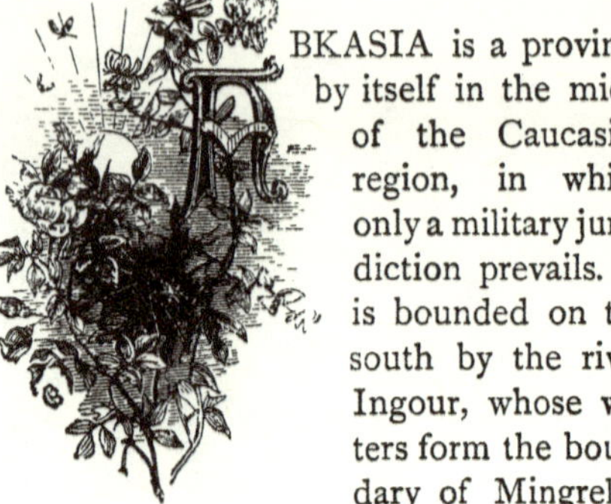

ABKASIA is a province by itself in the midst of the Caucasian region, in which only a military jurisdiction prevails. It is bounded on the south by the river Ingour, whose waters form the boundary of Mingrelia, one of the principal divisions of the government of Koutais.

It is a beautiful province, one of the richest in the Caucasus, but the prevailing system is not one to display its wealth to the best advantage. The inhabitants have scarcely yet begun to be proprietors of the soil, which belongs almost entirely to the reigning princes, descended from a Persian dynasty. So the native is still in a semi-savage condition, possessing little idea of time, without any written language, and speaking a kind of *patois* which his next neighbours can scarcely understand; and such a poor *patois* too, that it lacks words to express the most elementary idea.

Van Mitten was not slow to remark the great difference which existed between this country and the districts through which he had already passed. On the left of the road were fields of maize, very few of corn; goats and sheep, well tended; oxen, horses, cows wandered at liberty in the meadows; there were fine trees, white poplars, fig-trees, nut-trees, oaks, limes, plane-trees, extensive thickets of box and holly: such is the appearance of Abkasia. As an intrepid traveller—Madame Serena—has remarked, "If one compares the three provinces of Mingrelia, Samourzakan, and Abkasia, one may say that their civilization respectively is in the ratio of the culture of the hills which surround them. Mingrelia, which socially is the foremost, has wooded and cultivated heights; Samourzakan, already behindhand, presents a half savage aspect; Abkasia, last, remains in almost a primitive condition, and has only a line of uncultivated hills, which are at present untouched by manual labour." Such is Abkasia, which, of all the Caucasian districts, will be the last to enjoy the blessings of individual liberty.

The first halt which the travellers made after crossing the frontier was at the village of Gagri, which is a pretty place, possessing a beautiful church, the sacristy of which is used as a cellar; a fort, which is a military hospital; a torrent, which was then dry, named the Gagrinska: on one side is the sea, on the other a fruitful country, planted with fine accacias, and dotted with rose plantations. In the distance extends the boundary chain between Abkasia and Circassia, whose inhabitants, after their defeat by the Russians in the terrible campaign of 1859, have abandoned the beautiful coast.

The chaise, which reached this place at nine o'clock at night, remained till next day. Seigneur Kéraban and his companions slept in one of the *doukhans* of the village and quitted it early. At mid-day, six leagues farther on, Pizunda afforded them a change of horses, and Van Mitten had half an hour to admire the church wherein the patriarchs of the western Caucasus formerly resided. This edifice, with its brick cupolas, formerly covered with copper, the design of its naves, which followed the shape of the Greek cross, the frescoes on the walls, the façade shaded by elms, is raised to a position amongst the most curious monuments of the Byzantine style of the sixth century.

Then the same day our travellers passed the villages of Goudouati and Gounista: at midnight, after a rapid journey of eighteen leagues, they snatched some repose at Soukhoum-Kalé, which is built upon a wide bay which reaches to the south as far as Cape Kodor.

Soukhoum-Kalé is the principal port of Abkasia; but in the last war in the Caucasus the town was partly destroyed. In it there was a motley crowd of Greeks, Armenians, Turks, Russians even in greater numbers than natives. Now the military element is predominent, and the steamers from Odessa or Poti carry numerous visitors to the barracks, built near the ancient fortress, which was erected in the sixteenth century under the rule of Amurah at the time of the Ottoman dominion.

A very Georgian repast, consisting of an acid soup, a kind of chicken broth, a ragout seasoned with acid, saffron-flavoured milk —a repast little appreciated by two Turks and a Dutchman—preceded the departure of the party from the town at nine A.M.

Having passed the pretty little town of Kélasouri, built in the shady valley of Kelassur, the travellers crossed the Kodor twenty-seven versts from Soukhoum-Kalé. The chaise skirted enormous groves of trees, which one might compare to virgin forests (with inextricable jungles and thick scrub, penetrable only by water or fire; and in which were swarms of serpents, wolves, bears and jackals) forming a corner of tropical America, planted upon the shore of the Black Sea. But already the axe of the explorer is heard in these forests, which centuries have left untouched; and the beautiful trees will disappear ere long into the frame-work of houses or ships.

Otchemchiri, the chief place of the district, which includes Kodor and Samourzakan, is an important maritime town situated upon two streams. Ilori, whose Byzantine church is worth seeing, but could not be visited by our travellers, who were pressed for time; Gajida and Anaklifa were all passed during that day's travel, one of the longest and most rapid portions of the journey as regards the time and the pace. But about eleven o'clock in the evening, the travellers reached the frontier of Abkasia, passed the river Ingour, and twenty-five versts farther on stopped at Redout-Kalé, the chief town of Mingrelia, one of the provinces of the government of Koutais.

The remainder of the night was passed in sleeping. Tired though he was, Van Mitten rose early with a view to see something before they started again. But he found Ahmet already stirring, though Kéraban was still asleep in the fairly good room which had been assigned him at the principal hotel.

"Out of bed already?" said Van Mitten, when he perceived Ahmet. "Is my young friend inclined to join me in a stroll this morning?"

"Have I time for it, M. Van Mitten?" said Ahmet. "Must I not replenish our stores for the journey? We shall soon pass the Russo-Turkish frontier, and it will not be an easy matter to revictual in the deserts of Lazistan and Anatolia. So, you see, I have not a moment to lose."

"But when you have done that," said the Dutchman, "have we not plenty of time?"

"When I have seen to the provisions," replied Ahmet, "I must look to our carriage and get the wheelwright to examine the screws and grease the axles; I must examine the reins and the drag. It will never do to find any repairs are required after we have passed the frontier. I intend to put the chaise in thorough repair, and I depend upon its lasting to the end of this wonderful journey of ours."

"Quite right. But when you have seen to all that?"

"Then I will examine the relays, and I must go to the postmaster to arrange that."

"Very well; but after that?" said Van Mitten, who would not relinquish his idea.

"After that it will be time to start," replied Ahmet, "and we shall be off. So I must leave you."

"One moment, my young friend" said

"The beautiful trees will disappear ere long."

the Dutchman. "Let me ask you a question."

"Speak, but quickly please, M. Van Mitten."

"You are doubtless aware of what is worth seeing in this province of Mingrelia?"

"Pretty well!"

"It is the country watered by the poetic Phasis, whose waters deposited gold dust upon the marble steps of the palaces built upon its banks."

"Quite so."

"Here is the legendary Colchis, where Jason and his Argonauts, assisted by the magician Medea, obtained the Golden Fleece guarded by a formidable dragon, without mentioning the terrible bulls which vomited flame."

"I do not deny it."

"Finally now in those mountains yonder is the rock of Khomli, overlooking Koutaïs, to which Prometheus was bound, and where the vultures eternally feed upon his entrails as a punishment for having stolen the bolts of heaven."

"Nothing is more true, M. Van Mitten, but I repeat I am in a hurry. But what are you coming to?"

"To this, my young friend," replied the Dutchman in his most amiable manner: "Several days spent here in this part of Mingrelia, and as far as Koutaïs, would be well spent: and——"

"So you propose that we should remain some days in Redout-Kalé?"

"Oh, four or five days would suffice."

"Would you make that suggestion to my uncle Kéraban?" said Ahmet somewhat maliciously.

"I! Never, my young friend," replied the Dutchman. "It would give rise to a discussion, and since that regretable dispute about the tobacco I declare I will never enter into an argument with that excellent man again."

"And you will act wisely."

"But at this moment I am not addressing the terrible Kéraban. I am speaking to my young friend Ahmet."

"You are mistaken, M. Van Mitten," said the young man, taking his hand: "You are not speaking to him at this moment."

"To whom then?"

"To the *fiancé* of Amasia: and you know that he has not an hour to lose."

As he finished speaking Ahmet hurried away to complete his preparations: and Van Mitten, much disappointed, was obliged to content himself with a promenade of a very unsatisfactory nature in the little town, accompanied by his faithful but discouraging Bruno.

At mid-day all the travellers were ready to start again. The chaise, which had been carefully examined and repaired, promised to last for many long journeys. The provision lockers had been replenished, so there was nothing to fear on the score of food for many versts, or rather "*agatchs*," since the provinces of Asiatic Turkey were to be traversed during the second portion of the journey; but Ahmet might well congratulate himself on having forestalled every eventuality which might arise either in food or in locomotion.

Seigneur Kéraban was delighted, as he perceived the journey was being accomplished without accident or incident. How his self-love as an "old Turk" would be flattered when he arrived upon the left shore of the Bosphorus, notwithstanding the Ottoman authorities and the tax-collectors, it is needless to insist.

Redout-Kalé being only ninety versts from the Turkish frontier, in four-and twenty hours the most headstrong of Turks might depend upon stepping once more upon Ottoman territory. Then he would be at home.

"*En route*, nephew," cried Kéraban good-humouredly. "May Allah continue his protection!"

"*En route!*" said Ahmet.

They took their places, followed by Van Mitten, who in vain endeavoured to find out the mythological peak of the Caucasus on which Prometheus had expiated his crime. The chaise started with much cracking of the whip and neighing of horses.

In an hour the chaise passed the frontier of Gouriel, which since 1801 has been annexed to Mingrelia. Poti is the capital—a considerable port on the Black Sea, whence a railway is laid to Tiflis, the capital of Georgia.

The road ascends gently through and into a fertile country. Here and there are villages or houses scattered amid the fields of maize. The appearance of these structures is curious: they are not built of wood, but of platted straw like basket-work. Van Mitten made a note of this. Indeed there are only these petty details to be noted in the journey across the ancient Colchis. Subsequently perhaps he will be more happy when he reaches the banks of the Rion—the river of Poti—the celebrated Phasis of antiquity, which many geographers believe to have been one of the four Rivers of the Garden of Eden.

In another hour the travellers were stopped by the railway which runs from Poti to Tiflis; and which crosses the highway a verst below the Sakario Station. They were obliged to cross the line, to reach Poti, by the left bank of the stream. The horses were pulled up at the gate of the level-crossing. The windows of the carriage were

"'Stand aside! cried Kéraban, as the horses were halted face to face."

down; so Kéraban and his friends could see all that passed.

The postilion began to call for the gateman, who had not put in an appearance.

Kéraban put his head out of his window.

"Are we to lose our time on account of a wretched railway company?" he cried, "Why is the gate closed?"

"No doubt a train is due," said Van Mitten quietly.

"Why is a train due, then?" retorted Kéraban.

The postilion continued to call out, without achieving any result. No one appeared either in the hut or in the garden.

"May Allah choke him!" exclaimed Kéraban "If he do not come, I will open the gate myself!"

"Calm yourself, uncle," said Ahmet,

restraining him, for Kéraban was about to descend from the chaise.

"Calm myself?"

"Yes, here is the gate-keeper."

In fact, the man appeared at that moment and came very leisurely towards the chaise.

"Now then, are we to pass, or not?" exclaimed Kéraban.

"You can pass," replied the man, "the train from Poti will not come up for ten minutes."

"Open your gate, then, and do not delay us needlessly here: we are in a hurry."

"I am going to open it," replied the man.

So saying, he proceeded to open the gate at the opposite side first; and then the gate before which the chaise was waiting, but all deliberately, and with complete indifference to the demands of the travellers.

Kéraban was already boiling over with impatience.

Finally the way was clear, and the chaise began to cross the line.

At this moment, on the opposite side, appeared a party of travellers. A Turkish noble, mounted upon a splendid horse, and attended by four riders as an escort, prepared to cross the line.

This personage was evidently an important individual. He was about thirty-five years old; tall; and comported himself with the peculiar nobility of the Asiatic race. He was good-looking enough; his eyes only sparkled when he was moved by passion. His forehead was bronzed; his beard black, and flowing to his chest; teeth white, and lips which seemed unused to smiling. In fine his was the physiognomy of an imperious man, powerful by position and fortune, accustomed to have everything he desired, and a man whom opposition would drive to excesses. There was still something of the savage in his nature, in which the Turk bordered on the Arab.

This gentleman wore a simple travelling costume cut in the fashion usual with rich Osmanlis, who are more Asiatic than European. No doubt he wished to conceal the fact of his real importance under his sombre cafetan.

Just as the chaise reached the centre o the railway, the riding party also arrived there. Owing to the narrow space between the gates, only the chaise or the riders could pass at a time. One party or the other must give way.

The chaise stopped. So did the cavalcade: but it did not appear that the newcomer was at all inclined to yield to Kéraban. Turk against Turk could hardly fail to bring about some complication.

"Stand aside!" cried Kéraban, as the horses were halted face to face.

"Stand aside yourselves!" replied the new-comer, who seemed determined not to budge an inch.

"I arrived first!"

"Well then you will pass second!"

"I will not give way."

"Neither will I."

Begun in this fashion, the discussion threatened to reach an unpleasant pitch.

"Uncle," said Ahmet, "it will not matter to us——"

"Nephew, it matters very much."

"My friend——" began Van Mitten.

"Leave me alone," replied Kéraban, in at tone which drove the Dutchman into his corner.

Then the gate-keeper cried—

"Make haste, make haste! the train will be here directly, make haste!"

But Kéraban scarcely heard him. Having opened the door of the chaise he got out, followed by Van Mitten and Ahmet, while Bruno and Nizib jumped from the "cabriolet."

Kéraban walked up to the chief cavalier and put his hand on the horse's bridle.

"Will you let me pass?" he cried, with a violence he could not control.

"Never."

"We will soon see that."

"See that?"

"You do not know Kéraban."

"Neither do you know Saffar."

It was, in fact, Seigneur Saffar, who was

proceeding to Poti after a rapid journey in the Southern Caucasus. But the name of Saffar, the man who had anticipated the relays at Kertsch, only excited Kéraban still more. To yield to this man, who had already annoyed him—never! He would rather be trampled under his horse's feet.

"Kéraban put his hand on the horse's bridle."

"Ah, so you are the Seigneur Saffar! Well then, go back, Seigneur Saffar!"

"Forward!" exclaimed Saffar, signing to his men to force their way across.

Ahmet and Van Mitten, feeling assured that nothing would make Kéraban yield, prepared to assist him.

"Pass on, pass on!" cried the gate-keeper. "Here is the train."

At that moment the whistle of the approaching locomotive was heard as it came round the curve.

"Go back!" exclaimed Kéraban.

"Go back!" cried Saffar.

The whistle of the locomotive became more audible and warning in tone. The gate-keeper waved his flag with the intention to stop the train. He was too late. It came round the curve rapidly.

Seigneur Saffar, seeing that he had only

just time to escape, retreated quickly. Bruno and Nizib threw themselves aside. Ahmet and Van Mitten, seizing Kéraban, dragged him through; and the postilion, whipping his horses, impelled them outside the rapidly closing gates.

At that moment the express passed. But it struck the hinder portion of the chaise,

"'We have no longer any postchaise,' said Ahmet."

which it knocked to pieces, and disappeared without the travellers having experienced any injury from the broken part.

Seigneur Kéraban, almost beside himself, wanted to throw himself upon his adversary; but the latter, spurring his horse, crossed the line, disdaining even to look at Kéraban; and then, followed by his escort, galloped away on the other road, which followed the right bank of the river.

"The coward! the wretch!" exclaimed Kéraban. "If ever I meet him again!"

"Yes; but meantime we have no longer a post-chaise," said Ahmet, looking at the injured vehicle as it lay in the road.

"That may be, nephew; but nevertheless I passed over first."

This was Kéraban all over!

At that moment, some Cossacks who were charged with the care of the road approached. They had seen all that had occurred.

Their first move was to arrest Kéraban. He protested, and his nephew and Van Mitten vainly interfered. Then came violent resistence from the man who, after breaking the rules of the road, was threatening to complicate matters by resisting lawful authority.

One can no more argue with Cossacks than with gendarmes. It is no use to resist. So Kéraban was carried off to the Sakario station in a towering passion; while Ahmet, Van Mitten, Bruno, and Nizib, remained by the damaged vehicle.

"Here is a pretty state of things!" said Van Mitten.

"But what about my uncle?" said Ahmet. "We cannot abandon him!"

Twenty minutes later the train from Tiflis to Poti passed. They looked at it and——

In a compartment appeared the dishevelled head of Kéraban, red with fury, beside himself with rage, and none the less because he, for the first time in his life, had been compelled by the ferocious Cossacks to travel in a train.

But he could not be left alone in such a situation. It was necessary to release him from the consequences of the false step his impetuosity had induced him to take, and not to imperil the return to Scutari, by a delay which might be prolonged.

Leaving the remains of the chaise which was now useless, Ahmet and his companions hired a cart to which the postilion harnessed his horses; and then as rapidly as possible they proceeded to Poti; where they arrived in two hours.

Ahmet and Van Mitten, as soon as they reached the town, went to the police-station with the intention to release Kéraban. There they learned one circumstance which reassured them in a measure, and eased their minds concerning more delay.

Seigneur Kéraban, having been heavily fined for breaking the law and resisting its authority, had been put under the charge of the Cossacks and sent across the frontier.

It was necessary that they should rejoin him as quickly as possible, and with this view they sought to procure means of transport.

As for Saffar, Ahmet made it his business to endeavour to ascertain what had become of him. He had already embarked in the steamer which had quitted Poti for various ports of Asia Minor. But Ahmet could learn nothing concerning this grand personage, and he did not perceive the trail of smoke which hung over the steamer that was carrying the Seigneur Saffar to Trebizond!

# KÉRABAN THE INFLEXIBLE

## OR, ADVENTURES IN THE EUXINE.

## PART TWO

# KÉRABAN THE INFLEXIBLE;

## OR, ADVENTURES IN THE EUXINE.

BY JULES VERNE.

TRANSLATED BY HENRY FRITH.

### CHAPTER I.

### IN WHICH WE FIND SEIGNEUR KÉRABAN VERY ANGRY AFTER HAVING TRAVELLED BY RAILWAY.

HE reader, no doubt remembers that Van Mitten, much disappointed at not having been able to visit the ruins of the ancient Colchis, had made up his mind to indemnify himself by exploring the "mythological" Phasis, which, under the less euphonious name of the Rion, now flows into the sea at Poti, where it forms a little harbour in the littoral of the Black Sea.

But in truth the worthy Dutchman was again destined to have his hopes crushed. He was certainly very desirous to trace out the course of Jason and of the Argonauts, to explore the celebrated places through which the bold son of Æson penetrated on his search for the Golden Fleece. No! Van Mitten was just at present in a great hurry to quit Poti, so as to follow up Seigneur Kéraban, and to rejoin him on the Russo-Turkish frontier.

But at the very outset a fresh disappointment awaited him. It was already five o'clock in the afternoon. They intended to start on the following morning, 13th September. Of Poti, then, Van Mitten could only see the public gardens, in which are the ruins of an ancient fortress; the houses (built on piles), the abodes of some six thousand or seven thousand people; the wide streets flanked by ditches in which frogs croaked incessantly; and the harbour, well-filled with shipping, which is guarded by an excellent lighthouse, a guiding star of the first magnitude.

Van Mitten could only console himself for having so little time in which to make these observations, as he had to leave the town so quickly, by recollecting that it is situated in the midst of the marshes formed by the Rion and the Capatcha; and that by his rapid departure he would run no risk of the fever which is so prevalent there.

While the Dutchman was thus abandoning himself to all these kinds of reflections, Ahmet was busying himself in endeavouring to replace the chaise, which would have still done good service but for the indefensible imprudence of its proprietor. Now to find another post chaise, new or second-hand, in the little town of Poti was not to be expected. A *pereclad-naia*—or Russian *araba*—might indeed be obtained, and Seigneur Kéraban's purse was available to pay the cost, whatever it might be. But the available vehicles in fact were only more or less of a cart-like and primitive character, very uncomfortable, and had nothing in common with the travelling carriage. However willing the horses which might be yoked to it, they could not possibly proceed at the same pace as with a chaise. So there were many delays to be feared before the journey could be accomplished.

However, we may remark that Ahmet

was at any rate not likely to be embarrassed in the choice of a carriage, for nothing in the nature of a conveyance could be obtained! It was most important that he should rejoin his uncle as quickly as possible, for Kéraban's obstinacy would surely engage him in some deplorable adventure. So Ahmet decided to perform that journey of twenty leagues on horseback, for that was the distance which lay between Poti and the Turko-Russian frontier. He was an excellent horseman, and Nizib had often accompanied him in his rides. Van Mitten, when consulted, confessed that he had had some lessons in the principles of equitation, and he answered, if not for the actual skill of Bruno on horseback, at any rate for his obedience in following him under those conditions.

It was thus arranged that they should take their departure the following morning at an early hour, so as to be able to reach the frontier the same evening.

This settled, Ahmet wrote a long letter to the address of Selim the banker: a letter which naturally commenced with the words, "Dear Amasia." To her he related the various incidents of the journey: what had happened at Poti, why he had been separated from his uncle, how he hoped to rejoin him. He added that their return would be in no way retarded by this adventure: that he knew very well how to make both men and animals "step out," to accomplish the remainder of the journey in the shortest possible time. So he suggested that she should proceed with her father and Nedjeb to Scutari on the day fixed, or indeed, a little sooner, so that their meeting should not fail.

This letter—in which Ahmet scattered broadcast the most tender phrases and compliments—was intended to go by the regular mail-steamer next day. In eight-and-forty hours it would reach its destination, be opened and read—perhaps pressed to Amasia's heart, which Ahmet believed he could hear beating across the Black Sea. The fact being that the young lovers were at that time farther apart than at any other period of the journey—at the ends of an immense ellipse as it were, whose curves must be followed ere the young people could meet again.

Now while Ahmet was writing to console Amasia, what was Van Mitten doing?

The Dutchman, having dined at the hotel, was walking about the streets of Poti with curiosity—under the trees of the Central Garden, along the quays and piers, which were in course of construction. But he was alone. Bruno, this time, did not accompany him.

But why did Bruno not go with his master, free to make respectful but just observations upon the complications of the present and the chances of the future?

Because Bruno had an idea. If there were no carriages of any kind in Poti, he might, perhaps, find a pair of scales. For this emaciated Dutchman it was now or never to compare his actual weight with his former figure.

So Bruno had quitted the hotel, taking care to carry with him his master's "guide," which gave him in Tartar pounds the value of the Russian weights and measures, with which he was unacquainted.

On the quays of a maritime town, near the custom house, there are always some large scales in which a man can ascertain his weight at his leisure.

Bruno had no misgivings on the subject. In consideration of a few kopecks the proprietor of the scales made no objection to the lad's fancy. They placed a considerable weight in the one scale, and Bruno, not without secret misgivings, ascended into the other.

To his great disgust the latter remained upon the ground, and Bruno, notwithstanding his efforts, could not move the scale.

"The devil!" he muttered, "this is as I feared."

Then a less weight was substituted, but the scale remained as immovable as before.

"Is it possible!" exclaimed Bruno, who felt all the blood rushing to his heart.

At that moment his gaze fell upon a

pleasant face, which appeared quite benevolent in its regard.

"My master!" exclaimed Bruno.

It was Van Mitten, sure enough; who, by the chances of his promenade, had been led to the quay precisely at the time when his servant was undergoing the weighing operation.

"You here, sir!" said Bruno.

"Yes, myself," replied Van Mitten. "I see you are in the act of——"

"Of weighing myself, sir. Yes."

"And what is the result of the operation?"

"The result is that I do not know whether there are any weights light enough to weigh me!"

Bruno made this reply with such a dolorous expression of countenance that the plaint went direct to the heart of Van Mitten.

"What!" he exclaimed. "Have you grown so thin since you left home, my poor Bruno?"

"You may judge for yourself, sir," replied the man.

Then a third weight, less than the previous one, was placed in the scale.

This time Bruno, by slow degrees, managed to tip the scales, and put them *in equilibrio* on the horizontal beam.

"At last!" he exclaimed. "But what is such a weight as that?"

"Yes, what is that weight?" asked Van Mitten.

It was exactly, in Russian measure, four pounds, neither more nor less.

Van Mitten immediately took the guide-book, which Bruno still retained, and referred to the tables of weights and measures of the various nationalities.

"Well, sir?" asked Bruno, who was a prey to curiosity mingled with a kind of agonized feeling. "What is the value of the Russian pound weight?"

"About sixteen and a half Dutch '*ponds*,'" replied Van Mitten, after a little mental arithmetic.*

"And that amounts to——?"

* M. Van Mitten must be wrong. He meant about 18½ "*ponds*," we presume; 16½ × 4 gives only 66 *ponds*, not 75½.—TRANSLATOR.

"That makes exactly seventy-five and a half *ponds*, or one hundred and fifty-one pounds."

Bruno uttered a cry of despair and suddenly leaped from the scale, the other platform of which fell heavily to the ground, and he fell upon a bench half fainting.

"One hundred and fifty-one pounds!" he repeated, as if he had lost a considerable slice of his existence.

In fact, at his departure from home, Bruno had weighed eighty-four *ponds*, or one hundred and sixty-eight pounds. Now he weighed only seventy-five and a half *ponds*, or one hundred and fifty-one pounds. He had then lost seventeen pounds in twenty-six days of comparatively easy traveling without any great privations or fatigue. And now that the evil had begun where was it to stop? What would become of the stoutness which Bruno was hoping to possess, which had taken him twenty years to gain, thanks to his observance of a well calculated treatment? How would he now fall away from the honourable condition in which he had formerly maintained himself, particularly at the present juncture, when, for want of a carriage travelling through a country without supplies, in daily threatening fatigues and dangers, this absurd journey was about to be continued under new and less favourable conditions?

That was the question which the anxious servant of Van Mitten kept asking himself. He pictured to himself, in a rapid glance into the probable future, terrible eventualities, in the midst of which appeared a quite unrecognizable Bruno reduced to a perambulating skeleton.

So he made up his mind without a moment's hesitation. He rose, and dragging away his master who had not the strength to resist him, stopped him on the quay before entering the hotel.

"Master," he said, "there are limits to everything, even to human folly. We will go no farther."

Van Mitten received this statement with his usual placidity, from which nothing could move him.

"What do you mean Bruno? Do you intend us to stay for ever in this corner of the Caucasus?"

"No, sir, no. I merely would suggest that we leave Seigneur Kéraban to return as he pleases to Constantinople, while we go back in one of the steamers from Poti. The sea does not disagree with you nor me, and

"Weighing myself, sir, yes," said Bruno.

I run no risk of becoming thinner, a contingency which will certainly happen if I continue to travel under present conditions."

"The idea is perhaps wise from your point of view, Bruno," said Van Mitten, "but with me it is different. It requires some consideration before I can abandon my friend Kéraban after three parts of his journey have been accomplished."

"Seigneur Kéraban is no longer your friend," replied Bruno. "He is the friend of Seigneur Kéraban—that is all! Besides, he is not and cannot be my friend, and I will not sacrifice what little stoutness I still possess for his caprices. Three quarters of the journey accomplished, you say! That is true; but the fourth quarter seems to me to present many more difficulties in crossing this savage country. That nothing personally disagreeable to you may occur, I grant;

but I repeat—if you will insist on going—take care; something unfortunate will eventuate!"

The insistence of Bruno, that something serious would happen, had its effect upon Van Mitten. The suggestions of his faithful servant had some, if not a great, influence. Indeed the contemplated journey beyond the Russian frontier, through the district almost entirely uncontrolled by the Turkish government, was one which could not be undertaken without consideration. So, being rather weak, Van Mitten felt somewhat shaken; Bruno, perceiving this, redoubled his efforts. He added a most convincing argument, by showing how loosely his clothes hung upon him around his waist, which was growing smaller daily. Insinuating, persuasive, even eloquent under the domination of profound conviction, he induced his master to share his ideas and to see the necessity to separate himself somehow or other from his friend Kéraban.

Van Mitten was reflecting: He nodded his head in the right places; and, when this serious conversation was finished, he was only restrained by the fear of having a discussion on the subject with his incorrigible travelling companion.

"Well," said Bruno, who had combated all objections, "the circumstances are favourable. Since Seigneur Kéraban is no longer present, let us take French leave of him, and leave his nephew Ahmet to meet him at the frontier."

Van Mitten shook his head.

"There is only one obstacle to that;" he said.

"That is?" enquired Bruno.

"Because I left Constantinople with very little money, and now my purse is empty!"

"Can you not procure sufficient from the bank at Constantinople?" said Bruno.

"No; that is impossible. The deposit has not yet arrived from Rotterdam."

"So, to obtain the necessary money for our return——?" asked Bruno.

"We must address ourselves to my friend Kéraban," replied Van Mitten.

This reply by no means re-assured Bruno. If his master once met Kéraban again and mentioned the project, there would be a discussion, in which Van Mitten would come off second best. But what was to be done? Should they speak to Ahmet? No, decidedly. Ahmet would never supply them with means to desert his uncle. There was no use in thinking of that.

At length it was decided between the master and man, after a long discussion, that they would leave Poti in Ahmet's company, and proceed to rejoin Kéraban on the Turko-Russian frontier. There Van Mitten, under a pretext of failing health, and in view of the fatigue in prospect, would declare that he could not continue the journey. Under such circumstances, his friend Kéraban would never refuse to lend him the necessary funds to enable him to reach Constantinople by sea.

"No matter," thought Bruno, "a conversation between my master and Seigneur Kéraban on this subject, will, nevertheless, be a serious one."

They then returned to the hotel where Ahmet was awaiting them. They said nothing to him of their projects, for he would have endeavoured to combat them. They dined and slept. Van Mitten dreamed that Kéraban was chopping him into mince-meat. They awoke early next morning and found four horses at the door ready to "devour space."

Bruno was a curious spectacle while he was attempting to mount his steed. This was a new grievance against Kéraban. But there were no other means of travelling, and so Bruno was obliged to resign himself to the inevitable. Fortunately, his horse was an old hack, incapable of misconducting himself, and easy to manage. Van Mitten's and Nizib's steeds likewise were not formidable animals. Ahmet only rode a spirited horse; but, as he was quite at home in the saddle, he had no other anxiety than to moderate his pace so as not to distance his companions on the journey.

They quitted Poti at five o'clock in the morning. At eight they took their first breakfast at the village of Nikolaja, after a ride of thirty versts; a second breakfast at Kintryschi, fifteen versts farther on about eleven o'clock; and, towards two o'clock in the afternoon, Ahmet, after a stage of twenty versts more, halted at Batoum in that part of northern Lazistan which belongs to the Muscovite empire.

This was formerly a Turkish port, very

"Bruno was a curious spectacle."

conveniently situated at the mouth of the Tchorock, the Bathys of the ancients. It is very unfortunate that the Turks have lost it, for the harbour contains excellent anchorage for a number of ships even of great draught. The town is simply an important bazaar, which lines the principal street. But the hand of Russia is being extended slowly over all the Transcaucasian regions; and it has seized Batoum, as it will seize, eventually, the farther limits of Lazistan.

There Ahmet was not quite so much at home as he had been in the place some years before. It was necessary to pass Gùméh, at the mouth of the river, and at twenty versts from Batoum, the town of Makrialos, to attain the frontier, ten versts further on.

In this place, by the wayside, a man was

waiting under the scarcely paternal observation of a party of Cossacks. This individual's feet were placed at the very limit of Ottoman territory, and he was in a state of fury more easy to imagine than to describe.

The man was Seigneur Kéraban. It was six o'clock P.M., and since the midnight previous—the precise moment at which he had been ejected from Russian territory—Kéraban had been in a towering rage.

A wretched hut, badly furnished and miserably supplied, had been his only shelter, or rather his only place of refuge.

Half a verst away Ahmet and Van Mitten had respectively perceived their uncle and friend; and, pressing their horses, dismounted near him.

Seigneur Kéraban was just then pacing up and down, gesticulating, and talking to himself since no one took any notice of him, and he did not appear to see his friends approaching.

"Uncle!" exclaimed Ahmet, extending his arms. Nizib and Bruno took care of the horses.

"My friend!" cried Van Mitten.

Kéraban seized the hands of both; and, indicating the Cossacks, who were still patrolling the road, he exclaimed—

"On a railway! Those wretches actually compelled me to travel in a train! I, I!"

Evidently he had been reduced to that mode of locomotion, so unworthy of a true Turk, and the indignity had excited in the breast of Seigneur Kéraban the most violent indignation. No! he would never put up with that. His meeting with Seigneur Saffar, his quarrel with that insolent personage and its consequences, the breaking down of the post-chaise—the obstacles to the continuation of the journey: he forgot all these in face of the one great enormity! He had been in a railway carriage! He! a true Believer of the old school!

"Yes, it *is* an insult," replied Ahmet, who thought it best not to contradict his uncle under such circumstances.

"Yes, an insult indeed," added Van Mitten. "But after all, friend Kéraban, nothing serious has happened to you."

"Ah! you had better mind what you are saying, Monsieur Van Mitten," cried Kéraban. "Nothing serious, say you?"

Ahmet made a sign to the Dutchman to warn him that he was on the wrong tack. His old friend had addressed him as "Monsieur Van Mitten," and was continuing—

"Just tell me what you mean by those indefensible words 'nothing serious!'"

"I meant, friend Kéraban, any of the usual accidents which happen on railways—neither derailment, nor break-down, nor collision——"

"Monsieur Van Mitten, it were better to have run off the line," exclaimed Kéraban. "Yes, by Allah! better to have run off the line; to have broken an arm, a leg, or even my head, than to have put up with such an indignity—do you hear?"

"You may readily believe, friend Kéraban," continued Van Mitten, who did not know how to palliate his unfortunate words, "you may believe——"

"It does not matter what *I* may believe," interrupted Kéraban, walking up to the Dutchman, "but what *you* believe! It is a question of how you regard what has happened to a man who for thirty years has believed himself your friend."

Ahmet was anxious to change the conversation of which the evident result had been to make matters worse.

"Uncle," he said, "I can assure you, you have quite misunderstood M. Van Mitten."

"Really!"

"Or rather M. Van Mitten has not expressed himself clearly. He, quite as much as I do, resents with the greatest indignation the treatment which those confounded Cossacks have inflicted upon you."

Fortunately all this conversation was carried on in the Turkish language, and the "confounded Cossacks" did not understand a word of it.

"But really, uncle, it is to another person you must attribute all that has happened.

"STANDING ON THE VERY LIMIT OF OTTOMAN TERRITORY."—p. 32

Another is responsible for all this; and he is that impudent individual who obstructed your crossing the railway at Poti—Seigneur Saffar!"

"Yes, that Saffar!" exclaimed Kéraban, very opportunely put on this new trail by his nephew.

"A thousand times yes—that Saffar!"

Kéraban indulged himself with a last menace.

added Van Mitten, hastily. "He was the fellow I wished to speak of, friend Kéraban."

"The infamous Saffar!" said Kéraban.

"The infamous Saffar!" repeated Van Mitten, putting himself in accord with his companion.

He would have employed even a more forcible epithet, had it occurred to him.

"If we ever meet him again"—said Ahmet.

"And cannot we return to Poti to pay him out for his insolence," cried Kéraban; "to pick a quarrel with him, to tear his heart from his body, to hand him over to the executioner——?"

"To cause him to be impaled!" added Van Mitten, who adopted a ferocious tone, in order to preserve harmony.

This suggestion, so very Turkish, was successful in compromising matters, and gained for Van Mitten a grasp of his friend's hand.

"Uncle," said Ahmet, "it would be no use to return in pursuit of this Saffar now."

"Why, nephew?"

"Because he is no longer in Poti," replied Ahmet. "When we arrived there he had already embarked in the coasting packet, which skirts the shore of Asia Minor."

"The shore of Asia Minor—But our way lies along the coast!"

"Quite so, uncle."

"Well, then," exclaimed Kéraban, "if this infamous Saffar comes in my way—*Vallah billah tillah*—woe betide him!"

After pronouncing this formula, which is the sacred oath, Seigneur Kéraban could add nothing more terrible, and he was silent accordingly.

But how were they to travel now that they had no carriage? It was obviously useless to propose a journey on horseback to Seigneur Kéraban. His stoutness precluded any such suggestion. If he would suffer from riding, the horse would also have a bad time of it; and so it was arranged that they should all proceed to Choppa, the nearest town—which was not far off—and Kéraban could walk so far as that. Bruno also preferred to walk, as he could no longer sit his horse.

"And about that request for money you were going to make?" said he to his master, aside.

"At Choppa," replied Van Mitten; but it was not without considerable trepidation that he perceived the moment approaching when he must touch upon such a delicate topic.

Soon afterwards the travellers descended the gently sloping road which skirts the littoral of Lazistan.

Seigneur Kéraban turned round to indulge himself with a last shake of his clenched hand towards the Cossacks, who had so very rudely carried him—him!—in a railway carriage; and then a curve in the road hid the Russian frontier from sight of the travellers.

## Chapter II.

### In which Van Mitten decides to yield to the importunities of Bruno; and what came of his compliance.

"A curious country," writes Van Mitten in his note-book, as he hastily jotted down some random impressions of the journey. "The women work in the fields and carry burthens, while the men spin flax and knit in wool."

The worthy Dutchman was not mistaken: such are still the customs in the distant provice of Lazistan, where the second portion of the journey was commenced.

It is still a little-known country, this territory which extends from the Caucasian frontier; this portion of Turkish Armenia comprised between the valleys of the Charchout of the Tschorock, and the shore of the Black Sea. Few travellers, since the Frenchman M. Deyralles, have ventured across these districts of the pachalik of Trebizond, between the mountains which extend in an irregular manner, from the coast to the Lake Van, and embrace Erzeroum, the capital of Armenia, the chief place of a district which includes more than twelve hundred thousand inhabitants.

Nevertheless, this country has witnessed many grand historical events. When quitting the plains in which the two branches of the Euphrates rise, Xenophon and his Ten Thousand retreated before the armies of Artaxerxes Mnemon, and reached the banks of the Phasis. This Phasis is not the so-called Rion, which flows into the sea at Poti, but the Kour, which comes down from the Caucasian region, and not far from the province of Lazistan, across which Seigneur Kéraban and his companions were about to travel.

Ah! if Van Mitten had only had time, what precious observations he might have made, and which are now all lost for the erudite Hollanders! And why should he not have discovered the precise spot on which Xenophon, general, historian, and philosopher, gave battle to the Taochians and Chalybians when quitting the country of the Charduchians; and the mount Chenion, on which the Greeks welcomed, with loud acclamations, the appearance of the long-wished-for fleet in the Black Sea?

But Van Mitten had no time to see nor to study; or, rather, they did not give him time. And then Bruno returned to the charge concerning the loan from Kéraban, in order that they might separate from him.

"At Choppa," was Van Mitten's invariable reply.

So they all journeyed towards Choppa. But should they then find some means of proceeding—some vehicle which would replace the comfortable chaise that had been broken at Poti?

The situation was sufficiently grave. The travellers had still 240 leagues to traverse in seventeen days only. It was on the 30th of that month that Kéraban was due at home. It was on that day that Ahmet hoped to find in the villa at Scutari the youthful Amasia, who was waiting for the celebration of their marriage. One can quite understand then that both uncle and nephew were equally impatient; and on this account they were greatly embarrassed as to the means by which the second portion of the journey was to be accomplished.

It was not to be expected that they would find a post-chaise or even an ordinary carriage in the out-of-the-way towns of Asia Minor. Their only chance was to make use of one of the vehicles of the country, which are of a most rudimentary kind.

Under these circumstances, silent and pensive, Seigneur Kéraban proceeded along the coast-road on foot, Bruno also leading his own and his master's horses by the bridle, for Van Mitten preferred to walk beside his friend. Nizib was mounted, and rode in front. Ahmet had already hurried on in advance, so as to prepare the lodgings at Choppa, and to make enquiries concerning a carriage, so that the journey could be continued at sunrise next day.

The road was followed slowly and in silence. Kéraban smothered the anger which was burning within him, but it was every now and then manifested by such exclamations as, "Cossacks!" "railway!" "waggon!" "Saffar!" Van Mitten longed to converse with him upon the idea of the projected separation, but he did not dare—not thinking the time favourable in the state of mind in which his friend was, for the least suggestion would have upset him.

They reached Choppa at 9 o'clock in the evening. This stage accomplished on foot necessitated a night's rest. The inn was second-rate, but fatigue made amends for want of accommodation, and the four travellers all slept for ten hours consecutively, while Ahmet that very evening set off into the country to procure a vehicle.

Next day, 14th September, at seven o'clock A.M., an *araba*, already horsed, was standing ready at the door of the inn.

Ah! how they regretted the old post-chaise, now replaced by a kind of rough cart on two wheels, and in which there was scarcely room for three persons! Two horses would not be one too many to drag such a heavy vehicle. Ahmet had fortunately been able to procure a waterproof awning, stretched upon a wooden framing, so as to protect the occupants from wind and rain. They were obliged to put up with this *araba*, pending better accommodation, but it was improbable that they would find better before they reached Trebizond.

One can easily understand how, at the sight of this rough cart, Van Mitten, philosophical as he was, and Bruno, absolutely knocked up, could neither of them repress a grimace, which, at a look of Kéraban's, disappeared in an instant.

"That is the only conveyance I could find, uncle;" said Ahmet.

'It is all that is necessary," replied Kéraban, who for the world would not have permitted anyone to perceive the shadow of a regret for the excellent post-chaise.

"Yes," replied Ahmet, "with a good litter of straw in this *araba*——"

"We shall feel like princes, nephew," interrupted Kéraban.

"Theatrical princes!" muttered Bruno.

"Eh?" said Kéraban.

"Besides," continued Ahmet, "we are only sixty leagues from Trebizond, and there, I am assured, we shall find a much more comfortable mode of conveyance."

"I tell you this will do very well," said Kéraban, with a warning frown, as if he

"So we are going to ride in that thing?"

suspected his companions of some meditated contradiction.

But everyone, crushed by this formidable glance, preserved a passive demeanour.

So it was arranged that Kéraban, Van Mitten, and Bruno should occupy the *araba*, one of the horses being ridden by the postillion, who had charge of the relay, after each stage. Ahmet and Nizib, who were accustomed to ride, followed on horseback. By these means they hoped to reach Trebizond without much delay. Thence they determined to finish the journey in the quickest and most comfortable manner possible.

Then Seigneur Kéraban gave the signal for departure, after the *araba* had been furnished with provisions, &c., not forgetting the two *narghilés*, fortunately saved from the collision, carried by their respective owners. The towns in this portion of the littoral are not far apart. They are rarely more than four of five leagues distant from each other. So the travellers could easily repose or replenish their stores—supposing that the impatient Ahmet would consent to accord them a few hours' rest, and that the villages had sufficient store of provisions.

"*En route!*" repeated Ahmet after his uncle, who had already taken his place in the *araba.*

At this moment Bruno approached his master, and in a grave but almost imperious tone said:—

"How about that proposition you have to make to Seigneur Kéraban?"

"I have not yet had the opportunity," replied Van Mitten evasively. "Besides, he does not appear to me very well disposed to——"

"So we are going to ride in that thing?" continued Bruno, indicating the *araba* with a gesture of contempt impossible to describe.

"Yes, for the present."

"But when do you intend to ask for the money which will ensure our liberty?"

"At the next town."

"At the next town?"

"Yes: at Archawa."

Bruno shook his head in disapprobation and seated himself in the *araba* behind his master. Then the heavy conveyance proceeded at a fair pace along the slopes of the coast-road.

The weather was not all that could be wished. Stormy-looking clouds were massed in the west and held out threats of disturbances beyond the horizon. This portion of the road, swept by the winds, is not an easy route to follow; but one cannot command the weather, and the faithful fatalists of Mahomet know how to "take things as they come" better than all other people. In any case there was reason to fear that the Black Sea would not justify its classic name of *Pontus Euxinus* or "well-disposed," but rather the Turkish name of *Kara Dequitz,* which is of less fair augury.

Very fortunately the route no longer crossed the elevated and hilly regions of Lazistan. There roads were entirely wanting, and one cannot venture into the forests without axes to clear the way. The passage of an *araba* would be well-nigh impossible to accomplish. But the coast-road was much more practicable, and there was no failure in the path from one town to another. The route curved amid fruit-trees under the shade of nut-bushes and chestnut-trees, amid clumps of laurels and Alpine roses intertwined by the inextricable tendrils of the wild vines.

But if this side of Lazistan offers a safe road to travellers, it is not remarkable for its sanitary condition in the low districts. There pestilent marshes extend: endemic typhus reigns from May until August. Fortunately it was now September, and the travellers ran no risk. Fatigue they would encounter; diseases, no. But if they could not always keep well they could always rest! And when the most headstrong of Turks reasoned thus his companions had no answer to make.

# KÉRABAN THE INFLEXIBLE;

## OR, ADVENTURES IN THE EUXINE.

BY JULES VERNE.

TRANSLATED BY HENRY FRITH.

### CHAPTER II.

THE *araba* stopped at the little town of Archawa about 9 A.M. They were ready to start again in an hour without Van Mitten having found time to touch upon his famous project of the loan from his friend Kéraban.

Accordingly Bruno questioned him.

"Well, sir, have you done it?"

"No, Bruno, not yet."

"But it is time."

"At the next town."

"At the next town?"

"Yes: at Witze!"

And Bruno, who in a pecuniary sense depended on his master as Van Mitten was dependent upon Kéraban, took his place in the *araba*, not without ill-humour which he failed to conceal.

"What is the matter with that fellow now?" asked Kéraban.

"Nothing," replied Van Mitten hastily, with a view to turn the conversation. "He is a little fatigued perhaps."

"He!" exclaimed Kéraban. "He looks splendid. I think he is growing fatter!"

"I?" cried Bruno, touched to the quick by this remark.

"Yes: you have all the appearance of becoming a good Turk of a majestic corpulence."

Van Mitten seized his servant's arm, for Bruno was ready to explode at this left-handed compliment. So Bruno was silenced.

Meanwhile the *araba* continued its rapid course, and with the exception of the jolting which caused somewhat rough shocks, and consequent contusions to the occupants, there was nothing to complain of.

The route was by no means deserted. Some Lazes were visible descending the slopes of the Pontic Alps, on business connected with their wants or their commerce. Had Van Mitten been less occupied with his meditated request, he would have noted the difference in the costume, which exists between the Caucasians and the Lazes. A kind of Phrygian bonnet, the ribbons of which are tied around the head in the manner of a "coiffure," replaces the Georgian cap. These fine, tall, well-made mountaineers of fair complexion, carry two cartridge-pouches arranged like pan-pipes. A short gun, a long-bladed poignard stuck in a girdle edged with copper, constitute their ordinary accoutrements.

Some donkeys followed after them, and carried to the villages on the coast the fruits of all kinds which grow in the "middle zone." In fact, had the weather been less unsettled, the travellers would have had little to complain of in the journey, even made under such conditions.

At eleven o'clock in the forenoon, they reached Witze on the ancient Pyxites, whose Greek name *buis* ("box") is sufficiently justified by the abundance of that plant in the neighbourhood. At Witze they had breakfast, too quickly as it seemed to Kéraban's taste, who, this time, made no concealment of his ill-humour.

Van Mitten, then, of course, found no favourable opportunity to mention his little business; and at the moment of departure, Bruno, drawing him aside, said—

"Well, master?"

"Well, Bruno, at the next town——"

"What?"

"Yes; at Artachen."

Bruno, disgusted at such weakness, lay down, grumbling, in the *araba*, while his

The mountaineers of Lazistan.

master took a rapid survey of the romantic country which unites in itself all the cleanliness of Holland with the picturesqueness of Italy.

It was the same at Artachen as it had been at Witze and Archawa. They arrived at three, and started at four P.M. with fresh horses; but after a serious protest by Bruno, who would hear of no more temporising, his master pledged himself to make the demand at Atina, where it had been agreed to pass the night.

There were five leagues to be traversed before this next town was reached, and then fifteen leagues of the journey would be accomplished. This, after all, was not excessive; but the rain which was threatening, would no doubt render the roads heavy and less practicable.

Ahmet saw with anxiety the period of bad weather obstinately setting in. The stormy clouds grew larger. The heavy atmosphere rendered breathing difficult. It was evident that, during the evening or in the night, a storm would break over the sea. After the first peals of thunder, the squall would be let loose, and the tempest would bring up the vapour to be discharged in rain.

There was only room for three travellers in the *araba.* Neither Ahmet nor Nizib could find shelter under the tilt, which would, perhaps, not resist the force of the tempest. So the riders, as well as the others, were anxious to urge the horses on to the next village.

Two or three times Kéraban put his head outside the awning, and studied the sky, which became more and more overcast.

"Shall we have a storm?" he asked.

"Yes, uncle," replied Ahmet. "Let us endeavour to reach the next relay before the rain commences."

"As soon as it begins to fall, you can come inside here," said Kéraban.

"And who will give up his place?"

"Bruno. That brave fellow will take your horse."

"Certainly," added Van Mitten, quickly, for his faithful follower. The Dutchman would have had bad taste to decline.

But we may be sure Van Mitten did not look at Bruno when he made this answer. He did not dare to do so. It was as much as Bruno could do not to break out. His master felt it was so.

"The best thing we can do is to push on as quickly as possible," said Ahmet. "Should the storm come on, the covering of the *araba* will be torn away in an instant, and the place will be untenable."

"Hurry on," cried Kéraban to the postillion, "and do not spare your cattle."

And, indeed, the postillion, who was quite as anxious as the travellers to arrive at Atina, did not spare his horses. But the poor beasts, exhausted by the sultriness of the atmosphere, could not maintain the trot upon the road, which had not yet been macadamized.

How Seigneur Kéraban and his companions envied the "Cahapar," whose carriage passed their *araba* about seven o'clock in the evening. This is the English courier, who every two weeks carries European despatches to Teheran. He only requires twelve days to go from Trebizond to the Persian capital, with two or three horses, which carry his valises, and his escort of Zapties. But in the matter of relays, he has the preference over all other travellers, and Ahmet began to be afraid that, when they arrived at Atina, they would find only jaded cattle.

Fortunately, this idea never occurred to Kéraban. Else he would have had legitimate occasion to make more complaints, and would have gained a great deal by them, no doubt! Perhaps he was seeking such an opportunity elsewhere. At anyrate one was furnished by Van Mitten.

The Dutchman could no longer avoid the performance of his promises made to Bruno, and at length he took the chances, but with all the skill of which he was master. The bad weather appeared to afford him an excellent text.

"Friend Kéraban," he began, in the tone of a man who has no wish to give advice, but to seek it, "what do you think of the state of the atmosphere?"

"What do I think?"

"Yes; you know the autumnal equinox is close upon us, and it is to be feared that the latter portion of our journey may not be so pleasant as the former."

"Well then, it will be less pleasant, that's all," was Kéraban's dry reply. "I cannot alter atmospheric conditions at will; I am not aware that I command the elements, Van Mitten!

"No, evidently," replied the Dutchman, who was not particularly encouraged by this opening. "But that was not what I meant, my worthy friend."

"What did you mean then?"

"That after all, perhaps, it is only threatening a storm, and that it will pass over us."

"All storms pass over, Van Mitten. They continue for a greater or less time—like discussions—but they pass away, and fine weather succeeds, naturally."

"At least, if the atmosphere were less disturbed," continued Van Mitten, "if the period of the equinox were not so near——"

"When it is the equinox, it is as well to resign oneself to the conditions," replied Kéraban. "I can't do anything to prevent it. One might imagine that you are finding fault with me, Van Mitten!"

"No, I assure you. Reproach you? I find fault, friend Kéraban?" replied Van Mitten.

Things were not progressing favourably, that was plain. Perhaps, had Bruno not been behind him, Van Mitten would have abandoned this dangerous topic of conversation and resumed it later. But there were no means of retreat, particularly as Kéraban pointedly enquired as he bent a frowning brow upon him—

"What possesses you, Van Mitten? It would appear as if you had some hidden meaning in this!"

"I?" exclaimed Van Mitten.

"Yes you. Let us consider this. Be frank with me. I do not like people who put on these lugubrious looks without giving any reason."

"I—have I appeared discontented?"

"Have you anything to reproach me with? If I have invited you to dinner at Scutari, am not I taking you thither? Is it my fault if that chaise was smashed by that confounded train?"

Oh yes, indeed, it was his fault and his fault solely. But the Dutchman was careful not to reproach him.

"Is it my fault that the weather is not favourable?" continued Kéraban, "or that an *araba* is the only means of conveyance? Come, let us see. Speak!"

Van Mitten, sorely perplexed, had no answer to make to this. He forced himself, however, to ask his peremptory companion whether he intended to remain at Atina for the night, or at Trebizond in the event of the journey proving more difficult in consequence of the bad weather.

"Difficult is not the same as impossible, is it?" retorted Kéraban, "and, as I intend to reach Scutari by the end of the month, we will continue our journey though all the elements warred against us."

Van Mitten then screwed up all his courage, and, not without evident hesitation, formulated his famous proposition.

"Well, Kéraban," he said, "if it will not inconvenience you very much, I would request permission for Bruno and myself—yes, permission to remain at Atina."

"You ask my permission to remain at Atina," repeated Kéraban, dwelling on each syllable.

"Yes, permission—authority—for I do not wish to run counter to your wishes—and——"

"You wish to separate from me, is that so?"

"Oh, temporarily, only for a very short time," Van Mitten hastened to add. "We are very much fatigued—Bruno and I. We would rather return to Constantinople by sea—yes, by sea."

"By sea!"

"Yes, friend Kéraban. Oh, I am aware you do not like the sea—I do not say so to annoy you. I can quite understand that the idea of crossing the sea is distasteful to you. So it is only natural that you should continue to follow the route along the shore. But fatigue makes this jolting very disagreeable to me, and you can plainly perceive that Bruno is growing much thinner."

"Ah, Bruno is growing thinner, is he?" said Kéraban, without even turning towards the unfortunate servant, who with a shaking hand was clutching the ample garments which covered his emaciated figure.

"These are the reasons, friend Kéraban, why I beg you not to be offended with us if we remain at Atina, whence we may reach European territory again under more pleasant conditions. I repeat, you will find us again at Scutari, and you may depend upon us not to keep you waiting to solemnize the wedding of our young friend Ahmet."

Van Mitten had now said all he wanted to say and he waited for Kéraban's answer. Would it be a simple acquiescence with so natural a demand, or would he burst into an angry one-sided argument?

The Dutchman bent his head, without daring to lift his eyes to his terrible companion's face.

"Van Mitten," said Kéraban, in a calmer tone than had been anticipated, "Van Mitten, you must admit that your suggestion is calculated to astonish me, and even of a nature to provoke——"

"Friend Kéraban," interrupted Van Mitten, who at this juncture began to fear some violence was imminent.

"Let me conclude, if you please," said Kéraban "You must admit that I cannot regard this separation without real pain, and I may add that I could not have anticipated such conduct on the part of a correspondent bound to me by business relations extending over thirty years."

"Kéraban," said Van Mitten——

"Eh, by Allah, cannot you let me finish?" exclaimed Kéraban, who could not restrain his habitual gesture. "But after all, Van Mitten, you are free. You are neither my relation nor my servant; you are only my friend, and a friend may permit himself anything, even to break the bonds of old friendship."

"Kéraban, my dear Kéraban," replied Van Mitten, much distressed by this reproach.

"You will accordingly remain at Atina if you please to stay there, or at Trebizond if you prefer it."

Then Seigneur Kéraban withdrew into his corner with the air of a man who has no association with any others present, whom he regards as mere strangers that chance has thrown in his way, *en route*.

In fact, if Bruno were pleased at the course which things had taken, Van Mitten was much moved at having caused so much pain to his old friend. But, after all, his plan had succeeded, and although it came into his mind to withdraw the suggestion he did not do so: besides Bruno was present.

The question of the money still remained: the loan must be arranged, for they might have to remain in that country for some time, or to continue the journey under new conditions. There would be no difficulty on this point. The important sum which stood to Van Mitten's credit in Rotterdam would soon be transmitted to the Bank at Constantinople, and Seigneur Kéraban would only have to repay himself the sum lent by means of the cheque which the Dutchman would hand to him.

"Friend Kéraban," said Van Mitten, after a silence of some minutes' duration, which had been interrupted by no one. "Friend Kéraban——"

"What is it, monsieur?" asked Kéraban, in the tone he would have addressed to an intruder.

"When we arrive at Atina," continued Van Mitten, who felt cut to the heart by the word "monsieur."

"Well, when we reach Atina, we will separate," replied Kéraban. "That is understood."

"Yes—no doubt, Kéraban."

Van Mitten did not dare to say, "my friend Kéraban," but he continued—

"Yes, of course; but I would ask you to lend me a little money."

"Money! what money?"

"A small sum, which I will repay you through the Bank of Constantinople."

"A small sum?"

"You know," said Van Mitten, "that I left with very little money, as you were so generous as to defray all the expenses of this journey——"

"The expenses concern me only."

"Quite so—I do not wish to discuss that."

"I would not have permitted you to spend a single livre," said Kéraban. "Not a single one."

"I am extremely grateful to you," replied Van Mitten. "But at this moment I do not possess a single pará; and I should be much obliged if——"

"I have no money to lend you," replied Kéraban, brusquely. "I have only sufficient remaining to carry me through this journey."

"Nevertheless you may give me——"

"Nothing—I tell you."

"What?" exclaimed Bruno.

"Bruno, I think, is permitting himself to make an observation," remarked Kéraban, in a menacing tone.

"Certainly," replied Bruno.

"Hold your tongue, Bruno," said Van Mitten, who did not wish the discussion embittered by any observations from his servant.

Bruno was silent.

"My dear Kéraban," continued Van Mitten, "it is after all only a question of a relatively insignificant sum, which will suffice to maintain me at Trebizond for a few days."

"Insignificant or not, monsieur," replied Kéraban, "you must expect absolutely nothing from me."

"A thousand piastres would suffice."

"No, not a thousand, nor a hundred, nor ten, nor one," replied Kéraban, who was beginning to get angry.

"What? nothing at all?"

"Nothing at all."

"But then——"

"Then you have only to continue your journey with us, Monsieur Van Mitten. You shall want for nothing. But as for lending you a piastre, a pará, or half a pará to enable you to travel by yourself—never!"

"Never?" echoed Van Mitten.

"Never!" replied Kéraban decisively.

The tone in which this "never" was pronounced was quite enough to carry conviction to Van Mitten, and even to Bruno, that the resolution of the Inflexible One was irrevocable. When he had once said "No," he had, as it were, said it ten times.

Whether Van Mitten was really hurt at this refusal of his quondam friend and correspondent, it would be difficult to explain, so reserved and phlegmatic is the human heart—particularly the human Dutch heart! Bruno, however, was outraged! What! was he to continue his journey under such conditions, and, it might be, in worse? He might be compelled to prosecute this mad journey in a cart, on horseback, even on foot—who could tell? And all because it suited a headstrong Osmanli before whom his master trembled! He (Bruno) was perhaps condemned to lose even the little rotundity he still possessed, while Seigneur Kéraban, in spite of crosses and fatigues, continued to maintain his usual corpulence.

Yes, but what was to be done? Bruno had no resource but to grumble, and so he did grumble in his corner. For one instant he thought of staying by himself, to abandon Van Mitten to all the consequences of such tyranny. But the money question arose before him, as it had uprisen before his master who had not sufficient to pay his wages even. So he was obliged to remain with him.

While these discussions were proceeding the *araba* continued its way with difficulty. The sky had become very threatening and the clouds seemed to be resting on the water. The roaring of the breakers on the shore indicated the rising of the sea, and in the offing the wind was already blowing a gale.

The postillion pressed his horses as hard as he could, but the poor animals only proceeded with great difficulty. Ahmet, on his part, encouraged them, as he was in a great hurry to reach Atina, which it was now evident would not be gained before they were overtaken by the storm.

Kéraban remained silent with his eyes closed. This silence weighed upon Van Mitten, who would have preferred to hear some snappish remark from his old friend. He felt that by the latter complaints were being accumulated against him, and when the shell burst the explosion would be terrible.

At length Van Mitten could contain himself no longer, and leaning towards

"The 'ARABA' Continued its way with difficulty."--p.92

Kéraban so that Bruno should not hear, he said—

"Friend Kéraban!"

"What is it?" asked Kéraban.

"How could I yield to this idea of leaving you, for a moment?"

"Yes—how?"

"Indeed, I cannot understand it."

"No more can I," answered Kéraban.

That was all. But the hand of Van Mitten sought the hand of Kéraban, who acknowledged the repentance by a generous squeeze, which made the Dutchman's fingers tingle for a long time.

It was then 9 P.M. The night was very dark. The storm burst with tremendous violence. The horizon was illuminated by frequent flashes of lightning, but the thunder was as yet inaudible. The hurricane soon became so violent that many times the occupants of the *araba* fancied it would be overturned. The horses, worn out and weary, stopped every minute and reared and backed so that the postillion had great difficulty to maintain his seat.

What was to be done under such circumstances? They could not halt in such an unsheltered locality, swept by the fierce west wind; and there was yet half an hour's journey before they could reach the town.

Ahmet, who was very uneasy, did not know what to do, when on turning to the right, a light became visible like a flash from a gun. This came from the lighthouse of Atina, which, built on the cliffs in advance of the town, projected a bright gleam of light into the surrounding darkness.

Ahmet had conceived the idea of asking for shelter for the night from the caretakers of the lighthouse, so he knocked at the door of the hut erected at the foot of the building.

Some minutes later, Seigneur Kéraban with his companions, unsheltered, must have succumbed to the fury of the tempest.

---

## CHAPTER III.

### IN WHICH BRUNO PLAYS NIZIB A TRICK WHICH THE READER WILL KINDLY PARDON HIM.

AN immense wooden structure, divided into two chambers, with windows opening seawards, a scaffolding supporting a catoptric apparatus—that is to say, a lanthorn with reflectors, and topping the roof by sixty feet—such was the very primitive lighthouse of Atina.

But such as it was, it rendered very excellent service to navigation in the midst of that wild water. It had been only erected a short time, so what a number of vessels must have been driven ashore before the difficult channels of the port had been illuminated! Against the power of adverse winds, from north to west, a steamer can scarcely make headway, and much less could sailing vessels withstand the storm which drives them upon a lee shore.

Two light-keepers resided in the small wooden hut erected at the base of the lighthouse. The first chamber was the common sitting-room, another contained the two beds, which were never occupied at the same time. One of the men was on duty every night, as much to attend to the lanthorn as to signal any ships which might venture without pilots into the intricate channels of Atina.

The door of the hut was opened in response to a loud knocking, and Seigneur Kéraban, under the violent impulse of the storm—a storm in himself—entered precipitately, followed by Ahmet, Van Mitten, Bruno, and Nizib.

"What do you want?" enquired one of the lighthouse keepers; while his companion, rudely awakened from sleep, joined his associate almost immediately.

"Shelter for the night," replied Ahmet.

"If that is all you want, the house is open to you," replied the man.

"Shelter till daybreak, and something to appease our hunger meanwhile," added Kéraban.

"Very well," replied the keeper. "But you would do better at one of the inns in Atina."

"How far is the town from here?" asked Van Mitten.

"About half a league under the cliffs,' replied the man.

"Half a league in such weather as this!" exclaimed Kéraban. "No, my brave fellows, no! Here are benches upon which we can

"What do you want?'

pass the night. If our *araba* and our horses can find shelter under the lee of your lighthouse, that is all we shall require for them. To-morrow, as soon as it is light, we will proceed to the town; and may Allah find us some more convenient vehicle——"

"And one more rapid," added Ahmet.

"And less rough," muttered Bruno between his teeth.

"—Than this *araba*," continued Kéra ban, "of which it will not do to speak slightingly, nevertheless," he concluded bending a severe brow upon Van Mitten's spiteful follower.

"Seigneur," replied the keeper, "I repeat that our habitation is quite at your disposal. Many travellers have before now availed themselves of its protection from the weather, and have been satisfied."

"And with which we will know how to content ourselves," replied Kéraban.

Then the travellers made their arrangements for passing the night in the little house. In any case they could not but congratulate themselves upon having discovered such a refuge, uncomfortable though it was, when they listened to the wind, and to the torrents of rain which raged and fell outside.

But as to sleep—that was very well, on the condition that rest was preceded by some supper. Naturally it was Bruno who made this observation, at the same time calling attention to the fact that the supplies which had been carried in the *araba* were all consumed.

"Well, what have you to offer us, my fine fellows—on payment, of course?" asked Kéraban.

"Good or bad," replied one of the keepers, "there is only what there is, and all the gold in the imperial treasury would not avail to discover anything more than the little which remains of the provision allotted to the lighthouse."

"That will do very well," replied Ahmet.

"Yes, if there is enough of it," muttered Bruno, whose teeth were growing longer under the influence of real hunger.

"Go into the next room," replied the keeper, "what you will find on the table is at your service."

"And Bruno shall wait upon us," said Kéraban, "while Nizib assists the postillion to put up the horses and carriage as comfortably as possible under the lee of the lighthouse.

At a sign from his master, Nizib went out immediately to make things as snug as possible. Meanwhile Kéraban, Van Mitten, and Ahmet, followed by Bruno, entered the other room and sat down before a flaming wood fire beside a small table. On this they found some large dishes of cold meat, to which the travellers did full justice. Bruno, as he watched them eat, kept thinking that they were going rather far!

"But we must not forget Bruno and Nizib," said Van Mitten at last, after a quarter of an hour of mastication, which to the servant appeared interminable.

"No, certainly not," replied Kéraban, "there is no reason why they should die of hunger any more than their masters."

"That is very true," murmured Bruno.

"Nor is it necessary to treat them like the Cossacks," added Kéraban. "Ah, those Cossacks! I would hang a hundred of them."

"Oh!" exclaimed Van Mitten.

"A thousand—ten thousand—a hundred thousand," said Kéraban shaking his friend's hand violently. "Yes, until none were left. But it is getting late. Let us go to sleep."

"Yes, that will be better," said Van Mitten, who by his thoughtless "Oh!" had apparently provoked the massacre of a great part of the nomad tribes of the Russian Empire.

Kéraban, Van Mitten, and Ahmet retired to the first chamber at the moment when Nizib came in to join Bruno at supper. Then the three, wrapped in their cloaks, lay down upon the benches and sought to pass in slumber the long hours of the tempestuous night. But it must have been very difficult to sleep under such conditions.

Meantime Bruno and Nizib seated themselves opposite each other at table, and prepared to give a good account of such viands as remained; Bruno all the while "lording it over" Nizib, who was extremely deferential *vis-à-vis* of Bruno.

"Nizib," said Bruno, "my opinion is that when the masters have supped it is only right that the servants should eat all that is left."

"You are always hungry, Monsieur Bruno," said Nizib, admiringly.

"Always, Nizib, particularly after twelve hours have elapsed since the last meal."

"You do not look like it!"

"Not look like it! Don't you perceive

that I have lost ten pounds in eight days? My clothes have become loose enough to accommodate a man twice my size!"

"It is very extraordinary that you should do so. I have grown rather stouter."

"Ah, you grow fatter, do you?" murmured Bruno, looking askance at his companion.

"Let us see what is in that dish," said Nizib.

"Hum! not much," replied Bruno, "There is scarcely sufficient for one indeed —not enough for two."

"When travelling one must put up with what one can get, Monsieur Bruno."

"Ah, you are playing the philosopher," said Bruno to himself, "and yet you manage to get fat upon it!"

Then, pulling Nizib's plate towards him, he continued—

"Eh! what the deuce have you got here?"

"I don't know, it looks to me like mutton," replied Nizib, recovering his plate.

"Mutton!" exclaimed Bruno, "I say, Nizib, take care! I believe you are making a mistake."

"I will soon ascertain," replied Nizib, putting a piece in his mouth.

"No, no," cried Bruno, seizing his friend's hand. "Don't be in such a hurry. By Mahomet I believe it is the flesh of an animal forbidden to a Turk—not for a Christian—do you understand?"

"Do you think so, Monsieur Bruno?"

"Let me assure myself on the point," said Bruno.

So saying he transferred the food from Nizib's plate to his own, and under the pretext of tasting it, ate it in a few mouthfuls.

"Well?" asked Nizib, with a certain uneasiness of manner.

"Well," replied Bruno, "I was not mistaken. It is pork. Horrible! Fancy you were about to eat pork!"

"Pork!" exclaimed Nizib; "that is forbidden."

"Absolutely!"

"Nevertheless it seemed to me——"

"What do you mean, Nizib? Are you going to dictate to a man who knows so much better than yourself?"

"But then, Monsieur Bruno——"

"Then—in your place!—I would content myself with this morsel of goat's-cheese."

"It is very poor," replied Nizib.

"Yes, but it looks excellent."

# KÉRABAN THE INFLEXIBLE;

## OR, ADVENTURES IN THE EUXINE.

By JULES VERNE.

Translated by HENRY FRITH.

### Chapter III.

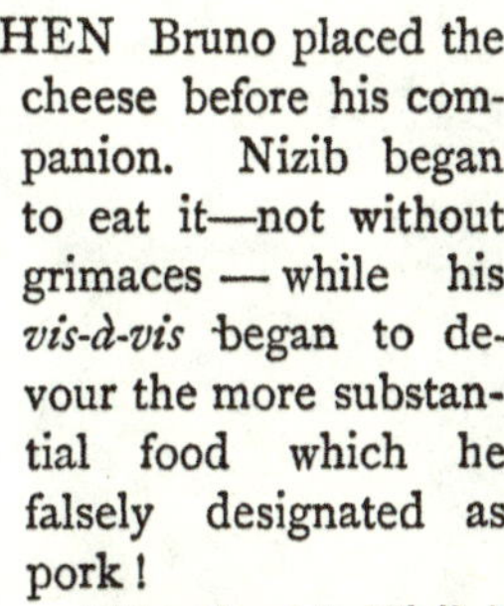

THEN Bruno placed the cheese before his companion. Nizib began to eat it—not without grimaces — while his *vis-à-vis* began to devour the more substantial food which he falsely designated as pork!

"Your health, Nizib," he said, filling a goblet from a jug on the table.

"What is that drink?" asked Nizib.

"Hum," replied Bruno, "it seems to me——"

"What?" said the other, holding out his glass.

"It seems to me that there is brandy in it, and a good Mussulman cannot partake of it," replied Bruno.

"But I cannot eat without drinking."

"Without drinking—no—and here is a jugful of fresh water, which ought to satisfy you, Nizib. How happy you Turks ought to feel in being accustomed to such a wholesome beverage."

And while Nizib was drinking, Bruno muttered, "Get fat, my friend; get fat!"

But just then Nizib, turning round, perceived another dish on the mantel-shelf, in which some food of appetising appearance still remained.

"Ah!" he exclaimed, "I shall have something more satisfying after all."

"Yes: this time, Nizib, we will share like good comrades. Indeed, I was quite sorry to see you reduced to sup upon goat's cheese."

"This seems to be mutton, M. Bruno."

"I believe it is, Nizib."

And the Dutchman, taking the dish, began to cut the morsel which Nizib was devouring with his eyes.

"Well," he said at last.

"Yes, it is mutton," replied Bruno; "it ought to be mutton, for we have met with so many flocks of sheep on our journey. Indeed, I believe that there are only sheep in this country, now I come to think of it!"

"Very well," said Nizib, holding out his plate.

"Wait a moment, Nizib, wait. In your interest I must make certain of this. You understand, though we are at some distance from the frontier, the cooking is still Russian, and we must beware of the Russians."

"I tell you, M. Bruno, that in this case no mistake is possible."

"No," said Bruno, who was busy eating. "No, it *is* really mutton, nevertheless——"

"Eh?" said Nizib.

"One might say," continued Bruno, as he bolted piece after piece. "One might say——

"Not so fast, M. Bruno."

"Hum. If this *is* mutton it has a most peculiar taste."

"Ah! I will just know what it is," cried Nizib, who, despite his calm temperament, was beginning to be angry.

"Take care, Nizib, take care!"

So saying, Bruno quickly swallowed the remaining morsels of the food.

"That is the end of it, M. Bruno!"

"Yes, Nizib, that is the finish. I am convinced you were quite right this time."

"It was mutton then."

"Decidedly, mutton."

"I will soon ascertain," replied Nizib.—*See page* 96.

"Which you have devoured!"

"Devoured, Nizib! Ah, that is a word which I cannot admit. Devoured? No! I have merely tasted it."

"And a nice supper *I* have had!" said Nizib, in a piteous tone. "It seems to me, M. Bruno, that you might as well have left me my share, and not have eaten it all to satisfy yourself that——"

"That it was mutton in fact," said Bruno. "My conscience obliged me——"

"Say, your stomach rather."

"Obliged me to ascertain what it was," continued Bruno. "After all, there is not much room for regret, Nizib."

"But if——"

"No; you could not have eaten it."

"Why not?"

"Because it was dressed with lard, Nizib; you understand, lard! Lard is not orthodox."

Then Bruno rose from table with the air of a man who has supped well, and re-entered the common room, followed by the discomfited Nizib.

Seigneur Kéraban, Ahmet, and Van Mitten lay extended upon the benches, but had not been able to snatch a moment's repose. The tempest was increasing in fury. The planks of the wooden structure creaked loudly. The occupants feared that the lighthouse would be demolished. The hurricane shook the door and rattled the window-shutters as if they were being "butted" by a mad bull; and they had to be firmly secured. But by the shocks of the lighthouse "scaffolding" encased in the wall they were enabled to estimate what the force of the wind was fifty feet above the roof. Would the lighthouse be able to resist the tempest? would the gleam of the lanthorn be extinguished? would it still illumine the straits of Atina, when the sea now ran in "mountains high?" All this was doubtful, and such doubts were full of grave eventualities. It was then half-past eleven at night.

"It is quite impossible to sleep here," remarked Kéraban, as he rose and paced the apartment.

"No, indeed," replied Ahmet, "and if the storm should increase, this hut will be endangered. I think we should be prepared for any eventuality."

"Are you asleep, Van Mitten? Can you sleep?" asked Kéraban, as he shook his friend.

"I was dozing," replied Van Mitten.

"Look what placid people can do!" cried Kéraban. "Under circumstances in which no one else can snatch a moment's rest, a Dutchman will manage to sleep!"

"I never remember such a night as this," remarked one of the light-keepers. "The wind is dead ashore, and who knows but by morning the sea will be strewn with wreckage."

"Were there any vessels in sight this evening?" asked Ahmet.

"No, fortunately, at least not at sunset," replied the keeper. "When I went up to light the lanthorn I could see nothing in the offing. That is lucky, for the channels of Atina are dangerous; and even with the light, which can be seen for five miles, it is difficult to weather them."

At that moment a gust of more than ordinary fury blew the door into the middle of the room as if it would knock the whole thing to splinters.

But Seigneur Kéraban threw himself against the door, and, struggling with the furious wind, succeeded in closing the aperture with the assistance of the keeper.

"What a headstrong wind," he cried, "but I was the more determined!"

"A terrible tempest indeed," said Ahmet.

"Terrible," acquiesced Van Mitten. "It is almost comparable with the storms from the Atlantic which beat upon the coast of Holland."

"Oh!" said Kéraban, "you can scarcely compare them!"

"Just think a moment, Kéraban," said Van Mitten. "They are storms which come all across the ocean from America."

"And how can the tempests of the Atlantic compare with those of the Black Sea, Van Mitten?"

"Friend Kéraban, I do not wish to contradict you, but really——"

"Really you are about to contradict me," replied Kéraban, who was not in the best of tempers.

"No, I merely say——"

"You say——?"

"I say that, compared with the ocean—with the Atlantic—the Black Sea is but a lake!"

"A lake!" exclaimed Kéraban, drawing himself up! "By Allah! Did you say a lake?"

"An immense lake, if you please," replied Van Mitten, who sought to modify his terms, "a large lake, but a lake nevertheless."

"Why not a pond?"

"I said nothing about a pond."

"Why not a pool?"

"I did not say a pool."

"Why not a cistern?"

"I never hinted at a cistern."

"No, Van Mitten, but you thought so."

"I assure you——"

"Very well, so be it—a cistern, but when some cataclysm occurs and throws your Holland into this cistern it will be entirely swallowed up in it. Cistern indeed!"

And muttering this word between his teeth Seigneur Kéraban continued to pace the room.

"I am quite certain I never used the word cistern," remarked Van Mitten, who was quite disconcerted. "Believe me, my young friend," he added, adressing Ahmet, "that I never even thought of such a term. The Atlantic——"

"Quite so, M. Van Mitten. But I do not think this is either the time or place to discuss the question," replied Ahmet.

"Cistern," muttered the inflexible Kéraban. Then he halted to look his Dutch friend in the face, but Van Mitten did not dare to take up the cudgels for Holland, which Kéraban had threatened with submersion in the Black Sea.

For quite an hour after this the tempest continued to increase in fury. The caretakers, very anxious, went out from time to time to observe the wooden structure which sustained the light. Their guests, overcome by fatigue, had once more stretched themselves on the benches, and sought repose for a few hours.

Suddenly, about two o'clock in the morning, masters and servants were all aroused from their lethargy. The windows, the shutters of which had already been wrenched off, were blown in with a crash; and, during the momentary lull which succeeded the furious gust, the report of a cannon was heard from the offing.

---

## CHAPTER IV.

### IN THUNDER AND LIGHTNING.

ALL the occupants of the hut rose hurriedly and rushed to the windows to look out upon the sea. The waves, scattered in foam by the wind, were dashing more violently against the lighthouse. The darkness was profound, and it was impossible to see anything, even at a few paces distant, unless when the vivid flashes of lightning illuminated the horizon.

It was in one of these flashes that Ahmet reported some object which appeared and disappeared in the distance.

"It must be a ship!" he cried.

"If there be a ship there, the crew must have fired that cannon," remarked Kéraban.

"I will ascend into the gallery," said one of the light-keepers as he advanced towards a little wooden staircase which opened and led upwards from one of the corners of the sitting-room.

"I will accompany you," said Ahmet.

All this while, Kéraban, Van Mitten, Bruno, and the other guardian, notwithstanding the tempest and the spray, remained standing in the bays of the broken windows.

Ahmet and his companion were not long in reaching the platform, which, on a level with the roof of the hut, served as a base for the scaffolding which sustained the lanthorn. Thence in the spaces between the beams which were fixed by cross-ties and formed the "tower," a rough staircase ascended in sixty steps to the upper part of the structure which contained the light.

The hurricane was so fierce, that it was an undertaking of no small danger to ascend this stairway. The solid supports oscillated from their bases. Ahmet frequently was obliged to cling to the balustrade so firmly that he began to imagine he would never be able to let go; but, taking advantage of a slight lull, he was able to ascend a few more steps, and, following the keeper, who was quite as embarrassed as Ahmet himself, he managed to reach the upper gallery.

What a sight he beheld! A terrific sea dashing its enormous waves against the rocks; thick clouds of spray drove like rain above the lanthorn, while great mountains of water reared their crests in the offing still distinguishable by the atmospheric reflection; a sky of inky hue, covered with low clouds which chased each other with tremendous speed across the firmament, sometimes discovering as they parted, other masses of vapour more elevated, from which at times escaped the long livid flashes—so silent and so pale—reflections which told of another storm raging at a still greater distance above.

" It was an undertaking of no small danger."

Ahmet and the light-keeper, crouching and holding tightly to the supports of the gallery, right and left, gazed seaward, seeking either the moving point already noticed or the flash of the cannon which would indicate the direction of the vessel.

Neither of the men spoke—it would have been impossible to hear each other, but their view embraced a considerable segment of the sea. The light of the lanthorn, surrounded by powerful reflectors, could not dazzle them, as it threw its brilliant rays of light before them to a distance of several miles.

But there was also a continual fear that the lanthorn would be extinguished, and frequently the gusts of wind would reduce the flame to the very lowest ebb of light, threatening to extinguish it altogether. Birds, too, blinded by the storm, came dashing blindly against the lanthorn, like so many insects attracted by the light of a lamp, and bruised themselves against the iron grating which protected the apparatus. The force of the wind was so great that the upper part of the lighthouse oscillated frightfully. Nor need we be surprised at this, for the stone lighthouses in Europe, at times, rock so much that the pendulums of the clocks are stopped. All the more reason therefore for the oscillation of these wooden structures, which cannot possess the solidity of stone-work. In the particular case of which we are writing, Seigneur Kéraban, who felt ill while crossing the Bosphorus, would have experienced all the horrors of sea-sickness had he stood on the gallery of the lighthouse.

Ahmet and the light-keeper sought to perceive the moving speck which they had already noticed in the sea. But, either it had disappeared or the flashes of lightning did not illuminate the spot it occupied. If it were a ship it was but too probable that the vessel had already been dashed to pieces by the tempest.

Suddenly Ahmet pointed towards the horizon. His eyes did not deceive him. An extraordinary meteor came along the surface of the sea, extending from the edges of the clouds.

Two columns, of vesicular shape, gaseous at the tops, liquid at the bases, united by a conical point and animated by a simultaneous rotatory movement of extreme velocity, presented a vast concavity to the wind, which was blowing fiercely over the waters, and causing the waves to form a whirlpool. In the intervals of the storm a sharp whistling noise could be heard, of such intensity that it must have been audible at a great distance. Frequent vivid flashes of forked lightning showed out the enormous body of the water-spout in strong relief, and then again it was lost in the darkness.

Suddenly, at a little distance from these water-spouts, the exact cause of which has never been accurately determined, a vivid flash was succeeded by a loud detonation.

"A cannon!" exclaimed Ahmet, extending his hand in the direction of the sound.

The light-keeper also concentrated his gaze upon the spot indicated.

"There, there!" he exclaimed; and by the glare of a tremendous flash of lightning, Ahmet perceived a vessel of considerable tonnage battling with the storm.

It was a felucca, disabled, her great lateen-sail in ribbons: without any power of resistance, she was driving helplessly on shore. With the rocks to leeward, and in the vicinity of the water-spouts which were proceeding towards her, it appeared impossible that she could escape destruction. It seemed merely a question of minutes, whether she was dashed to pieces or swamped.

Nevertheless, she bore up bravely. Perhaps, if she could escape the water-spouts, she would find a current which would carry her towards the harbour of Atina. Even scudding under bare poles, she might hit upon the channel, the direction of which was indicated by the lighthouse. It was her sole chance.

So the vessel was endeavouring to rid herself of the nearer of the two columns of water which threatened to drag her into the vortex around its base. Hence the firing of the cannon: the shots were for defence, not signals of distress. It was necessary to break these columns of water, and the gunners succeeded in their aim, but imperfectly. A shot cut through the column about one-third of the way up; the two portions separated, floating in space like the "trunks" of some fantastic animal; then they re-united and resumed their rotatory movement, sucking up the air and water as they revolved.

It was then three o'clock in the morning, and the vessel was still driving towards the opening of the channel. At that moment, a tremendous blast shook the tower from base to summit. Ahmet and the keeper feared the timbers would be uprooted from the ground. They found it therefore advis-

"A cannon," exclaimed Ahmet.

able to descend and seek shelter in the hut as quickly as possible. But the descent was not accomplished without difficulty and danger.

"Well?" asked Kéraban, when they again appeared in the room.

"There is a ship," replied Ahmet.

"In danger?"

"The doomed vessel rushed to destruction."

"Yes," replied the keeper—"at least unless it happens to find the channel of Atina."

"But can it do so?"

"Yes, if the captain is acquainted with the straits; the light indicates their direction."

"Can we do anything to guide the crew, or carry them assistance?" asked Kéraban.

"Nothing!" was the reply.

As he spoke, a fearful flash of lightning, followed immediately by a tremendous peal of thunder, almost paralysed Kéraban and his companions. It was a miracle that none of them were struck, if not directly, by the return-stroke. At the same time, a loud noise was heard, and a heavy mass came falling through the roof. The furious wind entered through the aperture, and levelled the wooden walls of the hut to the ground.

Providentially, none of those who were within were injured. The roof had fallen towards the right, while the travellers and their hosts were gathered in the left corner near the door.

"Outside, outside!" exclaimed one of the keepers, rushing out upon the rocks. They all followed him, and at once understood the cause of the catastrophe. The lightning had struck the lighthouse, and loosened the upper part, which in its fall, had demolished the roof, and the storm had completed the destruction of the hut.

Now, there was no longer a light to indicate the channel into the harbour of refuge. So, even if the vessel should escape the water-spouts, nothing could prevent her from being dashed to pieces on the reefs.

The spectators could perceive her carried helplessly along, while the columns of air and water whirled around her. Scarcely half a cable's length intervened between the vessel and an enormous rock which stood out of the water, some fifty feet or more from the north-west extremity of the harbour. On this rock, the vessel would inevitably strike, break up, and perish.

Kéraban and his companions paced the beach, regarding with horror the sad and terrible sight; powerless to assist the crew of the distressed ship; scarcely able themselves to resist the violence of the wind which covered them with spray and sand mixed with sea-water.

Some fishermen came hurrying up, perhaps to dispute over the timbers of the doomed ship which the hurricane was driving to destruction on the rocks. But Kéraban and his companions did not regard the men in that light. They wished them to do all they could for the rescue of the shipwrecked crew: they desired more—that they would indicate the passage, and guide the steersman to the channel; for might not some current carry them in, and so avoid the shoals right and left?

"Torches! bring torches!" cried Kéraban. Immediately some resinous pine-branches, torn from the adjacent trees, were lighted, and their dusky glare replaced in a measure the light of the lanthorn which had been extinguished.

Nevertheless, the doomed vessel rushed to destruction. While the lightning flashes lasted, the spectators could see the men on board working the ship. The captain was endeavouring to rig up a square sail, so as to steer her upon the beach, but, scarcely had he succeeded in getting it up when it was blown to ribbons, and the fragments were carried ashore like a covey of stormy petrels.

The prow of the little vessel was sometimes elevated high in air, and then plunged into a gulf where it was swallowed up, and appeared as if it had struck upon a submerged rock and would never rise again.

"Poor creatures!" cried Kéraban. "Can nothing be done to save them?"

"Nothing," replied the fishermen.

"A thousand piastres—ten thousand—a hundred thousand—to any who will afford them assistance," exclaimed Kéraban, excitedly.

But these offers were not accepted. It was impossible to swim in such a sea. Perhaps, with a rocket apparatus, one could have established communication; but no such apparatus was to be had, and the little port of Atina did not even boast a life-boat.

"But we cannot let the people perish!" repeated Kéraban, who could contain himself no longer.

Ahmet and his companions were perfectly powerless.

Suddenly a cry from the deck of the doomed vessel made Ahmet start violently. He fancied he heard his name called—yes, his name had been pronounced distinctly amid all the uproar of the elements. In fact this was the case, for during a lull the cry was repeated plainly—

"Ahmet! Ahmet! Help!"

Who could be calling on him thus? His heart beat violently under the pressure of a terrible presentiment. That vessel! he seemed to recognize it, he had seen it before! Where? Was it not at Odessa, in front of the villa of the banker Selim, on the very day when he had left it?

"Ahmet—Ahmet!"

Again the cry resounded through the storm.

Kéraban, Van Mitten, Bruno, Nizib came close to the young man, who with his arms

"Ahmet succeeded in pulling himself up on the rock."

extended towards the sea remained as if petrified.

"Your name—it is your name," said Kéraban.

"Yes, yes," replied Ahmet — "my name."

At that moment a flash of lightning which must have lasted two seconds—for it extended from one side of the horizon to the other—lit up the scene. In the midst of that brilliant illumination the vessel appeared as clearly as if it had been designed in white by some electrical effulgence. The main-mast was struck by the lightning, and burned like a torch in the midst of the hurricane.

At the stern of the felucca, two females, two young girls, stood wrapped in a close embrace, and from their lips escaped the supplication—"Ahmet, Ahmet!"

"She! 'Tis she—Amasia!" exclaimed the young man as he leaped upon one of the rocks.

"Ahmet, Ahmet," cried Kéraban in his turn warningly.

He rushed towards his nephew, not to prevent but to assist him if necessary.

"Ahmet, Ahmet!"

Once more the name was carried across the raging water. Doubt was no longer possible.

"I come, I come," screamed Ahmet, and precipitating himself from the rock into the foaming water, he disappeared.

Almost at the same moment, one of the water-spouts reached the bow of the vessel, which was sucked into the vortex and cast upon the reefs to the left, not far from that particular rock which rose from the waves near the north-west point. On this the little vessel was beaten with a noise which was audible over the roaring of the tempest, then it sank in an instant, and the water-spout as if it too had been broken by the shock against the rock, exploded like a gigantic bomb-shell; the watery base mingling with the sea, while the whirling vapoury column was dissipated in the atmosphere.

It seemed certain that all on board the felucca had been lost, as well as the courageous young man who had gone to the assistance of the two girls.

Kéraban himself wished to plunge into the waves, and was only withheld forcibly by his companions from certain death.

Meanwhile, by the light of the flashes, Ahmet could be perceived. He had, by almost superhuman efforts, succeeded in pulling himself up on the rock, holding on his arm one of the shipwrecked maidens. The other clinging to his garments climbed up with him. But no others appeared. No doubt the crew had all perished, as they had cast themselves into the sea when the water-spout struck the ship; so these two were the only survivors of the shipwreck.

Ahmet, as soon as he had climbed out of reach of the waves, paused for an instant to gaze upon the distance which separated him from the point of the channel. The space was more than fifteen feet, but, taking advantage of the retreat of an enormous wave which left but little water upon the sand, he rushed ashore with his burthen, followed by the other young woman, and reached the beach in safety.

A moment later he was surrounded by his friends, and fell on the shingle, overcome by emotion and fatigue, after he had placed in their arms the girl he had saved.

"Amasia, Amasia!" cried Kéraban.

Yes, it was Amasia, indeed: Amasia whom he had left at Odessa, the daughter of his friend Selim. She had been on board the felucca, and had been shipwrecked three hundred leagues away from Odessa, at the other extremity of the Black Sea! With her was Nedjeb, her servant. What could have happened? But neither Amasia nor the young Zingara could just then explain matters, for both girls had fainted.

Seigneur Kéraban took Amasia in his arms, while one of the lighthouse keepers assisted Nedjeb. Ahmet soon came to himself, but seemed like a man in a dream; he did not appear to realize the actuality of the scene. The whole party then made their way towards the little town of Atina, where one of the fishermen had offered them shelter.

Amasia and Nedjeb were placed before the hearth, on which a bright fire of vine-stalks was burning.

Ahmet bent down and raised up Amasia's head. He called her by her name, and said—

"Amasia, my dear Amasia! She does not hear me! She does not answer. Ah! she is dead. I will die too!"

"No, she is not dead," replied Kéraban. "She breathes, Ahmet. She is alive!"

# KÉRABAN THE INFLEXIBLE;

## OR, ADVENTURES IN THE EUXINE.

By Jules Verne.

Translated by HENRY FRITH.

### Chapter IV.

AT that very time Nedjeb recovered consciousness; and, throwing herself upon Amasia, exclaimed—

"My mistress, my dearest mistress! Yes, she lives—her eyes are opening."

And in fact the lids were slowly rising and discovering the girl's eyes.

"Amasia, Amasia," cried Ahmet.

"Ahmet, my dear Ahmet," she replied. Kéraban enfolded them both in his embrace.

"But what felucca was that?" asked Ahmet at length.

"The same we visited, Seigneur Ahmet, after you left Odessa," replied Nedjeb.

"The *Guidare*, Captain Yarhud's ship?"

"Yes, he carried us off."

"For whom was he acting, then?"

"That we do not know."

"Whither were you bound?"

"That we are also ignorant of," replied Amasia. "But you are here: I can remember nothing else."

"*I* will not forget," said Kéraban sternly.

If he had turned round at that moment, he would have perceived a man, who had been spying at the door of the hut, hurry away at top speed.

It was Yarhud, the Maltese Captain, the only sailor surviving. Almost immediately he rushed away unnoticed in a direction opposite to the little town of Atina.

Yarhud had heard everything. He knew now that, by some inconceivable fatality, Ahmet had reached the coast when the *Guidare* was wrecked, just as Amasia was about to perish.

Having passed the last houses, Yarhud stopped at a turn of the road.

"It is a long way from Atina to the Bosphorus," he muttered, "and on the road I will find a way to carry out Seigneur Saffar's orders."

### Chapter V.

#### How our Travellers Talked, and what they Saw, on the road between Atina and Trebizond.

How happy the young lovers were to be thus united again; how grateful they were to Allah for bringing Ahmet to the very place where the storm wrecked the vessel; and how they experienced one of those mingled impressions of joy and terror the remembrance of which is ineffaceable—it is useless to describe.

But it will be readily understood that Ahmet, as well as Kéraban, was very anxious to know all that had taken place since their departure from Odessa; so Amasia, aided by Nedjeb, could not delay to inform them of all the details.

It is of course understood that change of costume had been procured for the young girls, and that Ahmet himself was arrayed in rustic garb; that everyone, master as well as servant, was enjoying the fire, without any regard for the storm which was now blowing itself out.

With what feelings did the listeners learn all that had passed at the villa a few hours after Kéraban's departure. No, it was not to sell precious stuffs that Yarhud had cast anchor in the little bay. It was to carry out his vile plot, and everyone perceived that the scheme must have been maturing for some time.

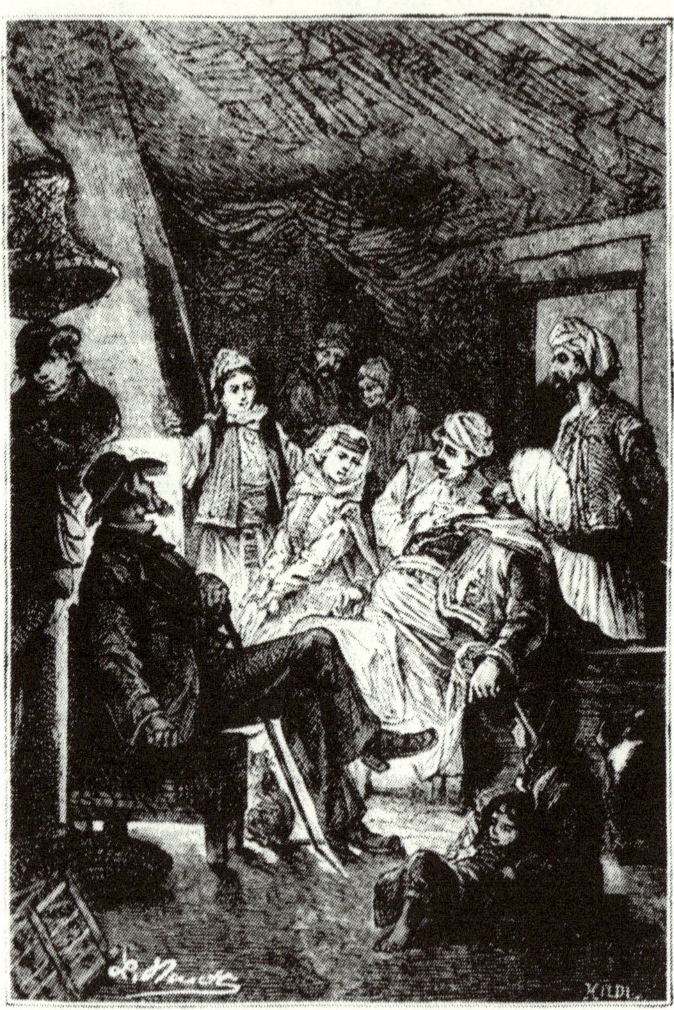

" Everyone - master as well as servant—was enjoying the fire."

The vessel had put to sea as soon as the girls had been taken on board, but neither of them could tell that Selim had heard their cries and that he had rushed out just as the *Guidare* had cleared the rocks at the extremity of the bay, that he had been wounded and had fallen—perhaps had died —without having been able to put anyone on the track of the ravishers.

Amasia had little to tell concerning their treatment on board. The captain had evidently taken particular care of her and Nedjeb, under powerful authority. The cabin occupied by the girls was most comfortable, and there they ate and slept. They were permitted to go on deck when they pleased; but they were closely watched, for fear they should attempt to escape

"The passage had at first been good."

by death the fate which threatened them.

Ahmet listened to their recital with beating heart. He wished to know whether the captain had acted on his own account, and carried off the girls to sell them in one of the slave-markets of Asia Minor; or whether he was acting for some rich citizen of Anatolia.

To that question neither Amasia nor Nedjeb could reply. To all their demands and protestations, Yarhud had vouchsafed no reply. They could not tell for whom the captain had acted, nor—and this was what Ahmet particularly desired to ascertain—whither the *Guidare* had been bound.

The passage had at first been good, but slow because of calms. These delays were evidently very galling to the captain, who was at no pains to conceal his impatience. So the prisoners concluded—and Ahmet and Kéraban were of the same opinion—that Yarhud had arranged to arrive at a specified time;—but where? Of that they were ignorant, though it was certain that the *Guidare* was expected at some port of Asia Minor on the Black Sea.

At length the calms ceased, and the vessel sailed eastwards, or, as Amasia said, towards the rising sun. For two weeks she proceeded thus without incident to break the monotony of the voyage. Many times vessels were perceived; steamers, war ships, and merchantmen passed or overtook the *Guidare;* but Captain Yarhud always obliged the prisoners to go below on these occasions, for fear they would give the alarm or show some signal of distress.

Then the weather began to look threatening: it got worse, and then very bad indeed. Two days before the *Guidare* was wrecked, a violent tempest arose. Amasia and Nedjeb perceived, from the anger of the captain, that he had been obliged to alter his course and that the storm was forcing him out of his way. The girls rather enjoyed the storm, inasmuch as it was removing them from the dreaded termination of the voyage.

"Yes, dear Ahmet," said Amasia in conclusion. "When I reflected on the fate that awaited me, carried away where I should never see you again, my resolve was taken. Nedjeb knew it: she would not have prevented me. Before the vessel had reached her destination, I would have thrown myself into the sea. But the tempest came. The very thing which threatened to destroy us, was the means of our safety. My own Ahmet, you came through the furious waves to my assistance. Never shall I forget that: never!"

"Dearest Amasia," replied Ahmet, "Allah willed that you should be saved, and saved by me! But if I had not anticipated my uncle, he would have rushed to your assistance."

"By Mahomet, that is true, I believe," exclaimed Kéraban.

"Fancy such a hard-headed man having such a soft heart!" murmured Nedjeb, involuntarily.

"Ah! that little lady aroused me," said Kéraban. "And now, my friends, confess that my obstinacy does good sometimes!"

"Sometimes?" exclaimed Van Mitten, very incredulous on this point; "I should just like to know——"

"No doubt, friend Van Mitten. If I had yielded to Ahmet's fancies, if we had travelled by railway instead of skirting the shore, Ahmet would not have been at the place to save his *fiancée* from shipwreck."

"No! quite right," replied Van Mitten, "but if you had not compelled him to quit Odessa, the abduction would not have taken place, and ——"

"Ah! that is the way you argue, is it?" retorted Kéraban. "You want to discuss the subject?"

"No! no!" exclaimed Ahmet, who knew, that in a discussion of this kind, the Dutchman would come off second-best. "It is too late to go into all the *pros* and *cons* now; much better take some rest——"

"In view of our departure to-morrow," added Kéraban.

"To-morrow, uncle! To-morrow! Why Amasia and Nedjeb must have some repose."

"Oh! I am quite strong, Ahmet, and to-morrow——"

"Ah! nephew," said Kéraban, "you are not in such a hurry now you have got my little Amasia with you. Nevertheless, the end of the month is approaching—the fatal day draws near, and we have interests we cannot afford to neglect. You must permit an old merchant to be more practical than you. So let each one sleep as well as he, or she, can; and to-morrow, when we have found a conveyance, we will continue our journey."

They installed themselves as well as they could in the fisherman's hut, and were quite as comfortable as they could possibly have been in one of the inns of Atina. Every member of the party, after so much excitement, was quite ready to rest for some hours. Van Mitten dreamt that he was again engaged in a discussion with his intractable friend: the latter dreamed that he was face to face with Seigneur Saffar, upon whom he was heaping all the maledictions of Allah and his prophet.

Ahmet only could not sleep. The desire to ascertain for what purpose Amasia had been carried away by Yarhud disquieted him, not only as regards the past, but for fear in the future. He kept thinking whether all danger had disappeared with the *Guidare.* Certainly he had reason to believe that not one of the crew had escaped, and he was quite unaware that Captain Yarhud had emerged from the shipwreck safe and sound. But the catastrophe would soon become known in the adjacent districts. The person for whom Yarhud had been acting—some rich merchant no doubt, or perhaps some pacha of the Anatolian provinces—would soon become acquainted with what had occurred. It would not be very difficult for him to put himself upon the girl's track. Between Trebizond and Scutari, across the deserted province through which the highway ran—what dangers might not be accumulated, what traps set, what ambushes prepared!

Ahmet, therefore, made up his mind to watch most carefully. He would never again separate himself from Amasia. He would himself undertake the leadership of the caravan, and would, when necessary, select some trustworthy guide who would be able to lead the party by the shortest route along the shore.

At the same time Ahmet determined to put the banker Selim in possession of all the circumstances relating to the abduction of his daughter. It was most important that Selim should be informed concerning Amasia's safety, so that he might appear at Scutari on the appointed day—in a fortnight. But a letter forwarded from Atina or Trebizond would not reach Odessa in time. So Ahmet resolved to "wire" without saying a word about it to his uncle—who would almost have a fit at the very mention of the word "telegram"—and forward a telegraphic message to Selim *viâ* Trebizond. He made up his mind to advise him that probably all danger was not over, and that Selim must not hesitate to come to meet the little caravan, *en route.*

Next morning, the 15th September, as soon as Ahmet met Amasia he acquainted her with his designs—partly at least—and without laying any particular stress upon the dangers which he fancied would ensue. Amasia perceived only one idea, viz., that her father would be re-assured concerning her safety, and in the very shortest possible time. So Ahmet and Amasia were very anxious to reach Trebizond, whence a telegram might be despatched without Uncle Kéraban knowing anything about it.

After some hours' sleep, Kéraban was more impatient than ever; Van Mitten resigned to all the caprices of his friend; Bruno endeavouring to ascertain how much of his figure still remained within his loose clothing, and only replying to his master in monosyllables.

First of all Ahmet searched Atina through. It is an unimportant town, which, as its name indicates, was formerly the "Athens" of the Black Sea. There are still existent some columns of the Doric order of architecture remaining in the Temple of Pallas. But if these ruins interested Van Mitten they had no attraction whatever for Ahmet. He would have much preferred to find some means of conveyance less rough, less primitive than the cart he had secured on the frontier. But it was absolutely necessary to return to the *araba*, which was specially reserved for the two young girls. Then there was need to provide mounts—horses, donkeys, or mules—so that masters and servants might reach Trebizond.

Bruno complained of the journey.

Ah, how Kéraban regretted the post-chaise smashed at Poti! And what recriminations and menaces did he not send to the address of the haughty Saffar, who was responsible, according to Kéraban, for all the mischief.

As for Amasia and Nedjeb nothing could be more agreeable to them than the journey in the *araba*. It was a quite new and unexpected experience. They would not have exchanged the vehicle for the finest carriage of the Padischah. How comfortable they would be under the tilt upon a litter of fresh straw, which could be easily renewed at every stage. From time to time they would offer a place beside them to Seigneur Kéraban, or young Ahmet, or Van Mitten! And the riders would escort them as if they were princesses! In fine it was perfectly charming!

It will be surmised that these foolish ideas emanated from the brain of the simple Nedjeb, who was so transported as to look upon things only on the good side. Amasia could not complain, since Ahmet was near her, and the journey was about to be completed under conditions so different, and with so little delay, to Scutari.

"I am certain," repeated Nedjeb, "that if we stood on tip-toe we should see the place!"

In fact, in the whole company there were only two individuals who had any misgivings—Seigneur Kéraban, who feared some delay in consequence of not finding a proper conveyance, and Bruno, who found that thirty-five leagues—and thirty-five leagues on mule-back—intervened between him and Trebizond, where, as Nizib confided to him, some more comfortable means of transport would surely be obtainable to cross the plains of Anatolia.

So, on the morning of the 15th September at eleven, the cavalcade quitted Atina. The tempest had been so violent that it had quickly subsided, and a perfect calm reigned in the atmosphere. The clouds which floated high in the air remained almost motionless though still lacerated by the wind. The sun shot out a few rays now and then, and lighted up the landscape. The sea alone was still agitated and beat fiercely on the beach.

Seigneur Kéraban and his companions traversed Western Lazistan as quickly as possible, with the intention to reach Trebizond before nightfall. The roads were by no means deserted. The travellers passed many caravans in which camels were numbered by hundreds, and the ear was deafened by the clang and jingle of the various bells which the animals carried round their necks, while the eye was amused by the varied and brilliant colours of their trappings. These caravans were coming from Persia or proceeding thither.

The sea-shore was not any less lively than the roads. The entire fishing population seemed to have assembled there. The fishermen at night-fall, their boats lighted up at the stern with burning resin, took in considerable quantities of the species of anchovy known as *khamsi*, of which they cure thousands all along the coast of Anatolia, and even as far as Central Armenia. The hunters on the other hand had no reason to envy the fishermen, for game was quite as plentiful as fish. Thousands of sea-birds of the grebe species—*konkarinas*—flock to these districts of Asia Minor. So the immense number slain for their feathers, which are much sought after, recompense the hunters for the time, the trouble, and the expense of ammunition incurred in procuring them.

About three o'clock in the afternoon the little caravan halted at Mapavra, situated at the mouth of the river of the same name, the waters of which are mixed with an oily stream of petroleum, which falls from the neighbouring springs. Three o'clock was a little too early for dinner, but as the party could not reach their camping place until quite late in the evening, it seemed only prudent to take some sustenance. This was at any rate Bruno's advice, and it had due weight.

Of course there was an abundance of *khamsis* on the table, which are the most esteemed food of the district. These anchovies are served cured and fresh, to please all palates; but there were, besides, more substantial dishes, to which our travellers paid their attention. So good humour reigned amongst them, and good humour is the best seasoning after all.

"Well, Van Mitten," said Kéraban, "do you regret the wilfulness—the legitimate obstinacy — of your friend and correspondent, which has compelled you to make this journey?"

"No, Kéraban, no," replied Van Mitten, "and I will continue it whenever you please."

"We shall see — we shall see," said Kéraban. "And you, my little Amasia, what do you think of your wicked uncle who carried away your Ahmet?"

"That he is what I have always known him to be—the best of men," replied Amasia.

"And the most accommodating," added Nedjeb. "It seems to me that Seigneur Kéraban is not quite so obstinate as he used to be."

"Good!" cried Kéraban, with a loud laugh, "that stupid girl is quizzing me!"

"No, indeed, seigneur—no, indeed."

"But, yes, indeed! Bah! you are right: I no longer argue—I am no more obstinate. Even Van Mitten here would not succeed in provoking me."

"Oh! that remains to be proved!" replied the Dutchman, shaking his head dubiously.

"It has been proved, Van Mitten."

"If they were to get you on certain subjects——"

"You are quite mistaken, I swear!"

"Do not swear."

"But I will swear!" replied Kéraban, becoming excited. "Why should not I swear?"

"Because it's so often difficult to keep an oath."

"Less difficult to keep than to hold one's tongue, in any case, Van Mitten; for it is quite evident at this moment, and just for the pleasure of contradicting me——"

"I, friend Kéraban!"

"Yes, you; and when I tell you that I am resolved never again to be obstinate about trifles, I beg you will not be so, just to prove the contrary."

"You see you are quite wrong this time, Monsieur Van Mitten," said Ahmet, "absolutely wrong!"

"Entirely wrong," continued Amasia, with a smile.

"Altogether wrong," added Nedjeb.

So the worthy Dutchman, finding the majority against him, thought it best to say no more.

But, after all the lessons he had received, and particularly during this journey so imprudently entered upon, and which might yet end disastrously—was Kéraban so "tamed" as he wished people to believe? That was to be seen; but no doubt everyone was secretly of Van Mitten's opinion. It was indeed an open question whether the bump of combativeness was reduced on the head of this Inflexible One.

"*En route*," said Kéraban, when dinner was over. "This meal has been an excellent one, but I know a better!"

"Which is that?" asked Van Mitten.

"The dinner which awaits us at Scutari!"

The party resumed their journey at four o'clock, and at eight the same evening reached the village of Rize. Then they found they must pass the night in a rather uncomfortable khan—so uncomfortable, indeed, that the young women of the party preferred to remain in the *araba*. The important question turned on rest and forage for the horses; fortunately straw and corn were in sufficiency in the racks. Kéraban and his companions had only one litter at their disposal, but it was dry and fresh, and they contented themselves with it. Next night they hoped to rest in Trebizond, with all the comfort that the best of the hotels in that town could afford.

As for Ahmet, whether the sleeping accommodation was good or bad, it made no difference to him. He would not be able to sleep with suspicion in his mind, for he was always in fear for the safety of Amasia, and confessed to himself that all danger had not been passed with the wreck of the *Guidare*; so he stood sentinel, well armed, near the khan.

Ahmet was right to do so. He had reason to fear, for Captain Yarhud had not lost sight of the party all day. He followed in their tracks, but kept out of sight; for Ahmet knew him as well as the two girls did. As he watched, he resolved upon his plans to recapture the prey which had escaped him, and at all hazards—he had written to Scarpante. This creature of Saffar's, as had been already arranged, was waiting at Trebizond, and Yarhud had appointed to meet him at the caravanserai of Rissar, about three miles from the town, without, however, telling him of the shipwreck and its sad consequences.

So Ahmet had only too good reason to be

on his guard. His presentiments did not deceive him. Yarhud approached near enough to assure himself that the young girls were sleeping in their *araba*. Fortunately for himself, he also saw Ahmet on the watch, and was enabled to retire without being perceived.

But this time, instead of remaining behind the caravan, he started westward along the road to Trebizond, so as to get in front of Kéraban and his party. Before their arrival in the town he wished to confer with Scarpante. So, mounting his horse, which he had ridden from Atina, he proceeded rapidly towards the caravanserai of Rissar.

Next day, the 16th September, as soon as daylight appeared, the whole party were on foot and in high spirits, except Bruno, who was wondering how many more pounds he would lose before he reached Scutari.

"My little Amasia," said Kéraban, rubbing his hands together, "come and let me embrace you."

"Willingly, uncle," she replied, "if you will let me always call you so."

"If I will permit you, my dear child! You may call me your father. Is not Ahmet as a son to me?"

"He is so, uncle Kéraban," said Ahmet, "so much so that he comes to give you an order, as it is right a son should do!"

"What order?"

"To depart at once. The horses are ready, and we must reach Trebizond this morning, you know."

"And so we will," cried Kéraban, "and quit it at sunrise to-morrow. Well, Van Mitten, you see it is fated that you shall visit Trebizond."

"Yes, Trebizond! What a splendid name for a town," exclaimed the Dutchman. "Trebizond and its hill where the Ten Thousand under Xenophon exhibited their games and combats under the presidency of Dracentius, if I may believe my guide-book. In truth, friend Kéraban, I shall not be at all sorry to see Trebizond."

"Well, you will carry away some important reminiscences of this journey, Van Mitten."

"They might have been fuller, perhaps."

"At anyrate, you have had nothing to complain of."

"It is not over yet," whispered Bruno to his master, like an oracle of evil omen charged to remind men of the instability of human affairs.

The caravan left the khan at 7 o'clock A.M. The weather was improving, and the sky was rapidly clearing.

At mid-day, they halted at Of, on the Ophis of the ancients, where the old Grecian race still survives. They dined at a small inn, on the supplies obtained from the *araba*, which were, however, nearly exhausted.

Besides, the innkeeper did not trouble himself about his guests, for his wife was very ill, and he was at his wits' end. There was no doctor in the district, and to send to Trebizond for one would be too great an expense for a poor hotel-keeper.

So it followed that Kéraban, aided by Van Mitten, undertook the office of *hakim*, or physician, and prescribed some simple drugs which could be obtained easily at Trebizond.

"May Allah protect you, seigneur," said the stingy husband; "but what will these drugs cost me?"

"Twenty piastres," replied Kéraban.

"Twenty piastres!" exclaimed the man; "why, for that sum I can buy another wife!"

And so saying he turned away, not without thanking the visitors for their advice, by which, however, he did not intend to profit.

"There is a practical husband for you," said Kéraban. "You ought to marry in this country, Van Mitten!"

"Perhaps I ought," replied the Dutchman.

At five o'clock in the evening the travellers halted at Surmeneh. They continued their journey at six, with the intention to reach Trebizond before day declined. But there was delay occasioned by the breaking of a wheel of the *araba* some six miles from the town,—about nine o'clock in the evening,—and they were thus compelled to pass the night in the caravanserai at the road side, a building well known to all travellers in that part of Asia Minor.

---

## CHAPTER VI.

### CONCERNING THE STRANGERS MET BY KÉRABAN AT THE CARAVANSERAI OF RISSAR.

THE caravanserai of Rissar, like all other buildings of its class, is entirely appropriated to the service of travellers. The host, or guardian, of this particular halting-place near Trebizond, was a certain Turk named Kidros, a cunning rogue and more "tricky" than are members of his race: he usually took great care of the place. He sought to please his guests, with much advantage to his own interests, which he understood thoroughly; he was always of their opinion, even to the extent of reducing their bills (which he had previously "swollen" with a view to this very reduction, and still left himself a handsome profit) out of pure regard for such honourable travellers!

The arrangement of the caravanserai was as follows:—A vast court-yard, encircled by four walls, out of which a gate opened into the country. At each side of this gate were two watch-towers, whence one could overlook the environs in case the roads were unsafe. In the thickness of the walls were doors giving access to separate rooms in which travellers could pass the night, for they were seldom occupied during the day. A few sycamore trees planted round the court-yard threw a little shade upon it. In the centre was a well, worked by an endless chain pump, the buckets of which could empty themselves into a trough which formed a semi-circular basin. Outside was a line of boxes in sheds where the horses found food and litter. Behind were the pickets, to which mules and dromedaries were attached as being less particular than horses in the matter of accommodation.

That evening of which we are writing, the caravanserai without being full, had a good many occupants; some on the way to Trebizond, others to the eastern provinces, Armenia, Persia, or Kurdistan. Twenty chambers were full, and the occupants were for the most part asleep.

About nine o'clock, only two men were walking up and down the court-yard; they were talking earnestly, and only interrupted their conversation to cast a suspicious look around occasionally. These two individuals, dressed so as not to attract particular notice, were Seigneur Saffar and his steward Scarpante.

"I repeat that it is here, Seigneur, that Yarhud has appointed to meet us. Here is the caravanserai Rissar," said the steward.

"Dog!" exclaimed Saffar. "Why is he not here then?"

"He will not tarry now."

"And why has he thought of bringing Amasia here instead of carrying her direct to Trebizond?"

Saffar and Scarpante, it must be remembered, were ignorant of the wreck of the *Guidare*, and of the succeeding events.

"Yarhud's letter to me came from the harbour of Atina," said Scarpante. "It makes no mention of the young lady, but begs me to meet him here."

"And he is not come," exclaimed Saffar, advancing towards the gate. "Ah, he had better beware how he tries my patience! I have a presentiment that some accident has occurred."

"Why, seigneur? The weather has been stormy, and perhaps the vessel could not reach Trebizond, so she put in at Atina."

"But who can tell whether Yarhud succeeded in the first instance in carrying Amasia away from Odessa?"

"Yarhud is not only a skilful seaman," replied Scarpante, "he is also a very sharp fellow!"

"Yet his sharpness is not always successful," replied the calm voice of the Maltese captain himself, who had for a few moments been standing motionless on the threshold of the caravanserai.

Seigneur Saffar and Scarpante both turned round suddenly, and the latter exclaimed—

"Yarhud!"

"At last you are here," said Saffar, roughly, as he advanced towards the captain.

"Yes, Seigneur Saffar," he replied, bowing. "Here I am—at last!"

"And Selim's daughter? Did you succeed in carrying her away from Odessa?"

"The banker's daughter," replied Yarhud, "was carried away by me about six weeks ago, soon after the departure of Ahmet, who was obliged to accompany his uncle in his journey round the Black Sea. I at once set sail for Trebizond, but my vessel was carried to the eastward, and, notwithstanding all my efforts, was wrecked on the rocks near Atina, and all my crew were drowned!"

"All your crew?" exclaimed Scarpante.

"Yes."

"And Amasia?" enquired Saffar, who seemed little affected by the loss of the *Guidare.*

"She was saved: saved with the young servant, whom I carried off with her."

"But if she was saved——" said Scarpante.

"Where is she?" interrupted Saffar.

"Seigneur," replied the Maltese. "Fate was adverse to me—or rather, to you."

"Speak," cried Saffar, menacingly.

"The banker's daughter," replied Yarhud, "was rescued by her *fiancé*, Ahmet, who was by some unfortunate chance on the spot."

"Saved by him!" exclaimed Scarpante.

"And at this moment?" enquired Saffar.

"At this moment she is under the protection of Ahmet, of his uncle, and his companions on the way to Trebizond. Thence they propose to proceed to Scutari to celebrate their marriage."

"Bungler!" roared Saffar. "Why did you let her escape instead of saving her yourself?"

"I would have done so at the peril of my life; if Ahmet had not come up, she would now be safe in your palace at Trebizond."

"Ah, you are quite unworthy of any mission," replied Saffar, who could not restrain an angry movement.

"Will you listen to me, seigneur?" said Scarpante. "When you are calmer you will recognize the fact that Yarhud did all that was possible."

"All," added the Maltese.

"All is not enough," replied Saffar, "when the accomplishment of my orders fails."

"The past is past, Seigneur Saffar," said Scarpante. "Let us look at the present and see what chances it offers us. Amasia is not yet Ahmet's wife—nothing is lost!"

"No, nothing," added Yarhud. "After the shipwreck I followed her; I have watched Ahmet and his companions ever since their departure from Atina. They are travelling without any suspicion. The way is long across Anatolia from Trebizond to the shores of the Bosphorus. Now neither Amasia nor her servant have any idea whither the *Guidare* was bound. Besides, no one in the caravan knows Seigneur Saffar nor Scarpante. Can we not take them in a trap?"

"Scarpante," said Saffar coldly: "this girl is necessary to me. If fate is against me I will fight against fate. It shall never be said that my wishes cannot be complied with."

"It shall be as you desire," replied Scarpante. "Yes; between Trebizond and Scutari, in those deserted plains, it is possible, even easy, to lie in wait for the caravan, perhaps to find a guide for it who will know how to lose his way: then you may attack it with your men. But that is force—better succeed by stratagem if we can."

"But in what manner?" inquired Saffar.

"You said, Yarhud," replied Scarpante, turning to the Maltese, "that Ahmet and his companions were making for Trebizond?"

"Yes, and they will soon arrive here, and will certainly pass the night in the caravanserai," said Yarhud.

"Well then," said Scarpante, "cannot

we stir up some excitement which will detain them here—which will separate Amasia from her betrothed?"

"I have more faith in force," remarked Saffar, brutally.

"Very well," replied Scarpante. "We

"Silence, we are not alone!'

can use force if stratagem fail. But leave me here to watch what goes on."

"Hush, Scarpante," said the Maltese. "We are not alone."

As he spoke, two men entered the courtyard. One was Kidros, the other an important personage—at least by repute—who must be introduced to the reader.

Seigneur Saffar, Scarpante, and Yarhud moved away into an obscure corner apart. There they could listen at their ease, and so much the more easily, as the personage in question always spoke in very loud tones, and very haughtily.

This person was a Kurdish "lord," and his name was Yanar.

# KÉRABAN THE INFLEXIBLE;

## OR, ADVENTURES IN THE EUXINE.

BY JULES VERNE.

TRANSLATED BY HENRY FRITH.

---

## CHAPTER VI.

THE mountainous region of Asia which includes ancient Assyria and Media, is now called Kurdistan. It is divided into Turkish and Persian Kurdistan, and the former province contains many hundreds of thousands of inhabitants, not the least considerable amongst them being this Seigneur Yanar, who, with his sister, the noble Saraboul, had arrived at the caravanserai the day before.

Seigneur Yanar and his sister had quitted Mossoul two months previously, and were travelling for pleasure. They came to Trebizond, where they intended to remain some weeks. The "noble Saraboul," as she was generally called in her native *pachalik*, was at this time thirty or thirty-three years of age, and had been for some years a widow. The Turkish governor to whom she had been married had been only able to devote to her a very brief existence. The widow was of pleasing and agreeable appearance, and was not altogether unwilling to enter into matrimonial bonds for a second time. This was a more difficult aim to accomplish than at first sight would appear, for, though rich and well born, she was of a violent and impetuous temper; and, being a Kurd, extremely fond of her own way; so any suitor for her hand might not unnaturally be alarmed at her temper. Her brother Yanar, who also constituted himself her body-guard, had advised the journey—chances are so many while travelling! And that is the reason why these two "personages," having quitted their native Kurdistan, found themselves on the highroad to Trebizond.

Seigneur Yanar was a man of about forty-five years old, tall, imperious, and with a stern countenance; one of those hectoring fellows who are born with a frown. His aquiline nose, his deep-set eyes, his shaven head, and enormous moustaches, indicated him as a specimen of the Armenian, rather than of the Turkish, type. His head was adorned with a felt cap, tied round with brilliantly red silk. He wore a robe with wide sleeves under an embroidered vest; large trousers which fell to his ankles, and embroidered leather boots. His middle was girt about with a scarf, in which he carried a varied assortment of poignards, pistols, and yataghans. He had a truly terrifying appearance.

So Kidros always addressed him with extreme deference, and bore himself like a person who was obliged to bow and scrape before a cannon loaded with grape-shot.

"Yes, Seigneur Yanar," said Kidros emphasising his words with suitable gestures. "I repeat that the judge will arrive here this very evening, and to-morrow morning, at daybreak, will begin his quest."

"Master Kidros," replied Yanar, "you are the host of this caravanserai, and may Allah choke you if you do not take care of your guests' safety and comfort here."

"Certainly, Seigneur Yanar. By all means."

"Well then, last night some ruffians, robbers, or others, penetrated, had the audacity to enter the chamber in which my sister, the noble Saraboul, reposed." And Yanar indicated the particular opening in the wall to which he referred.

"The ruffians!" exclaimed Kidros.

"And we will not quit this caravanserai," continued Yanar, "until they have been discovered, arrested, condemned, and hanged!"

Master Kidros was not quite assured that any real attempt at robbery had been made. One thing alone was certain. For some reason or other the affrighted widow had rushed from her chamber, screaming and calling for her brother; the whole establishment had been upset, and the malefactors, supposing there had been any, had managed to escape, without leaving a trace of their presence.

At any rate, Scarpante, who had not lost a word of the conversation, at once began to think how he might turn this business to his own profit.

"Now we are Kurds," continued Yanar, drawing himself up proudly to give full effect to his words, "we are Kurds of Mossoul, the splendid capital of Kurdistan, and we will never admit that any slight can be put upon Kurds without reparation being obtained by law, or by force!"

"But, seigneur, what injury has been done?" asked Master Kidros, with some temerity, but prudently retreating a pace or two as he spoke.

"What injury!" exclaimed Yanar.

"Yes, seigneur. No doubt some scoundrels *did* endeavour to enter last night, into the chamber apportioned to the noble Saraboul, but they took away nothing!"

"Nothing; as a matter of fact, nothing; but only thanks to my sister's energy and courage! She can handle a pistol as well as a yataghan!"

"So the malefactors, whoever they might have been, ran away?" remarked Kidros.

"A very good thing for them that they did, Master Kidros. The noble and valiant Saraboul would have exterminated them two by two—four by four! That is the reason why she will remain armed, as I am, to-night; and woe to anyone who ventures near her room!"

"You may well believe, Seigneur Yanar, that there is nothing to fear now. The robbers—if there were any—will not again hazard——"

"How, *if* there were any *robbers!*" roared Yanar. "Who do you think these bandits were then?"

"Perhaps some venturesome—some foolish people; or some one who, smitten by the charms of the noble Saraboul,——"

"By Mahomet," exclaimed Yanar, seizing his weapon. "Here is a pretty affair. The honour of a Kurd is at stake! Ah! arrest, imprisonment, impalement will not suffice in this case! No; the most horrible tortures will not be sufficient—unless the ruffian has position and fortune sufficient to repair his fault!"

"Calm yourself, Seigneur Yanar," replied Master Kidros. "The enquiry, which will be instituted, will discover the author, or authors, of this insult. I tell you again, the judge has been summoned. I myself sought him in Trebizond, and when I told him the particulars he assured me that he possessed means of ascertaining—sure means of discovering—who the malefactors are."

"And what means are these?" enquired Yanar ironically.

"I cannot tell," replied Kidros, "but the judge maintains they are infallible."

"Be it so," replied Yanar. "We shall see when to-morrow comes. I will retire, but I will watch. I will watch, armed. Oh, my sister, my noble sister!"

So saying, the terrible Yanar turned away to his apartment, which was next to his sister's. There he paused at the door for a moment, and shook his fist at the keeper of the caravanserai.

"You cannot play tricks with a Kurd," he cried in a loud voice; then he disappeared within his chamber.

Master Kidros gave vent to a long sigh of relief.

"At last," he said. "We shall soon see how this will end. But it is as well that the thieves—if there were any—have decamped!"

Meanwhile Scarpante was talking in an undertone with Saffar and Yarhud. "Yes," he was saying, "thanks to this affair of Seigneur Yanar there can be some plan attempted."

"You propose——" said Saffar.

The Caravanserai of Rissar.

"I propose to stir up here some unpleasant circumstances which will have the effect of keeping that Ahmet here for some days, and of separating him from his betrothed, perhaps."

"Good; but if the *ruse* fail?"

"We must use force then," replied Scarpante.

At that moment Kidros perceived Saffar, Scarpante, and Yarhud, whom he had not previously noticed. He advanced towards them and in the most amiable manner said,

"What do you require, gentlemen?"

"We are waiting for some travellers who may arrive at any moment now," replied Scarpante.

Just then a noise was heard from the outside; a caravan was evidently approaching; mules and horses halted at the door.

"Here they are, no doubt," said Master Kidros, as he crossed the court-yard to admit the travellers.

"Here are rich personages," he muttered, "on horseback. I had better go out and offer them my services." So he did.

But Scarpante had advanced to the door also, and looked out.

"Are these people Ahmet and his companions?" he enquired of the Maltese.

"Yes, yes; they are," replied Yarhud, who retired hastily so as not to be recognized.

"They!" exclaimed Saffar advancing in his turn, but without going outside the door.

"I am not mistaken," replied Yarhud, "there is Ahmet and his *fiancée*, with her servant."

"Let us be on our guard," said Scarpante, signing to Yarhud to keep out of sight.

"You can already recognize Kéraban's voice," continued the Maltese.

"Kéraban!" cried Saffar quickly, as he rushed towards the door.

"What is the matter, Seigneur Saffar?" asked Scarpante, much astonished. "Why does the name of Kéraban agitate you so?"

"Ha! Yes he is there, 'tis he indeed," replied Saffar. "That is the traveller who encountered me on the Caucasian railway; and who wanted to prevent my carriage from crossing!"

"He knows you?"

"Yes, and he will not find it difficult to continue the quarrel; to stop him——"

"Ah! that will not stop the nephew," remarked Scarpante.

"I know how to disembarrass myself of the nephew as well as of the uncle," replied Saffar.

"No, no; we must have no quarrelling, no noise," insisted Scarpante. "Take my advice, Seigneur Saffar. Let Kéraban once suspect your presence, let him only be made aware that Yarhud carried off Amasia on your account, and all will be lost."

"Very well, I will retire and trust to your skill, Scarpante. But succeed!"

"I will succeed, Seigneur Saffar, if you will allow me to act. Go back to Trebizond, to-night."

"I will," replied Saffar.

"And you too, Yarhud, leave the caravanserai at once," continued Scarpante. "They know you, and they may recognize you if you remain."

"Here they are," said Yarhud.

"Leave me; go," cried Scarpante pushing the captain of the *Guidare* away.

"But how can we go unobserved?" asked Saffar.

"This way," replied Scarpante, opening a door cut in the wall which led to the fields.

Signor Saffar and the Maltese passed out at once.

"Just in time," muttered Scarpante, "and now I must keep my eyes and ears open."

---

## Chapter VII.

### In which the Judge of Trebizond proceeds with his Enquiry in a very Ingenious Fashion.

Seigneur Kéraban and his friends, having left their horses in the sheds outside, entered the caravanserai, attended by Master Kidros in a most obsequious fashion. He had placed his lanthorn in a corner, and but very little light was thrown into the interior of the court.

"Yes, seigneur, come in," he continued, bowing to the ground. "This is the caravanserai of Rissar."

"And we are only two leagues from Trebizond?" said Kéraban.

"Two leagues—at most."

"Good. Let our horses be cared for, as we intend to leave here at daybreak."

Then, turning to Ahmet, who had led Amasia to a seat, where she was sitting with Nedjeb, he continued, good humouredly—

"There! since my nephew has found

this little one, he thinks of no one but her, and leaves to me the arrangements for our journey?"

"That is only natural, Seigneur Kéraban; what is the use of being an uncle, else?" said Nedjeb.

"You must not blame me," said Ahmet, smiling.

"'You can give us rooms for the night?' asked Kéraban."

"Nor me," added Amasia.

"Oh, I am blaming no one," replied Kéraban. "Not even this fellow, Van Mitten, who actually had conceived the idea —the unpardonable idea—of leaving us!"

"Oh, do not speak of that," cried Van Mitten, "not now, nor ever."

"By Mahomet, why not? A little discussion upon it, or on some other subject, would stimulate us."

"I thought, uncle," observed Ahmet "that you had made a resolution to have no more discussions!"

"That is so—quite right, and I will never break it—even if I have a hundred reasons for so doing."

"We shall see that," murmured Nedjeb.

"Besides," continued Van Mitten, "the best thing for us now would be a sleep for some hours"

"If we can sleep here at all," muttered Bruno, who was as usual in a bad temper.

"You can give us rooms for the night?" asked Kéraban of Kidros.

"Yes, seigneur, as many as you please."

"Good, excellent!" exclaimed Kéraban. "To-morrow we shall reach Trebizond, and Scutari ten days later. There we will have a good dinner—the dinner which I promised you, Van Mitten."

"You certainly owe us that, friend Kéraban!"

"A dinner at Scutari," whispered Bruno to his master, "yes, if we ever get there."

"Get out, Bruno! Have a little courage, man, if only for the honour of Holland."

"Eh, I am something like Holland, myself," replied Bruno, touching his loose garments, "I am all *en côtes!*"

Scarpante, standing apart, listened to this conversation, and waited for the moment when it would suit his interests to interfere.

"Well,'" said Kéraban, "which room is intended for these young ladies?"

"This one," replied Master Kidros, indicating a door in the wall on the left.

"Good night, my little Amasia," continued Kéraban, "and may Allah give you pleasant dreams."

"The same to you, Seigneur Kéraban," replied the girl. "Till to-morrow, dear Ahmet!"

"Till to-morrow, dearest Amasia," replied the young man as he embraced her.

"Come, Nedjeb," said Amasia.

"I follow you, dear lady," replied the maid; "but I know on what subject we shall converse for the next hour!"

Then the girls entered the chamber the door of which was held open by Kidros.

"Now, where are these good fellows to sleep?" asked Kéraban, indicating Bruno and Nizib.

"In one of the exterior rooms," replied Kidros, "I will show it to them."

So saying, he advanced towards the door, and beckoned to the servants to follow. Nizib and Bruno, feeling tired, obeyed without hesitation, after bidding their masters good-night.

"Now, or never!" muttered Scarpante to himself.

Kéraban, Van Mitten, and Ahmet were pacing the court waiting the return of Kidros. The uncle was in high spirits. Everything was going well. He would soon reach the Bosphorus, and was already chuckling over the visages of the authorities when they would see him appear. For Ahmet, the return to Scutari meant his long-desired union with Amasia: for Van Mitten, the return meant—well, the return and no more.

"It seems they have forgotten us," said Kéraban. "Where is our room?"

Turning round he perceived Scarpante, who immediately advanced towards the party, slowly.

"Were you seeking the room allotted to Seigneur Kéraban and his friends?" he enquired with a low bow, as if he were one of the servants of the caravanserai.

"Yes."

"Here it is."

Scarpante then indicated, on the right, the door which opened into a corridor in which the chamber of the Kurdish lady was situated; next to that occupied by Yanar.

"Come along, my friends," said Kéraban, pushing at the door indicated by Scarpante. The door, slightly fastened, gave way at once.

All three men entered the passage, but ere they had time to close the door a terrible clamour arose—cries succeeded—and an alarming female voice made itself audible, quickly sustained by the deeper tones of a man.

Kéraban, Van Mitten, and Ahmet, quite at a loss to understand what it all meant, retreated precipitately to the court-yard again.

Immediately doors were opened on all sides, and travellers came out of the rooms. Amasia and Nedjeb re-appeared. Bruno and Nizib came in again; while in the semi-darkness, the form of the fierce Yanar loomed threateningly. Finally a woman precipitated herself from the passage into which Kéraban and his friends had so imprudently entered.

"Robbery—assault—murder!" screamed this woman.

She was the noble Saraboul; tall, strong, and of firm carriage; her eyes flashing, her cheeks burning, her black hair flowing, her teeth disclosed by the haughty upper lip;—in a word, the Seigneur Yanar in female shape.

"The noble Seraboul" and her brother Yanar.

Evidently the lady had been watching in her room, at the moment that Kéraban and his companions had forced open the door, for she had not taken off her yellow, gold-embroidered costume, nor had she discarded any of the weapons which she carried in her girdle. She still wore the fez from which hung a long *puskul* like a bell-rope, and her leather boots, concealed by the *chalwar* or Oriental pantaloons. Some people might have taken her for a wasp in her present costume. Well, the noble Saraboul would not have been annoyed at the comparison—she *was* a wasp, and with a very formidable sting!

"What a woman!" ejaculated Van Mitten.

"And what a man!" replied Kéraban pointing to Yanar.

The Kurd then exclaimed—

"Another attempt of the scoundrels! Let everyone be arrested!"

"We must be on the alert here," said Ahmet to his uncle, "or I fear we shall be convicted as the cause of the uproar."

"Nobody saw us," replied Kéraban, "and Mahomet himself could not recognise us."

"What is it, Ahmet?" cried Amasia, who nestled to her lover's side.

"Nothing, dearest, nothing," he replied.

At this instant Master Kidros appeared on the door-step at the end of the court, saying—

"You have arrived in the very nick of time, Monsieur le Juge."

In fact the judge had arrived from Trebizond, intending to pass the night at the caravanserai, so as to proceed leisurely upon the enquiry demanded by the Kurdish pair. He was followed by his clerk, and stood upon the door-sill.

"Ah," he exclaimed. "So the malefactors have repeated their attempt of last night!"

"It would appear so, monsieur," replied Kidros.

"Let the gates be all closed," said the magistrate in an authoritative voice. "Let no one quit the caravanserai without my permission."

His orders were immediately executed, and all the travellers thus became virtually prisoners.

"Now, judge," cried the noble Saraboul, "I demand justice upon the wretches who have not scrupled a second time to attack a defenceless woman."

"Not only a woman," added Yanar with a threatening gesture, "but a Kurd!"

Scarpante, as may be imagined, followed every incident carefully.

The judge, a sly-looking individual, with a pointed nose, little gimlet eyes, and wearing a long beard which concealed his closed mouth, sought to examine the faces of all the travellers, a by no means easy task in the dim light which was diffused by the single lanthorn in the corner. This examination rapidly concluded, he addressed himself to the noble lady tourist—

"You swear, that last night some people attempted to enter your apartment?"

"I swear it!"

"And that they repeated their criminal offence?"

"They, or others. Yes."

"Only just now?"

"Just this instant."

"Could you recognise them?"

"No: my room is dark and I could not see their faces."

"Were there many of them?"

"I do not know."

"We *will* know, sister!" exclaimed Yanar. "We will know; and then, woe to the scoundrels!"

Kéraban then whispered to Van Mitten—

"There is nothing to fear. No one perceived us. Mahomet himself could not discover us."

"Fortunately it is so," replied the Dutchman, who was by no means completely assured as to the consequences of the adventure. "With these devilish Kurds, the affair might have turned out badly for us."

Meanwhile, the judge kept walking about. He did not know which side to take, to the great indignation of the plaintiffs.

"Judge," said the noble Saraboul, folding her arms across her chest, "is justice to remain inactive in your hands? Are not we subjects of the Sultan, and entitled to his protection? Is a woman of my station to be insulted, and are the guilty to escape punishment?"

"She is really superb," remarked Nedjeb.

"Superb, but alarming," replied Van Mitten.

"How do you decide, judge?" asked Yanar.

"Let them bring torches!" exclaimed Saraboul, "then I shall see, I will seek, and perhaps recognize, the perpetrators of this outrage, who have dared——"

"It is useless," remarked the judge. "I charge myself with the discovery of the perpetrators."

"Without lights?"

"Without lights!"

As he made this reply, the judge whispered to his secretary, who nodded, and left the court-yard.

The Dutchman at this time could not help whispering to Kéraban—"I do not know why, but I am by no means assured respecting the issue of this affair."

"The Secretary returned, dragging a Goat into the Courtyard."

"By Allah, you are always afraid," retorted Kéraban.

Then they were silent, and waited like the rest, in anxious silence, the return of the secretary.

"Come, judge," said Yanar at length, "do you pretend that in this gloom you will indicate——"

"I? no," replied the judge, interrupting him. "But I am going to enlist in my service an intelligent animal which has before now assisted me in my investigations."

"An animal!" exclaimed the lady.

"Yes, a goat; a fine cunning beast, that will denounce the criminal if he be present. Now, he must be here somewhere, for no one has quitted the caravanserai since the assault was attempted."

"This judge is an idiot," muttered Kéraban.

At this juncture the secretary returned, dragging a goat into the court-yard. This animal was of the species that furnishes the "bezoar," a stony concretion which is found in the entrails and much esteemed for its supposed medicinal qualities. The intelligent-looking goat looked quite worthy of the *rôle* of "diviner" which his master was about to call upon it to play. It lay gracefully upon the sand, and watched the audience with his cunning eyes.

"What a pretty animal," remarked Nedjeb.

"But what is the judge going to do with it?" asked Amasia.

"Some 'sorcery' no doubt," replied Ahmet, "by which these ignorant natives will be 'taken in.'"

Kéraban was of the same opinion, and shrugged his shoulders; while Van Mitten looked on uneasily.

"How now, judge?" said the noble Saraboul. "Is it by means of this goat that you hope to ascertain who the culprits are?"

"Just so," replied the judge.

"And it will answer?"

"It will answer."

"In what way?" asked Yanar, who, in his Kurdish heart was quite ready to accept anything that "smacked" of superstition.

"Nothing is more simple," replied the judge. "Every traveller will approach and place his or her hand upon the back of the goat, and as soon as the animal feels the touch of the guilty person it will designate him by bleating."

"This fellow is simply a humbug," muttered Kéraban; "a common conjuror."

"But, judge," said the noble Saraboul, "surely such a silly animal as that——"

"You will soon see," replied the judge.

"And why not?" remarked Yanar. "I will set the example and begin the trial."

So saying, Yanar approached the goat, which remained quite still, and passed his hand down the animal's back, from head to tail.

The goat remained silent.

"Now the rest," cried the judge.

Then in succession all the others present imitated Seigneur Yanar, and caressed the back of the animal. But none of those who touched her were apparently guilty, for the goat made no sign nor did she utter any accusatory bleatings.

---

## Chapter VIII.

### Which concludes in a Manner very Unexpected, particularly by Van Mitten.

While the trial was proceeding, Seigneur Kéraban had taken his nephew and Van Mitten apart, and, forgetting all his good resolutions, sought to bend them to his own mode of proceeding.

"Well, my friends, this sorcerer is simply the biggest idiot——"

"Why?" interrupted Van Mitten.

"Because there is nothing to prevent the guilty parties, ourselves for instance, from *appearing* to caress the goat, and we can pass our hands over instead of upon its back, without touching it. The judge should at anyrate have tried this test with lights, so as to check any evasion. In this semi-darkness it is absurd!"

"Well," said Van Mitten——

"That is what I am going to do, and I advise you strongly to follow my example," said Kéraban.

"But, uncle, whether we caress the goat or not, you know it cannot tell the innocent from the guilty."

"Certainly not, Ahmet, but since that stupid judge is acting in this way, I claim to be less simple than he, and I will not touch the beast, and I beg you to do as I do."

"But, uncle,——"

"Ah, are we going to have an argument?" exclaimed Kéraban, who was beginning to get excited.

"Nevertheless," began Van Mitten.

"Van Mitten, if you are so foolish as to put your hand on the back of that goat, I will never forgive you!"

"Very well; I will pat nothing at all, if I should disoblige you," replied Van Mitten. "Besides, they will not see us in the dark."

By this time the majority of the travellers had submitted to the test, and the goat had accused nobody.

"Now it is our turn, Bruno," said

"'Nothing is more simple,' replied the judge."

Nizib. "How stupid these Orientals are!"

So, one after the other, they caressed the goat, which did not bleat for them any more than for the rest.

"But your animal says nothing!" remarked the noble Saraboul to the judge.

"Is this a practical joke?" demanded Seigneur Yanar. "You will find it expensive to joke with Kurds!"

"Patience," replied the judge, bowing. "If the goat has not bleated, it is because the guilty person has not yet stroked her."

"We are now the only ones left," muttered Van Mitten, who, without knowing why, felt some vague presentiment of evil.

"It is our turn," said Ahmet.

"Yes, mine first," said Kéraban.

So saying, he advanced before his nephew and Van Mitten.

"Now, take care you do not touch it," he repeated in a low voice.

Then extending his hand above the animal's back he pretended to caress it slowly, but without touching one of its silky hairs.

The goat did not bleat.

"That is so far comforting," said Ahmet, and, following his uncle's example, he passed his hand over the animal's back, without touching it.

The goat did not bleat.

Then it came to the Dutchman's turn. Van Mitten, last of all, was compelled to try the ordeal. He advanced towards the goat, which seemed to eye him askance; but he also, fearing to displease Kéraban, only pretended to stroke the goat.

The goat did not bleat.

There was a general exclamation of astonishment. "Ohs" and "ahs" were heard from every one of the audience.

"Decidedly your goat *is* a beast," remarked Yanar, angrily.

"She has not discovered the culprit after all," cried the noble Kurdish woman, "and nevertheless the guilty one is here."

"Ha!" exclaimed Kéraban, "this judge is making himself very ridiculous, Van Mitten."

"Not a doubt about it," replied Van Mitten, now reassured as to the result of the trial.

"Poor little goat," cried Nedjeb to her mistress. "Are they going to do it any injury because it has said nothing?"

Every person present looked at the judge, whose eyes scintillated in the obscurity like carbuncles.

"Now, Monsieur le Juge," said Kéraban sarcastically, "now that your enquiry has terminated, there is no reason, I suppose, why we should not retire to our rooms?"

"That must not be," exclaimed the angry Lady Kurd. "Certainly not: an assault has been attempted."

"Eh, madame?" replied Kéraban, not without some asperity. "You cannot have the assurance to keep honest people out of their beds when they want to go there!"

"You are giving yourself airs, Monsieur le Turc!" said Yanar.

"I speak as it suits me, Monsieur le Kurd," retorted Kéraban.

Scarpante, who deemed that the trial had failed, was not sorry to perceive this quarrel arising between Yanar and Kéraban. Some further complication of a nature favourable to his own projects might arise from it.

In fact, the dispute was becoming serious, and Ahmet was about to assist his uncle, when the judge interposed and said quietly—

"Range yourselves in line, and let lights be brought."

Master Kidros, to whom the latter order was addressed, hastened to comply with it. In a moment four servants, carrying torches, appeared, and the court was brilliantly illuminated.

"Let each one hold up his right hand," said the judge.

At this order each right hand was elevated, and everyone was black—with the exception of those of Kéraban, Ahmet, and Van Mitten!

The judge at once pointed to the three men.

"There are the culprits!" he said.

"What?" said Kéraban.

"We?" exclaimed Van Mitten, who did not understand anything.

"Yes, you," repeated the judge. "Whether these men were or were not afraid of being denounced by the goat, matters little. One thing is certain, and that is, knowing themselves to be guilty, instead of caressing the animal, whose back was rubbed with soot, they only passed their hands above the fur, and so accused themselves."

# KÉRABAN THE INFLEXIBLE;

## OR, ADVENTURES IN THE EUXINE.

By Jules Verne.

Translated by HENRY FRITH.

### Chapter VIII.

A COMPLIMENTARY murmur pervaded the audience at the judge's ingenuity, while Seigneur Kéraban and his companions, greatly disappointed, hung their heads!

"So," began Yanar, "these are the three culprits, who last night——"

"Last night we were ten leagues from here," said Ahmet.

"Who can prove that!" exclaimed the judge. "In any case you have this evening attempted to make your way into the apartment of this lady."

"Well, yes," replied Kéraban, who was furious at having been caught in such a snare. "Yes, we did enter the passage, but under a misapprehension on our part, or rather on the part of one of the servants of the caravanserai."

"Indeed!" said Yanar ironically.

"Yes, indeed! The lady's room was shown to us as ours."

"That won't do!" remarked the judge.

"They are caught," muttered Bruno, "all three!"

Seigneur Kéraban, indeed, was so absolutely put out of countenance that he had lost all his usual assurance; and he was entirely upset when he heard the judge say, "Let them be taken to prison."

"Yes, to prison," cried Seigneur Yanar, while all the crowd echoed the order, "To prison! To prison!"

When Scarpante perceived the turn things had taken he congratulated himself upon what he had done. Seigneur Kéraban, Van Mitten, and Ahmet in custody, the journey would be interrupted and the wedding postponed. Above all, an immediate separation would be effected between Amasia and her betrothed; and there was thus a possibility of acting with success, and of renewing the attempt in which the Maltese captain had failed.

Ahmet, when he thought of the consequences and of his separation from Amasia, felt very angry with his uncle. Was it not Kéraban who by his obstinacy had placed them in this dilemma? Had not he prevented them from caressing the animal in order to spite the foolish judge, who had nevertheless got the better of them? It was Kéraban's fault that they had fallen into the trap, and were now menaced with imprisonment, for some days at least.

Kéraban, too, on his part was very angry, for he remembered how little time remained to him to complete his journey, if he would arrive at Scutari at the appointed time. One bit of obstinacy, as useless as absurd, had cost a fortune to his nephew.

As for Van Mitten he kept balancing himself on either leg alternately, very much embarrassed, and not daring to look Bruno in the face: while the valet seemed to be repeating the ominous words—

"Did I not tell you that we would come to grief sooner or later?"

Then Van Mitten, addressing Kéraban, said—

"Now, why did you prevent us caressing the goat's back?"

For the first time in his life Kéraban was unable to make any answer to a question addressed to him.

" To prison ! to prison ! "

Meanwhile the cries of, "To prison!" continued, and Scarpante joined in them heartily.

"Yes, send these malefactors to prison," cried the vindictive Yanar, who was well disposed to aid the law by force. "Away with them, all three!"

"Yes, all three, unless one will take upon himself the responsibility of the act," replied the noble Saraboul, who did not wish that two innocent persons should suffer with the guilty one.

"That is only fair," assented the judge. "Well now, which of you really attempted to enter this lady's apartment?"

There was a momentary indecision in the minds of the accused, but it was not of long duration. Kéraban requested permission to confer with his friends. This favour was accorded. Then, taking Van Mitten and Ahmet aside, he said in a tone which admitted of no discussion—

"My friends, there is only one way out of this. One of us must be the scapegoat for the others: the matter is very serious."

Here the Dutchman, as if he had a presentiment of what was coming, "pricked up his ears."

"Now," continued Kéraban, "there can be no question of choice. The presence of Ahmet is necessary at Scutari to celebrate his marriage."

"Yes, uncle, yes," assented Ahmet.

"My attendance also is necessary," proceeded Kéraban, "in my capacity of guardian."

"Ha!" ejaculated Van Mitten.

"So, friend Mitten, there is no alternative. You must sacrifice yourself."

"I—? What?"

"You must accuse yourself. What risk do you run? A few day's imprisonment. Bagatelle! We will soon have you out!"

Van Mitten, who felt he was being disposed of rather unceremoniously, began to protest.

"My dear M. Van Mitten, you really must," said Ahmet. "I beg you to do so in Amasia's name. All her future will be blighted unless we reach Scutari at the appointed time."

"Oh, Monsieur Van Mitten," pleaded the young lady who had approached him.

"Well, as you will," replied Van Mitten.

"Hum," muttered Bruno, "here is another act of folly they are making my master commit!"

"Monsieur Van Mitten," began Ahmet—

"Well done!" exclaimed Kéraban, wringing his friend's hand.

While this conversation was proceeding, the cries of "To prison!" became louder.

The unhappy Dutchman did not know what to say or do. He wished to say "Yes," and then "No," but the approach of the people to arrest the three culprits finally decided him.

"Stop," he cried. "Stop, I confess that I am the person who——"

"Foiled," muttered Scarpante, with an angry gesture of disappointment.

"It was you then," said the judge.

"I—yes—I——"

"Dear M. Van Mitten!" murmured Amasia in his ear.

"Ah yes, indeed," added Nedjeb.

But what was the noble Saraboul doing all this time? Well, that admirable lady was observing with some curiosity the man who had dared to attempt to enter her apartments.

"So then," cried Yanar, "*you* are the individual who had the temerity to enter the rooms allotted to this noble Kurdish lady?"

"Yes, I," replied Van Mitten.

"You have not the appearance of a thief!"

"A thief! I? I am a merchant—a Dutchman;" exclaimed Van Mitten, with much indignation.

"But then——" continued Yanar.

"Then," interrupted his sister, "you had other and more dishonourable motives."

"To insult a Kurdish lady," roared Yanar, grasping his yataghan.

"After all, he is not so bad, this Dutchman," remarked the noble lady mincingly.

"Not all your blood will suffice to wash out this insult," continued Yanar.

"Brother, brother!" remonstrated Saraboul.

"If you refuse to make reparation," added Yanar.

"Ah!" said Ahmet.

"You shall marry my sister, or else——"

"By Allah!" said Kéraban, "here is another complication now."

"Marry! I marry!" repeated Van Mitten, raising his hands to heaven.

"You refuse?" roared Yanar.

"If I refuse,—if I refuse," replied Van Mitten, in the depths of despair. "But I am already——"

Van Mitten had not time to conclude his sentence. Kéraban seized him by the arm, and said—

"Not another word. Consent you must. Don't hesitate."

"Consent? Why, I am married already," pleaded Van Mitten. "It would be bigamy."

"No matter in Turkey whether it be bigamy, trigamy, or quadrigamy,—it is perfectly lawful. So now say 'Yes'!"

"But——"

"Marry her, Van Mitten, marry her. Then you will not have an hour in prison. We shall be able to continue our journey all together. Once at Scutari you can be off the shortest way, and bid the new Madame Van Mitten good evening!"

"But you demand impossibilities, Kéraban," replied the Dutchman.

"You must, or all will be lost."

At that moment Seigneur Yanar came over, and grasping Van Mitten by the arm, said——

"He must!"

"He must!" repeated the noble Saraboul, seizing the other arm.

"Since I must, then," replied Van Mitten, whose shaking limbs could scarcely sustain him.

"What! are you going to give in again?" cried Bruno.

"Needs must, Bruno," muttered Van Mitten, in a feeble voice.

"Come! stand up!" cried Yanar, giving his future brother-in-law a violent push.

"And firmly," continued Saraboul, with a reminder on the other side to her intended husband.

"As becoming a brother-in-law!" said he.

"And the husband of a Kurdish lady!" added she.

Van Mitten stood upright under the influence of these repeated shocks, but his head was swimming round as if it was only half fixed on his shoulders.

"A Kurd," he muttered. "I, a citizen of Rotterdam, the husband of a Kurd!"

"Have no fear, it is only a mock ceremonial," whispered Kéraban. "A joke."

"You can't joke with these people," replied Van Mitten, piteously, and so comically withal, that his friends could scarcely keep from laughter.

Nedjeb, indicating the noble Saraboul, said to her mistress—

"I am very much mistaken it this is not all got up by the widow to secure a second husband."

"Poor M. Van Mitten!" said Amasia.

"I would rather have eight months in prison than eight hours of such married life," said Bruno, sadly.

Seigneur Yanar turned to the audience and said loudly—

"To-morrow we will celebrate, with all due pomp at Trebizond, the betrothal of Seigneur Van Mitten and the noble Saraboul."

At the word "betrothal," Van Mitten and his companions began to hope that the consequences of the adventure would be less serious than they had feared.

Here it may be remarked that, according to the usages of Kurdistan, these betrothals constitute an indissoluble bond of marriage. They may be compared to the "civil contract" of certain European nations, and that which follows it to the religious marriage. But in Kurdistan, though after the betrothal the man is only "engaged," he is bound for life to the *fiancée* he has chosen—or, as in the present case, to the lady who had chosen him!

All this was duly explained to Van Mitten by Seigneur Yanar.

"But after all," whispered Kéraban, "it can make no difference to you whether you are betrothed or married."

Scarpante, who quitted the caravanserai as soon as the gates were re-opened, muttered this threat—

"The trick has failed. Now we shall try force!"

Then he disappeared, unnoticed by either Kéraban or any of his friends.

"Poor M. Van Mitten," said Ahmet, as he watched the discomfited mien of the Dutchman.

"We must make light of it," replied Kéraban. "The betrothal is nothing. In ten days the whole affair will be at an end. That will not matter!"

"No; but ten days' engagement to such an imperious lady as the Kurdish woman is, must count for something!" replied Ahmet.

Five minutes later the court of the caravanserai was empty. Everyone had gone to bed. Van Mitten was guarded by his terrible brother-in-law, and silence fell upon the scene of the tragic comedy, the principal part in which had fallen so heavily upon the unfortunate Dutchman.

---

## Chapter IX.

### In which Van Mitten has the Honour to become the Brother-in-Law of Seigneur Yanar.

A town which dates from the year (A.M.) 4790, which owes its existence to the inhabitants of a Milesian colony which was conquered by Mithradates; fell under the power of Pompey; submitted to the rule of the Persians and Scythians: which was "Christian" under Constantine the Great, and Pagan to the middle of the 6th century (A.D.): which was relieved by Belisarius and enriched by Justinian; which was owned by the Comneni, of whom Napoleon I. was said to be the descendant; then by the Sultan Mahomet; till the end of the 16th century, when the Empire of Trebizond came to an end, after lasting 250 years:—this town, as will readily be conceded, has some right to figure in the history of the World. So neither will any one be surprised that Van Mitten had been very anxious to see such a celebrated place, and one so renowned in the annals and romances of chivalry.

But when this delightful anticipation possessed Van Mitten, he had been free from all care. He had only to follow his friend Kéraban round the antique Euxine; but now an engaged man, for some days provisionally, but still engaged to the noble lady who held him in leash; he was not altogether in the vein to appreciate the historic splendours of Trebizond.

It was on the 17th September, about 9 A.M., two hours after quitting the Caravanserai of Rissar, that Kéraban and his companions, Yanar, his sister, and their respective attendants, entered the capital of the modern pachalik, built in the midst of an Alpine country, including valleys, mountains, and waterfalls, which recall the scenes of central Europe, and make one fancy that a slice of Switzerland or of the Tyrol has been transported to the shores of the Black Sea.

Trebizond, situated 325 kilomètres from Erzeroum, the important capital of Armenia, is now in direct communication with Persia, by a route which the Turkish government has opened by way of Garnuch Kané, Baiborut, and Erzeroum, and by this means something of its ancient commercial prosperity is preserved.

The city is divided into the Turkish and Latin quarters. The former bristles with the minarets of at least forty mosques, which rise above the orange and olive groves. The latter, the Christian quarter, is the commercial centre in which the Grand Bazaar is situated, wherein are found all kinds of stuffs, arms, money, and precious stones. The harbour is served by a weekly line of steamers which keep open the communication with the principal points of the Black Sea.

In the town lives, or vegetates, according to the various elements of which it is composed, a population of 40,000 inhabitants,

Turks, Persians, Christians of the Armenian and Latin churches, orthodox Greeks, Kurds and Europeans. But when our travellers entered the city the population was augmented more than five times beyond its normal strength by the numbers of the Faithful who had come from all parts of Asia Minor to attend the festivities which were about to be celebrated in honour of Mahomet.

The little caravan had some difficulty in finding a lodging for the twenty-four hours they intended to remain in Trebizond, as Kéraban intended to quit the town the next morning for Scutari. In fact he had not a day to lose if he would arrive there by the end of the month.

The Little Caravan enters Trebizond

At length, in a regular district of caravanserais, khans, auberges, at a Franco-Italian hotel, they found accommodation near the Giaour Meidan, the commercial quarter, and consequently outside the Turkish city. But the hotel was comfortable, and Kéraban had not the shadow of an excuse for finding fault.

Now when Seigneur Kéraban and his friends had reached this stage in their journey, in the belief that they had passed all the danger, if they had not escaped all the fatigues of the way—a plot was hatching in the Turkish town, where their mortal enemy resided.

It was at the palace of Seigneur Saffar, which was built on the slopes of the Boshpeh mountain, which slopes gently towards the sea, that, early in the morning, Scarpante arrived, two hours after he had quitted the caravanserai of Rissar.

Seigneur Saffar and Yarhud had been awaiting him, and to them Scarpante related the incidents which had occurred the night before. He told them how Kéraban and Ahmet had been saved from imprisonment which would have left Amasia virtually unprotected, and how they had been released by the stupid unselfish devotion of Van Mitten. The plans discussed by the three men ended in the resolve to interrupt the travellers between Trebizond and Scutari. What the plan was, the sequel will tell; but we may say that a commencement was made that very day, for Seigneur Saffar and Yarhud, without thinking of the *fêtes*, quitted Trebizond, and took the western road through Anatolia, which leads to the Bosphorus shore.

The Harbour of Trebizond.

Scarpante himself remained in Trebizond.

He was not known to either Kéraban, Ahmet, or the ladies, and so could have full liberty of action. He was to play the important part in the drama which would in future substitute force in action for cunning.

So Scarpante was enabled to mingle with the crowd, and to stroll in the Giaour Meidan. He was not likely to be recognized by Kéraban or his nephew, for they had only seen him in the semi-darkness of the court-yard at the caravanserai of Rissar. It was easy enough for Scarpante to spy upon them unsuspected.

This is how it happened, that he perceived Ahmet, soon after his arrival, proceed through the encumbered streets, and obtain the direction of the telegraph office. Scarpante also noticed that Ahmet despatched a long telegram to Amasia's father.

"Bah," muttered the spy, "that message will never reach the hand for which it is intended. Selim was mortally wounded by Yarhud, and there is nothing to alarm us in this."

So Scarpante was quite easy in his mind, and thought no more of the telegram.

Then Ahmet returned to the hotel, and Amasia was convinced that in a few hours those at the Villa Selim would be reassured concerning her safety.

"A letter would have taken too long to reach Odessa," added Ahmet, "and besides I am always afraid——"

He checked himself suddenly.

"You are afraid of what, my dearest Ahmet? What do you mean?" asked Amasia, somewhat surprised.

"Nothing, dearest," replied Ahmet, "nothing, I wished to remind your father to be at Scutari to meet us, and even to be there before us, so as to make sure that no delay shall occur in our marriage."

The truth was that Ahmet, still distrustful of new attempts to carry Amasia away, had notified the banker that all danger had not passed: but, fearful of alarming Amasia, he had quieted her apprehensions, vague and only founded on presentiments though they were.

Amasia thanked Ahmet tenderly for the forethought he had displayed in telegraphing to her father, and for running the risk of Kéraban's malediction for using the wire.

But what had become of Van Mitten all this time? He had most unwillingly become the affianced husband of Saraboul, and the pitiful brother-in-law of Yanar the Kurd.

How could he resist? On one side was Kéraban, telling him he must carry out the sacrifice to the bitter end, or else the judge would send them all to prison—an act which would irreparably compromise the issue of the journey; that the marriage, though legal in Turkey, was a "dead letter" in Holland, where Van Mitten had a wife already: that he might if he pleased, have one wife in Europe or two in Turkey. But Van Mitten's choice was made; he was not going to be made game of.

On the other side there were a brother and sister who were not likely to let their prey escape. It was then only prudent to satisfy them, to give them the slip beyond the Bosphorus, and prevent them from exercising their pretended rights as brother-in law and wife respectively.

So Van Mitten made no attempt to resist, and calmly awaited events.

Fortunately Kéraban had got them to consent to proceed to Scutari, before returning to Mossoul, so that they might be present at the wedding of Ahmet and Amasia, and the Kurdish lady was not to carry off her *fiancé* till three or four days after the marriage.

It was arranged that Bruno, though thinking his master had got only what he deserved for his weakness, was not to leave him under the control of that terrible female. But we must confess that Bruno was seized with a fit of laughter which Kéreban could not repress, when they saw Van Mitten proceeding to attend the betrothal ceremony in the costume of Kurdistan.

"Is that really you, Van Mitten?" cried Kéraban. "Have you arrayed yourself in the Oriental dress?"

"It is I," replied Van Mitten.

"As a Kurd?"

"As a Kurd! Exactly."

"Well, it is not unbecoming to you, and I am sure when you become accustomed to it you will find the costume much more convenient than your scanty European garments."

"You are very good, friend Kéraban."

"Look here, Van Mitten, banish this sad

The Shore of the Bosphorus.

expression of yours. Tell yourself that it is carnival time, and that you are merely disguised for a mock marriage."

"It is not the disguise that troubles me," replied Van Mitten.

"What is it then that does?"

"The marriage!"

"Bah! Merely a temporary arrangement, Van Mitten. Madame Saraboul must put up with the loss. Yes, when you tell her that these betrothals are not binding on you as you have a wife already in Rotterdam, when you take leave of her and her terrible brother, I shall be there, Van Mitten. Truly, people must not be married against their wills. It is quite bad enough when they consent to it."

As everything tended to this end the

worthy Dutchman had finally accepted the situation. It was best after all to look at the matter from the comic side, since such a course helps one to resign oneself, while it also serves the interests of all.

Besides, on that day Van Mitten had hardly had time to look about him, or to think of himself. Yanar and his sister were not people to let the grass grow under their feet. They were for summary "execution," and the marriage gibbet was quite ready to hang up the child of Holland.

Still it must not be imagined that any custom or formality of Turkestan would be omitted or neglected. No, the brother-in-law took all these preparations under his own particular care, and in such a large town nothing would be wanting to give all possible solemnity to the marriage.

Amid the population of Trebizond are included a number of Kurds, and amongst them Yanar and his sister found some acquaintances and friends. These worthy people considered it their duty to assist their compatriots on the auspicious occasion, and to do all in their power to help their countrywoman to a second husband. So there was quite a clan on the side of the bride, while Ahmet, Kéraban, and their companions were engaged to figure on the side of the bridegroom. Nevertheless Van Mitten was closely watched and had never been permitted to see his friends alone since the time he had spoken to Kéraban about the change of dress.

But for one instant only Bruno was able to glide up to his side and whisper in a warning tone—

"Mind what you are about, master. Take care; you are risking a heavy stake in this game!"

"How can I act otherwise, Bruno?" replied Van Mitten in a resigned tone. "At anyrate if I am guilty of folly it will relieve my friends from embarrassment, and the consequences of it will not be serious."

"Hum!" muttered Bruno, "Master is going to be married, and says the consequences will not be—hum!"

If some one had not at that moment come for Van Mitten, there is no knowing what the termination of the sentence might have been.

It was mid-day and the Seigneur Yanar with the other Kurds came to Van Mitten whom they would not again leave until the ceremony had been performed.

Then the knot was tied with much ceremony. During the performance of the rite, Van Mitten would not permit his anxiety to appear; the noble Saraboul was delighted at having won a European to wed her a woman of Asia—what a glorious alliance was this of Holland with Kurdistan!

The bride was resplendent in her wedding-dress, which she carried about with her in case of need—a necessary precaution, as events proved. Her robe of cloth of gold, her jewellery and ornaments were all magnificent. Never had such a splendid bride been seen in the streets of Trebizond, which ought to have been laid down with a purple carpet, as they were at the birth of Constantine.

But if the noble Saraboul was superb, Seigneur Van Mitten was magnificent; while Kéraban congratulated him warmly—though the compliments could not fail to be of a somewhat ironical flavour from an old Believer who retained the ancient Oriental dress.

Van Mitten had quite a martial appearance in his new dress, a haughty air, and a somewhat forbidding aspect, quite at variance with the general appearance of a Rotterdam merchant. He could not be otherwise in such a costume, booted and spurred as he was; a fez ornamented with *yeminis* and the *puskul*, the enormous length of which indicated the rank which the Dutchman would shortly attain as the husband of the noble Saraboul.

"The Imaum offered up a simple prayer."—p. 307

# KÉRABAN THE INFLEXIBLE;

## OR, ADVENTURES IN THE EUXINE.

BY JULES VERNE.

TRANSLATED BY HENRY FRITH.

---

### CHAPTER IX.

THE great Bazaar of Trebizond had furnished all these adjuncts, which, had they been made to measure, could not have fitted better. Van Mitten had also procured a perfect armoury of weapons, damascened poignards, double-edged and jade-hilted daggers, silver-mounted pistols, a short handled sabre, saw-bladed and ornamented with silver; and finally a long-hafted steel weapon with designs in relief, and with a curving blade like the blades of the old scythes.

Ah! Kurdistan might declare war against Turkey. The army of the Padischah could not hope to vanquish such warriors as these! Poor Van Mitten, who could have ever imagined you in such a position? Fortunately, all his friends, except Bruno, kept tellinghim tha t it was "only a joke!"

During the ceremony nothing particular occurred, and if the bridegroom had not been found somewhat cold by his terrible brother-in-law, and his not less terrible sister, all would have been well.

At Trebizond there is no want of judges, acting as ministerial officers, who would gladly register such a marriage contract—so much the more as it was not unattended with profit. But the magistrate who had so sagaciously unfolded the mystery at the caravanserai of Rissar, was the person entrusted with the honourable duty, and he complimented in proper terms the future pair.

Then when the contract had been signed, the *fiancés* and their suite, in the midst of an enormous concourse of people, proceeded to the enclosed town, and to a mosque which had formerly been a Byzantine church, the walls of which were decorated with curious mosaics. Then there was some Kurdish chanting, which is more melodious and rythmical than the Turkish or Armenian chants, and some simple musical instruments of metallic tone, with some little flutes, united in the quaint concert. Then the Imaum offered up a simple prayer, and Van Mitten was legally affianced, tightly tied up, as Kéraban, with some "*arrière pensée*," assured the noble Saraboul when he felicitated her on her marriage.

Later on, the ceremony would be repeated in Kurdistan, where other fêtes would be carried on for many weeks. Van Mitten would have to conform to the customs of the country, or, at least, he would have to try to do so. The husband there has to carry off his wife unexpectedly in his arms when she reaches her future house, no doubt to save her blushes at the idea of going of her own will into a strange home. When he arrived there Van Mitten would do nothing to slight the customs of Kurdistan; but, fortunately, that country was still far distant.

But at that time the ceremonies of the betrothal were naturally eclipsed by those which were performed to celebrate the night of the ascension of the Prophet, the *eil-et-ul-my'râdy*, which usually takes place on the 29th month of Redjeb. That year, in consequence of the particular circumstances of a politico-religious ceremony, an ordinance of the chief Imaum had fixed the great *fête* for the same date as the marriage ceremony.

That evening, in the largest palace of the town, magnificently arranged for the purpose, thousands and thousands of the Faithful lent themselves to the ceremonial which had attracted them to Trebizond from every corner of Mussulman Asia.

The noble Saraboul could not resist the temptation to exhibit her husband in public. As for Seigneur Kéraban, his nephew, the two young girls, and their servants, what could they do better in order to pass the evening than to attend this marvellous ceremony!

And marvellous it is indeed! and how could it fail to be so in that country of the East in which all the dreams of the rest of the world become realities. It would be more easy for the painter to depict the scene than for the writer, even though he could command all the hyperbole, the imagery, the periods, of the most illustrious poets of the world.

"Riches are in the Indies; wit in Europe; but pomp is in the Ottoman Empire," is a Turkish proverb.

And it was really in the midst of incomparable pomp and magnificence that the poetic fable displayed itself, and to which the most charming daughters of Asia Minor lent their grace and beauty. The ceremony is based upon the legend imitated from the Christian record that, until his death, which happened in the 10th year of the Hegeira, his paradise was closed to all the faithful ones sleeping in the arms of space, pending the arrival of the Prophet. On that day he appeared on horseback on "El-borak," the hippogriff which waited his arrival at the gate of the Temple of Jerusalem. Then his tomb miraculously quitted the earth, ascended to the heavens, and remained suspended between the zenith and the nadir in the midst of the splendours of the Paradise of Islam. All the Faithful then awoke to render homage to the Prophet. The period of eternal happiness promised to them began, and Mahomet raised himself up in a dazzling apotheosis, while the stars of heaven in the form of innumerable houris circled round the resplendent throne of Allah.

In a word this *fête* is as the realization of the dream of one of the poets, who best interpreted the Oriental poetry when he said, *àpropos* of the ecstatic performances of the dervishes, carried away by their dances and strange rhymes——

"What saw they in those visions in which they rocked themselves? Forests of emeralds bearing rubies as fruit; the mountains of amber and myrrh; the kiosks of diamonds, and the tents of pearl of the Paradise of Mahomet."

---

## Chapter X.

### In Which the Hero of this Story loses no time.

The next day, the 18th of September, as the sun was beginning to light up the highest minarets of the town, a little caravan came out by one of the gates of the old fortification, and the travellers waved a last adieu to poetic Trebizond.

This caravan, *en route* for the Bosphorus, was proceeding along the coast, led by a guide, whose services Kéraban had willingly accepted. This guide ought, at any rate, to be acquainted with this part of Anatolia, for he was one of those nomads known in the country as *loupeurs*.

By this name are designated a certain class of woodcutters whose occupation it is to scour the forests of the districts for walnuts. On those trees grow large natural excrescences of remarkable hardness, the wood of which, inasmuch as it lends itself to all the requirements of the cabinet-makers, is particularly sought after.

This guide, having learnt that the strangers were about to quit Trebizond for Scutari, had come the previous evening to offer his services. He appeared intelligent, quite conversant with all the routes, with the windings of which he was familiar. So, after giving distinct and straightforward replies to the questions put by Kéraban, the *loupeur* had been engaged at a high price, which he was assured would be doubled if the caravan reached the hills above the Bosphorus within twelve days, the extreme period fixed for the celebration of the marriage of Amasia and Ahmet.

Ahmet, after having questioned the guide, and particularly having sought to discover in his inexpressive countenance and reserved manner that indescribable "something" which always speaks in favour of people, and to which one never hesitates to accord one's confidence, was satisfied. No one could be more useful than a man who had been perfectly well acquainted with these regions all his life, nothing could be more reassuring under such circumstances, when a journey had to be accomplished so speedily. So, then, the *loupeur* became guide to Seigneur Kéraban and his companions. To him the little troop turned for direction. He chose the halting places, and organized the encampments; he looked after them all; and when he was promised that his salary should be doubled on condition they arrived at Scutari with as little delay as possible, he replied—

"Seigneur Kéraban may be assured I will do my best, and, since he has proposed to double the money for my services, I pledge my word I will demand nothing if before twelve days he is not in Scutari."

"By Mahomet! that is the man for me," said Kéraban, when he told his nephew of the proposal.

"Yes, uncle," replied Ahmet; "but, however good a guide he may be, do not let us forget how imprudent it is to venture on the roads of Anatolia."

"Ah! always afraid of something, Ahmet!"

"Uncle Kéraban, I shall not think we are safe until we are at Scutari."

"And you will be married! Is it not so?" said Kéraban, taking Ahmet's hand. "Very well, in twelve days I promise you Amasia shall be the wife of the most distrustful of nephews."

"And the niece of ——"

"The best of uncles!" cried Kéraban with a roar of laughter.

The little caravan was made up of two "talikas" (a "talika" is a kind of not uncomfortable open carriage, which can be closed in case of wet weather; with four horses each "talika"), and two horses saddled. Ahmet was glad, even at the high price, to find such vehicles in Trebizond, so that he might finish his journey in comfort.

Seigneur Kéraban, Amasia, and Nedjeb were in the first talika, Nizib being in the seat at the back. At the back of the second the noble Saraboul was enthroned near her *fiancé*, and opposite her brother, with Bruno to act as valet.

Ahmet was mounted on one of the saddle horses, the guide on the other; the latter sometimes rode by the talikas, and sometimes showing by which way to go.

As the country was not very safe, the travellers were provided with guns and revolvers, besides the usual arms that Yanar and his sister carried in their belts, and Seigneur Kéraban's famous pistols. Although the guide assured Ahmet that there was nothing to be afraid of on the roads, he determined to take precautions against all aggression.

After all, there was no absolute difficulty in travelling two hundred miles in twelve days, without changing horses (as post-houses were rare in the country), even letting the horses rest every night. Then, unless any unseen or improbable accidents happened, this roundabout journey would be completed in the wished-for time.

The country that extends from Trebizond to Sinope is called "Djanik" by the Turks. It is on the other side that Anatolia—commonly called Ancient Bithynia—commences. It has become a great pachalic of Turkey in Asia, being on the west of Asia Minor. Kutaya is the capital, and Brusa, Smyrna, Angora, &c., the principal towns.

The little caravan started at 6 o'clock in the morning from Trebizond, arriving, at 9 o'clock at Platana, after a stage of five leagues.

Platana is the ancient Hermonassa. To get there one must pass through a sort of valley where barley, corn, and maize grow; where magnificent tobacco plantations prosper marvellously. Seigneur Kéraban could not help admiring these plantations, where the leaves become, without any drying preparation, a golden yellow. Very likely his correspondent and friend, Van Mitten, would also have been unable to restrain his admiration if he had not been altogether wrapt-up in the noble Saraboul. In all this country grow beautiful trees. The pines and the beeches may be compared to the most majestic trees of Holstein and Denmark; also the nut trees, the currant and wild raspberry bushes. Bruno, with an envious feeling, observed the natives of this country, even at an early age, were stout—this was rather humiliating for a Dutchman reduced to a skeleton.

At noon they passed the little market town of Tol, leaving on the left the first undulations of the Pontic Alps. Along the roads going towards Trebizond, or returning, were peasants, clothed in thick brown woollen stuff, and a bonnet made of sheep-skin for their head-dress, accompanied by their wives, wrapped in a piece of striped cotton cloth, which went well with their short red woollen petticoats.

All this country Xenophon made illustrious by his famous retreat of the Ten Thousand. But the unfortunate Van Mitten would cower under the menacing look of Yanar, without even being able to consult his guide book. So he had ordered Bruno to consult it for him and take notes. It is true Bruno would think of other things than the exploits of the great general, and that is why, in leaving Trebizond, he had forgotten to show his master the hill that over-looked the coast, and from the height of which the Ten Thousand saluted with their enthusiastic cries the waves of the Black Sea. In truth he was not a faithful servant!

That evening after a journey of 20 leagues, the caravan arrived and slept at Tirebola. There the "caiwak," a sort of cream obtained by lukewarm milk, made with lamb's rennet; and the "yaourk," cheese made with sour milk by means of pressure, were thoroughly appreciated by the travellers, who had gained an appetite from the long journey. Besides, mutton in all forms was not absent at the repast, and Nizib could now regale without fear of infringing the Mussulman law. Bruno this time did not cheat him out of his part of the supper.

This little market town, which is only a simple village, was left on the morning of the 19th of September. During the day they passed Zèpe and its narrow port where only three or four merchant ships of small draught are able to shelter. Then, still under the direction of the guide, who knew these roads perfectly, the party proceeded on the sometimes troublesome tracks, in the middle of long plains. They arrived, very late, at Kérésoum, after a stage of 25 leagues.

Kérésoum is built at the foot of a hill, in a double escarpment of its side. This, the ancient Pharnace, where the Ten Thousand stopped during ten days to recruit their strength, is very picturesque, with the ruins of its castle overlooking the entrance of the port. There Seigneur Kéraban would have easily been able to make an ample provision

"In all this country grow beautiful trees."

of cherry-wood pipes, which are objects of an important trade. In fact the cherry tree abounds on this part of the pachalic, and Van Mitten thought he ought to relate again to his *fiancée* the great historical fact, that it was to this same Kérésoum that the proconsul Lucullus sent the first cherry-trees that were acclimatized in Europe. Saraboul had never heard of the celebrated *gourmet*, and appeared to take but small interest in the learned dissertations of Van Mitten. The latter, under the dominion of this haughty person, became a sadder Kurd than one can imagine. In the meantime, his friend Kéraban, without anyone being able to guess whether he jested or not, did not cease to congratulate Van Mitten on the way in which he wore his new costume, which made him shrug his shoulders at Bruno.

"Yes, Van Mitten, yes!" repeated Kéraban, "that suits you perfectly; this robe, this 'chalwar,' this turban; but to be a complete Kurd, you want larger and fiercer moustaches, like Seigneur Yanar's."

"I have never had moustaches," replied Van Mitten.

"You never had moustaches?" cried Saraboul.

"He has never had moustaches?" repeated Seigneur Yanar disdainfully.

"Scarcely any, noble Saraboul."

"Very well, you shall have them," replied the imperious Kurd, "and I undertake to make them grow."

"Poor Monsieur Van Mitten!" murmured young Amasia, rewarding him with a kind look.

"Good! all that will end in smoke," repeated Nedjeb, while Bruno shook his head like a bird of ill omen.

The following day, the 20th of September, after having followed an enticing Roman road that Lucullus had constructed, they said, to reunite Anatolia to the Armenian provinces, the little troop, favoured by the weather, left behind them the village of Aptas, then towards noon the market town of Ordu was gained. This stage skirted the verge of splendid forests, that clothed the hills on which abounded the most varied species of trees; oaks, witch-elms, elms, maples, planes, plum-trees, wild olives, junipers, white poplars, pomegranates, white and black mulberries, walnut trees and sycamore. There the vine is an exuberant vegetable that grows like ivy in some mild country, twining as far as the tree-tops. All these! without speaking of the shrubs, hawthorns, barberries, filbert-trees, laburnums, elders, medlar trees, jasmines, tamarisks, nor of various other plants, blue and white saffron flowers, iris, rhododendrons, scabiouses, yellow narcissi, mallows, centaury, gilliflowers, oriental clematis, and wild tulips —yes, even tulips! that Van Mitten could not see without all the instinct of the amateur awakening in him, indeed the sight of these plants was rather of a nature to evoke some displeasing remembrance of his first union. It is true the existence of the other Madam Van Mitten was now a guaranty against the matrimonial pretentions of the second. So far the worthy Dutchman was happy, and ten times happier because he had been already married.

The Cape Jessoun Bouroun once passed, the guide directed the caravan across the ruins of the old village of Polemonium, towards the market town of Fatisa, where travellers and horses slept soundly all night.

Ahmet, always on the alert, had not, so far, had any great cause of suspicion. Fifty odd leagues had been got over since leaving Trebizond; during that time no danger had threatened Seigneur Kéraban and his companions. The guide was of a communicative nature, so was always discussing matters during the walks and stoppages, skilfully and shrewdly. Nevertheless, Ahmet felt for this man a certain mistrust that he could not overcome. So he neglected nothing that he ought to have done to assure the security of all, and he watched for the common safety without even letting them perceive his anxiety.

On the 21st, at daybreak, they left Fatisa; about noon they left on the right the Ouruck port and its erection of woodyards, at the mouth of the ancient Œnus. Thence the road proceeded to cross immense plains of hemp, as far as the mouth of Tchercherebet (where a rumour has placed a tribe of Amazons), so as to "turn" the capes and the headlands, that are covered with ruins, like all those upon that historical coast. The market town of Terma was passed in the afternoon, and in the evening the travellers halted at Sansoun for the night.

Sansoun is one of the most important ports on this slope of the Black Sea, although its roadstead is scarcely a safe one, and the harbour is rather shallow at the mouth of the Ékil-Irmak. However, trade is fairly active and cargoes of water-melons which flourish in the vicinity are forwarded, under the name of *arbute-berries*, to Constantinople. An old fort, picturesquely placed upon the margin of the coast, defends but imperfectly the place from attack by sea.

In the state of emaciation to which Bruno was reduced it seemed to him that the water-melons, on which Seigneur Kéraban and his friends were regaling, were scarcely sufficient nourishment, and he declined to partake of them. The fact was, the brave fellow, although already much reduced in size, found still an opportunity to grow thinner, and Kéraban felt constrained to remark it.

"This stage skirted the verge of splendid forests."

"But," he added, in a consolatory manner, "we are approaching Egypt; and there, Bruno, if he likes, may make a good bargain for his body."

"In what way?" asked Bruno.

"By selling yourself as a mummy!"

If this joke displeased the unfortunate valet, and if he wished for Kéraban a more unpleasant fate than his master's second marriage, he kept his wishes to himself!

"But you will see that nothing will happen to this Turk," muttered Bruno: "all the unpleasantness will fall upon the Christians, as we are!"

And indeed Kéraban was in capital form, for he did not consider that his good humour had been much tried, as all his plans were being accomplished under the best conditions of time and safety.

The travellers did not halt, except to rest the horses, either at Meletsch or by the Kysie, which was crossed by a bridge of boats, in the course of the 22nd September; nor at Gerse where they arrived next day, nor at Tschobanlar. Nevertheless Kéraban would have liked to explore, if only for a few hours, Bafria, or Bafra, situated a little inland, where a great trade in tobacco is carried on, the "tays" or packets of which, tied up between long laths, had so often replenished his stores in Constantinople; but it would have been necessary to make a detour of a dozen leagues or so, and it was thought wiser not to lengthen a journey already long enough.

On the 23rd the little caravan arrived without opposition at Sinope on the frontier of Anatolia proper.

Sinope, another important port of the Black Sea, situated on the isthmus of the same name, the ancient Sinope of Strabo and Polybius. The anchorage is always excellent, and ships are built in the place with the splendid woods of the Aio-Antonio mountains, which rise close by. There is a castle, with a double enceinte, but there are only five hundred houses at most, and scarcely six thousand inhabitants.

Ah, why had not Van Mitten been born two thousand or three thousand years sooner! How he would have admired that celebrated town, the origin of which is attributed to the Argonauts; which became such an important Milesian colony as to deserve the name of the Euxine Carthage; whose ships covered the Black Sea in the time of the Romans, and which ended by being ceded to Mahomet II. because it delighted the Commander of the Faithful! But it was now too late to recall the decayed splendour of the architecture of such various styles. It is only necessary here to recall the fact that it derived its name of Sinope from a daughter of the Asopus and Methone, who was carried away by Apollo to this place. On the present occasion the nymph was carrying away the object of her tenderness, and her name was Saraboul! This reflection caused Van Mitten some lively pangs.

# KÉRABAN THE INFLEXIBLE;

## OR, ADVENTURES IN THE EUXINE.

BY JULES VERNE.

TRANSLATED BY HENRY FRITH.

### CHAPTER X.

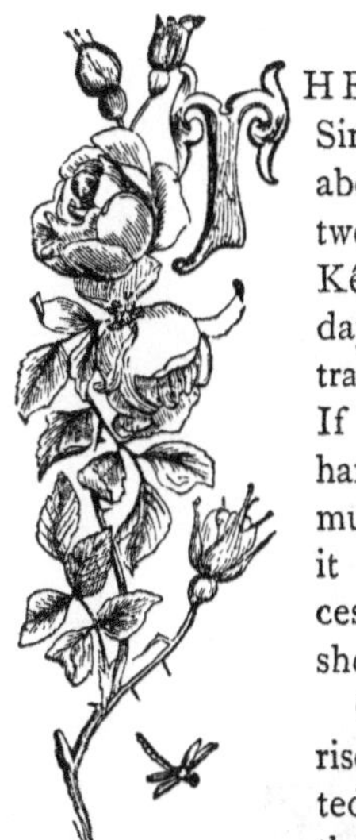

THE distance between Sinope and Scutari is about one hundred and twenty-five leagues, and Kéraban had only seven days left in which to traverse that distance. If he was not behindhand neither was he much ahead of time. So it was absolutely necessary that no time should be lost.

On the 24th, at sunrise, the caravan quitted Sinope to follow the Anatolian coast-line. About ten o'clock the little *troupe* reached Istifan, at mid-day Apena was passed, and in the evening, after a day's journey of fifteen leagues, the travellers stopped at Ineboli, which, open to all winds, has only unsafe anchorage for merchant vessels.

Ahmet then proposed to rest for two hours only, and to travel the rest of the night. Twelve hours gained would be well worth a little fatigue. Seigneur Kéraban accepted the situation. No one objected, not even Bruno. Besides, Yanar and Saraboul were anxious to reach the Bosphorus, so as to proceed towards Kurdistan; and Van Mitten was in no less haste, but to fly as far as possible from Kurdistan, the very name of which made him shudder.

The guide made no objection to this plan, and declared himself ready to start whenever they liked. By day or night the road was all the same to him, and this *loupeur*, accustomed to traverse thick forests by instinct, had no difficulty in following the coast road.

So, at eight in the evening, they started under a beautiful full moon, which was rising in the east after the sun had set. Amasia, Nedjeb, Kéraban, the noble Saraboul, Yanar, and Van Mitten stretched in the vehicles, permitted themselves to sleep, lulled by the quick motion of the carriages and the tramp of the horses.

They saw nothing of Cape Kerenebé, half hidden in the crowd of sea-birds whose cries filled the air. In the morning they passed Teniléh without any incident having occurred to trouble them: then they reached Kidros, and in the evening halted at Amastia. They had now a right to some hours' rest, after having made more than sixty leagues in thirty-six hours.

Perhaps Van Mitten—for we must always turn to this excellent man, who had been diligently reading up his guide-book—perhaps Van Mitten, had he been a free agent, and had time and money not been wanting, would have dug out the harbour in the hope of seeking an archæological object of which an antiquary would not dare to dispute the value.

Everyone knows that 290 years before Christ, Queen Amastris, wife of Lysimachus, one of Alexander's captains, and the foundress of this town, was enclosed in a leathern sack, and thrown by her two brothers into the harbour she had constructed. Now, what a glorious thing it would be for Van Mitten, if on the faith of his guide-book he could fish up this famous sack. But, as we have said, time and money were wanting and, without imparting his idea to anyone, not even to the noble Saraboul, the subject of his reverie, he kept his archæological regrets to himself.

Next morning, 26th September, at day-break, they left this ancient metropolis of the Genoese, which is now only a miserable village of toy-makers. Three or four leagues further on is the little town of

The caravan quitting Sinope.

Bartan, which was passed close by, and in the afternoon Jelias; at nightfall Ozina, and towards midnight Eregli was gained.

There the party reposed until daylight. This was indeed little enough rest, for the horses as well as the travellers began to feel greatly fatigued by the exigencies of the long journey, which had left them little time for repose since they had left Trebizond. Only four days remained—the 27th, 28th, 29th, and 30th of September—and the last day would have to be deducted from the total, as the 30th was intended to be passed in another fashion. So, if Seigneur Kéraban and his companions did not reach the shores of the Bosphorus very early on the morning of the 30th, the situation would be seriously compromised. There was not a moment to lose, and Kéraban hastened the start at sunrise.

Eregli is the ancient Heraclea, of Greek origin. It was formerly an immense city, whose walls, now in ruins, still indicate the extent. The harbour, at one time very important and well-sheltered, has degenerated with the town which boasts only six or seven thousand inhabitants. After the Romans, after the Greeks, after the Genoese, it fell under the domination of Mahomet II., and the city, which had known long days of splendour, became a simple market-town, devoid of any industry or commerce.

The happy *fiancé* of Saraboul would have still had some curiosity to satisfy there. Was it not at Heraclea, that peninsula of Acherusias, that the mythological cavern, one of the entrances to Tartarus, opened. Does not Diodorus of Sicily tell us that it was by this gate Hercules brought back Cerberus, when returning from the infernal regions? But Van Mitten still kept his desires deep down in his heart. Besides, as to Cerberus, did not he recognise in Yanar his faithful image—his watchful guardian. Of course the Kurdish gentleman had not three heads, but one was enough for him, and when he held that up with a ferocious air, it seemed that his teeth appeared under his thick moustaches as ready to bite as were those of the tri-headed dog, which Pluto had enchained.

On the 27th September the little caravan passed through the town of Sacaria, and towards evening reached Cape Kerpé, where sixteen centuries before the Emperor Aurelius was slain. There they halted for the night and took counsel as to the means by which the journey might be more readily completed, so as to reach Scutari within forty-eight hours—that is to say, on the morning of the last day fixed for their return.

---

## CHAPTER XI.

### IN WHICH SEIGNEUR KÉRABAN TAKES THE ADVICE OF THE GUIDE AGAINST THE OPINION OF AHMET.

THE suggestion made at the end of the last chapter had been advanced by the guide, and it was desirable that it should be taken into consideration.

What distance still lay between them, and the heights of Scutari? About sixty leagues. How much time remained to them to accomplish that distance? Forty-eight hours. That was little enough, if the cattle could not be made to proceed during the night.

Well then, by quitting the road, the windings of which lengthened the journey considerably; and by cutting across the extreme angle of Anatolia, which is included between the Black Sea and the Sea of Marmora—the travellers could shorten the journey by a good dozen leagues.

"This, Seigneur Kéraban, is the plan I would suggest to you," said the guide, in the cool manner which characterized him, "and I advise you to adopt it."

"But is not the coast road safer than the interior?" enquired Kéraban.

"There is no more danger to be feared in one than in the other," replied the guide.

"And are you well acquainted with these roads by which you offer to lead us?"

"I have traversed them twenty times, when I was working in the forests of Anatolia," replied the man.

"It seems to me that we ought not to hesitate in our choice," said Kéraban. "Twelve leagues is a considerable saving in our journey, and worth the extra fatigue we may have to endure!"

Ahmet listened, but said nothing.

"What are you thinking of, Ahmet," asked Kéraban, turning to his nephew.

Ahmet made no answer. He had certainly nursed suspicions against the guide—suspicions which, it must be confessed, were growing stronger as the termination of the journey was approaching.

In fact, the crafty manner of the man—his frequent inexplicable absences, during which he got ahead of the caravan—the care with which he always held aloof at camping time under the pretext of preparing the camp—the curious, even suspicious glances he bestowed upon Amasia—a care which he seemed specially to entertain for the young girl:—all these signs did not tend to reassure Ahmet. So he would not lose sight of this guide, accepted at Trebizond, of whom they knew nothing. But Kéraban was not a man to share these fears; and it would have been very difficult to make him accept as a fact what was still only a presentiment of ill.

Taking counsel for completing the journey.

"Well, Ahmet, before closing with this suggestion of the guide, I await your answer. What do you think of the itinerary proposed?"

"I think, uncle, that so far we have done well in following the coast road, and it would be imprudent to quit it."

"But why, Ahmet? Our guide is perfectly well acquainted with the roads of the interior, which he proposes we shall follow. Besides, the economy of time is worth the trouble."

"We can, by pushing our teams, very easily make up the——"

"You say this because Amasia is of the party," replied Kéraban. "But if she were waiting for us at Scutari, you would be the first to hasten our journey."

"Very likely, uncle."

"Well, for my part, as I have your

interests to serve, I think the sooner we arrive the better. We are at the mercy of the least delay; and since we can gain a dozen leagues by changing our route, we ought not to hesitate."

"So be it, uncle," replied Ahmet. "Since you desire it shall be so, I will not discuss the matter farther."

"It is not because I wish it, it is because you have nothing to advance against my argument," replied Kéraban, "and I am too much for you!"

Ahmet did not answer. At any rate, the guide could not fail to perceive that the young man had some distrust of the modification proposed by him. Their eyes met, but for a second; yet that glance was sufficient to measure swords, as they say in the fencing-school. So Ahmet determined to be on his "guard" in future, not merely on the watch. The guide seemed to him an adversary, only waiting the suitable moment to make a treacherous attack.

As for the others, the abridgment of the journey could not fail to please them, who had scarcely felt "at home" since they had quitted Trebizond. Van Mitten and Bruno were anxious to reach Scutari, to put an end to an irksome and unpleasant situation. Seigneur Yanar and the noble Saraboul, because they wanted to return to Kurdistan with brother-in-law and *fiancé* in the steamer; Amasia to be united to Ahmet, and Nedjeb to assist at the ceremony, and the rejoicings at the wedding.

So the suggestion was well received. It was decided that they would repose that night, 26-27th September, so as to be able to accomplish a long "stage" on the following day.

But there were some precautions to be observed, as the guide indicated. They must furnish themselves with food sufficient for forty-eight hours, for the region through which they proposed to travel was almost uninhabited. They would find neither "khans" nor "doukhans," nor inns, on the journey. So it was necessary to provide themselves with supplies for all requirements.

Fortunately they were able to procure what was wanted at Cape Kerpé on payment of a round sum, and they also acquired a donkey to carry the supplies.

It must be confessed that Seigneur Kéraban had a weakness for donkeys—the sympathy of one headstrong animal for another—and the ass he purchased at Cape Kerpé pleased him particularly.

It was rather a small animal, but it was strong enough to carry a horse's load about ninety "oks" or more than one hundred kilogrammes, one of those donkeys which one meets by thousands in Anatolia, where they carry cereals down to the various ports of the coast.

This frisky and active donkey had his nostrils artificially divided, so that he might the more effectually disembarrass himself of the flies which introduced themselves into his nose. This gave him a smiling appearance, quite a gay physiognomy and he quite merited the nickname of the "laughing jackass." He was a very different creature from those wretched-looking beasts described by Th. Gautier with drooping ears, and of a thin and scraggy backbone. The animal in question could be probably as obstinate as Kéraban himself, and Bruno maintained that the Seigneur had met his master!

A quarter of a sheep, cooked with "bourghoul," a kind of bread made with dried wheat, worked up with butter, was all the provision they needed for such a short journey. A small two-wheeled cart to which the donkey was harnessed served to carry the food.

On the 28th September, just before sunrise, the whole party were afoot. The horses were harnessed to the "talikas" in which each person occupied his or her accustomed place. Ahmet and the guide mounting their horses led the way. In an hour the vast expanse of the Black Sea had disappeared behind the hills. The country appeared undulating as it opened before them.

The journey was not very trying, though the condition of the road left much to be

"Ahmet followed him unseen."—p. 359

desired, a circumstance which gave Kéraban an opportunity to repeat a "litany of lamentations" against the neglect of the Ottoman authorities.

"One may easily perceive that we are approaching their modern Constantinople," he said.

"The roads in Kurdistan are infinitely superior to this," remarked Yanar.

"I can quite believe it" replied Kéraban, "and my friend Van Mitten will not have to regret Holland in that respect."

"In no respect" retorted the noble Kurd quickly, whose imperious character now displayed itself in all its grandeur!

Van Mitten would willingly have consigned his friend Kéraban to the Prince of Darkness, for the merchant appeared to take a malicious pleasure in tormenting him. But after all only eight-and-forty hours had to elapse before he should recover his liberty fully and completely, and then he would have *his* joke!

That evening the caravan halted near a dilapidated village, a mass of ruined huts scarcely fit to shelter cattle. There vegetated some hundreds of miserable beings who existed on milk and on meat of poor quality, and on bread which contained more bran than wheat. An unpleasant smell pervaded the place; this odour arose from the burning of "tezek" a kind of peat made of mud and dung, a fuel much used in the country, and of which the walls of the hovels are sometimes composed.

It was fortunate that as suggested by the guide, provisions had been provided by the travellers. There was nothing to be obtained in that miserable village, the inhabitants of which would have been much more likely to demand provisions than to supply them.

The night was passed, without incident, in a ruined cart-shed, wherein were some bundles of fresh straw. Ahmet kept watch with more than his usual circumspection, not without reason, for during the night the guide quitted the village and went off by himself some hundreds of paces in front.

Ahmet followed him unseen, and did not return to the encampment till just before the guide himself came back.

What was the man doing during the time he was absent? Ahmet could not make out. He assured himself that the guide held communication with no one. Not a living being had approached him. Not a cry had been heard in the deep silence of the night. Not a signal had been made from any point on the plain.

"Not a signal," said Ahmet to himself when he had returned to his place in the shed. "But was not the fire which appeared for an instant on the western horizon an expected signal?"

And then a circumstance which Ahmet had not at the time remarked, came vividly before him. He recalled very distinctly that while the guide was standing on a small hillock a fire had gleamed out in the distance—flashed three times distinctly, at short intervals, and then disappeared. Ahmet had at first put this down as a herdsman's fire, but now in the silence of the night, under the peculiar impression which the lethargy—which is not sleep—gives, he reflected: he recalled the appearance of the fire, and came to the conclusion—a conviction which was far beyond any presentiment—that the gleam was a signal.

"Yes," he thought, "our guide is betraying us, that is evident. He is acting in the interest of some powerful personage."

But in whose? Ahmet could not divine, though he was convinced the treachery had something to do with the abduction of Amasia. Though snatched from the hands of those who had carried her away from Odessa, might Amasia not be threatened by new perils? And now, when approaching Scutari, within a few days' journey of the goal, was there not all the more reason to fear!

Ahmet passed the remainder of the night in extreme anxiety. What was he to do? He did not know. Ought he at once to unmask the treason of the guide—treason of which there was no doubt—or to wait for the commencement of the execution of the plot before confronting and punishing him.

Daybreak found him more calm. He then decided to let things go on as they were for that day so as to ascertain more clearly the intentions of the guide. Resolved not to lose sight of him for an instant, Ahmet would not permit him to stray away either on the march or when the party halted. Besides, he and his friends were well armed, and, if the safety of Amasia had not been at stake, he would have had no fear of any attack.

Ahmet had once again resumed his wonted serenity. His features gave no indication of his feelings to any one of the party, not even to Amasia, whose affection could read his heart deepest; not even to the guide, who, on his part, did not cease to observe him with some considerable penetration.

The only resolution Ahmet made was to confide to his uncle Kéraban the suspicions he had confirmed, and that he would do as soon as occasion offered, even if he had to sustain the most stormy of discussions.

Next morning, very early, they quitted the miserable village. If it revealed neither treason nor mistake, this would be the last day of the journey undertaken to satisfy the *amour propre* of the most inflexible of Osmanlis. In any event the day would be a fatiguing one. The teams would have considerable difficulty in crossing the hilly country which belongs to the orographic system of the Elken. If only on this account, Ahmet had much to regret in having consented to an alteration in the route. Many times they had to dismount to lighten the carriages. Amasia and Nedjeb displayed great energy on these occasions. The noble Kurdish lady was not behind her companions in determination. As for Van Mitten, the husband of her choice, who had been very downcast since his departure from Trebizond, he was obliged to walk as he was bidden despotically.

There was, however, no hesitation as to the direction they had to take. The guide, evidently, was perfectly well acquainted with all the *détours* of the country. He knew it quite well, according to Kéraban—he knew it too well, according to Ahmet. So the latter could not accept the compliments of his uncle upon the conduct of the man so suspected. It must be stated that all that day the guide never quitted the travellers, but rode at the head of the caravan the whole time.

So things seemed to occur quite naturally, apart from the difficulties inherent to the condition of the roads—to their steepness when they ascended a hill-side, to their ruts when some places, which had been broken up by the late rains, were passed. However, the horses extricated the party from all these trials; for as it was the last day, the "cattle" were called on for some extra exertion. They would have plenty of time to rest afterwards.

Even the little donkey carried his burthen uncomplainingly, so Seigneur Kéraban took a great fancy to him.

"By Allah, this animal pleases me," he said; "and, to spite those Ottomans still more, I have a great mind to arrive on the shores of the Bosphorus on donkey-back."

This was quite understood to be only an idea of Kéraban's, but no one disputed the chances of its being carried out, so the author of it had no excuse for putting it in execution.

Towards nine o'clock in the evening after a really fatiguing day's march the caravan halted, and by the guide's advice began to form an encampment.

"How far are we from the heights of Scutari?" asked Ahmet.

Five or six leagues," replied the guide.

"Then why not push on?" continued Ahmet. "In a few hours we should arrive."

"Seigneur Ahmet," replied the guide, "I do not care to venture on this portion of the province at night. I am afraid I would lose my way. To-morrow at daybreak there will be nothing to fear; and, before noon, we shall arrive at the end of our journey."

"The man is right," said Kéraban. "We must not compromise our safety by too great haste. Let us camp here, nephew; let us take our last meal as travellers together, and to-morrow, before ten o'clock, we shall salute the Bosphorus."

Everyone except Ahmet was of Kéraban's opinion; so they disposed themselves in the best available manner under the circumstances.

The Gorge of Nerissa.

The place had been well-chosen by the guide. It was a somewhat straight defile between the mountains—or, more correctly, hills—of this part of Anatolia. The pass is called the Gorge of Nerissa.

At the end the high rocks united with the lower strata of the cliff, whose semi-circular shelves extended to the left in rising stages. On the right was a deep cavern, in which all the party could find shelter.

If the place was suitable for an encampment of the travellers, it was none the less adapted to the horses, which needed rest and food. A few hundred paces off, beyond the winding gorge, a plain extended, in which were water and grass in abundance. Thither the horses were led by Nizib who was appointed their guardian as usual during noctural halts.

"'Let us sup, my friends,' cried Kéraban."—p. 407.

# KÉRABAN THE INFLEXIBLE;

## OR, ADVENTURES IN THE EUXINE.

BY JULES VERNE.

TRANSLATED BY HENRY FRITH.

---

### CHAPTER XI.

NIZIB accordingly directed his steps towards the plain, and Ahmet accompanied him, at once to reconnoitre the district, and to assure himself that there was absolutely nothing to fear.

In fact Ahmet saw nothing suspicious. The prairie, which was bounded westward by an undulating range of hills, was absolutely deserted. The night was calm, and the moon, which would rise about eleven o'clock, was sufficiently old to give good light. Some stars shone between the light clouds, as if they were sleeping in the high zones of the heavens. Not a breath of wind stirred, and no sound was audible in the atmosphere.

Ahmet scrutinized the horizon most searchingly. Would some flame once again illumine the crests of the surrounding hills? Would some signal be made that the guide would come and detect afterwards?

No fire displayed itself on the boundary of the plain. No signal was sent from the distant horizon.

Ahmet desired Nizib to keep a most vigilant watch. He enjoined him particularly to return without a moment's delay in case of any eventuality occurring before the horses had been brought into camp. Then he himself, having given these orders, hurried back through the Gorge of Nerissa.

### CHAPTER XII.

IN WHICH IS REPORTED SOME CONVERSATION BETWEEN THE NOBLE SARABOUL AND HER FIANCÉ.

WHEN Ahmet rejoined his companions, the final arrangements for supping first and sleeping afterwards had been completed. The sleeping apartment, or rather the common dormitory, was the cavern, which, high and spacious, contained many convenient recesses wherein each member of the party might repose at his or her pleasure, comfortably. The dining-room was the level plain outside, whereon were scattered boulders and stones which would serve admirably for tables and chairs

Some provisions had been taken from the cart which had been drawn by the little donkey. The latter was amongst the number of the *convives*, having been specially invited by his friend Kéraban. A little forage, on which the animal had made an excellent meal, sufficed for his part of the feast, and he brayed his satisfaction.

"Let us have supper," cried Kéraban, in a cheerful tone, "let us sup, my friends. Let us eat and drink at our ease. There will then be so much less for this brave little donkey to drag to Scutari."

Of course, at an open-air meal, in the midst of the camp illuminated by resinous torches, every person placed himself as he pleased. Seigneur Kéraban seated himself on a rock, a true seat of honour, the "chair" of the meeting. Amasia and Nedjeb sat together, like dear friends, no longer mistress and servant, on smaller rocks; and reserved a place for Ahmet, who quickly joined them.

As for Van Mitten, he was flanked right and left by the inevitable Yanar and the inseparable Saraboul, and all three were seated before an immense slab of rock, which the sighs of the unfortunate Van Mitten ought to have softened.

Bruno, thinner than ever, with his mouth full waited upon the party.

Not only was Kèraban in a good humour as was natural to him fortune favoured, but, as was usual with him, his enjoyment escaped in joking, and some of his jests were directed at Van Mitten. It is a fact that ever since the Dutchman had devoted himself to save his friends, he had not ceased to excite the caustic humour of Kéraban. In twelve hours it is true the story would be told, and Van Mitten would hear no more of the Kurds, brother and sister, but that was precisely the reason why Kéraban continued to sharpen his wit upon his travelling companion.

"Well, Van Mitten, all goes well, eh?" he said rubbing his hands. "You are at the summit of your desires. Good friends accompany you, an amiable lady whom you have encountered in your travels is by your side. Allah could not have done more for you had you been one of the Faithful yourself."

The Dutchman looked at his friend and pulled a long face, but said nothing.

"Well, you are silent?" asked Yanar.

"No, no, I was speaking, inwardly," replied Van Mitten.

"To whom?" demanded the lady Kurd, imperatively.

"To you, dear Saraboul, to you," said the victim.

Then rising, he stretched out his arms and ejaculated, "Ouf!"

Seigneur Yanar and his sister rose at the same moment, and accompanied him in all his movements. "If you wish," said Saraboul, in that tender tone which admits of no contradiction; "if you wish, we will only stop an hour or two in Scutari?"

"If I wish it?" said Van Mitten.

"Are you not my master?" continued the insinuating lady.

"Yes," muttered Bruno, "he is her master, as much as one is master of a hound that every minute is flying at one's throat!"

"Fortunately," thought Van Mitten, "to-morrow we shall part. But what a scene in perspective will that breaking off be!"

Amasia regarded him with true commiseration; and, not daring to pity him openly, she whispered to his faithful attendant—

"Poor M. Van Mitten! This comes of his devotion to us."

"And of his pliability in the hands of Seigneur Kéraban," replied Bruno, who could not forgive his master for his weakness.

"At anyrate," said Nedjeb, "that proves that M. Van Mitten has a good and generous heart."

"Too generous," said Bruno. "Besides, since my master consented to accompany Seigneur Kéraban on this journey, I have never ceased to repeat that ill would come of it sooner or later. But such a misfortune as this! To become engaged, if only for a few days, to such a woman! I never could have imagined such a thing; no, never. The first Madame Van Mitten was a perfect dove compared with the second."

Meanwhile the Dutchman had again seated himself, still flanked by his body-guard, and Bruno came to offer him some food. But Van Mitten had no appetite.

"You do not eat, Seigneur Van Mitten," said Saraboul, looking him straight in the face.

"I am not hungry," he replied.

"Really, you are not hungry?" said Yanar. "But in Kurdistan everyone is hungry, even after a meal!"

"Ah! in Kurdistan;" said Van Mitten, as he swallowed the double helping, which he had been obliged to accept.

"And drink," said Saraboul.

"But I am drinking, I drink in your words——"

He did not dare to add, "Only I know they will disagree with me!"

"Drink," continued Yanar.

"But I am not thirsty."

"In Kurdistan we are always thirsty, even after a meal."

Meanwhile Ahmet, who was always on his guard, was watching the guide closely. The man sat apart eating his share of the supper, but he could not conceal some movement of impatience. At least Ahmet thought so, and how could he think otherwise believing him to be a traitor? The man was anxious that Ahmet and his party should take refuge in the cavern, when sleep would render them defenceless against any pre-arranged attack. Perhaps the guide wished to depart on some secret errand, but he did not dare while Ahmet, whom he feared, kept observing him.

"There, my friends," said Kéraban. "We have had an excellent meal for an open-air supper. We have well recruited ourselves for our last stage. Is not that true, my little Amasia?"

"Yes, Seigneur Kéraban," replied the girl. "I am quite ready to resume the journey if necessary——"

"You would continue it——?"

"To follow you."

"Particularly to make a certain halt at Scutari," returned Kéraban, laughing loudly; "a halt such as our friend Van Mitten made at Trebizond."

"He is laughing at me to boot," murmured Van Mitten, who was very angry, but did not dare to reply in the presence of the susceptible Saraboul.

"Ah," continued Kéraban, "the marriage of Amasia and Ahmet may not be so imposing as the betrothal of Van Mitten and the noble Kurdish lady; of course I cannot give them a *fête* like the Paradise of Mahomet, but I can manage a thing or two, I daresay. I want all Scutari to be present, and wish that my friends from Constantinople shall fill the gardens of the villa."

"There is no need for so much for us," said Amasia.

"Yes, yes, my dear mistress," exclaimed Nedjeb.

"And if I desire it, if I wish it," continued Kéraban; "would my little Amasia thwart me?"

"Oh, Seigneur Kéraban!" she said.

"Well then," continued he, holding up his glass, "let us drink to the happiness of the young people, who so well deserve to be happy."

"To Seigneur Ahmet, to the fair Amasia," cried the *convives* with one accord, in high good humour.

"And," continued Kéraban, "to the alliance of Kurdistan with Holland."

To this toast, given in a cheerful tone and with all hands extended towards him, Van Mitten was obliged to return thanks, whether he wished it or not.

The supper, rough, but very pleasant, was at length over. Now for a few hours rest, and the journey might be accomplished without fatigue.

"We will sleep until daybreak," said Kéraban, "and I order the guide to call us at that time!"

"Very well, Seigneur," replied the man. "But would it not be better for me to relieve Nizib in his guard over the horses?"

"No, stay where you are," said Ahmet quickly. "Nizib will do very well where he is, and I prefer you to remain here. We will keep watch together!"

"Keep watch!" exclaimed the man, who in vain endeavoured to conceal his chagrin. "There is no danger here, in this extreme district of Anatolia."

"Very likely not," replied Ahmet, "but a little excess of prudence can do no harm. I will myself replace Nizib in his charge. So remain here, you."

"As you please, Seigneur Ahmet," replied the guide. "Let us place everything in the cavern then, so that your friends may sleep more contentedly."

"Do so," said Ahmet, "and Bruno will assist you, if M. Van Mitten has no objection."

"Go, Bruno, go," said Van Mitten.

The guide and Bruno entered the cavern and carried in all the cloaks, cafetans and coverings which might serve as bedding. Amasia, Nedjeb, and their companions had not made any difficulty concerning the supper, and the question of bed would find them equally accommodating, no doubt.

While preparations were being concluded, Amasia approached Ahmet, and, taking his hand, said :

"So, my dear Ahmet, you are really going to pass the night without repose?"

"Yes," replied Ahmet, who did not wish Amasia to observe his anxiety. "Must I not watch over one who is so dear to me?"

"Well, this will be the very last time?"

"The very last. To-morrow all the fatigues of our journey will be ended."

"To-morrow," repeated Amasia, raising her eyes to his; "that to-morrow which seems never to come."

"But which will last for ever," replied Ahmet.

"For ever," murmured the girl.

The noble Saraboul, too, had seized Van Mitten by the hand, and, indicating Amasia and Ahmet, said with a sigh—

"You see them, Seigneur Van Mitten; you see those two?"

"Who?" asked the Dutchman, whose thoughts were far from such a tender course of ideas.

"Who?" retorted the lady sharply, "who but those two *fiancés*. In fact I find you curiously reserved."

"You know that Dutchmen are very self-contained," replied Van Mitten. "Holland is a country of dikes and barriers; dikes everywhere!"

"There are no dikes in Kurdistan," exclaimed the noble Saraboul, who was mystified by his coldness.

"No, indeed there are not," added Yanar, seizing his brother-in-law's arm violently, as if he would crush it in his vice-like grip.

"Fortunately," Kéraban could not help saying, "fortunately our friend Van Mitten will be free to-morrow."

Then, turning to the others, he cried, "Well, now the dormitory is prepared, a chamber wherein is room for all. It is nearly eleven o'clock; the moon is already rising, let us retire to rest."

"Come, Nedjeb," said Amasia.

"I follow you, dear mistress."

"Good night, Ahmet."

"Till to-morrow, dear Amasia, *à demain*," replied Ahmet, as he led the young girl to the entrance of the cavern.

"You will follow me, M. Van Mitten," said Saraboul in a tone which could scarcely be called "engaging."

"Certainly," replied the Dutchman; "but, all the same, if necessary I could remain with my young friend Ahmet."

"What did you say?" asked the imperious woman.

"What did he say?" asked Yanar.

"I said," replied Van Mitten, "I said, my dear Saraboul, that my duty obliged me to watch over you; and that——"

"Very well, you shall watch; *there!*"

She indicated the cavern, while Yanar shoved him by the shoulder, saying—

"There is one thing of which you may rest quite assured, Seigneur Van Mitten: you need have no doubt of it——"

"What is that, if you please, Seigneur Yanar?"

"That in espousing my sister, you have married a Volcano!" said Yanar.

Under the impulse of his vigorous arm, Van Mitten was hurried into the cavern, whither his *fiancée* had preceded him, and whither Seigneur Yanar immediately followed him.

Just as Kéraban was entering in his turn, Ahmet stopped him.

"Uncle, just one word," he said.

"Well, only one," said Kéraban, "I am tired, and want to go to sleep."

"Very well; but I want you to hear me."

"What have you to say?"

"Do you know where we are?"

"Yes; in the defiles of the gorges of Nerissa."

"At what distance from Scutari?"

"About five or six leagues."

"Who told you that?"

"Well, the guide."

"Have you confidence in that man?"

"Why should I distrust him?"

"Because the fellow, whom I have been

watching for several days, has been going on in a way more and more suspicious," replied Ahmet. "Do you know him, uncle? No. At Trebizond he came and offered to conduct us to the Bosphorus. You accepted his services without knowing who he was. We came away under his guidance——"

"Yanar seized him by the shoulder."

"Well, Ahmet, it seems to me he has proved his acquaintance with these roads."

"Undoubtedly, uncle."

"Do you wish to argue, nephew?" demanded Kéraban, whose brow began to knit ominously.

"No, uncle, no; and I beg you to believe that I have no intention to say anything disagreeable. But I am by no means easy in my mind, and I fear for those I love."

Ahmet's emotion was so evident as he spoke, that Kéraban was quite touched.

"Look here, Ahmet, my boy; what ails you? Why these fears, when all our trials are just over? I will confess to you—only to you, mind—that I must have been rather mad to undertake this journey. I confess, but for my obstinacy in causing you to leave Odessa, that the abduction of Amasia would not have been accomplished. Yes, all that was my fault. But here we are, at the end of our journey. Your marriage will not be retarded by a day. To-morrow we shall be in Scutari, and to-morrow——"

"But if we are not in Scutari to-morrow, uncle? Suppose we are much further from it than this guide tells us we are? Suppose we have been purposely led astray, after being advised to leave the coast-road? In fine, suppose this man is a traitor!"

"A traitor!" exclaimed Kéraban.

"Yes; what if this man be a traitor, and serving those who carried off Amasia?"

"By Allah, nephew, how did you conceive this idea? On what foundation does it rest? On mere presentiment!"

"No uncle, on facts! Listen to me. For several days this man has been in the habit of leaving us during our halts, on the pretext of examining the route. Last night he was away from the camp for an hour. I followed him, and I declare that a signal by fire was given to him from a certain point in the horizon, a signal that he was expecting!"

"This is a very serious matter, Ahmet," replied Kéraban. "But how do you connect the acts of this man with the abduction of Amasia by the captain of the *Guidare?*"

"Well, uncle, whither was the vessel bound? To Atina? Evidently not, for we know the storm drove her out of her course. My opinion is that she was bound for Trebizond, where the harems of the nabobs of Anatolia are often replenished. There it might have become known that the girl had been saved from the shipwreck, and the abductors put on her track may have despatched this guide to conduct our little caravan into an ambush."

"Yes, Ahmet. Yes, you may be right. It is quite possible that danger threatens us. You have watched and done well, and to-night I will watch with you."

"No, uncle, rest yourself. I am well armed, and at the first alarm——"

"I tell you I will watch," replied Kéraban. "It shall never be said that such an obstinate man as I am could bring about a new catastrophe."

"No; do not fatigue yourself unnecessarily. The guide by my orders will pass the night in the cavern. Go in."

"I will not"

"Uncle——"

"Once for all, are you going to withstand me? Ah, take care, Ahmet: it is a long time since anyone has contradicted me!"

"Very well, uncle, let us watch together."

"Yes, under arms; and woe to him who enters our encampment!"

So Kéraban and Ahmet paced up and down, their gaze fixed upon the narrow pass, listening to the least noise, and keeping watch and ward upon the cavern faithfully. Two hours, then a third, passed thus. Nothing suspicious happened—nothing to justify the fears of Kéraban and his nephew occurred. They began to hope that the night would pass without incident; but about three o'clock in the morning cries of terror arose from the direction of the pass.

Kéraban and Ahmet at once seized their weapons, which had been placed at the foot of a rock; this time Kéraban, mistrusting his pistols, had got a musket.

At that instant Nizib came rushing up, out of breath.

"Ah, master!"

"What is it, Nizib?"

"Master—yonder; below there——"

"Yonder?" said Ahmet.

"The horses——"

"Our horses?"

"Yes."

"Speak out, you stupid animal," exclaimed Kéraban, shaking the lad roughly. "Our horses?"

"Stolen!" said Nizib.

"Stolen!"

"Yes," continued the servant. "Two or three men came rushing out and carried them off."

"They have got away with our horses, you say?"

"Yes."

"On the road—that side?" asked Ahmet, pointing in a westerly direction.

"On that side—yes!"

"We must run after them; we must give chase," exclaimed Kéraban.

"Let us remain where we are, uncle," said Ahmet. "To hope to catch our horses is vain. We must, before all things, put our camp in a state of defence."

"Ah, master, look," cried Nizib. "See there—there!"

He pointed to the hollow of a large rock which stood up high, on the left of the place where they were consulting.

"Yes, we will watch—under arms."

## CHAPTER XIII.

### IN WHICH SEIGNEUR KÉRABAN, HAVING COME INTO COLLISION WITH THE DONKEY, FINDS HIMSELF OPPOSED TO A MORTAL ENEMY.

SEIGNEUR KÉRABAN and Ahmet turned round, and looked in the direction indicated by Nizib. What they saw caused them to retire and crouch down out of sight.

On the upper ledge of the rock, opposite the cavern, a man was crawling along, with the object, apparently, to reach the extreme angle—no doubt in order to watch the camp. It was only natural to conclude that some secret understanding existed between this man and the guide.

It must be confessed that Ahmet had been correct in his estimate of the machinations which had been formed against Kéraban and his companions: his uncle was forced to admit as much. It was pretty obvious, too, that the danger was imminent; that an attack in the dark was being prepared, and that very night the little caravan, after being surprised by an ambuscade, would be destroyed.

Kéraban, at first, unreflectingly, raised his musket, and was about to fire at this spy who had the hardihood to venture so close to the camp. In another second the gun would have been discharged, and the man would have been shot, no doubt; but such a course—which would have given the alarm—might have had serious consequences, and complicated a situation already sufficiently grave.

"Stop, uncle," whispered Ahmet, throwing up the levelled musket.

"But, Ahmet——"

"No; the report would only be the signal for attack; and, besides, we had better take that man alive. He must know on whose account these wrctches are acting."

"But, how are we to take him?"

"Let me manage that," replied Ahmet.

So saying, he disappeared towards the left, so as to "turn" the rock and climb it from the back. Meantime, Kéraban and Nizib held themselves in readiness to interfere, should occasion demand it.

The spy, crouched face downwards, had reached the extremity of the rock. His head alone protruded over the ledge; he was endeavouring to see into the cavern by the aid of the brilliant moonlight.

In about half-a-minute Ahmet re-appeared upon the upper ledge; and, creeping cautiously along, he advanced towards the spy, who had not perceived him.

Unfortunately, an unexpected incident put the man on his guard, and revealed to him the danger which threatened him.

Almost at that moment Amasia came out of the cavern. A feeling of anxiety, for which she could not account, prevented her from sleeping. She fancied Ahmet was threatened by some danger from the musket or the dagger of the assassin.

Kéraban at once made a sign to the girl to stop, but she did not understand him; and, looking up, perceived Ahmet just as he was raising himself upright on the rock. A cry of alarm escaped her.

At the sound of her voice the spy turned round rapidly and stood up. Perceiving Ahmet still bending down, he threw himself upon him.

Amasia, nailed by terror to the spot, cried to her lover. The spy, knife in hand, was about to stab his adversary, when Kéraban, shouldering his piece, fired.

The spy, hit full in the chest, let fall his dagger and rolled to the ground from the ledge of the rock.

In another instant Amasia was clasped in the arms of Ahmet, who had let himself down from the rock and rejoined her.

At the sound of the shot all the occupants of the cavern came hurrying out—all except the guide. Kéraban, brandishing his musket, exclaimed—

"That was a splendid shot, by Allah!"

"More dangers!" muttered Bruno.

"Do not leave me, Van Mitten," cried the noble Saraboul, seizing the arm of her *fiancé*.

"He shall not leave you, sister," said the resolute Yanar.

By this time Ahmet had advanced to the spot where the spy lay.

"The man is dead," he said, "and he would have been worth more to us living."

Nedjeb had joined him, and she immediately exclaimed—

"But that man is—is——"

Amasia now approached in her turn, and cried out—

"Yes, yes; 'tis he—Yarhud; the captain of the *Guidare!*"

"Yarhud!" exclaimed Kéraban.

"Ah, then, I was right," said Ahmet.

"Yes," continued Amasia, "that is the very man who carried us away!"

"I recognise him now," said Ahmet. "I remember him myself. He came to the villa to show us his merchandize just before my departure; but he cannot be alone. The whole band of ruffians is on our track, and to prevent us from continuing our journey they have stolen our horses!"

"Our horses stolen!" exclaimed Saraboul.

"If we had taken the road home to Kurdistan, this would not have happened to us," said Yanar.

And his look, as it rested on Van

"Ahmet appeared advancing towards the spy"

Mitten, seemed to hold him responsible for all these complications.

"But whom is this Yarhud acting for?" remarked Kéraban.

"If he were alive we would drag his secret from him," said Ahmet.

"Perhaps he carries some paper," suggested Amasia.

"Yes: let us search the body," said Kéraban.

"'Read it, Ahmet, read it,' said his uncle."—p. 453.

# KÉRABAN THE INFLEXIBLE;

## OR, ADVENTURES IN THE EUXINE.

BY JULES VERNE.

TRANSLATED BY HENRY FRITH.

### CHAPTER XIII.

AHMET bent over the corpse, while Nizib held a lantern which he had procured from the cavern.

"Here is a letter," said Ahmet, as he withdrew his hand from the dead man's pocket.

The latter was addressed to a certain "Scarpante."

"Read it, Ahmet, read it," said his uncle, who could not control his impatience.

Ahmet opened the paper and read as follows:

"The horses of the caravan once seized, while Kéraban and his companions are asleep in the cavern whither Scarpante will conduct them——"

"Scarpante!" exclaimed Kéraban, "that is the guide—the traitor!"

"Yes: I was not deceived in him," remarked Ahmet. "Then," he continued—"let Scarpante make a signal by waving a torch, and our men will descend upon them in the gorge of Nerissa."

"And that is signed——?" asked Kéraban.

"It is signed—Saffar!"

"Saffar—Saffar—so it is he then!"

"Yes," replied Ahmet, "it is evident it is the same insolent person whom we encountered on the railway line at Poti, and who some hours later embarked for Trebizond. Yes, it is this Saffar who caused Amasia to be carried off, and who wants to recapture her at any price."

"Ah, Seigneur Saffar," cried Kéraban, raising his clenched hand, and letting it fall on an imaginary head, "if ever I find myself face to face with you——!"

"But where is this Scarpante?" asked Ahmet.

Bruno hurried into the cavern, but returned almost immediately, and said—

"He has disappeared—by some other aperture, no doubt."

That was in fact what had occurred. Scarpante, his treason discovered, had made his escape from the other extremity of the cavern.

So the disgraceful plot was now disclosed in all its details. It was indeed the intendant of Saffar who had offered himself as guide; it was Scarpante who had conducted the party, first along the coast and afterwards across the mountainous regions of Anatolia. It was no other than Yarhud whose signals had been perceived by Ahmet the night before, and it was the Captain of the *Guidare* who had come secretly to convey Saffar's last commands to Scarpante.

But the vigilance and perspicacity of Ahmet had checkmated this manœuvre. The traitor unmasked, the criminal designs of his master were revealed. The name of the abductor of Amasia was known to be Saffar who had been threatened by Kéraban with his vengeance and reprisals.

But if the trap into which the party had been led was discovered, the peril was none the less imminent, and might befall them at any moment.

So Ahmet, with his usual quickness, perceived the only solution, and made his decision at once.

"My friends," he said, "we must at once quit these gorges of Nerissa. If we are attacked amongst these rocky defiles, not one of us will come out alive."

"Let us proceed," said Kéraban. "Bruno, Nizib, and you, Seigneur Yanar, have your weapons ready for any event."

"You may depend upon us, Seigneur Kéraban," replied Yanar. "You will see what my sister and I are capable of."

"Yes, indeed," responded the courageous lady, brandishing her yataghan with magnificent action. "I will not forget that I have an affianced husband to defend."

If ever Van Mitten experienced deep humiliation, it was when he heard the intrepid woman speak thus. But he also seized his revolver and was quite determined to do his *devoir*.

The whole party then proceeded to mount the defile and gain the plateau, when Bruno who could never escape from ideas of feeding remarked—

"But we cannot leave the ass here."

"There is something in that observation," remarked Ahmet. "Perhaps Scarpante has led us astray; or perhaps we are farther from Scutari than we imagine. The cart contains all the provisions we possess."

These hypotheses were both plausible. It was to be feared that the traitor had compromised the arrival of Kéraban and his party on the shores of the Bosphorus by leading the caravan astray.

But there was no time to argue the point, action was necessary and at once.

"Well," said Kéraban, "the ass will follow us—why should he not?"

So saying he took the animal by the bridle, and attempted to pull him towards him.

"Come on," said Kéraban.

The ass never moved.

"Will you come with good will?" asked Kéraban, giving the bridle a violent jerk. But the ass, which no doubt was inflexible in his way, declined to budge.

"Shove him, Nizib," said Kéraban.

Nizib assisted by Bruno then endeavoured to push the donkey from behind, but the animal moved backwards farther than he advanced.

"Ah! you intend to try conclusions with me, do you?" said Kéraban, who began to be angry.

"Good," muttered Bruno, "obstinacy against obstinacy."

"You resist me then! resist me!" repeated Kéraban.

"Your master has found his," said Bruno to Nizib in an undertone.

"That would astonish me," replied Nizib.

Ahmet then broke in impatiently—

"We must depart. We have not a moment to lose—let the ass alone—leave him where he is."

"I? yield to an ass? Never!" exclaimed Kéraban.

Then seizing the quadruped by the ears he pulled as if he would pull them out altogether.

"Will you come on?" he said.

The ass did not stir.

"Ah! won't you obey me? Well then, I will compel you to do so, somehow."

Then Kéraban entered the cavern, and emerged with some handfuls of hay which he twisted up and presented to the donkey. The animal made a step in advance.

"Ah, ha!" exclaimed Kéraban, "that makes you step out, and by Mahomet you shall go on."

The hay was then fastened to the extremities of the shafts of the cart, but in such a way as to be just without the reach of the ass, which by extending his neck could smell the hay, and so he proceeded, in a continuous but vain endeavour to reach the tempting morsels, towards the pass.

"Very ingenious," said Van Mitten.

"Well, then, imitate him," said the noble Saraboul, dragging him after the cart. She was also a tempting morsel, which continued progressing before him, but Van Mitten was, unlike the ass, not desirous to reach to it.

The whole troop, continuing in the same

direction, had soon cleared their camping-ground, which was a position quite untenable.

"So, Ahmet," said Kéraban, "in your opinion this Saffar is the same insolent individual, who by his obstinacy caused the destruction of our chaise on the Poti railway?"

"Saffar's mercenaries had attacked the caravan."

"Yes, uncle; but he is, above all, the miscreant who endeavoured to carry off Amasia, and his punishment belongs to me."

"Let us proceed two by two now," said Kéraban, "and may Allah assist us."

Scarcely had Kéraban and his company ascended fifty paces when they perceived the rocks surmounted by assailants, who utttered loud cries and fired a volley at them.

"Retreat, retire," cried Ahmet, who led his party back to the limits of the encampment.

It was too late to escape from the gorges of Nerissa : too late to seek a better position on the plateau. Saffar's mercenaries, to the number of a dozen, had attacked the caravan; their chief was exciting them to this criminal proceeding, and in the position they occupied they had the advantage.

Seigneur Kéraban and his companions were actually at their mercy.

"Keep together," cried Ahmet.

"The women in the centre," said Kéraban.

Amasia, Saraboul, Nedjeb, formed a group around which Kéraban, Van Mitten, Ahmet, Yanar, Nizib and Bruno ranged themselves. There were six men against twelve, one against two, and in a disadvantageous position besides.

Almost immediately the banditti, uttering horrible cries, came down the pass and dashed into the encampment.

"My friends," said Ahmet, "let us fight to the death!"

The combat at once began. Nizib and Bruno were immediately wounded, but slightly. Yet they did not give ground, they all fought valiantly, and none more courageously than the Kurdish lady, who fired many shots at the assailants.

It was evident that they had had orders to take Amasia alive, and that they preferred to fight cautiously with that object, so that no harm might befall her. So, notwithstanding superiority of numbers, the first success did not lie with the banditti, many of whom fell dangerously wounded.

At that juncture two new combatants appeared on the scene—Saffar and Scarpante.

"Ah! the villain; there he is," exclaimed Kéraban. "That is the railway-man!"

Many times Kéraban aimed at him, but could not fire on account of the attacks made by the assailants.

Ahmet and his friends fought valiantly. They all were possessed with the same idea to save Amasia at any hazard, at any price to save her from falling into the hands of Saffar.

But, notwithstanding all their courage and devotion, they had to yield to superior numbers. So, little by little, Kéraban and his companions gave way, became separated, and then had to take to the rocks in the defile; confusion was already setting in amongst them.

Saffar perceived this.

"Seize her, Scarpante, seize her," he cried, indicating Amasia.

"Yes, Seigneur," replied Scarpante, "and this time she shall not evade you."

Then, profiting by the disorder, he managed to seize Amasia, and endeavoured to drag her away.

"Amasia, Amasia," cried Ahmet, who attempted to advance to her rescue, but was opposed by the band, who intercepted him, and compelled him to fight.

Yanar also attempted to reach the young girl and to rescue her from the hands of Scarpante, but he could not, and the intendant succeeded in dragging her away some paces up the defile.

But Kéraban aimed at him, and Scarpante fell mortally wounded, letting go the young lady, who at once attempted to rejoin Ahmet.

"Scarpante is dead. Let us avenge him," exclaimed the chief of the bandits.

They at once threw themselves on Kéraban and his friends with a ferocity it was impossible to resist. Pressed so closely at all points, the assailed found it almost impossible to use their arms.

"Amasia! Amasia!" exclaimed Ahmet, as he vainly endeavoured to rush to the assistance of the girl, whom Saffar had now seized and was carrying away.

"Courage, courage," cried Kéraban continually.

But he felt that his party and himself, overpowered by numbers, must be soon destroyed.

At that moment a shot fired from the top of the rocks struck down one of the assailants. Other shots succeeded quickly, and more of the banditti fell. Their fall disheartened their companions.

Saffar stopped at once, and sought to find the cause of this diversion in his enemy's favour. What was this unexpected reinforcement?

Already Amasia had disengaged herself from the clutches of Saffar, for he had been disconcerted by the sudden attack.

"Father, father!" she cried.

It was indeed Selim, who, followed by

twenty men, well armed, had come to the assistance of the little caravan, just as it was in imminent danger of destruction.

"*Sauve qui peut,*" shouted the bandit leader, setting the example by running away. He quickly disappeared into the cavern, followed by his *troupe*, who were aware of the existence of the exit at the back.

"Cowards!" exclaimed Saffar, seeing

Death of Scarpante.

himself thus abandoned. "Well, they shall not have her living!"

So saying he dashed at Amasia, just as Ahmet was rushing on him.

Saffar discharged the last barrel of his revolver at the young man; it missed fire. But Kéraban, who had lost none of his coolness, did not fail. He rushed at Saffar, seized him by the throat, and plunged his dagger in his enemy's heart. One shudder and all was over. Saffar, in his death-struggle, did not even hear his foe exclaim—

"That will teach you how to smash my carriage!"

Seigneur Kéraban and his friends were saved. Scarcely any had been severely wounded. Nevertheless they had all fought valiantly: Bruno and Nizib, whose courage had not failed; Seigneur Yanar, who had performed prodigies of valour; Van Mitten, who had quite distinguished himself in the *mêlée;* and the energetic Saraboul, whose pistol had often been discharged in the thickest of the fight.

However, had not Selim so unexpectedly arrived, Amasia and her defenders would have been no more. All would have perished, for they had determined to die for her.

"My father, my father," cried the girl, throwing herself into Selim's arms.

"My old friend," said Kéraban; "*you* here!"

"Yes, I," replied Selim.

"What fortunate chance brought you hither?" asked Ahmet.

"No chance at all," replied Selim; "and I would long ago have started in search of my daughter, if at the moment of her abduction I had not been wounded."

"Wounded, father!"

"Yes, by a shot fired from the felucca. For a whole month I was condemned to remain at Odessa by my wound. But a few days ago Ahmet's telegram——"

"A telegram!" exclaimed Kéraban, whose attention was at once arrested by this hated word.

"Yes, a telegram from Trebizond."

"Ah, that was a——"

"No doubt, uncle," said Ahmet, embracing Kéraban; "but, for the first time that I have ventured to send a telegram without your knowledge, confess I did well."

"Yes, wrong well done," replied Kéraban, shaking his head, "but I will not reprove you, nephew."

"So," continued Selim, "learning from the telegram that danger threatened your little caravan, I assembled my brave servants, reached Scutari, and pursued the coast-road."

"By Allah, you arrived only just in time, friend Selim," said Kéraban. "We would have been lost without you. Nevertheless we fought well!"

"Yes, indeed," said Yanar, "and my sister proved that she could, in case of necessity, use her weapons!"

"What a woman!" muttered Van Mitten.

At that moment the first streaks of day began to appear on the horizon. Some clouds in the zenith variegated the first rays of sunlight.

"But where are we, friend Selim?" asked Kéraban; "and how have you managed to find us in this region, into which we have been misguided by a traitor!"

"And so far out of our way," added Ahmet.

"Not so, my friends, not so," replied Selim, "you are on the way to Scutari, only a few leagues from the sea!"

"Eh?" said Kéraban.

"The shores of the Bosphorus are yonder," continued Selim, pointing north-east.

"The Bosphorus!" exclaimed Ahmet. And all the party ascended the rocks to gain the plateau which extends above the gorges of Nerissa.

"There! see!" said Selim.

And in fact at that moment a natural phenomenon revealed to the travellers the desired locality. As daylight strengthened, a mirage presented, one by one, the objects situated below the horizon. One would have said that the hills which formed the boundary of the plain, had been engulfed in the earth as a theatrical scene sinks beneath the stage.

"The sea! the sea!" exclaimed Ahmet, and the cry was echoed by all present.

Although the appearance was only the effects of a mirage, the sea was distant but a few leagues.

"The sea! the sea!" repeated Kéraban. "But if it is not the Bosphorus, if it be not Scutari,—this is the last day of the month, and——"

"It is the Bosphorus. It is Scutari," said Ahmet.

The mirage grew more distinct and presented the profile of the town on the horizon.

"By Allah, it is Scutari," said Kéraban, "there is the mosque of Buyuk Djami!"

It was indeed Scutari, which Selim had left only three hours before.

"*En route!* EN ROUTE!" cried Kéraban; and like a good Mussulman, who in all circumstances acknowledges the greatness of Providence, he added—

"*Ilah il Allah!*" as he turned towards the rising sun.

A moment after, the little caravan was hastening along the road which lies close by the left shore of the strait. Four hours later, on that day, the 30th September, the last day permitted for the marriage of Amasia and Ahmet,—Seigneur Kéraban, his friends, and the donkey, having achieved the tour of the Black sea—gained the heights of Scutari, and with loud acclamations welcomed the shores of the Bosphorus.

# KÉRABAN THE INFLEXIBLE;

## OR, ADVENTURES IN THE EUXINE.

By Jules Verne.

Translated by HENRY FRITH.

### Chapter XIV.

### In which Van Mitten endeavours to make the Noble Saraboul understand the Situation.

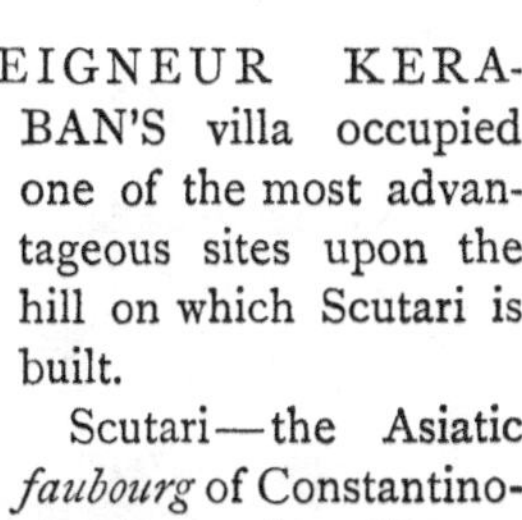

SEIGNEUR KERABAN'S villa occupied one of the most advantageous sites upon the hill on which Scutari is built.

Scutari—the Asiatic *faubourg* of Constantinople, the ancient Chrysopolis, with its gilt-roofed mosques, and all the medley throng of a population of fifty-thousand inhabitants; its floating landing-place, and the extensive grove of cypress-trees in the cemetery;—Scutari, the resting-place elected by rich Mussulmans, who are afraid lest the capital may be taken while the faithful are at prayers, according to the legend; then, a league farther on, is Mount Bouljourlon, which dominates the scene, and affords a prospect embracing the Sea of Marmora, the Gulf of Nicomedia, the canal of Constantinople :—nothing can give an idea of the grandeur of the panorama, which is unique, and of which the windows of the rich merchant's villa commanded a view.

The exterior of the villa—its terraced gardens, its beautiful trees and shrubs—were in worthy keeping with the interior of the mansion. Truly it was a pity to have deprived one's self of all this for the sake of a few paras demanded daily for crossing the Bosphorus.

It was mid-day. For three hours the owner and his guests had been installed in that elegant villa. Having made their toilette, they were reposing after the fatigues and trials of the journey. Kéraban, very proud of his success, was holding the Muchir and his imposts up to ridicule; Amasia and Ahmet, as happy as an engaged couple could be; Nedjeb, in a state of continuous laughter; Bruno, satisfied that he was growing fatter, but anxious on his master's account! Nizib, always calm even in the midst of the grand surroundings of the place; Seigneur Yanar, more ferocious than ever, no one knew why; the noble Saraboul, as imperious as if she were in the capital of Kurdistan; and, finally, Van Mitten, much pre-occupied concerning the issue of this adventure.

It was not without reason that Bruno fancied he was gaining flesh. He had enjoyed a *déjeuner* as ample as magnificent! This was not the famous dinner to which Kéraban had invited his friend Van Mitten six weeks before; but it was none the less magnificent. And now all the party, seated in the charming *salon*, whose bay windows opened on the Bosphorus, congratulated each other in animated sentences.

"My dear Van Mitten," said Kéraban, who moved about cordially among his guests, "I did invite you to a dinner, but you must not blame me if the hour has obliged us to——"

"I do not complain," replied Van Mitten, "your cook has done very well."

"Yes, excellently, in truth," added Yanar, who had eaten more than was convenient, even for a Kurd with a voracious appetite.

"One could not have done better in Kurdistan," replied Saraboul, "and, Seigneur Kéraban, if ever you come to Mossoul to pay us a visit——"

"Oh, I will come," replied Kéraban. "I will come and see you and my friend Van Mitten."

The Villa of Signor Kéraban.

"And we will endeavour to make you forget your villa; and you will not regret your native Holland," added the amiable woman, turning to her betrothed.

"Near you, noble Saraboul——" Van Mitten ought to have said; but he could not manage to finish the phrase, and gave it up.

Then, while the Kurdish lady turned towards the window which opened upon the Bosphorus, he said to Kéraban—

"The moment has come to tell her that the marriage is null and void."

"As void as if it had never been celebrated, Van Mitten."

"You will assist me a little, Kéraban, in this business: it will be unpleasant."

"Hum," remarked Kéraban, "there are some private matters which are best discussed *tête-à-tête.*"

"The devil!" was the Dutchman's reply. Then he retired to a corner to consider the best mode of action.

"Worthy Van Mitten," remarked Kéraban, to his nephew, "what a scene he will have with this Kurdish woman!"

"We ought not to forget that he was impelled into this scrape by his devotion to us," replied Ahmet.

"So we should assist him? Bah, he was married at the time he was affianced, and for an Occidental this is a final barrier. So he has nothing to fear."

"I know that," replied Ahmet, "but when Madame Saraboul receives this blow she will leap like an enraged panther! As for her brother, Yanar, he will explode like a powder-magazine."

"By Mahomet, but we will make them listen to reason," replied Kéraban. "After all, Van Mitten is not guilty of any misconduct."

"Certainly not, uncle, and it is equally certain that this tender widow wants to be married again at any price."

"No doubt, and she did not hesitate to put her hand upon good M. Van Mitten."

"A hand of iron, uncle Kéraban."

"Of steel, rather," replied her uncle.

"At anyrate, uncle, if it is necessary to undo this pretended marriage, it is——"

"Also necessary to perform a real one, eh?" interrupted Kéraban, rubbing his hands as if he were washing them.

"Precisely so—mine," replied Ahmet."

"Ours," said Amasia, who had approached the pair. "We have deserved it."

"Well deserved it," said Selim.

"Yes, indeed, my little Amasia; deserved it ten, a hundred, a thousand times! Ah, my dear child, to think that by my obstinacy, by my fault—that you were nearly——"

"We will not speak of that," said Ahmet.

"No, never, uncle Kéraban," said the girl putting her little hand on his mouth.

"So," continued Kéraban, "I made a vow—yes, I made a resolution—that I would never be 'pig-headed' again, no matter what happened."

"I must see that, to believe it," laughed Nedjeb.

"Eh, what does that quizzical Nedjeb say?" exclaimed Kéraban.

"Oh, nothing, Seigneur."

"Yes," continued Kéraban: "I will never again be obstinate, except in my affection for you both."

"When Seigneur Kéraban ceases to be the most head-strong of men——," began Bruno.

"That will be when he has no longer a head," remarked Nizib parenthetically.

"Just so," said Bruno.

Meanwhile the noble Kurdish lady approached her *fiancé*, who was seated very pensive in his corner—no doubt finding his task all the more difficult as the time approached for executing it alone and unaided.

"What is the matter with you, M. Van Mitten?" she asked. "You look very serious."

"Yes, indeed, brother-in-law," added Yanar. "What are you about? You surely have not brought us to Scutari for nothing, to see nothing. Show us the Bosphorus, as one of these days we will show you Kurdistan."

At this celebrated name the Dutchman started as if he had received an electric shock.

"Come, let us go, M. Van Mitten," said Saraboul, compelling him to rise.

"At your service, beautiful Saraboul," replied Van Mitten, aloud; but, mentally, he was thinking how he best could break the subject of separation to her.

At that moment the young Zingara, having opened one of the great bay-windows which was shaded by an awning, exclaimed, "Look, look! Scutari is all alive. It would be very pleasant to walk about the city to-day!"

The guests at once advanced to the windows.

"Indeed," remarked Kéraban, "the

**A Street in Scutari.—p. 492**

Bosphorus is covered with gaily decked boats. In all the squares and streets there are jugglers and acrobats, there is music, and the quays are crowded with people!"

"Yes" said Selim, "the town is *en fête*."

"I trust that will prove no bar to our marriage," remarked Ahmet.

"Certainly not," replied Kéraban. "We are going to have at Scutari a repetition of the feast at Trebizond, and these appear to be in honour of our friend Van Mitten!"

Scutari is all animation.

"He will make game of me to the end," muttered the Dutchman. "But he cannot help it, it is in the blood!"

"My friends," said Selim, "let us look at this important affair. To-day is the last day——"

"And we will not forget that fact," replied Kéraban.

"I will proceed to the judge's house, so that the contract may be drawn up," said Selim.

"We will meet you there," replied Ahmet. "You know, uncle, that your presence is indispensable."

"Almost as much as your own," replied Kéraban, laughing loudly by way of confirmation.

"Yes, uncle, more indispensable, if one may say so, in your position as trustee."

"Well," said Selim, "in an hour we will meet you at the house of the judge of Scutari."

As he quitted the room, Ahmet, addressing Amasia, said—

"Then, dear Amasia, after the signing of the contract, we pay a visit to the Imaun, who will put up his best prayer, and then——"

"Then we shall be married," exclaimed Nedjeb, as if the ceremony included herself.

"Dear Ahmet," murmured Amasia.

Meanwhile the noble Saraboul had a second time approached Van Mitten, who, more and more pensive, was seated in a corner of the room.

"Pending this ceremony," she said, "why cannot we go as far as the Bosphorus?"

"The Bosphorus!" exclaimed Van Mitten, with an abstracted air; "you are speaking of the—Bosphorus?"

"Yes, the Bosphorus," said Yanar. "One would almost imagine you did not understand."

"Yes, yes, I am quite ready," said Van Mitten, rising as his powerful brother-in-law placed his hand upon his shoulder. "Yes, the Bosphorus. But first I desire—I wish——"

"You wish?" repeated Saraboul.

"I would be happy to have an interview, a private interview with you, beautiful Saraboul."

"A private conversation?"

"Very well, I will leave you," said Yanar.

"No, stay where you are, brother," replied Saraboul, who was staring her *fiancé* out of countenance. "I have a presentiment that your presence will be needed."

"By Mahomet! I wonder how he will get it done," said Kéraban in his nephew's ear.

"It will be difficult," replied Ahmet.

"We will not go far away, so that we may be at hand to support Van Mitten."

"They will certainly tear him to pieces," remarked Bruno.

Seigneur Kéraban, Ahmet, Amasia, and Nedjeb, Bruno and Nizib, then moved towards the door so as to leave the field clear for the encounter.

"Courage, Van Mitten," said Kéraban, shaking his friend's hand as he passed him. "I will not go far away. I will remain in the next room, and watch over your safety."

"Courage, master," said Bruno, "or beware Kurdistan!"

A moment later, Van Mitten and the two Kurds were left alone in the room, and the Dutchman, as he rubbed his head, made a melancholy "aside"—

"If I only knew how to begin!"

Saraboul then advanced quickly towards him.

"What have you to say to us, Monsieur Van Mitten?" she asked in a tone which prevented too much pleasantness from being imported into the discussion.

"Yes, speak out," added Yanar.

"If we might sit down," began Van Mitten, who felt his limbs giving way beneath him.

"What you can say seated you can say standing up," replied Saraboul. "We are listening."

Van Mitten summoned all his courage, which had given way on hearing those words, so eminently calculated to embarrass a timid speaker.

"Beautiful Saraboul, you may be sure, first of all, and very much against my will, I regret that——"

"You regret?" said Saraboul, "you regret what? Is it our marriage? That is, after all, only a legitimate reparation——"

"Oh! reparation, reparation!" Van Mitten ventured to remark in an undertone.

"And I also regret," continued Saraboul. "Yes, certainly I regret——"

"Ah! you also regret——?"

"I regret that the intruder at Rissar was neither Seigneur Ahmet nor Kéraban. In either case I should have married a *man*——"

"Well said, sister," remarked Yanar.

"Instead of a——"

"Well said again, although you have not finished your sentence," continued Yanar.

"Excuse me," interrupted Van Mitten, who was injured by such personal remarks.

"Whoever would believe," continued Saraboul, "that the author of such an attempt was a Dutchman preserved in ice!"

"Ah! I can't stand this," cried Van Mitten, absolutely hurt at being thus compared to a sweetmeat. "First and foremost, Madame Saraboul, there was no intrusion at all!"

Cemetery of Scutari.

"Really?" said Saraboul, sacastically.

"No," continued Van Mitten, "It was a mistake. We—or rather I—under a false and perfidious direction, mistook the room."

"Indeed!" remarked Saraboul, sarcastically.

"A mere misdirection, which, under threat of imprisonment, has compelled me to perpetrate a preliminary marriage——"

"Preliminary or not," remarked Saraboul, "you are not the less married—married to me; and you may depend upon it, monsieur, that the ceremonial begun at Trebizond will be completed in Kurdistan."

"Yes? Let us talk of it in Kurdistan, then," retorted Van Mitten, who was beginning to lose his temper.

"And," continued Saraboul, "as I perceive that the society of your friends renders you insensible to my regard, we will leave Scutari this very day, and start for Mossoul, where I will infuse a little of the Kurd into your veins."

"I protest," exclaimed Van Mitten.

"Another word, and we will start this instant."

"You may depart, Madame Saraboul," replied Van Mitten, ironically, "you may depart if it is convenient, and no one will dream of detaining you, but I will not go!"

"You will not go?" cried Saraboul, much enraged at this defiance of two tigers by a sheep.

"No."

"And you have the temerity to resist us?" asked Yanar, crossing his arms.

"I have."

"Resist me, and her, a Kurdish lady!"

"Yes, were she ten times a Kurd!"

"Just remember, Mr. Dutchman, what kind of woman I am," said Saraboul, marching towards her *fiancé*, "and remember what I have been. Recollect that at fifteen I was already a widow."

"Yes," said Yanar, "and when one begins so early——"

"It may be so, madame," replied Van Mitten, "but one thing you can never be, notwithstanding your early habits——"

"And that is?"

"You can never be my widow."

"Monsieur Van Mitten," said Yanar, putting his hand on his yataghan, "one blow of this would suffice——"

"That is where you are mistaken," replied Van Mitten. "Your sabre would not make Madame Saraboul a widow, for the very excellent reason that I cannot be her husband."

"Eh?"

"And our marriage would be null."

"Null?"

"Because if Madame Saraboul has the happiness to be the widow of her first husband, I am not the widower of my first wife."

"Married? He is already married!" exclaimed the noble Saraboul, beside herself at the announcement.

"Yes," replied Van Mitten, now fairly in for it. "Yes, married! It was only to save my friends, and to prevent our arrest at the caravanserai of Rissar that I sacrificed myself!"

"Sacrificed!" screamed Saraboul, falling back on the divan.

"Knowing quite well that the marriage was not valid," continued Van Mitten, "since the first Madame Van Mitten is no more dead than I am a widower, for she is in Holland——"

The outraged "bride" rose, and, turning to Yanar, exclaimed—

"You hear him!"

"I hear."

"Your sister has been jilted!"

"Insulted!"

"And this traitor still lives!"

"He has only a few seconds more to live!"

"How savage they are," cried Van Mitten, really nervous at the turn the matter had taken.

"I will avenge you, sister," exclaimed Yanar, who, with uplifted weapon, advanced upon Van Mitten.

"I will avenge myself!" she cried.

So saying, the noble Saraboul rushed at the Dutchman, uttering cries of rage, which were fortunately audible in the next room.

---

## Chapter XV.

### In which Kéraban is more obstinate than he had ever been.

The door was immediately flung open, and Kéraban, Ahmet, Amasia, Nedjeb, and Bruno appeared on the threshold.

Kéraban quickly disengaged Van Mitten.

"Come, madame," said Ahmet, "you must not strangle people for a misunderstanding."

"*Diable!*" muttered Bruno, "it was quite time we arrived!"

"Poor Monsieur Van Mitten," said

Amasia, who felt sincere pity for her travelling companion.

"She is decidedly not the wife for him," added Nedjeb, shaking her head.

Meanwhile Van Mitten had recovered his spirits a little.

"It was rather hard, wasn't it?" asked Kéraban.

"Yes," replied Van Mitten, "a little more and I would have died!"

At that moment the noble Saraboul turned to Kéraban and, taking him aside, said—

"And have you lent yourself to this——"

"Mystification," interrupted Kéraban, "that is the proper word—mystification."

"I will be revenged. There are judges in Constantinople."

"Charming Saraboul," replied Kéraban, "you can only accuse yourself. You were anxious, on account of a pretended insult, to stop our journey. By Allah, we had to get out of the scrape as best we could. We extricated ourselves by a pretended marriage, and we assuredly had a right to this retaliation."

At this answer Saraboul fell a second time upon the divan, a prey to one of those attacks of nerves of which women, even in Kurdistan, possess the secret.

Nedjeb and Amasia hastened to her assistance.

"I am going—I am going!" she cried.

"*Bon voyage!*" said Bruno.

At this juncture Nizib came in.

"What is it?" demanded Kéraban.

"A telegram brought from the office at Galata," replied Nizib.

"For whom?"

"For M. Van Mitten. It came to-day."

"Give it to me," said the Dutchman.

He took the telegram, opened it, and looked at the signature.

"It is from my managing clerk in Rotterdam," he said. Then he read the message as follows—

"*Madame Van Mitten—five weeks ago—died!*"

The despatch was crushed in his hand. Van Mitten was thunderstruck, and (why conceal the fact?) his eyes filled with tears.

On hearing the last words Saraboul suddenly rose.

"Five weeks!" she exclaimed in rapture. "He said five weeks——"

"Imprudent man," muttered Ahmet, "what business had he to divulge the date at such a moment!"

"Yes," continued Saraboul triumphantly, "it is only ten days since he was affianced to me; and——"

"Mahomet choke you," muttered Kéraban, a little louder than he perhaps intended.

"You were then a widower, my dear spouse," said Saraboul, triumphantly.

"Absolutely a widower, dear brother-in-law," added Yanar.

"And our marriage is valid!"

Then Van Mitten, crushed by the logic of this argument, in his turn sank upon the divan.

"Poor man!" said Ahmet to his uncle, "nothing now remains for him but to throw himself into the Bosphorus."

"Good," replied Kéraban. "She will then throw herself after him and save him—for revenge!"

The noble Saraboul had already seized her property by the arm!

"Get up," she said.

"Yes, dear Saraboul," replied Van Mitten, hanging his head, "I am quite ready."

"And follow us," said Yanar.

"Yes, dear brother-in-law," replied Van Mitten, absolutely checkmated, "I am ready to follow you wherever you please."

"To Constantinople, where we will take the first steamer," said Saraboul.

"For——?"

"For Kurdistan," replied Yanar.

"Kurdistan! You will accompany me, Bruno? They live well there: that will fully compensate you."

Bruno could only make a sign in the affirmative.

The noble Saraboul and the Seigneur Yanar then dragged the unfortunate Dutchman away, though his friends in vain attempted to detain him, and his faithful servant followed him, muttering—

"I told him that some evil would befall him!"

Kéraban and the others remained stupefied and mute at this shock.

"Then he is married!" said Amasia.

"For his devotion to us," said Ahmet.

"For good and all this time," added Nedjeb.

"He will have only one resource in Kurdistan," said Kéraban with much seriousness.

"That will be, uncle——?"

"That will be—in order to neutralise her, he must marry a dozen!"

At that moment the door opened and Selim appeared quite out of breath as if he had been running.

"Oh, father, what is the matter?" exclaimed Amasia.

"What has happened?" cried Ahmet.

"My friends," replied Selim, "it is impossible to celebrate the marriage of Amasia and Ahmet."

"What do you say?"

"At Scutari at least."

"At Scutari?"

"It can only take place at Constantinople."

"At Constantinople!" cried Keraban, who began to prick up his ears, "why?"

"Because the judge of Scutari refuses to register the contract."

"He refuses?" said Ahmet.

"Yes, on the pretext that Kéraban's domicile, and consequently Ahmet's, is not Scutari but Constantinople!"

"In Constantinople," said Kéraban, frowning.

"Now," continued Selim, "this is the last day appointed for the marriage of my daughter, if she is to succeed to the fortune to which she is entitled. We must, therefore, without losing a moment, hurry to the house of the judge who will register the contract in Constantinople."

"Let us go," cried Ahmet, turning to the door.

"Let us go," added Amasia, following him. "Seigneur Kéraban, can you refuse to go with us?"

Kéraban remained silent and thoughtful.

"Well, uncle," said Ahmet turning to him.

"Will not you come?" asked Selim.

"Must I use force;" said Amasia, gently taking Kéraban by the arm.

"I have got a caique ready to cross the Bosphorus," said Selim.

"The Bosphorus!" echoed Kéraban, and then he added severely: "Is the tax of ten paras still demanded from those who cross?"

"Yes, certainly, friend Kéraban; but now that you have played such a fine trick on the Ottoman authorities as to go from Constantinople to Scutari without paying, I think you will not refuse——"

"I will refuse," replied Kéraban.

"Then they will not let you cross."

"Very well. I will not cross."

"And our wedding," exclaimed Ahmet. "Our marriage, which should take place to-day?"

"You can be married without me."

"That is impossible. You are my guardian," uncle Kéraban, "and you know quite well your presence is indispensable."

"Well then, Ahmet, wait till I have established my domicile at Scutari—and you can be married at Scutari."

# KÉRABAN THE INFLEXIBLE;

## OR, ADVENTURES IN THE EUXINE.

BY JULES VERNE.

TRANSLATED BY HENRY FRITH.

### CHAPTER XV.

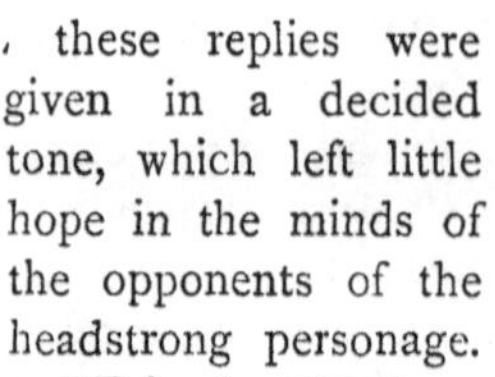

ALL these replies were given in a decided tone, which left little hope in the minds of the opponents of the headstrong personage.

"Friend Kéraban, to-day is the last day, and all the fortune which ought to come to my daughter will be lost—if——"

Kéraban shook his head, and accompanied the action with a more negative gesture.

"Uncle," pleaded Ahmet, "you cannot wish to——"

"If they compel me to pay ten paras," replied Kéraban, "never—no never, will I cross the Bosphorus. By Allah, I would rather go round the Black Sea again!"

And indeed he was just the man to do it.

"Uncle," said Ahmet, "this is bad—under such circumstances as these, let me tell you, this obstinacy is inexplicable in a man like you. You will cause misery to those who have always regarded you with true affection. It is wrong of you!"

"Ahmet, mind what you are saying," cried Kéraban, angrily.

"No, uncle, no. My heart is overflowing, and nothing shall prevent me from speaking. It is the act of a bad man!"

"Ahmet, dearest Ahmet, be calm," cried Amasia. "Do not address your uncle so. If this fortune on which you counted escapes you—renounce the marriage!"

"What—renounce you?" exclaimed the young man, catching her to his heart. "Never, no never. Come, let us leave this town forever. We have still enough left to pay the ten paras to cross to Constantinople."

Ahmet, scarcely master of himself, dragged the maiden towards the door.

"Kéraban," said Selim, who wished to make a last attempt to turn his friend from his determination—"Kéraban!"

"Leave me, Selim—leave me alone!"

"Alas! Let us go, father," said Amasia, casting a tearful look on Kéraban; and, restraining her emotion with difficulty, she directed her steps towards the door of the room, where she stopped, with Ahmet.

"For the last time, uncle," he said, "do you refuse to accompany us to Constantinople, to the house of the judge, where your presence is indispensable to our marriage?"

"What I refuse," said Kéraban, "is to pay the tax. That I will never submit to."

"Kéraban!" said Selim.

"No, by Allah, no!"

"Well then, farewell, uncle," said Ahmet, "your obstinacy will cost us a fortune. you will have ruined her who ought to be your niece. So be it. It is not the fortune I regret, but you have deprived us of our happiness. We will never see you again."

Then the young man led Amasia away, and, followed by Selim, Nedjeb, and Nizib, quitted the *salon*, then the villa, and shortly afterwards embarked for Constantinople.

Seigneur Kéraban remained alone, a prey to the greatest agitation.

"No, by Allah! no, by Mahomet!" he muttered; "it would be undignified. To have made the circuit of the Black Sea to avoid the tax, and then to pay immediately on my return! No. Rather than thus put foot in Constantinople, I will sell my house at Galata; I will retire from business; I will give all my fortune to Ahmet to replace

"I told him evil would come of it.

Amasia's. He will be rich, I shall be poor; but then I shall not have yielded! I will not yield."

As he continued, his anger became greater. "Yield—pay,—I, Kéraban! To arrive before the chief of the police who defied me; who saw me depart; who is waiting my return; who will snap his fingers at me before all the crowd as he claims the hateful tax? Never!"

It was quite evident that Kéraban was arguing against his conscience, and that he was fully aware that the consequences of his foolish obstinacy would fall on others as well as himself.

"Yes," he continued, "but would Ahmet accept my offer? He has gone away desolate, and angry at my obstinacy. I can conceive it. He is proud. He will refuse anything from me now. Let me see. I am an honest man. Am I about to snatch happiness from those young people by my stupid resolve? May Mahomet choke the whole Divan, and all the new *régime* of Turks besides."

Seigneur Kéraban paced his room irresolutely. He pushed the cushions and chairs aside. He sought some fragile object with the intention to break it to assuage his anger, and very soon two vases were smashed. Then he returned to the question.

"Ahmet, Amasia, no! I cannot be the cause of their misery, and only for a point of self-love. To delay this marriage will be, perhaps, to prevent it altogether. But to yield—to give way—I! Ah, Allah, guide me."

And with this invocation Kéraban, impelled by a rage he could no longer interpret, or give vent to, by words or actions, rushed out of the *salon*.

---

## Chapter XVI.

### Which demonstrates once again that there is no such thing as "Chance" in Human Affairs.

If Scutari was *en fête*, if on the quays from the harbour to the Sultan's Kiosk the crowd was surging to and fro—there was no less a concourse on the other side of the strait on the quays of Galata from the first bridge of boats to the barracks of Top-hané. The tranquil waters were likewise covered with caïques and other craft, laden with Turks, Albanians, Greeks, Europeans or Asiatics, which passed constantly to and fro. Certainly it was no ordinary attraction which had brought together such multitudes of spectators.

So when Ahmet and Selim, Amasia and Nedjeb, having paid the new tax, disembarked at the Top-hané steps, they found themselves in the midst of a regular "fair" with all its pleasures, in which however they had little inclination to take part.

But since the spectacle, whatever it was, had attracted such a crowd, it was only natural that Seigneur Van Mitten, who was quite well now and a Kurdish lord to boot, his *fiancée*, the noble Saraboul, and his brother-in-law, Seigneur Yanar, followed by the obedient Bruno, were among the curious.

So Ahmet found on the quay his former travelling companions. Was Van Mitten "shewing around" his new relatives, or were they showing him off? The latter case appeared the more probable.

However that might have been, the moment when Ahmet met them Saraboul was saying to her *fiancé*—

"Yes, Seigneur Van Mitten, we have more beautiful *fêtes* than this in Kurdistan."

And Van Mitten replied in a resigned tone—

"I can quite believe that, beautiful Saraboul."

This remark drew from Yanar the caustic comment, "You are wise to think so!"

However, some exclamations—one might say cries of impatience—were heard sometimes in the crowd; but Amasia and Ahmet paid scarcely any attention to them.

"No, dear Amasia," said Ahmet, "I know my uncle well, and, nevertheless, I would not have deemed him capable of pushing his obstinacy so far as hardness of heart."

"Then," said Nedjeb, "so long as this tax remains, will he never return to Constantinople?"

"He? Never!" replied Ahmet.

"If I regret the fortune which Seigneur Kéraban has deprived us of, it is not for myself, it is on your account, dear Ahmet, for your sake only."

"Let us forget all that," said Ahmet; "and the easier to forget it, and to break with this intractable uncle, who has been hitherto a father to me, let us leave Constantinople, and return to Odessa."

"That Kéraban ought to be tortured," said Selim, who felt greatly outraged.

"Yes," replied Nedjeb, "married to this Kurdish lady, for instance—why did not she espouse him?"

It need scarcely be said that Saraboul

heard neither Nedjeb's pert observation, nor Selim's reply to this effect—

"He? Why he would subdue her by his obstinacy as he would conquer a wild beast."

"Perhaps so," muttered Bruno, "but, meantime, it is my poor master who has entered the cage."

So Ahmet and his companions took but a lukewarm interest in what was going on.

Crossing the Bosphorus.

In such a temper the proceedings interested them but little, and they did not hear one Turk say to another—

"An audacious fellow, this Storchi, indeed, to venture to cross the Bosphorus in such a fashion."

"Yes, in a manner never contemplated by the tax-gatherers."

But if Ahmet paid no attention to these observations, he was obliged to reply when he heard himself accosted.

"Ah! here is Seigneur Ahmet!"

The speaker was the chief of the police, the man who had incited Kéraban to make the tour of the Black Sea.

"Ah! it is you, monsieur," said Ahmet.

"Yes, I congratulate you indeed. I have just heard that Seigneur Keraban has performed his promise. He has reached Scutari without crossing the Bosphorus."

"Yes, indeed," replied Ahmet, bitterly.

"It is heroic. For the sake of ten paras he has spent thousands of pounds."

"Just so."

"Well, he has made great progress, truly," continued the chief of police, ironically. "The tax still exists, and if he continues as obstinate, he will have to go back the same way to reach Constantinople again."

"If he wishes to, he will," answered Ahmet, who, furious as he was against his uncle, could not refrain from replying to the mocking observations of the officer.

"Bah, he will give in at last," continued the man, "and he will cross the Bosphorus. But the tax-collectors let the caiques, and attend at the landing-places. So, unless he swim or fly across——"

"Why not, if it suits him?" replied Ahmet, coldly.

At this juncture a general movement of curiosity agitated the crowd. A murmur arose. Many hands were extended towards the Bosphorus in the direction of Scutari. All heads were elevated, and the people cried—

"There he is: Storchi, Storchi!"

Ahmet and Amasia, Selim and Nedjeb, Saraboul, Van Mitten, and Yanar, with Bruno, found themselves at the angle of the quay of the Golden Horn, near the landing-place of Top-hané, and all had an excellent view of the spectacle now offered to the public.

On the Scutari bank, about six hundred feet from the margin of the Bosphorus, in the water, rises a tower miscalled the Tower of Leander. This portion of the strait is the Hellespont, the real Dardanelles, across which the classic swimmer passed from Sestos to Abydos to join Hero, the beautiful priestess of Venus—an exploit afterwards performed by Lord Byron, who was very proud of having swam in one hour and ten minutes the twelve hundred *mètres* of water which stretch between the banks.

Was this feat going to be emulated by some amateur, jealous of the mythological hero, and the author of the *Corsair?*

A long rope was stretched between the Scutari side and the Tower of Leander, the modern name of which is Keuz-Koulessi, which means the Tower of the Virgin. From that point the rope, about thirteen hundred *mètres* in length, being thus firmly supported, crossed the strait, and was attached to an elevated scaffolding, raised at the angle of the quay of Galata with the Place Top-hané.

Now it was upon this rope that the celebrated acrobat Storchi, an imitator of Blondin, was about to try to cross the Bosphorus. True, Blondin had risked his life when crossing the Niagara Falls. Here Storchi had only to fear a plunge into the smooth waters, whence he could be rescued without serious injury.

But as Blondin had crossed Niagara carrying a very brave friend upon his shoulders, so Storchi was about to cross now with an acrobatic friend. Only he was not going to carry him on his back: he was going to wheel him in a barrow, the wheel of which traversed the rope securely in a groove.

Storchi appeared on the first portion of the cord which connected the Asiatic side with the Tower of the Virgin. He wheeled his companion in the barrow, and reached the tower without any misadventure. Cheers greeted this first success.

Then the gymnast adroitly descended the rope, which nearly touched the water in the centre, and wheeled him so far with consummate coolness. It was superb! When Storchi had reached the centre, the difficulty commenced; for he had to ascend the sloping cord to the top of the scaffolding. But his muscles were firm, his arms and legs worked mechanically. He continued to wheel the barrow, while his companion remained perfectly motionless, and did not by the slightest movement endanger the stability of the wheelbarrow.

At length a shout of relief and congratulation arose. Storchi had reached the summit of the scaffolding, and then he descended with his companion at the angle of the quay where Ahmet and his companions had remained as spectators. The bold enterprize had succeeded, but the man who had been wheeled over had a right to half the congratulations which Asia sent to Europe in their honour.

But why does Ahmet exclaim, "Can he believe his eyes?" The companion of the celebrated acrobat, after shaking hands with Storchi, stopped before Ahmet and smilingly regarded him!

Seigneur Kéraban overcomes the difficulty.

"Kéraban—my uncle Kéraban," cried Ahmet, while the ladies, with Van Mitten, Yanar, Selim, and Bruno pressed round him.

It was, indeed, Kéraban himself.

"Yes, my friends, it is I—I, who, finding the brave acrobat ready to start, took the place of his companion. Yes, I have passed the Bosphorus—or rather over it—to sign the marriage contract, Ahmet."

"Ah, Seigneur Kéraban—uncle," cried Amasia, "I felt sure you would not abandon us."

"This is splendid," exclaimed Nebjeb, clapping her hands.

"What a man this is," said Van Mitten,

"you would not find his equal in the whole of Holland!"

"Just my opinion," remarked Saraboul drily.

"Well, you see, I have crossed without paying," said Kéraban to the chief of the police. "Yes, without paying—at least only two thousand piastres for my place in the barrow, and the eight hundred thousand expended in going round the Black Sea."

"I congratulate you with all my heart," replied the officer, who could only bow to this unparalleled obstinacy.

Loud cries greeted Seigneur Kéraban from all sides, when that good-natured if inflexible man embraced Ahmet and Amasia heartily.

But he was not a man to lose time, even in the midst of his triumph.

"Now," said he, "let us go to the judge of Constantinople."

"Yes, uncle, to the judge's house," said Ahmet. "Oh, uncle, you are indeed the best of men."

"Well, what did I tell you?" replied Kéraban. "I am not at all headstrong unless I am thwarted!"

We need not dwell upon the succeeding events. That very afternoon the judge received the contract, the Imaum said prayers in the mosque; then, on returning to Galata, Ahmet was married, and well married, to his dear Amasia, the rich banker's daughter, on that 30th September, before the clock struck midnight.

That same evening, Van Mitten, quite subdued, was preparing to depart for Kurdistan with Yanar and Saraboul, and in that distant country the last ceremony would finally make Saraboul his wife.

As they were bidding farewell to Ahmet, Amasia, Nedjeb, and Bruno, Van Mitten could not help saying to Kéraban in a reproachful tone—

"When I think, Kéraban, that because I did not like to thwart you, I am married a second time——!"

"My poor Van Mitten, if this marriage turns out anything but a dream, I will never forgive myself," replied Kéraban.

"A dream! Does it look like it! This telegram——"

As he spoke, he unfolded it again, and perused it mechanically.

"Yes, this despatch:—'*Madame Van Mitten, who five weeks ago deceased,—to rejoin her husband.*'"

"Deceased to rejoin!" exclaimed Kéraban, "what does that mean?"

Then, snatching the telegram, he read, "Madame Van Mitten, who five weeks ago *decided* to rejoin her husband, has started for Constantinople." "*Decided*, not *deceased!*"

Then he is not a widower!

These words escaped everyone, and Kéraban, not without reason, added—

"Another error in these stupid telegrams. They never make anything else but mistakes."

"No, I am not a widower, not a widower," repeated Van Mitten, "and too delighted to return to my first wife, for fear of the second!"

When Yanar and Saraboul understood the case, there was a terrible explosion, but they were obliged to yield at last. Van Mitten was a married man, and that day he was reunited to his wife, who brought him, as a peace offering, a magnificent *Valentia* bulb.

"We shall do better, my sister," said Yanar, "much better than——"

"That icicle of a Dutchman," said Saraboul. "That will not be a difficult matter."

So they departed for Kurdistan, but it is probable that the handsome indemnity paid by Kéraban tended to render their return less irksome.

However, Kéraban could not always have a rope extended between Constantinople and Scutari, to cross the Bosphorus. Did he, therefore, cease to cross?

No. For some time he would not yield, and remained firm. But one day he offered to buy up the tax on caiques, and the offer was accepted by the government. This cost him a large sum, no doubt, but he became more popular than ever; and strangers never fail to pay a visit to KÉRABAN THE INFLEXIBLE as one of the most astonishing curiosities of the capital of the Ottoman Empire!

www.ingramcontent.com/pod-product-compliance
Lightning Source LLC
LaVergne TN
LVHW091040080826
845145LV00002B/565

*9781589634640*